LEGACY

Book 1 of the
Resonance Tetralogy

Hugo Jackson

Inspired Quill Publishing

Published by Inspired Quill: September 2013

First Edition

Contact the author through their website:
http://www.hugorjackson.com

Chief Editor: Sara-Jayne Slack

Paperback ISBN: 978-1-908600-22-6
eBook ISBN: 978-1-908600-23-3

Inspired Quill Publishing, UK
Business Reg. No. 7592847
http://www.inspired-quill.com

Acknowledgements

I'd most gratefully like to thank all those who've supported me in writing this novel.

Most important thanks go to my wife, Madison, who in herself has consistently provided me with an undying inspiration. To my Mum, Coral, who built the foundations of my story-telling abilities, my Dad, Rob, for providing a roof over us, my sisters Dulcie and Venetia for their unyielding enthusiasm and encouragement. To my mother- and father-in-law Dionne and Ray, and my sister-in-law Morgan, for allowing me to steal Madison from North Carolina, and for keeping me safe when we moved back. To Paul Ullson for helping with my geography; to Daniel Hill for getting me to start the book in the first place; and to Jeremy Graves for getting me to finish it! To Lawrence Tate, who rescued me from a spiralling plothole and ignited the second book's storyline. To the Goodwood Actors' Guild and Raven Tor Living History Group for their support and friendship, and for giving me an escape when I needed it. To noxi-kun on DeviantArt for giving me the amazing first concept art of the characters. To Minna Sundberg and her phenomenal work on the front cover. To members of FictionPost.com, OtakuBoards.com and the Chichester Festival Youth Theatre for their feedback, interest and support. To Bognor Regis Memorial War Hospital for providing me such warm encouragement. To the amazing denizens of Meatopia, who enveloped me within their circle of friendship and found me a place to belong. To Sara-Jayne Slack and Inspired Quill, for discovering me among the lists of fantasy books and her patience despite my initial misgivings, and for crafting new creativity and inspiration from a story I had thought complete, and making it only more so.

Thank you.

Cover artwork by Minna Sundberg – http://www.minnasundberg.fi

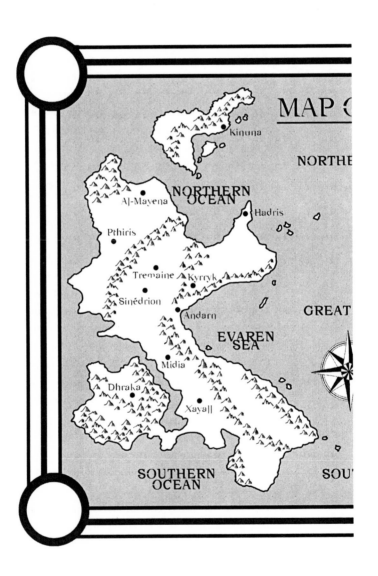

MAP O

NORTHE

Kinuna

NORTHERN
OCEAN

Al-Mayena

Hadris

Pthiris

Tremaine

Kyrryk

Sinédrion

Andarn

GREAT

EVAREN
SEA

Midia

Dhraka

Xayall

SOUTHERN
OCEAN

SOU

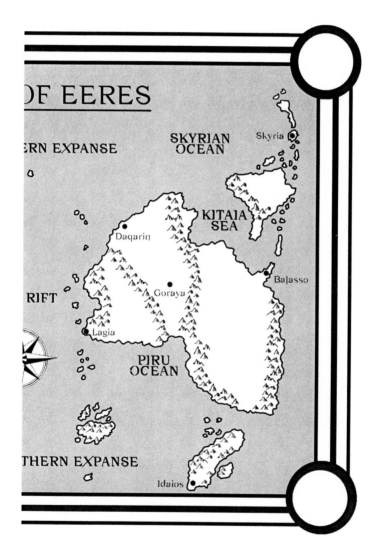

Centuries had passed. The ancient tales were forgotten, lost in the winds of time. Many who knew them died without uttering a single breath of their secrets, the memory of them too harrowing to endure.

Two and a half thousand years ago, a great cataclysm struck. It reshaped the world, purging its surface of millions of lives. The only evidence that civilisation ever existed before this point were tiny clues in buried ruins and the vague remembrance of stories whispered through the generations. One word consistently appeared time and again, a single clue of the world that existed before—Nazreal.

That this was once a city was the only certainty. Where it lay, why it disappeared and the fate of its inhabitants remained as myth and speculation. The world had barely escaped from its spiralling plunge into chaos and virtual extinction. Those who survived fought over ancient artefacts unearthed by chance; the promise of old technologies fuel for their battle to remain alive. They were desperate to find out what happened to prevent it from happening again.

While the world was currently stable, its foothold was tentative at best. Tense diplomacy and uneasy peace had reigned for many years now, but fresh arguments and border disputes erupted on a near-daily basis.

But then, something stirred deep at the heart of the world. A new discovery had just been made.

Chapter One

"**I**mpossible! Nazreal does *not* exist! If it did it wasn't anything more than the cities which stand today. How could it be anything else?"

Sinédrion, grand central city of the Cadon continent, was alight with debate.

"Show some intelligence, Pthiris! We can't draw conclusions until we've examined the evidence."

There was nothing unusual about the Senate holding audience. It happened every seventy days. But those who knew the meeting's agenda were waiting impatiently outside the illustrious pantheon structure of the Senate building while the representatives conducted their speeches within its lavish halls. The massive amphitheatre was under higher security than it had ever been before. The stern guards standing by each massive oak door would brandish their spears at anyone who tried listening in, the metal weapons almost as sharp as their harsh, forbidding glares. The anticipation had everyone on edge.

"And how long will that take? Months, years, decades? Our time is better spent on the problems that plague our land *now*, not thousands of years in the past!"

This was unlike the Senate gatherings people were used to. Normally they were rigid, sparse affairs. The city-state nations of the Senate, known as 'sovereigns', usually ignored their calling due to disinterest and unwary preoccupation with their own matters. This time the hall was full to bursting. This meeting had brought news that the entire world had been waiting to hear: a breath of evidence that could help explain Eeres' greatest myth, the disappearance of Nazreal, and so bring hope of new solutions to their ongoing struggles. Dhraka, a sovereign to the Southwest, had unearthed a new artefact.

"Representatives, silence!" came a gruff, rumbling growl. "You disgrace yourselves!"

News of the discovery had spread quickly as Dhraka sent out its messengers to pique the interest of other nations. The word sunk into people's minds, creating widespread controversy. Some sovereigns even tried to keep their people uninformed to prevent unnecessary excitement; nothing could be decided until the claims were proven true. People were sceptical of a hoax attempting to channel resources and money, or an immature exaggeration of easily identifiable debris, as had happened before. But every new find sent ripples of anxiety through the world: underground ruins crushed by seismic activity, scraps of metal from unknown sources. These told very little, but spoke volumes in their implications. The largest sovereigns had been continually researching Nazreal since its likely existence first came to light, but nothing conclusive had ever been proven.

A tense quiet descended upon the members of the Senate as one of the Dhrakan Representatives, the current despotic ruler and military commander Fulkore Crawn, stood at the central plinth, awaiting his chance to continue. He was tall and muscular, with amaranth scales and a dark grey suit of armour. On the chest plate was the Dhrakan emblem: a dark red dragon with blazing yellow eyes, spitting fire, set against a black pyramid. That he had been allowed free entry to the Senate Hall was contentious enough given the dragon race's violent history. Thought extinct and virtually unknown, they re-emerged some decades ago with great vehemence. The fact that Dhraka had persisted so urgently in taking their discovery to the Senate in the first place had surprised many, as few believed they possessed interest in anything other than themselves.

Deep red claws clicked on the stone surface with disdainful calculation as Fulkore stood before his audience, barely even attempting to conceal the satisfaction at the furore his claims caused. His sharp, angular wings, boasting a span of at least twelve feet, were folded behind his back. It was forbidden for any creature to open their wings inside the Senate chamber, but they twitched and swung with his body, in constant threat of breaching the code.

With his piercing yellow eyes he glanced around at the rows of anxious dignitaries, taking in every detail of their extravagant ceremonial clothes and their ornate gilded chairs. He looked to the transcribers on the next level up, quills in hand, fervently awaiting his next word. Everyone was watching him, a glorious moment he savoured while brandishing his presence before them. He craned his neck back to the stained glass ceiling and gave an arrogant scowl. It was overcast.

"Such a pity," he thought, *"that the sun cannot see my glory today."*

"Representative Dhraka," the crisp, old voice barked from behind him. He turned round to meet the gaze of Chief Senator Tyrone, a hulking badger in the elaborate green and gold uniform of the Senate House. He governed the Senate meetings and had done so for the last twenty-five years. His distinguished features and imposing figure were shaded with an air of tiredness; one of his eyes was half-closed and his fur was greying quite considerably. The once perfectly-fitting tailored dress uniform sagged in places about him and his head was noticed to drift slowly closer to his chest as meetings progressed. His voice, however, still contained enough authority to make younger delegates jump in their seats and for the entire room to straighten themselves out of respect. The dragon looked at him expectantly, the ridge of spines down his back flexing at the gall of his interruption.

"Yes, my Lord?" he replied, with as little respect as he could get away with.

Tyrone was nonplussed at the dragon's indulgent antagonism. "You were saying?" the badger growled, glaring at him with increasing boredom.

Fulkore turned swiftly back to face the rest of the Senate, fast enough that his armour gave an indignant rattle.

"Yes…" he spoke very deliberately, just enough to not appear patronising, "the piece our workers found was of substantial size and of a material so far undocumented in our scientific endeavours. The material and the area it was discovered in have led us to believe it is from the city of Nazreal. In the interests of the—"

"Where did you find it?" a voice called from the higher seats. The noble figure of a red fox rose stood at the rail; suddenly all eyes had turned to him. Aidan Phiraco, the Emperor of Xayall, stood before him. Although of more youthful appearance than most of his fellow Representatives he was an experienced dignitary, taking an active role in the politics of the continent, and often sought as a mediator to reconcile disputes between sovereigns. While this gained him respect it also made him a number of enemies who saw his efforts as overbearing and manipulative, or a conceited effort to take over the Senate for himself.

The Dhrakan rustled his wings, his grin ebbing. "A rather forward outburst, Xayall," he growled, unimpressed at being interrupted a second time. "That's unlike you." He gave the slender fox a steely glare before continuing. "It doesn't matter where it was found. The point is—"

"But you said that 'the area' led you to believe it was from Nazreal," the middle-aged fox pressed, his voice rising but remaining calm. Under his stiff imperial robes he held a sense of veteran experience, somewhat belying his outward years. His eyes were cerulean, faded slightly through chronic illness, but still alight with sagacity. "How are we supposed to quantify that if we don't know where it was from?"

The dragon clenched his fist. "I'll forgive your inappropriate interruption, *Xayall*," his voice so full of acidity it seemed poisonous even to listen to, "as this is a matter of the world's importance… But I admit that I have made an error. I apologise," he said, "I meant that given the location of *previous* pieces thought to be from Nazreal, this ties together those smaller proofs to create a larger, more detailed picture of our history."

Aidan studied the dragon with a narrow stare, guarded by suspicion.

The lizard's grin re-appeared as he fixed his gaze directly on his Xayall counterpart. "Ironically, you are quite apt to stand, as I have a proposition for your sovereignty. Given the previous discoveries, we of Dhraka are in agreement that it is in the world's interest to access these artefacts in order to study the possibilities more closely. Specifically, we need to see the extensive library collected within the Xayall vaults, and hence express an interest in a joint venture to excavate areas within your borders for further research."

Aidan stood unmoved. "That's impossible. We cannot grant you permission to tear up our land on the basis of an object that has not even been described to us." Whispered murmurs began coursing through the other seats. "As the Senate is aware, we have already opened our reports to Sinédrion's library in accordance with the requirements of the law regarding ancient histories. You are free to look at those for your examinations, if you so wish."

Where Xayall's heritage was one of respect and co-operation, Dhraka's had done nothing but bicker and oppress since its reintroduction to the world. The dragons would frequently raid the tiny villages and towns that neighboured them, but threats and mass disappearances in the correct application allowed many trespasses to go unreported until the damage had been discovered and the culprits safely obscured behind their wall of reptilian wings. Violence was not their only machine, however—further subversive operations conducted in dark corners and shady streets negotiated hungry, destructive agreements. They were not to be trusted, but difficult to pin to their crimes, and harder yet to strike an alliance against, due to their intimidating diplomatic nature and secret agreements.

Crawn, being the head of the civilisation since its reappearance, had been throwing his might around in search of Nazreal since whispers of its existence caught the air, and although information was scarce, under his rule Dhraka had engaged many troops in legal and illegal artefact hunts.

Everyone looked back at Fulkore, who, although keeping his body absolutely still behind the plinth, had a vicious fire in his eyes. His claws closed around the edges of the wooden lectern, gouging bits of it free. "You are being unreasonable, Xayall," he seethed. "Don't you understand the importance of these finds? How are we to understand the ancient disaster that confined our race to the darkness if you forbid us from investigating it? How can we rebuild what was lost to history without sharing its knowledge?"

"We don't even know that Nazreal was involved in the disaster," Aidan said calmly. "But there is still nothing of ours that you have not already seen. The interest in our libraries aside, with Dhraka's border relations being as they are, we cannot let you inside our sovereign. I'm sure you don't need reminding that your continued encroachment on numerous territories, including our own, has still not been rectified to the Senate's satisfaction. And you have not yet fulfilled your obligation to the Senate under the Ancient Histories Decree to reveal what this new artefact is. Until these matters are resolved, we have to respectfully deny your request."

A new murmur swept around the hall.

Aidan didn't allow himself to look around, focusing solely on the dragon at the pulpit. The smile had completely drifted from Fulkore's face, replaced with a stark, jagged snarl.

"*You still persist in your vile impertinence. You'll suffer for this,*" the dragon thought, bile rising in his throat. "The matters of our country are none of your business, Xayall." A flicker of hatred flashed across his eyes as he addressed the fox. "Petty accusations aside, is our request unreasonable? This is in the interests of the entire world; do not forget your responsibilities."

"*You mean* your *interests…*" Aidan growled internally. His knowledge of the Dhraka and Nazreal ran deeper than anyone else in the Senate. He was not prepared to back down.

Fulkore took on a more obnoxious, patronising tone, his conceit grating like claws on glass. "Perhaps Xayall has another reason to forbid us access," he tested harshly, pacing around the plinth again. "Perhaps these artefacts hold more than the reports dictate: that there are more waiting in your vaults, their benefits being secretly reaped by the nation for your own gain."

"What are you suggesting?" Aidan growled.

"I am not 'suggesting' anything," the creature fawned, feigning a mock calm. "I'm merely… *speculating* as to why a sovereign that has always had such an interest in Nazreal and proposed the Ancient Histories Decree in the first place would be so protective over its release of information. After all, without having an outside nation to verify your reports, there is no way of knowing they are genuine. I'm sure you don't believe us any more than we do you, but this piteous mistrust must be resolved or we may never discover the truth of our world."

Aidan could hear whispers creeping across the room. He withdrew from the parapet and straightened himself, content not to continue the debate any further. He was aware that Nazreal was a contentious issue for the entire Senate, and he didn't trust Dhraka not to have coerced other smaller sovereigns into supporting their cause, or to act independently to gain the knowledge they sought.

"I understand your concerns, Dhraka. But we cannot approve your request at this time," he said firmly, before sitting back down.

Fulkore flicked his tail dismissively. "Then there is little point in continuing." He bowed to Chief Senator Tyrone. "I am finished in my address, My Lord." With a final glare aimed at Aidan, he stalked across the stage and made his way to the Dhrakan seats, where more dragons gloated and sneered to each other in uncivil tongues. An unsettled quiet sunk into the Senate as the hope for detailed news dissolved into the air, unfulfilled.

The badger rapped his gavel on the desk before him, displeased by the rising tension in the seats. "Perhaps Xayall would be more willing to accede to your request if a third party oversaw the operation, Representative Dhraka. Shall we put it to discussion at the next meeting?"

Fulkore craned his fearsome head round to give the old boor a look of absolute disgust. "It shall be considered, My Lord," he oozed.

Tyrone nodded sagely, satisfied in his resolution. "To further matters, then. I trust we shall hear no more than necessary of this pointless, cyclic argument? What an anticlimax," he sighed. "Skyria, your Representative?"

A female pine marten stood up, clutching a note in her claws. "My Lord, and fellow Representatives, we have still not received any word about the Skyrian abductors who disappeared to the Cadon mainland over two months ago…"

Once the meeting had finished, the delegates filed out of the amphitheatre, flanked by guards.

Aidan was shadowed by his bodyguard Kier, a younger fox with three white crystal earrings in each ear and bold, silver eyes. He had been standing behind his master for the whole meeting, and now he matched his pace to Aidan's urgent stride as they marched to the outer wings of the building. Once they were out of sight, Aidan slowed dramatically. He let out a heavy, rattling sigh, massaging a pain in his ribs. The blue imperial robes were heavy, and tired him as much as the debate had, the long sleeves and tight, high collar constricting his already weakening circulation. He ripped the headdress off and bundled it towards Kier's chest. Hurriedly, he pulled open the collar of his jacket, allowing the oxygen to flow back into his lungs. His mind pulsed with the weight of the meeting.

"Are you all right, Your Majesty?" Kier said, taking his arm in support.

Aidan brushed him away, breathing through his teeth. "Yes, I'm fine, Kier. It was just… troublesome."

"I did offer to go in your stead, Majesty," the younger fox said quietly.

Aidan let out a slight laugh, his pain slowly subsiding to a dull ache. "This isn't... something you'd be able to debate. You'd never be allowed to speak if you weren't a Representative anyway. It had to be me..."

Compounding his worries from the Senate was the journey back to Xayall, at least two days by carriage if the journey was smooth. As soon as he returned he'd have to make plans to leave again, and Faria would not make it easy for him.

They rounded a corner and descended a set of large, sweeping stairs; this was one of the main entrances to the building. Aidan could hear the bustling of the citizens in the streets outside.

When they reached the large iron door at the base, two bulky guards hauled it open, revealing the eminent city of Sinédrion laid out before them, colours ablaze in the late evening's low vermillion sun. A large river curved majestically around the Senate chamber, wearing luxurious bridges like a uniform of office.

Their carriage awaited them: an elegant design in dark wood with green and gold trim. Tall, horse-like dinosaur creatures with long tails, Theriasaurs, stood proudly at its head awaiting their command to move. The Xayall emblem, a white fox on a shield of blue flame, had been carved into the vehicle's doors. A troop of mounted soldiers were stood to attention behind it; a silent, respectful welcome to their Emperor.

A footman held the door for them as they climbed inside, and seconds later the carriage began to move. For a while

Aidan watched the shifting cityscape with a distant, grave expression.

"The world ended once already…"

"I'm sorry, Your Majesty?"

Aidan pulled a piece of parchment from a chest under the seat, along with a quill and a bottle of ink.

"Nothing. Kier, I need you to deliver a letter to a friend of mine in Andarn," the older fox explained, his serious tone sounding all the darker in the half-light of the carriage. "We'll stop near the city for you. I'm sorry, but it may take a while to find him."

Kier nodded. "I will, Majesty."

"I take it you still have my staff?"

The younger fox instinctively moved a hand to his back to check, even though he knew the Emperor's charge was still safe in its cloth shroud. "Yes. Do you want it now?"

"No. But I'll take it with me. Make sure you leave it when you go."

"Yes, Majesty."

The carriage fell into silence. As they passed through Sinédrion's gates and the voices of the crowd subsided, Aidan let himself relax a little. The meeting had not filled him with optimism. He only hoped that his concerns regarding the Dhrakans would not be proved right. Xayall did not have the military strength to repel the dragons if anything were to happen.

The Emperor's procession passed the city's gates and broke into the forest. Some seconds after the last armoured creatures thundered away, a black carriage ground into motion, following in their tracks.

Chapter Two

The city of Xayall stood on a low hill in the centre of a wide, shallow valley, surrounded by an immense forest with lush, green trees that rippled gracefully in the mid-afternoon breeze. Its sandstone walls shone lustrously in the brilliant sunlight, the many spires and grand archways creating an image that complemented the forest surrounding them. On top of the firm bastions archers and sentries took turns lounging in the sun while the others kept guard. A wide, glistening moat hugged the bank below the city, fed by a river to the southeast. Proud bridges arched over the river from the treeline to the three gates of the city; every passenger on their stony backs could not help but be impressed by the city's commanding, inspiring presence.

At the city's heart stood the Tor, a stone tower rising high above the city walls, dominating the other buildings and dwarfing even the oldest of the trees in the forest. The building's gentle taper held it boldly against the hue of the sky, the sentinel of the surrounding lands. At its peak were two gold and white wing-like spires gently reaching into the sky, as if part of a huge bird readying itself to take flight. The city below was made in the same light stone as if it were the tower's nest, with smaller spires and flat-topped buildings echoing the central structure's design.

Within the Tor's outer defensive walls lay its gardens. The brilliant flowers and gleaming trees presented themselves to the clean air, filling the proud building with the gentle sound of their rustling leaves.

In these gardens, in the centre of a large grass circle, stood a figure. The young vixen with brilliant orange-red fur clutched a short metal rod, at the end of which was a spear-head of blue-green crystal that shimmered gently in the sunlight. The crystal was laid in intricate veins that wrapped their way down the rod's handle, pulsing with a faint glow where she held it.

Faria Phiraco was seventeen, with a light frame and a gentle face. Given her short muzzle, her height and her ears she looked a lot like a fennec fox—from her mother's side of the family, she was told. The rest of her bold markings, her black ears, hands and feet, were like her father's.

She let out a deep breath, the strong sunlight uncomfortably warm on her Imperial jacket of deep blue, black and gold. The coat flared out below the waist; over her shoulders was a black shoulder cape that reached down to the small of her back, held in place by a wide blue strap. The turned-back sleeves displayed her elegant, gentle arms, on which she was wearing black fingerless gloves reaching to just below her elbow, with channels of gold braid running down them. Her legs were covered by a modest, formal skirt, and black knee-length gaiters, fastened at the back with gold buttons.

Her deep, cobalt-blue eyes examined the staff, taking in all the details on its surface, beautifully crafted in crystal and silver. And this was only a practice rod, nowhere near as elaborate as her father's.

Almost camouflaged in his green and grey armour, her bodyguard, an ocelot called Bayer, watched from the shadow of the nearest tree as she began her resonance practice. This was an important routine for Faria. If she fell behind she could lose her affinity with the crystals she commanded. She would train for hours every day honing her skills, and even longer when her father was away, never entirely confident that she could follow in his footsteps as ably. He'd always said she was gifted, potentially better than he was, but she hadn't truly believed in herself despite her powers being second nature, almost instinctive. The application was key, and she kept finding new ways to use the crystal. Their diversity was intimidating.

She insisted that nobody watch her train, so she would always move into the gardens to be away from prying eyes. The resonance shared by her and her father was unknown to most of Xayall. It could prove dangerous if people knew of their abilities. But more than that, it distracted her if people saw her mistakes.

Faria raised the staff in her right hand and held it aloft, tightening her grip. The crystal veins swam with a flowing, organic light, spreading to the smooth, sharp blade of the head. Light streamed from the point and mist, drawn from the air, began condensing around the rod's tip. As more water was sucked in it formed large, erratically pulsating spheres of the clear liquid. When she shifted the position of her fingers along the haft, one sphere shot from the staff and burst a few feet away, showering the grass with a spray of water. Quickly grabbing the haft in her left hand, she twirled it round and in moments the remaining water solidified into ice. Her coat whirling, she spun around and aimed the icy ball at the nearest tree. With a deft movement of her hands, the rod shone and a burst of wind erupted behind the sphere, punching it through the air in a spiralled blast.

Something was wrong.

Bayer drew his sword just in time, slicing through the iced ball with ease. She stopped, clutching the staff to her chest with a fearful look in her eyes.

"Bayer!" she cried. "Are you all right?"

The ocelot sheathed his sword, smiling wryly. "I'm fine, Your Highness. You should be proud of your aim."

She ran to him. "Not if it's going to hit you!"

He leant back against the tree. "It didn't hit me. Anyone watching you less closely, unknowing of your abilities, would have been stopped in their tracks."

She shook her ears indignantly. "I'm not just doing this for self-defence. I need to understand the resonance to help people. I mean… we shouldn't need to fight, should we? The border disputes never get that bad…"

Bayer lowered his sleek frame into a sitting position, nestling between two roots of the tree. His russet eyes, alight and piercing, kept a vigilant watch on the young Empress-to-be. In the few years he'd been guarding the Phiraco family he'd grown a great respect for their power and humility, and took pride in protecting them. "If you'll pardon my saying so, Your Highness, it would be naïve to think you would never have to fight someone at least once in your life. And since your life is so important, it is imperative that you survive anything you face."

She accepted silently, although currently she was more concerned with aiding those around her than protecting herself. She took great pride in being in a position to help others, and she was determined to do it successfully and powerfully, even if the prospect scared her senseless sometimes. Now mindful of where Bayer had positioned himself, she returned to the circle to start again. She shuffled awkwardly in her clothes, trying to squeeze some of the heat from the fabric. The blue redingote of the Xayall reigning family, with its heavy braids and intricate patterning, was not practical wear, especially for resonance training, but in her father's absence she had to keep up appearances. And she wanted to look her best for when he returned. For all their cumbersome embellishments, she did like the Imperial robes.

She pointed the rod at the ground, a little less elegantly than she had done before, and with the glowing crystals coaxed a patch of grass to grow to the height of her waist. With a sweep of the point across the ground she created mounds of soil, plucking the earth from under the surface as if it were attached to an invisible thread.

She paused for a second, surveying the mess she'd created. Thinking guiltily of the work the gardeners faced, she held her staff to the monstrous molehills and angled it down, slowly pushing the soil underground again. The oversized grass stood defiantly before her, however. Swapping to her other hand, she took the edge of the spearhead and ran it along the grass blades. The crystal, sharpened to a razor-sharp blade, sliced effortlessly through the greenery, which then fluttered to the ground.

Her hands tingled. She pumped her fingers to try and alleviate the irritating sensation, but unfortunately it was a near-permanent side effect of having an affinity with the crystals. It worsened when she practiced. Her father's staff was far larger—about three feet long, double-ended, and contained a greater amount of crystal. She felt sick just thinking about the amount of energy it would take to wield, and the pain she would inevitably receive if she ever had to use it.

The crystal's pulse faded to a soft glow. She watched it distantly, wondering after her father's health.

She knew about the history of resonance, of course, and how she and her father had both come to wield it. Millennia ago a huge meteor had stuck Eeres' moon, casting a thunderous storm of debris towards the planet. As the splintered fragments pierced the atmosphere they twisted and melted in the heat, transforming into thousands of glowing crystals that rained over the lands of Eeres.

Over time these were discovered to contain an organic energy that, if used correctly, could sympathise, or 'resonate', with materials and forces around them: everything from rock to electricity. This was the phenomenon known as resonance. Occasionally a person was born with the ability to change the crystals' shape and the way the energy flowed through them; those who had this power were known as 'resonators', such as Faria and her father.

Bayer rose to his feet. Someone was approaching from the Tor. A sprightly meerkat attendant came to a quick halt and bowed graciously to Faria.

"Your Imperial Highness, The Emperor is approaching the city."

Her face lit up with a wide, excited grin. She looked eagerly to Bayer, who smiled and gestured to the attendant to lead them away.

Faria found it difficult not to race ahead. She wasn't allowed to meet him by the carriages—for her own safety, she was told. No attempts had been made on either of their lives yet, but that didn't mean it wasn't going to happen, and her father was deeply concerned about her safety, far more so than his own.

The attendant led her into a large room midway up the Tor, lavishly decorated in tapestries and huge detailed maps of the region, where Xayall officials met to discuss running the sovereign. The far end of the room opened out to a sprawling balcony, presenting a panoramic view of the city and the forests beyond to the north. She strode outside and leant on the stone rail, watching the gates for signs of her father's carriage. Bayer stood at the balcony threshold, resting his hands on the pommel of his sword.

Faria sighed and let herself disappear in the view, feeling the warmth of the sun on her face. The city was beautiful in the sunlight. She enjoyed looking out over the landscapes and watching people wander around the streets. The best view was to the east, though. There you could see part of the striking, jagged mountain range that ran past the sovereign's borders. She wanted to be taken there one day, along with many other places she'd heard about. Her father was always evasive about letting her out of the city, and whenever she was it was under close guard. She couldn't always see why, though she surmised it might be to do with her resonance.

She held the short staff aloft, against the light, letting the rays play through the crystal and observing them pensively.

Most people considered stories of resonators to be fanciful at best, relegated to myths and popular heroic legends. She knew of no others aside from herself and her father, although there had to be more, if for no other reason than the number of different known crystal types. The most versatile were the blue-green ones found inside Aidan's staff. These were apparently the most common, and also the hardest for one person to control.

Since most people had no understanding of using crystals for elemental manipulation, they were often used as jewels. Faria had seen a number used on ceremonial hats, which always amused her. She knew a little about the different crystals and their properties, but mostly that their potential was virtually limitless.

Her father warned her of the dangers of being a resonator when she was very young. Due to the alien nature of their abilities and common superstitions, resonators, once discovered, could be stalked by bounty hunters and overzealous scholars, or shunned by communities as a freak or witch, if not forced into self-imposed exile out of fear for the lives of others. It was a grievously misunderstood power.

As such, it was unknown how many resonators existed. With the crystals' rarity, it was unlikely for any resonator to come across the type of crystal they could use. They had a number of symptoms relating to their resonance, though, making them at least a little easier to identify. Aside from the constant tingling sensation in their hands (often misinterpreted as physical damage or illness), particular resonance abilities also affected the colour of their eyes. Neither Faria nor her father's eye colours were natural as such, both reflective of the crystals they could control.

Her father had been born with resonance, and had married into the Xayall reigning family when it was revealed that the Empress Kaya Phiraco, Faria's mother, also had a degree of resonance inherited from her ancestors. When Faria was born they'd said that her resonance potential was in excess of anything either of them had ever seen. Nothing had come to pass so far where she'd had to utilise her skills in anything other than training (although she had been prepared for more serious events), but the strength of her power could work both in her favour and heavily against her.

In the distance, the northern city gates rumbled open. Through them, a carriage moved briskly towards the Tor. Faria smiled, her tail flicking excitedly from side to side.

The cart rattled into the walled plaza in front of the Tor and slowed to a halt by the eminent archway. No sooner had it stopped than a footman pulled open the door with a flourish and bowed respectfully to the Emperor within. Aidan stepped outside, looking weary, still carrying the staff wrapped in its sheath. The footman closed the carriage door and lifted the chest containing His Imperial Majesty's belongings, then handed it to another attendant. A third moved to Aidan's side and led him up the stairway.

Ascending the Tor became harder for the weakened fox every time. The thought that someday he would lose the strength to get out of bed plagued him constantly. There was still so much left to do. Currently, knowing that Faria was waiting upstairs drove him steadily forwards. He rested just by the entrance of the room to regain the breath rasping out from his throat. The attendant watched with concern, but Aidan had dismissed the need for a doctor. He shakily waved the attendant away, and dutifully, albeit reluctantly, he left. Aidan reached into his shirt and took hold of the crystal pendant around his neck. A soft blue light blossomed under the material. Within a few seconds he was able to breathe normally again and the paleness in his skin subsided.

Faria noticed him immediately as he pushed through the veil. She leapt towards him and flung her arms around his waist, burying her head in his chest.

"Father!" she cried happily. Aidan smiled, but was finding it difficult to keep upright. He held his arms on her shoulders.

"It's good to see you, Faria," he sighed, a deep sense of relief in his voice. Bayer bowed respectfully and left, keen to preserve their privacy. "I missed you."

She pulled away to see her father's face, and the eyes that looked at her with all the love in the world. She smiled. "I'm glad you're back. I was worried you'd become sick again."

He smiled back, a hint of pain creeping into his face. "I was all right. How were you?"

She took his hand and led him onto the balcony. She gestured to the view over the city with wide arms. A flock of birds took flight from the easternmost wall and flew across the sky. "Things have been fine. It's been really beautiful here…" she sighed. He leant on the parapet, saying nothing but agreeing all the same.

"But nothing's really happened," she continued, looking at the rod she was holding. "I've been practicing again."

"You'll wear yourself out if you train too much," he said, still looking out over the city. It occurred to him that while he didn't want her training excessively, if he was correct in his assumptions then she'd soon have more than resonance burnout to deal with.

He clutched his own staff tightly. She stood next to him, watching with concern. "How was the Senate meeting?" she asked quietly.

He stroked his ears back, the tips of which were beginning to grey. "It was... disconcerting. The Dhrakans say they've found an artefact from Nazreal, and they wanted to gain access to the city to aid their research."

She scrunched her nose dismissively. "How would that help them?"

"It could help them a lot, if they found the right thing," he muttered, staring into the middle-distance. "Faria... I need to go to Skyria. I know—"

"Already?" She tried to hide the protest in her voice. "But... you've only just arrived. You should have a few days' rest, at least. You'll only make yourself worse if you leave for such a long journey so soon." She took his arm, her pleading eyes betraying the hidden desperation to keep him close.

He sighed. "I'm sorry, Faria. I have to. We can't risk Dhraka taking control of what they've found."

She held the rod to her chest. "But... I was hoping you could train me a little more," she said quietly. "I'm not very good."

Aidan gave a quiet laugh. "Not very good?"

She turned away bashfully. Before she knew it he'd wrapped his arms around her shoulders and was resting his head on top of hers, swaying her playfully. She almost lost her balance. "So even though you've mastered the major elemental effects *and* can change the physical shape of the crystals *and* can manipulate solid, compound and granular materials, you're still not very good? Some people would kill to have the powers and control that you do."

She folded her arms in a sulk and turned pointedly to the view. He couldn't help but smile, releasing her, but taking her hand in his.

"So, why do you think you're not very good, my dear?"

She pretended to ignore him, but accidentally caught his gaze when glancing to him out of the corner of her eye. She threw her arms in an exasperated sigh.

"I don't feel ready," she grumbled, pacing. "I don't know what I'm supposed to do with my resonance. I've kept it secret, so I can't go out and help people with it without someone discovering it; there's no-one to fight, and without either of those it's just a weird ability to keep me from getting bored. I have mended some of the cracks in the walls, though, for all the good that'll do in the world."

He chuckled, cracking an understanding smile. He stepped closer to her again and gently unwrapped the cloth that veiled his crystal staff. The weapon was a beautiful construction of gold, silver and the blue crystals. It glistened brilliantly in the sun, far more lustrous than her training rod, with shining veins of the aquamarine stone far finer and more intricate. Large spearheads glinted at either end; masterfully crafted, but deadly.

He knelt down before her and rested the staff on the floor, pinching the haft between his fingers. "These crystals," he began, sending a flow of energy through the staff that made sparks erupt from the higher end, "while you control and command them, they also react to your instincts. The resonance is a part of you—your mind, your body and your will. They will help protect and move you when you need them, in the ways that you need them to. You can bend them to your will or let your subconscious take control. If you can find a way to control it, there is nothing you cannot do. But…" he hesitated for a moment, his gaze distant, disturbed. "…there will be a time when you will need to defend yourself, and those around you."

She gave him a quizzical look; the seriousness in his face was worrying her.

"Faria… things may get very dangerous for us both very soon. The Dhrakans are becoming aggressive. They may approach Xayall before long, and in force. You cannot trust them if they enter the gates. If Crawn has found something significant, it may affect the whole of Eeres. I need to find out what they've discovered, and destroy it. Skyria's our only ally in this. There are things from Nazreal that should never have existed. You need to be able to protect yourself, the city… and me."

"But… Nazreal disappeared, Father. I don't under-stand—"

He placed a finger on her nose to quiet her for a moment. He held out his staff to her. "I want you to try this out for me until I get back," he said, a trusting look in his eyes.

"But… this is yours," she whispered, feeling the massive latent energy of the crystals without even touching them. "Won't you need this if it's getting dangerous?"

He gestured to her training rod. "I can make do with that one. But for the moment I want you to take this for me."

The crystals glowed appreciatively as she gently ran her fingers down the golden metal. Gently, she took it in her right hand and turned it over in the sun. For being so much larger, it felt more balanced than her training rod.

He took the smaller staff from her and tucked it into his belt. "This will be a lot more powerful than you're used to. It will hurt a little more, but if you can use it effectively, you'll have finished all the training you need."

The ornate tool fixed itself in her view, stern and imposing. She didn't want it. "I…" she croaked. "I don't want you to leave."

He pulled her into a warm embrace, feeling the sun's kind rays flow over them. Moments like this, with her, were worth living for. "You mean more to me than the world, Faria. I want you to be safe wherever I am. I promise I'll be careful."

She gave a reluctant grunt into his body. After a short time, he slipped his arms from her and stood up. "I need to get things prepared. I'll see you at dinner."

Holding the staff sadly against her chest, she watched him disappear behind the softly flowing curtains.

Chapter Three

Dinner came and went far too soon for Faria. Within three short hours she was standing on a pier outside Xayall's east gates while her father's provisions were loaded onto a barge to take him to the port. He was on the deck, organising where everything went and discarding anything unnecessary. She simply watched dejectedly as the inevitable parting drew ever nearer.

He was aware of her feelings, but the painful decision to put them aside had to be made. After all, this would be for her safety as well, and that was paramount. Soon, however, he could find no more little excuses to keep the barge there any longer. He had already requested different supplies, letting him stay by her for a few minutes more while the matter was attended to.

Slowly, he stepped off the barge and approached her, trying not to look as regretful as he felt. She fidgeted with her robes, looking at the ground in front of him.

"I'll return as quickly as possible," he said softly.

"It's not that…" she replied, speaking more to her jacket than to him. "You're still sick. If something happened on the way…"

Her voice disappeared in her throat, swallowed by the distressing thoughts that flooded her. She clung onto his long, flowing robe and held him tightly as he enveloped her in a warm embrace.

He stroked a loving hand down her cheek. "Don't worry about me, Faria. I know things could get dangerous, but… I'll look after myself. And you must do the same. Can you promise me that?"

She nodded.

"I love you, Faria."

"I love you too," she mumbled, pressing her head to his chest.

Slowly, he pulled himself away and stepped onto the barge. She wiped her eyes and stood straight, reluctantly reminding herself that now her father was leaving again, she was effectively the head of the sovereign. She still had an image to uphold. As the wooden vehicle drifted into motion, he waved to her with a gentle, tired smile. She waved back and smiled in reply, although she still brimmed with worry.

Once the barge was out of sight she gave a deep, lonely sigh, then turned and walked slowly along the pier. Bayer had been waiting close by the whole time, and together they walked back into the city towards the Tor.

It was night. The stars shone brightly against the obsidian backdrop of the sky, the ghostly white moon looming silently among them. The crater caused by the ancient meteor impact was easily visible on the moon's surface. On some nights the shadow of the massive scar turned the satellite into an eerie, unwavering eye watching over the planet.

The moon used to scare Faria when she was younger. She always felt it was leering at her like some possessed astral giant. It caused her many nightmares that only subsided when her father told her where the crystals came from and showed her a map of the moon from the library. Now that she knew what it was, it didn't bother her as much. She almost felt a degree of closeness to it in some small way, perhaps because of her connection to the crystals.

She couldn't sleep. She sat on her bed, still in her grand Imperial robes, staring at the starry sky.

Restlessness had plagued her all evening. Unpleasant thoughts about her father, Nazreal and the Dhraka swirled through her mind. His staff, although resting across the room, buzzed with an energy that forbade her to relax. She looked at it accusingly, studied it for a minute or so, then pulled on her cloak and marched out to the gardens.

The stave held a beautiful blue-green hue in the moon-light. She turned it over in her hand and watched the light play through the crystal winding along the haft.

Standing in the same spot as earlier, Faria took a deep breath and readied herself, the staff pulsing in her hand. She held it aloft and, as she had that afternoon, tried to draw water out of the air to the staff's tip. Instantly, far quicker than before, a light spiralled up the shaft's crystal web and burst into the spearhead above her. A cloud of mist appeared and shrank back to the tip; milliseconds later an orb of water quivered over the end of the staff, still growing as more mist swirled into it. Able to ignore for now the creeping burn in her hands, she watched in awe as a power she never thought she could wield coursed through the weapon. The waves of tingling heat intensified, running through her veins in hot stabs.

She pointed the stave towards a tree, the ball of water becoming so big that it could hardly support its own weight, rippling and quaking. With another shift of her fingers and pulse of energy the ball froze instantly around the staff's head. Suddenly it became too heavy for her and she dropped it forwards, hitting the grass with a dull thud. She couldn't lift it up. Instead, she grabbed the haft with both hands and sent a small, sustained energy through it that heated the crystal and melted the ice around it, letting it slip free.

She observed the frozen ball with a mild sense of accomplishment, albeit veiled by new frustrations that she still lacked the control her father had. The pain in her hands wouldn't subside—it felt as though someone was plucking her fur with red-hot tweezers. She dropped the staff and loosened her gloves, massaging her hands while holding them to the cool night air to try and calm the prickling burn. As she blew on her palms, she sensed something in the darkness behind her.

She jumped round. "Who's there?"

A familiar shadow emerged from under the tree. "It's me, Your Highness," Bayer said, wearing his armour as comfortably as if he slept in it.

She turned away and gave a silent, impatient sigh, picking up her staff. She held her hands to the ball of ice to see if that was a more effective treatment for the resonance's feedback. It wasn't.

"Well, at least I know I can use it," Faria said idly, tapping the staff against the ice.

Bayer was silent. Her frustration at his presence knotted in her stomach.

"Did you want something?" she asked, feeling impertinent.

Bayer bowed his head. "It's my duty to protect you, Your Imperial Highness. I was concerned when I saw you heading outside."

She folded her arms. For her to be wandering around by herself at night with no guard given her father's worries was, admittedly, a little irresponsible. Although irritated by his common sense, she was grateful for his protection. "Yes, well… thank you. But I'm all right."

"Are you sure? It's not like you to be awake this late, Your Highness," he said softly.

It wasn't true—Faria often didn't sleep at night. She would just read or talk with her father instead of wandering around outside by herself. She sighed. "I know. I'm just… I've never seen Father look so worried."

"He has great concerns about Nazreal. All of Eeres is unsettled by it."

"Yes, but…" She knew that. This time there was something different. It had scared her to the core. The deep, almost infinite apprehension in her father's eyes…

She shook her head to try and rid herself of her doubts. Drawing a tired hand over her ears, she looked into the sky wistfully. "Xayall's never the same without him. I hate having to make these decisions by myself. I'm worried I'll do something wrong." There had never been such a long stretch of time where he wasn't present at the daily government meetings. He and the Councillors made the major decisions and she was always there to watch their recommendations, but, for the moment at least, she was now the higher authority they would report to. Holding the reins of an entire sovereign wasn't a role she enjoyed. She likened it to driving a heavy Theriasaur down a gravelled slope.

Bayer looked up at the Tor. "Your Highness shouldn't worry about the city. For the most part it governs itself."

She didn't listen. "And then the Dhrakans... I know they're aggressive, but do you think Father's right? Would they really try attacking us?"

There was a tense pause. The night's heavy air pressed in around them.

"You will be protected, Your Highness."

She looked uneasily to the grass. "I see..."

The dark forest of Xayall's thick leaves lay still; an oppressive silence descending over the landscape. Even the wind seemed to be lost among its shield of branches.

A sound pierced the blinding shadows.

Rumbling towards the city, a carriage's wheels thrashed the stones below it, the wooden framework creaking agitatedly as it raced past the raised torches illuminating the path to the north gate. Four pike-bearing coati guards and their sergeant marched into place, brandishing their weapons as a signal for it to stop. The Theriasaurs drawing the vehicle skidded to a violent halt, panting raggedly.

"What's your business?" the sergeant called to the hooded driver, moving around the large creatures to give a closer address.

From underneath the hood spoke a sharp female voice. "We're here for your city."

"Xayall's gates are barred. What do—"

Something pierced the sergeant's neck, strangling his voice. He felt a tearing in his throat and a warm trickle down his collar. Just ahead of him his men had slumped to the ground, two black-clad Dhraka to each, their swords dripping with blood. He dropped his shield and spear as the sounds around him faded to muffled noise and more bodies were cast from the sentry towers above him. The last thing he saw before he died was his blood-covered hand, clawing vainly at the crossbow bolt lodged in his neck.

The driver leapt from the seat. She gave the sergeant's body a contemptuous kick and looked to the large metal gates before her. The team of thin, snake-like Dhrakans waited hungrily for their next order, bristling in their armour painted black to match the darkness, hiding them from the glare of the city's torches. Above, the ones who had dispatched the sentries looked to the other gates, which were by now suffering the same brutal assault. They looked obediently to their commander.

She was a vicious hybrid, not quite recognisable as any particular species. The different patterns of her body had been forced onto a shape that didn't fit them. Her ears were similar to a lynx's, her fur mottled like a hyena's. Her face was feline, squat and gaunt. Patches of her fur were wearing thin; underneath could just be seen the sheen of scales. The fur on her arms disappeared at the wrist, leaving scaly hands with savage, jet-black claws. Around her head was a ragged bandanna with a purple crystal sewn in the centre.

Another dragon appeared from the darkness behind her.

"The army is ready, Commander Vionaika."

"Good," she snarled, her reptilian eyes glinting with violent promise above her unfeeling scowl. She gave a quick glance to the carriage. A silent metal body sat within, awaiting its release.

In front of her the gates opened with a deep, ominous rolling.

She licked her lips.

The forest shook under the weight of the army that stirred in the darkness.

Faria and Bayer were inside the Tor. She had been hoping for more reassuring conversation from him, but the dedication to his role as a bodyguard seemed to prevent him from expressing anything greatly personal. She wondered whether it was down to her age, too. Whatever the reason, at present he was only a sounding board for her woes. His assurances that she would be kept safe for as long as he could stand didn't aid her quest for peace of mind.

She stopped by a window and looked outside, gazing at the stars. A shadow moved across the sky. She couldn't discern it; it disappeared against the night seconds later. Dismissing it, she turned back to her ocelot guardian.

"I'm sorry, Bayer. I'm boring and selfish." she said solemnly. "I hate sounding so spoilt. I need to stop complaining and make myself stronger."

"You train a lot already, Your Highness."

She idly raked a claw along the stone windowsill. "I mean more than just training. I won't be much of an Empress if I just sit in a tower and whine all day. I want to be someone Xayall can be proud of. That my Father can be proud of... so he doesn't have to worry."

Bayer said nothing, staring her way with a slowly darkening squint. She gave him a puzzled look in reply. A shadow flashed behind her.

"Bayer, what—"

Suddenly he leapt for her; she was thrown to the floor. The bulk of a creature swept through the window and careened into the wall, sneering and spitting.

The dragon's piercing steel blade lodged itself in the stone. In a second, Bayer drew his sword and sliced at its neck. With a whimpering snarl it collapsed to the floor, dead. The lithe cat looked out of the window and immediately saw more dark shapes flying hungrily towards them. From the streets below came the harsh sounds of fighting as more of Xayall's guards discovered the brutal invaders.

"RAISE THE ALARM!" he roared, his voice booming down the corridors. Grabbing Faria, he sprinted away around a corner, just in time for two more dragons to swoop through the window over the body of their dead comrade.

He quickly led Faria to the upper levels of the Tor, rushing past scores of imperial guards hurrying to defend the tower. Her heart was pounding, the crystal in the staff oscillated urgently.

This wasn't real. It couldn't be real.

What should she do?

Behind them rang the clash of blades. She looked over her shoulder to see the battle's shadows on the wall when Bayer came to an abrupt stop. She turned forwards; a moment later something punched through the air and hit her guard squarely in the jaw, sending him reeling across the floor.

The creature flexed its metal claws, fixing its big, black eyes on her with a cold, empty glare.

Were it not for the metal enhancements, she would have recognised the intruder as a raccoon, a being far removed from this thing's vision of emotionless menace. Its arms and claws gleamed in sharp, forbidding metal; the top of its head and its left ear were plated with the same harsh steel.

"What is that?" she choked.

The raccoon flashed into action. Its forearm detached and cannoned forwards with an explosion of steam, a long metal chain rattling behind it from deep within the creature's shoulder. It hurtled past her left flank, carving deep gouges in the wall next to her. Startled, she spun around just as the raccoon's other arm rocketed forwards, aimed at her skull— Bayer pulled her clear just in time. The metal fiend began reeling his arms back into their sockets at break-neck speed, ripping up the tiled floor with his knifelike claws.

She only had a second. Her mind raced. Desperately, she threw one end of the staff against the wall. A ripple surged through the stone, shaping it into long, finger-like structures that chased after and snapped around the raccoon's wrists like snakes, hardening in place moments later. He pulled against the rocky shackles and hurled his body into it, trying frantically to break free. Ignoring the searing pain in her hands, Faria pulled Bayer up and, with the path in front of them now blocked by the uselessly wrestling raccoon, turned back. Metres before they reached the corner a figure tore into their path and loosed a volley of crossbow bolts at them.

Bayer barged Faria aside. One bolt bounced off the wall and snapped, the others impaled the ocelot in the right shoulder and hip. He collapsed backwards, sword clattering to the floor.

"Bayer!" Faria ran to him, trying to lift him up by his shoulders. He grimaced in pain, glaring at the creature that had shot him, barely keeping hold of his blade.

Vionaika's piercing, sardonic grin filled Faria with equal fear and anger. The crossbow magazine's final bolt was pointing between her eyes; even the fox's most defiant stare wasn't enough to sway the ruthless hyena hybrid in front of her.

Vionaika licked her teeth through a wicked grin. "I haven't had this much fun in a long time," she hissed.

Faria clutched the staff tightly, trembling. "What do you want?"

Vionaika shot her a contemptuous sneer and forced the crossbow closer to Faria's skull. The vixen reeled back in fear and tripped, but as her staff hit the ground a pillar of rock burst from the floor and punched the snarling hyena back into the wall.

From behind the thrashing raccoon a Dhrakan appeared. His destruction-hungry eyes saw Bayer and Faria, and with greedy malevolence he lit a grenade with a firebrand on the wall. He tossed it forwards, eyes alight with anticipation. He didn't see his Commander until the bomb flew from his grasp.

Vionaika looked up in a stupor to see the grenade roll along the floor. In her line of sight was Aidan's staff. Fear torched through her body as the explosive's fuse fizzled down to nothing.

"Wait, you fool!"

Boom.

Chapter Four

Vionaika dived behind the corner as the blast rocked the building. Stone shards exploded sideways like a wall of needles; a thick veil of ash, dust and debris shrouded the corridor. With the throb of the shockwave still clouding her head, she stumbled back to see if the staff, or the one holding it, was still intact.

The grenade had freed the cybernetic raccoon from his stone restraints, save for a small ring of rock still binding his right arm. He rolled over, dazed and bruised. The Dhrakan who threw the grenade was unconscious, though he deserved more than that for being so reckless. Vionaika hurriedly searched the corridor for a sign of the fox or her staff. All that met her grasp was sharp, fractured rock, charred by the grenade's wrath. As the smoke and dust lifted however, where the fox and ocelot had lain was a solid, sinkhole-like depression in the floor, as if it had been sucked away from underneath. She pounded her fist on the stone, spitting venomously.

"Damn it!"

A group of Dhrakan soldiers appeared, alerted by the blast. She wrenched herself to her feet, her claws shuddering as they raked down the wall in her shaken rage.

"Get downstairs, immediately! The vixen with Phiraco's staff—she's a resonator! Find her, now!"

They growled in reply and sprinted forth to their duty.

Downstairs, Faria was moving as quickly as she could with the heavy Bayer leaning on her for support. His breath was unsteady and ragged, her own was ripping from her throat with the strain of the resonance burst. She still wasn't sure what had happened, it was so quick. She felt almost detached, but with the frenzy of the battle she knew if she slowed down even for a second she would collapse under its horrific brutality.

"I'm sorry, Your Highness," Bayer groaned.

She dragged him around a corner, checking ahead for Dhrakans. "No," she grunted. "You saved my life."

The walls were strewn with craters and slices where blades and shields had recently clashed. Bloody sprays marred the walls and darkened the floor. She tried not to look at them.

Suddenly ahead there came a shout. She froze; Bayer tried to raise his sword. They heard metal strike metal, a short yell and a gurgling, stifled moan. A fisher marten in Xayall armour slid down the wall, his descent punctuated by a Dhrakan blade slicing into his head as he fell. Faria forced back the scream that tried to rip from her throat.

It was too late to run. The dragon was already marching towards them, his blade raised. Another followed.

She dropped Bayer and slammed her staff on the floor with a fierce cry. A flash of blue shimmered from the bladed tip between the stones, skirting around the dragons' feet. The slabs beneath them shook loose and collapsed inwards, taking the shocked dragons with it. Before they could fly up and retaliate, another blue burst sealed the hole with the remaining stones.

Bayer sat for a second, stunned by her powerful demonstration.

"Your Highness—"

Something shifted behind him. He whirled up and round, his sword catching the Dhrakan's dagger inches from his neck. Faria spun around in shock. The reptile was forcing his blade toward Bayer's shoulder; the ocelot bashed the dragon away with his hilt, then swung the blade back in an arc that sliced the creature's throat. It spun back and hit the wall, clutching its torn neck. Bayer almost dropped his sword, the pain of the bolt in his shoulder feeding down his arm and pulsing in his chest. Faria pulled him away as the bloodthirsty cries of more Dhrakans rang down the halls.

In their desperate sprint they reached the room Faria had met her father in earlier that day. She pushed shut the heavy doors as quickly as she could. The clash of swords and screams echoed close by, tearing her mind with fear. She couldn't stop shaking. Bodies lay on the floor. She wanted to ignore them, knowing that she'd recognise them, but she kept helplessly glancing and each time had to pull her vision away in fear.

The young fox leant on her palms against the now-closed door. Her hands burned with the ferocity of the resonance's after-effects, and a feeling in her stomach threatened to make her throw up any second. She didn't know how she'd reacted so quickly before the grenade exploded. Her mind raced; she couldn't remember, but her body still quaked with adrenaline. Bayer startled her with a spitting groan as he grabbed hold of the bolt in his shoulder, and with a painful grimace ripped it out and threw it spitefully to the floor, before doing the same to the one in his leg.

"What are we going to do?" she asked quietly, her voice quaking.

He moved to the balcony and scanned the city. The buildings around the east gate had been virtually destroyed, bathed in a fiery orange light. Screams of anger and terror pierced the sounds of battle, and a thick, acrid smell of charred flesh drifted through the air. Scenes of horror and brutal devastation played around the walls. From the forest the Dhrakans were launching bombs into the city, aimed directly at the defending soldiers. Elsewhere, a handful of Xayall troops were coming round to attack the northern artillery while other soldiers raced about the city, trying to evacuate or safely barricade the civilians through any means possible.

She ran to look; he thrust his arm out to halt her.

"Don't. There's nothing you can do for them," he said gravely. "What we have to do… is guarantee your safety."

Faria was horrified. "What do you mean?"

"You must escape Xayall."

She turned to him desperately, a pleading look in her eyes. "We can't fight through all those Dhrakans! We'd never make it! I'm not strong enough!"

He took her arm, grabbing her tightly to make her focus. "Your Highness, you know that isn't true!" He gave a calculating look to the balcony ledge. "You don't have to fight. Escape. With your resonance abilities, you have the greatest chance of getting away safely. You have the power to free yourself and warn other sovereigns of our danger."

She tightened her grip around the staff. "But what about you?"

He gave her a stern glance. "I am not your concern, Your Highness."

"But—"

Footsteps echoed in the corridor, followed by the sound of something light and round hitting the floor. Bayer threw Faria to the ground behind the massive wooden table. Moments later the bomb exploded, showering the room with piercing oak splinters. Four reptilian warriors barrelled inside; Bayer grasped his sword with both hands and hurled it at the shoulder of one, forcing the dragon into his follower. The other two rounded on Faria.

The first raised his twin blades above the vixen's head for a killing stroke. A surge of energy rippled through Faria's body as she thrust the stave into the chest of the snarling beast. The staff erupted with light and the dragon's armour exploded inwards, crushing his chest. He let out a strangled roar, stumbling backwards, desperately trying to rip his armour off.

One of the lizards attacking Bayer thrust his swords towards the feline's head; he kicked himself back and dived left, the dragon's blades sweeping down his tail. He swung his sword round to strike at its scaly throat. A parry by the creature from its first sword stopped it dead and a thrust from its second almost impaled Bayer's stomach.

The other Dhrakan lunged at Faria, landing his free hand on the staff in an attempt to wrench it out of her grasp. She held it fiercely as she tried to wrest it back; it flashed and shook violently, light pulsing towards the Dhrakan's claws. His flesh ruptured and burst open; with an agonising yell he dropped her weapon and stumbled against the wall, clutching his torn, fissured claw.

Suddenly, with a powerful blow to the chest by the pommels of the Dhrakan's swords, Bayer was knocked down. With a vicious kick the dragon hit him across the floor and into a pillar, the other rounding him with teeth bared.

Faria ran to protect him but the dragons wheeled round and advanced on her, swords outstretched. Trapped, she began to panic. They closed distance, drawing back for a final thrust—

"Halt!"

The Dhrakans stopped with their blades inches from her chest. The hyena commander and her robotic minion marched in, the latter still trying to rid himself of the stone around his wrist. Vionaika's face contorted to a sickening smirk.

"So this is his daughter! How fortunate he neglected your safety."

The hackles stood up on the back of Faria's neck; she growled fiercely back at her. "What do you want with my father?"

"He holds information that's the key to a new era," Vionaika sneered with vicious pride, moving closer, the crossbow aimed at the vixen's throat. "But in his absence, it won't take much to tear Nazreal's secrets out of you instead."

Faria bristled with anger. She kept a tight grip on the staff; none of them noticed the breeze begin to strengthen. "I don't know anything about Nazreal!" she shouted defiantly.

"Don't patronize me!" Vionaika scoffed. "You're a resonator, *his* daughter, and you're hiding within Xayall's Imperial Tor. Your father already knew of the dangers of such a powerful legacy; it's quite pitiful he'd leave it so poorly guarded. But perhaps if you really don't know, then we should find him instead…" Her eyes flashed with glee. "…not that we haven't already been tracking his ship, of course. They may have him by now."

"NO!" Faria screamed.

A savage whirlwind erupted in the room, forming the scattered remnants of wooden door into a barrage of debris that Faria then cast at the attackers. The other edge of her staff she formed into a razor-sharp blade; whirling it behind her she sliced through the third Dhrakan's breastplate to tear a splitting gash across his stomach.

The raccoon leapt for her. She screamed; a bolt of electricity snapped from the staff, jolting up his mechanical arm, causing it to twitch uncontrollably and him to howl in pain. She turned round just as Vionaika, briefly distracted by the whirlwind, trained the crossbow on her chest.

At that instant a sword knocked the stock upwards. Bayer dropped his weapon and grabbed the hyena's arms, wrestling for control of the bow.

"Go, Your Highness!" he yelled, struggling against his injuries. "Get out and find your father!"

She was out of time. More Dhrakans spilled into the Tor below. With a last, lingering look back at Bayer she ran to the balcony and vaulted over the side.

Vionaika freed one of her claws and ripped into Bayer's already injured shoulder. He yelled and fell back. Wresting the crossbow free, she jammed it against his chest.

"Fool."

Faria plummeted towards Xayall's streets, the force of the rushing wind stopping her breath as she fell. Almost losing herself in the descent, she grasped the staff desperately and willed for a wind to catch her, keep her steady, save her from a messy death on the streets.

In answer, two huge vortices from the staff's tips whirled underneath her, slowing her plunge just above the rooftops. They were unsteady, fluctuating; too much power either way would send her rocketing into the air or falling to the ground again. She swayed violently as she tried to direct herself to the south-western wall on the pillars of air, constantly near to throwing herself to the stone beneath.

Below and around her the battle raged, the Xayall guard desperately outnumbered and caught by surprise. Streets burned—the eastern part of the city was already lost to flames. Those who tried to evacuate found the main gates barred by the arrival of more Dhrakan troops.

As she neared the wall the ache in her hands was almost unbearable—she couldn't even tell if she was holding the staff any more. With the pain rising, she almost smashed herself against the city's outer walls. She meant to land on the battlements but in her panicked state she overshot and withdrew her power on the other side, spiralling down into the river. She hit the water with an impact she was sure would break her; her lungs burnt as the air was punched from them. She almost lost her staff as she broke the surface. Faria surfaced with a rattling gasp and stabilised herself as best she could, shaking uncontrollably in a rush of panic and in shock at the water's deep chill. The river's current was taking her into the forest. She had to swallow a cry as she saw the Dhrakan army marching into the city, each looming reptile as bloodthirsty as the ones before.

As the calmly sweeping waters washed her away from the terror wrought on her city, the cries of battle softened, until eventually all she could hear was the dull roar of distant soldiers, and all she could see was the Tor, lit by the streets' raging fires.

After a time the river slowed and, struggling to swim while saving her father's weapon, she managed to haul herself onto the bank. Still shaking, she lay helpless on the grass, waiting for her breath to return and her brain to stop thumping inside her head. Her mind was telling her to run, to run now and get away. The Dhrakans would be looking for her, but the shaking would not leave her. Heaving to a stand, she looked straight ahead and ran, hitting the foliage at full speed, careening through it, tearing past branches and bushes that bruised, battered, scratched her body and caught on her clothes as she went.

The streaking shadows merged into a dizzying blur. Each heavy, frantic footfall pounded through her, rattling the breath from her chest. She ran for what seemed like hours, but every glance over her shoulder still brought the image of the city's faint glow. The sickening scent of the bombs' inferno was carried on the breeze. She fell to her hands and knees, quaking, her stomach surging so heavily she felt she would throw up at every movement. For a second she stayed there, staring at the dark ground. Groggily, she pulled herself up and began stumbling ahead.

Faltering through the thick plants, her body gave up a few feet later. Her legs could no longer hold her and she crashed to the floor, breathing heavily, sweat dripping down her muzzle. A dull thud echoed in her ears; they burned with the heat of the blood coursing through her veins. Her hands were shaking uncontrollably, her vision swimming.

She knew she had to hide herself or else be found unconscious later, and Bayer's sacrifice would have been for nothing. Fumbling beside her for her staff, it took all her strength to raise it up. It glowed softly, almost invisibly in her weak and unfocused state. In response, the branches around her began to reach down and intermesh, forming a wooden, leafy web to conceal her. It wasn't perfect, but it was all she could manage.

As the world twisted around her she was overcome by exhaustion and grief, and let out a quiet, pitiful sob before falling into a deep sleep.

Chapter Five

Xayall gleamed ethereally in the midday sun, the hazy air giving the sky a golden hue that reflected from the city's walls. A wonderful, buzzing calm filled the streets as bodies moved in and out of the buildings, gliding along as they always had, serene and secure.

Faria swaggered confidently along the street that rocked with the steps of the people around her, all walking past her in the opposite direction. She was ten. Her new dress, a rich blend of gold and green, had just been finished by special commission. She insisted on walking all the way back to the Tor so she could show it off and watch it gleam beautifully in the sun. She did her best not to focus on the other occupants of the street; she didn't want to catch their eye in case they disapproved of her boasting. She fixed herself on her goal—to head home to the Tor.

Striding ahead of her, a few big steps away, was her father. He cut a penetrating swathe through the respectful crowd. She was always proud of her father. He was the best father in the world; strong, generous, and he cared for her more than any other father could. The people of Xayall were right to move out of his way.

A whisper in the crowd caught her ear. Someone hissed his name. It was harsh, accusing. She hadn't heard the rest of what they were saying; they were walking too fast in the opposite direction. She dismissed it.

Again, from the other side she heard it. She turned to see the voice's face, but couldn't place it. Then another. And another. Again and again his name pierced her ears, rising into a cacophony of whispers threatening to split her head open. The faces of the people grew eerily dark, their eyes hidden but staring at her with a crushing force. She whimpered for her father. He didn't hear. She called for him again, louder. Still he didn't turn, marching alone through the crowd ahead. The figures all turned against him, their harsh whispers ripping her ears. She screamed, her voice silent under the frightening rumble of the crowd, and lunged forward.

He turned. Just before she could see his face, she tripped. Her arm went out instinctively and grasped hold of his staff. A flash of white burned her eyes, her fingers stung with electric stabs.

When she opened her eyes she was seventeen again. Xayall's streets were black as charcoal, the walls and ground cracked and burnt. Smoke rose from fissures beneath her. Deep, dark red clouds rolled overhead, and an ominous rumbling shook the buildings. The hyena's piercing laughter echoed in the distance. Up ahead, the Tor had been twisted, distorted. Faria rose to her full height, Aidan's staff in her hand. As she looked at it, a dark shape burst from the Tor's highest window, shrieking madly. Deep red eyes flashed with hate.

"Your death shall be my glory!"

It surged towards her, speed so great she was powerless to avoid it. She screamed, raising her arms against it in vain. It struck her in the chest and a deep, soft pain blossomed through her body. As she fell backwards, she felt her father calling.

"Faria… I'm sorry…"

Faria's eyes drifted open, flickered slightly, then closed again for a moment. Instantly opening them again, the young vixen sat bolt upright, scraping her ears against the wooden canopy she'd created last night. She cursed under her breath, and then froze, suddenly remembering the Dhrakan presence in the forest. The nightmarish scenes of the previous night shot through her mind. The young vixen was almost sick again with their remembrance but she quelled it, breathing slowly and deliberately to calm herself down. She had not been found yet, but wagered that the dragons were already creeping around close by, or would be soon. She had to leave. But…

Faria pulled the staff closer and nudged the branches that hid her. Peering out, she scanned the area for movement. Nothing obvious. Tentatively, she waved the staff and the branches withdrew, leaving her sat quietly between the two trees. The young fox looked around her before standing up and, confident that no scouts were nearby, crawled back in the direction of the city.

When the city was back in proper sight, she climbed and hid in a dense, leafy tree, straining to get a good view of the destruction. The walls she could see were mostly intact, although the gates where the loyal Xayall guards used to stand were now marshalled by fierce Dhrakan bruisers with shields bigger than she was. The only thing she could really see was the Tor, and aside from one or two scorch marks, its clean, decorated structure completely belied the devastation wrought elsewhere.

A lamenting but determined sigh escaped her. She had to find her father before the Dhrakans did. He could convince the Senate to liberate the city, she was sure of it. Andarn and Tremaine's armies were the biggest in the world; the Dhraka wouldn't stand a chance against them if they were to help. If she could get *near* either sovereign, it would be a start.

But her father was on his way to Skyria already—an island almost on the other side of the world, and it seemed even more unreachable for all the trouble it would take getting there. At the least, she hoped with all her heart that he *was* on his way, and hadn't been caught up in the Dhrakan attack somewhere outside Xayall's borders. But if she could reach Andarn, she could board a boat to Skyria. She had to try. For her sake, her father's, Xayall's, and if her father's misgivings were true, possibly Eeres' itself.

The doubts and fears that plagued her yesterday began creeping into her consciousness. Why couldn't he have taken *her* to Skyria too? How dangerous can a lost, ruined city like Nazreal be?

She rapped her knuckles for being defeatist and checked herself for her frustration. She had to trust his judgement, and if nothing else she was thankful for him not to have been in that horrifying siege.

The guards by the gates began to move. She had to leave. Now. Frenzy shadowing her movements, she jumped from the branch and moved deeper into the forest, beginning a wide circle around the city to the north-leading Andarn road. She moved swiftly between trees, using large bushes for cover as much as she could. Thankfully the trees were large, with thick leaves that kept the forest floor shady, cool and at least a little more concealing. She knew partially colour-blind Dhrakan eyes couldn't see well in green forests, with their lands being mostly red and their homes underground, but her cobalt jacket was hardly discreet. Coupled with her orange fur and big, black ears, she felt she might as well be waving a flag with her name and address on it.

The forest stretched for miles, from far beyond Xayall in the south to the borders of Tremaine in the north. A ridge of mountains ran through the centre like the spine of a massive, ancient dinosaur. The temperate region covering Xayall boasted a proud variety of life. Some trees were massive, having survived for over a thousand years to tower eminently over the landscape. Others were smaller, not even breaking through the canopy. Huge areas were carpeted in a fine green moss that crept up the trunks of the wooden giants, engulfing the barky husks of felled trees and turning them into a paradise for insects and small mammals.

She was rarely allowed into the forest, and had never been by herself before. It was hauntingly beautiful, but her admiration for its scenery was tainted by her sense of panic and looming dread. She climbed, crawled and darted along as quickly as she could, all the time seeking out pursuers through the leaves. Her staff, although dormant, retained a faint, hollow glow as if it were also on guard.

Soon enough she saw the road, its stone and sand pathway flanked by a protective row of trees. She could see a number of Dhrakans marching malefically along it to halt a caravan travelling towards the city. Crouching, peering through a large fern, she observed them. She couldn't hear what they were saying, but the caravan was turned away and hurried off at a pace while the Dhrakans smiled secretively to one another. She could risk following after it and hitching a ride, but she feared the dragons would be patrolling the road elsewhere, looking to raid travellers' cargo in the hope of unearthing something they could capture. Instead, she shadowed the road's path as best she could.

The Dhrakans she passed didn't seem to enjoy guarding the road. Most of the time they looked surly and bored, except when coaches appeared. Faria saw them spit and jeer at a mongoose family who refused to turn around; from what she could ascertain one of their children was sick and they wanted to see a Xayall physician.

Those who were turned back (and eventually, everyone was) were faced with sneers by the loathsome dragons, stationed along the road at regular intervals. As she moved further away from Xayall the guards became more infrequent, and she was even tempted to talk to a group of travellers she passed when no scouts were around. She grudgingly decided against it for fear of being recognised, although she desperately wished that she could tell someone, anyone, about the city's invasion. She had never been left unprotected before. While her powers had helped her escape so far, this was the first time she needed to defend against anything other than her imagination. It was unsettling, alien, and the thought of being alone in a forest full of enemies sent chills up her spine.

She'd dropped her staff out of tiredness a few times, and every time she picked it back up with increased ambivalence, not wanting to part with it but blaming the whole situation on it for lack of any other explanation. Whenever a dragon appeared on the road it took all her strength not to bolt and turn back to the city just to be somewhere she knew, regardless of what the Dhrakans wanted from her. She couldn't escape them alone, she knew that much. But a gaping pit of fear opened within her when the prospect of revisiting the bodies of the invasion and facing that hyena hybrid again flashed in her mind. Turning back was no option.

She hadn't eaten since the previous day, and unsurprisingly her stomach growled in frustration, with greater volume each time. She would have given anything to run into a lost Xayall patrol, or an inn which hadn't yet received news of the siege, or better yet, her father. It was no challenge to imagine Dhrakan sentries around every mound or tree, however, and even if she did stumble across a friendly lodging, she had no money to pay for food.

Aside from the small groups of travellers, there were very few other people on the road, which surprised her. Normally the roads to and from Xayall were bustling, especially as the north led to all the major cities, including Sinédrion. It all added to her apprehensions.

She clambered over a large tree-trunk, catching her coat on one of its protruding branches. As she pulled herself free a flash of red in the middle-distance caught her eye. In a wave of panic she looked around, trying to find the shape or a movement to match her fleeting glance. Nothing appeared, leaving her alone in the rustling leaves amid the faint calls of the forest's inhabitants. After a few seconds, cautiously, she began moving again, holding her staff as a guard in front of her body. Low pulses of energy twisted through it, ready to protect her.

A loud snap to her right caused her harried gaze to swing around—again, nothing. She continued forwards, quickening her pace. Her heart boomed in her chest, a rush of fear sweeping down her shoulders. She broke into a run.

With a crack of branches to the left a Dhrakan appeared from the road, pounding the earth with powerful legs to match her speed with ease, closing distance.

"Found her!" he screeched. He whirled a bolo over his head, the weapon thrumming with impending malice. She darted right to evade him and was faced with another dragon, armed with sword and shield. Behind her she could hear tree branches creaking under the weight of something bounding from limb to limb, but she couldn't afford a warning glance.

The Dhrakan with the bolo cast it at her; at the same time, the swordsman leapt forward. A funnel of wind from her staff sent the bolos flying into the trees, and with a deft twist she brought the other end crashing against the sword's blade, snapping it in two. Her adversary threw his broken weapon aside and charged towards her, putting his full force behind the shield. She didn't have time to react; the heavy impact sent her through the air and brought her to the ground with a jolt a few feet away. She thrashed around, trying to right herself as the shield-baring dragon raced to her again.

She panicked. Gripping the staff tightly, shaking, she ducked underneath the closest tree and willed for something to save her. Desperately trying to focus her thoughts, she could feel energy spewing from her palms. A deep whooshing sound came from above her, followed by a dull impact and a painful groan.

By her power, the tree had swung its huge, low branch and brained the beast, now lying prostrate in the ferns. Timidly, she stood up to be faced by the last dragon. He cracked his shoulders menacingly and let out a threatening growl. Just as she thought to move, he made a contemptuous beckoning gesture to something in the trees above.

The same metallic raccoon that had attacked her inside the Tor landed in front of her, the ring of stone still attached to its wrist.

"You again!?" she gasped.

The Dhrakan licked his lips and stepped back for his companion beast to take the stage, his eyes gleaming with a thirst for blood.

"Take her alive, if you want."

The raccoon fixed his empty stare on her and shot his left fist out; she fell backwards to avoid its crushing impact, watching it cannon past her face and crash into the foliage beyond. She scrambled round the tree, trying to find an escape.

The tree bark cracked behind her right ear. She rolled forwards just in time to see the raccoon swoop past, claws outstretched, having used his arm as a slingshot to catapult

himself towards her. As he passed he fired his other arm;
Faria just managed to block it with her staff but he latched
hold, throwing it, and her, behind him. Hurtling towards a
tree she aimed the staff to the ground and a mountain of soil
rose to cushion her fall. She scrambled away as the raccoon
wound up for another attack. With a frantic yell she bran-
dished the staff towards him, her body aching under the strain
of her power.

His wrist fired. At the same time the staff pulsed and a
shrill, piercing sound shrieked through the woods, following a
ripple of air shot from the point of her stave. The bullet of
sound smashed into the creature's metal headplate. He yelped
and cradled his head with his remaining arm, the one he fired
veering off course into the ferns.

This was her chance!

Its arm started to reel back in, gaining speed. She grabbed
hold of the chain and jumped, letting it carry her straight
towards her foe. In his eyes was a faint flicker of surprise
moments before the end of her stave flashed with electricity
and struck his head. He collapsed backwards, unconscious,
one of his arms only half-wound. Landing heavily the other
side of him, she turned to face her last opponent, the unarmed
Dhrakan. She tried to keep upright, fighting against legs that
insisted they should give way.

"I don't care how many of you there are," she barked
shrilly, "but if you so much as come near me again I'll take
your head off!" Her ferocity surprised even her, and for a
brief second the dragon looked warned by her brave display.
He cracked his shoulders again and with vicious confidence he
drew a long, thin blade from a scabbard on his back, twirling

it through the air with a disgusting grimace. As he moved to advance, a determined snarl from Faria stopped him in his tracks. Moments later he fell downwards with a roar, disappearing below the plants. She ran forwards to see his head just visible above the ground, the rest of him tightly encased in the soil that had swallowed him from below. Before he could free himself she swung the flat edge of the staff against his head with all her strength, rendering the beast unconscious.

She breathed an exhausted sigh. That was more than she needed.

Suddenly though, the muscles in her hands went into spasm; she dropped the staff and yelped as she tried to fight against the pain coursing from her fingers to her forearms. She'd used too much energy, and her body was beginning to take damage from the resonance. It felt as though hot needles were being pressed into her muscles. Sweat poured down her muzzle, her breathing was ragged; desperately, she tried not to scream with agony and alert more dragons to her presence.

Eventually the pain subsided to a dull throb, and after a minute or so of gently massaging her hands she was able to pick up her staff.

"They'll be back, I know it," she muttered angrily, glaring to the bushes beyond.

Shaking her head clear, she stood and restarted her trudge north, the thought of seeing her father, and being in his protection, the only motivation she could find.

The cyborg raccoon twitched as she passed. She paused, crouching over it for a closer look. She'd never seen anything so bizarre. It was a fascinating creature, but there was something unnerving about it. It wasn't the harsh metal claws and half-face that grasped her attention; it was the technology behind them. She had seen metal limbs before—physicians were working on replacement legs that had hinges—but nothing this sophisticated. She wasn't sure she wanted to think about where it came from, or how the poor thing came to be in that state. Either way, she hoped it would stay there and leave her alone.

She straightened quickly, remembering her situation. Later would do for answers.

As she darted away into the forest, the raccoon's half-wound arm began to trickle back into its mechanical socket.

Its eyes flickered open.

Chapter Six

The forest's uneven ground and the sun radiating through the leafy canopy were unforgiving to one in such a weary state. Faria had not stopped once since waking, and still didn't know what she was going to do when she reached the next town... if she even made it that far. If the Dhrakans were lurking around the gates there, too, then she'd be trapped outside, separated from any help. The unconscious bodies she'd left behind had probably been discovered by now. She was only glad so few dragons had found her so far, although each of the forest's unfamiliar sounds rushed fresh panic to her ears that she had been sighted.

A growl escaping her throat, she slashed at a low shrub with her staff, snapping it in two, and slumped by a tree. Her head in her hands, she tried vainly to ignore the feeling that her stomach was going to collapse in on itself with hunger. Her clothes were scratched and dirty, as were her tail and ears. She had countless bruises running up her body from being battered with branches, and a heavy pain in her chest from the Dhrakan's shield.

"Maybe I should hand myself in... they might at least feed me before killing me," she whispered, leaning back against the tree. Hearing a faint noise in the bushes to the right, she absently rolled her head to look. A figure, partly obscured by the plants, stepped forwards. Its metal ear caught the sun. She leapt up and readied her staff, shaking with apprehension and the aching strain of rising so quickly.

The raccoon stopped.

"Go away! I'll hurt you if I have to!" she yelled.

The raccoon tilted its head in response. His mouth moved as if speaking, but the voice was absent, lodged in his throat. He then stepped forwards again.

"I'm warning you!" she called, this time louder, bracing the staff under her left arm like a lance.

The raccoon stopped a short distance away. It looked to the floor and spoke again, silently at first, trying to get its voice to surface. "...n... ou... elp me?" it croaked eventually, like the gears of an old, rusty machine grinding into action.

She raised her staff higher; the tip danced with electric sparks. "What do you want?" she snapped, her voice cracking. She barely had the energy to stand, let alone shout at this stalker. "If you don't answer I'll strike you again!"

It gave a few short coughs and a loud hum, pushing its voice back into the air.

"Oh... I was just... wondering if you could help me get this stone off my wrist," it sighed in a young male voice, twisting the rocky handcuff round to try and prise it off, to no avail. He gave a small, relieved smile, looking grateful for the return of his powers of speech.

She watched him cautiously. His stance was completely different to when she'd first seen him in the Tor. He had a spark of curiosity in his eyes and a youthful brightness in his face. He walked closer, his tail flicking in alert regard as he looked her up and down. She didn't move, but still held the staff threateningly in his direction, unsure of what to do.

He stopped about three feet away, his gaze fixed on her strange, ornate weapon. He craned his neck to see it closer; she instinctively pulled it back even though she wanted to jab it into his face as a warning.

"I like your sword," he chimed. "Can I have a look?"

She was about to correct him about it being a staff rather than a sword, but tried to keep focus on her situation, watching for an ambush. "No!" she barked. "Get back!"

"Why?"

Faria wished the tree wasn't behind her. "It's—I'll hurt you if you come any closer, I promise! Just get away! Um…" The crystal rippled in warning light.

He gave her a quizzical, playful look. "Um?" he repeated. "You know… I'm really glad I can speak again, but it looks like you're having problems this time," he said playfully. He then gave her a rather disgruntled pout. "But you're being rude."

She didn't take her eyes from him for a second. Her chest heaved with harsh, defensive breaths as they watched each other tensely for a few seconds.

"Who are you?" she asked, her voice hushed, guarded.

The raccoon stepped back and straightened his worn jacket with mismatched sleeves. His trousers, slightly too long for him, wore a coating of black dust so thick it was impossible to tell what colour they were originally. Around his neck was a folded scarf, carefully bunched around his neck to cover the space between his jacket and black undershirt. A thick belt sat on his hips, not actually serving its purpose to support anything. "I'm Tierenan. Tierenan Cloud, from Skyria."

"That's where…" Faria blurted before she could stop herself. "…I'm going."

His ears pricked up as he smiled. "Oh, what for?"

"I'm not telling you!" she spluttered. "Look, I don't know what you're trying to do but just… leave me alone!"

Tierenan did a proud little pirouette, adding to the confusion that was quickly swamping Faria's exhaustion-addled mind. "Okay then," he cooed, a little disheartened. Almost instantly he turned back, an excited grin lighting up his face. "Well, Skyria's a lovely place! It's got trees bigger than you can imagine, and mountains, and waterfalls, and lovely birds! I'll show you around when you get there if you like." He paused for a second, looking at her suspiciously. "You're not going to walk there, are you?"

She leant back against the tree, studying him with utmost suspicion. Was it a trick, or had she done something to alter his personality? She had to choose her words carefully. "I'm… not going to walk all the way."

"I just mean, there's a road there," he said, pointing at the pathway not that far from them. "Why are you walking through the forest?"

"Yes, I know there's a road, but it's complicated…"

Since he seemed open to conversation, she thought now might be a good time to get some answers of her own. "Why are *you* here, Tierenan?"

He didn't answer, but folded his arms and pouted again. "You haven't told me your name yet."

"What?"

"Your name!" he said emphatically. "I introduced myself, but you haven't. We can't have a proper conversation if I don't know your name. It's just rude."

She opened her mouth to protest but thought better of herself. If he already knew her as a target it wouldn't make a difference whether she used a pseudonym or not. "My name is Faria Phiraco. I'm from Xayall."

"See? Your name's cool! You should be proud of it," he chirruped, giving her a satisfied smile and turning to the trees. "This is a nice forest," he said happily, skimming the flowers with his hands. She clenched her fists, frustrated that he avoided her original question. He didn't seem to react at all to her name, so perhaps he'd forgotten his mission. As he swept his fingers through the low leaves surrounding him, he only now seemed to notice his metal claws. He froze for a moment, then turned them over and began examining them urgently.

She watched silently as he slowly closed and opened them, staring distantly at the joints. "Are you okay?" she asked quietly.

Tierenan didn't answer for a second. He ran his hands over his head, feeling his real right ear, then his left metal one, and then pulled at his sharpened claws.

"I've changed," he said flatly.

She hesitated, sensing his sudden quiet. "Do you... remember what happened?"

He looked at her, puzzled. "The metal? That was years ago. What I mean is I've changed *again*. My old metal hands were different. I don't understand..."

"Years ago?" she asked, subconsciously pulling at one of her ears, stroking out a scratch.

"Yeah" he said, smiling slightly. "There was a fire in Skyria when I was younger. A burning branch fell on me, crushed my arms and took off my ear. It burnt most of my face off too," he said, a little more cheerfully than he'd intended. His body sunk slightly. "Heh, not very nice. Anyway, I had a lot of surgery to put me right, but those parts of my body were too damaged to repair themselves. In the end my family gave me new ones instead." He held out his claws to her, grinning. "But these new ones are pretty cool, aren't they?"

She didn't want to agree. "Ah... Does your family make them?"

"No, somebody else did. But my parents are important in Skyria, so they let me have them, my old ones. They wanted to see if they'd work..." He trailed off, distrait. "Hey, where are the others?" he asked, looking around.

Faria flicked her tail and gave him a sideways look. "What others? The Dhrakans, you mean?"

"What? No," he replied. "The people I was travelling with. That's what I wanted to ask when you ran away. Did you see any of the people from my carriage here?"

She shook her head slowly, still wary of him. "You weren't in a carriage. You were with the Dhrakans, and a... someone else. You..."

He looked concerned. "Dhrakans?! What Dhrakans? Where have I been?"

"You attacked me last night. You besieged Xayall and tried to capture me."

His hand rushed to his mouth, his knees buckling slightly as the cold shock hit him. He looked terrified.

"And you attacked me in the forest a while back. Your arms flew off and tried to punch me. I hit you with my staff."

He looked at his hands, scars of battle already etched into their sharp edges. The claws twitched and flicked, as if impatient to be released once more. Swallowing hard, he shrank back.

"I'm sorry," she said quietly.

Tierenan looked ruefully at his right claw. "You don't need to apologise. Did I... really do that? I can't remember much..." Suddenly he rushed to her, concern gripping his voice. "I didn't hurt you, did I? I'm really sorry if I did! Please tell me you're okay!"

She chuckled weakly, pushing him back. She wasn't expecting his apologies. "Yes, I'm okay. But were there more of you?"

He nodded. "I was being taken to the Senate to show the academics what they could do with this technology. But I fell asleep on the way, and..."

There was a long, tense pause.

"...my arms 'flew off'?"

Faria smiled nervously. "Er...yes. They have chains attached to them. But, um..."

Tierenan immediately gazed wide-eyed at his arm and turned around, aiming his fists at a nearby tree. Just before he was about to shoot them into its trunk to see for himself, he paused. "You say 'um' a lot, Faria," he said, smiling over his shoulder at her. She couldn't help but smile nervously back— she could hardly believe this was the same creature that tried to attack her before. His eyes were completely different now, alive with life. His fluffy tail flicked playfully around when he spoke or moved, and even standing still he seemed to brim with energy that threatened to make him climb on everything in sight. There was a loud '*thunk*', followed by an ecstatic gasp from the raccoon.

"Wow, you were right!" he trilled. "Look, I grabbed it without moving!"

She scratched the back of her head as he tried for a few seconds to bring the tree back with his hand, then gave up, satisfied with a clawful of bark instead. Once retracted he lifted his hand to the light, and his face lit up in awe as a small green bird with a long tail came to rest on his finger, studying him curiously.

While Faria watched him inspect the elegant avian, a flash of danger sparked through her mind. She was wasting time here. With Tierenan stood before her, such a drastic change between his personality now and the monster of the previous night, she had to measure her plan carefully. Trusting him could be a fatal mistake, but for the moment he was her best chance of help in reaching her father without a Dhrakan escort. Regardless of whether or not this was a ploy to capture her, he certainly didn't seem like a threat at the moment...

The bird fluttered away, disappearing into the canopy. He watched it leave, smiling serenely.

"Tierenan, we can't stay here," she said eventually. Staying with him was probably safer than being found by the Dhrakans outright, at least for the moment. She'd have to watch him carefully, though. "Will you take me to Skyria?"

"Yeah!" he said gleefully. "I want to go home anyway."

"Thank you," she said, smiling despite the impending worry that she may have betrayed herself already. "But we need to leave, now. And I need to explain something to you about why I'm here."

"Can you take this stone off my arm first, please?"

Night in the forest was no quieter than the daytime. Night birds and insects sang, chirruped, croaked and wheezed in content, blissfully ignorant of the larger struggles on the land below.

When Faria told Tierenan the full story about the Dhrakan assault on Xayall and why she was escaping to Skyria, he'd fallen very quiet for quite a long time. For a while she wondered whether he'd been offended, thinking she distrusted him, or if he was worried he'd been found out and was calculating an opportunity to capture her. He seemed less skittish as they travelled, and wore a look of guilt that didn't suit him. When he did finally say something again it was to point out a species of tree he particularly liked, and soon afterwards he acted as if nothing had happened.

They were now sat under a roof of low branches she'd formed using her staff. He'd watched enraptured as the limbs twisted around each other like long woody fingers, although upon seeing her drop the staff and grasp her hands in pain, he quickly rushed to her side to see if she was all right.

He held an incredible knowledge of forest plants. While Faria was nursing herself he'd disappeared into the trees and within minutes had brought back numerous edible nuts, berries and fungi for them to share.

"I couldn't get any insects," he'd said. "I'm not used to my new claws, so all I get is squish."

Normally Faria would turn her nose up at any kind of mushrooms (especially uncooked ones), but having had little else to eat all day, she wolfed them down to appease her stomach and restore some energy. It had reached the point where had a rat wandered past, she'd have launched herself on it and eaten it whole, but she held her polite reserve. After all, she didn't want to upset Tierenan. He'd spectated eagerly as she chomped on the seeds he'd brought her, which she guiltily found dry, grainy and tasteless. The young vixen gave as approving a look as she could muster without retching. He smiled and lay back on the ground, running his metal claws along the lines of the wooden canopy.

"So it hurts, doing this?" he asked quietly.

"Yeah," she said, trying to scrape the taste of the seeds off her tongue against her teeth. "It takes a lot of my energy. If I do it too much it feels like my body's being sucked out through my skin."

Tierenan grimaced. She quickly tried to right the conversation.

"It's to do with the structure of the crystals. I can change their shape, and that affects how they react when energy passes through them," she continued, blindly. She tried to stop herself, but guessed that if he wasn't a resonator there was little he could do with the staff anyway, and if he had wanted to capture her he'd had plenty of opportunities to do so by now. "I can alter the way certain elements behave, and move, and change their shape. I have to use the crystals in the staff, though. I can't do it by myself."

He sat up. "Do you think I could do it?"

"I… don't think so. I only know one other who can. It's a hereditary thing—you can't learn it." She looked at his metal limbs and surreptitiously tossed the remainder of her nuts outside while he was distracted elsewhere. "Besides, you have your claws. They're pretty impressive."

"I guess so," he mused. "But I'd love to do stuff like that as well! What else can you change?"

It occurred to her that she'd never been asked this before. Even by Bayer or Kier, the only two others who knew about it. She looked up thoughtfully. "Metal—that's pretty easy. Rock is more difficult, because it'll shatter if you're not careful, and earth, because it's loose and is made of lots of different elements. Wind, water, sound, erm… electricity…" She paused as her mind taunted her with the thoughts of the Dhrakan's exploding hand back in Xayall. "…fire, and a few other things. I'm still discovering what I can do myself."

There was another pause. Tierenan drew in breath as if to speak several times, each time faltering into silence. Although she was interested in knowing what he wanted to say she didn't prompt him, preferring to wait until he could find the right words.

Eventually, he did. "I'm sorry for attacking you," he said solemnly.

"It's… okay," she said, smiling faintly.

"They must have done something to me. I still don't remember much. It just makes me worry, because… because there could be important things I've forgotten. I hope I've not hurt anyone."

Faria rested her muzzle on her hands. He'd done much less than the dragons had. She'd hurt people, too. She'd had to, otherwise she could have been in a far worse situation than she was now. But knowing what she'd done pulled at her core. Pangs of regret tugged at her mind, regardless of how often she asserted to herself the need to escape and survive.

"I don't think we can always help what happens in a fight," she said. "It's not as if you have much of a choice. If you're powerful, even the smallest actions can have the biggest repercussions. That doesn't make it right, but you just have to hope that what you decide can be justified later. Or that you make proper recompense."

She glanced over to him. He didn't respond, still looking a little doubtful. He had been under their control, after all; it wasn't a matter of choice.

"And if you're forced into something, then you have to hope that something good will come from it anyway." She gave him a little tap with her staff. "If you hadn't attacked me, I wouldn't have been able to knock you back to your senses. So that's good, right?"

Tierenan grimaced comically. "Well, I dunno. You have to put up with me until Skyria now! I hope you know what you're in for, Faria."

She smiled again. "Oh, I'm sure I'll manage."

Chapter Seven

A low mist hung in the air. The dawn's light cast splinters of silver through the trees while two figures drifted between them, trudging steadily onwards in spite of their tiredness. They had been travelling for two days now, and had crossed the wide river that marked Xayall's sovereign borders early last morning.

The forests heaved with Dhrakan soldiers. The areas between Xayall and Andarn were only sparsely inhabited, and the city patrols didn't venture this far out. As such, the dragons' web was spreading wider, unhindered, hoping to catch the young fox in its vicious, barbed threads. The progress she and Tierenan made during the day was slow, with a lot of time spent hiding from leering eyes and moving between safe positions. They had fought more Dhrakan squads together; while she was grateful for Tierenan's help, she was having difficulty maintaining her energy, and was conscious of becoming more of a hindrance than a help. It took all her strength just to run, let alone wield the crystal stave. Their only other advantages were the Dhrakan's poorly-adjusted eyesight and Tierenan's uncanny ability to climb. Many of the dragons seemed to be affected by pollens from the plants, making stealthy movement past them considerably easier. It was still terrifying for Faria, with the fear of their hungry glares always pressing into her back.

The nights were worse still. They could hear patrols and scouts marching past their cover every few minutes. Never completely knowing if the dragons had left, neither she nor Tierenan dared to fall asleep for fear of one or both of them being discovered and taken away. Once it was light enough for them to move they carried on.

Their current heading was a small town called Midia, a frequent stop for travellers and merchants. It was a slight deviation from Andarn's hopeful goal, but here they would be able to find food, and perhaps (at Tierenan's most ecstatic suggestion) a bodyguard.

"We'd be completely safe! They'd be strong, and fast, and good with weapons, and have that dark-and-brooding-but-really-a-softie-on-the-inside look about them, and be hero-ic…"

Tierenan trailed off, happily lost in his own vision of the ideal bodyguard, while Faria struggled to remain enthusiastic about the adventure he seemed to accept so readily. At least she was convinced of his loyalty now. After all, if he were still allied with the Dhrakans he would have called a patrol over to claim her or turned on her in one of the fights. What she was less convinced about now was Midia as a safe stopping point. She had heard a lot of stories about this particular town, none of which filled her with optimism.

It was a 'free town' in the sense that it wasn't governed by any of the major sovereigns, and as such had its own laws and a crude number of soldiers to guard it. Both of these could, however, be easily corrupted by whoever managed to come to power in the city. Due to the sheer amount of competition the governors changed at an incredible rate, leaving Midia near enough unmanageable. Despite this, it didn't have nearly as many problems as other cities, as most of the people travelling to and from it were mercenaries or merchants, none of whom stayed for more than a few days.

The town mostly kept the peace with an almost unspoken code of conduct that only dissipated if someone tried to preach religion or start a fight. Particular objection was taken to larger sovereigns' soldiers entering the town walls in formation, especially on raids for fugitives. But it was the city's own inhabitants that gave Faria greatest cause for worry: drunks, swindlers and other hard characters she didn't particularly want to risk meeting. At least though, she considered drolly, it would be a change from being hunted by dragons.

Aside from the reptilian troops, the roads she and Tierenan kept close to were eerily quiet, which gave her yet more misgivings. They hadn't seen anyone travelling in either direction for over a day.

As they approached the city they began to hear the low murmurs of a massive, bustling crowd of people. Increasing pace, they moved closer, hiding themselves amongst the leafy bushes, and there they witnessed the answer to the quiet roads.

At Midia's southerly gate were twenty Dhrakan soldiers blocking the way, a wall of plate armour and scales. Opposing them was a mass of people pressing to get through, all of them bristling angrily and throwing irate yells at the blockade. A short, thick-set dragon climbed onto a nearby barrel and gave a bellowing roar:

"LISTEN UP! Xayall's infected with a fatal disease and it's spread to the forest around it. Until we know it's all safe, Dhraka is governed with policing these entrances and we're not letting anyone through, understand?"

He was met with a wave of bewildered protests and confused, angry questioning. He raised an arm to silence them. It didn't work.

"AND," he yelled over the unruly mob, "The one who spread the disease is a fox disguised as the Princess of Xayall. She's fled the city dressed in her blue robes and there's a reward for the one who brings her to the Dhrakan authorities!"

The crowd fell silent. Faria could see the attention shift from irritation to curiosity, and some quickly bore greedy, glinting leers. A low murmur rippled through them as the squat Dhrakan officer jumped back down again, smiling wryly before disappearing behind the wall of shields. Faria watched, sickened, as his soldiers licked their lips and grinned their sinister grins at one another.

"You're a Princess?" Tierenan hissed.

Faria bristled angrily. "'Princess' is a title for prissy, entitled waifs. I'm not a Princess, thank you, and don't ever call me that. I'm an Empress, or at least I will be." There was a tense pause as Faria ground her teeth; Tierenan picked mud from his claws and said nothing more until she calmed down.

"Let's see if there's another way round," she said to him eventually, slipping away. So not only would the Dhrakans be after her, but now *anyone* could try and bring her in. She did her best not to dwell on it. The thought of being pursued all the way to Skyria threatened her already fragile resolve.

The walls of Midia weren't as high as Xayall's. It was never rich enough to afford anything grand. About thirty years ago a foppish dandy rose to power and completely wrecked the city's economy, leaving it to become overrun by bullies and opportunists, and setting the standard for every successive governor. As such, maintenance of the buildings and city defences was never a high priority.

None of the turrets held any guards. There were several children playing behind the crenelations, who upon seeing Faria and Tierenan became incredibly interested in what the two strays were trying to do. Thankfully, as with most children, they weren't preoccupied with world affairs and were all too helpful assisting them breach Dhraka's 'quarantine' rules by finding them a lower section of wall for Tierenan to latch his claws onto. They gasped and whooped in excitement as his forearms shot away and grabbed a secure piece of brickwork. Faria wrapped her arms around him and he slowly climbed up, reeling his arms in as he did so. The children all applauded their safe arrival on Midia's walls.

"Let me see your arms again!"

"That was cool!"

"I like your dress—you look pretty."

They smiled. "Thank you," Faria said soothingly, trying to hide her fear that the children would get them noticed. "We have to go now, though. You'll play safely up here, won't you?"

They nodded affirmatively. One of the younger otters idly chewed his tail as he gave them a shy wave goodbye. They ran off along the walls, laughing and pretending to be able to shoot their arms out as well.

"I love kids," Tierenan mused as he slid down a ladder onto a mucky cobbled street below. "I help run a nursery back in Skyria."

Faria was only half-listening; she was preoccupied with their next move, reluctant to dive recklessly into the city in case she was spotted, but unwilling to stand on the wall for too long. "Ah, that's nice."

Hesitantly, she climbed down.

As soon as her feet touched the ground she flung herself flat behind a stack of crates in an attempt to be stealthy. Tierenan let out a burst of laughter.

"What are you *doing?*" he giggled.

Faria blushed, half hiding behind her staff. "Oh, off with you! I was just trying to be discreet. We're wanted, you know."

"Well, *you* are. I can go where I please," he said smugly.

Faria scowled angrily, upset. "Fine, alright," she snapped. "*You* go and sort everything out, then. You don't exactly blend in when you're made of metal."

Tierenan could tell she was getting irritable and was tempted to tell her that she needed to eat something, but decided against making a silly comment in favour of actually being helpful. "Well, if I find you a place to hide, why don't I grab us something from the market? Maybe I'll find someone who can help us too, hmm?"

Faria nodded, peeling herself from the wall with a sulky, miserable look on her face. She didn't like Midia. The streets were filthy. She could hear coarse, raucous voices from almost every direction and she could tell they were going to have difficulty getting away without being seen. Sullenly, she followed Tierenan down a street, around a corner and along an alleyway, dodging a drunken weasel and avoiding lumps of something that smelt like it was either dead, rotten or had recently been excreted.

They arrived on a busy street that appeared to lead from one end of the town to the other. Theriasaur-drawn carts took no prisoners when pushing through, and in every direction could be seen countless numbers of drunk, dangerous and ill-tempered-looking animals shuffling along the road. Opposite them stood a three-storey wooden building with dirty glass windows, stains on the walls and a faded sign that read 'Rosa's Retreat' across the door frame.

Tierenan gave a quick look around, then pointed her towards it. "You hide in there. I'll see if I can find the market."

He went to leave but Faria lunged possessively at his arm and hauled him back. "I don't want to! It looks horrible..."

Tierenan remained patient but was getting worried about the number of suspicious eyes passing Faria as they stood by the alley entrance. "Faria, you need to hide. Everyone's going to see you out here. You can bet those stupid dragons are at every gate, and they'll all be telling that disease story."

She suddenly became aware of the people around her. All of them appeared to be looking her way, or if they weren't she was sure they were deliberately avoiding her out of suspicion. She struggled around for a place to conceal her staff. As big as it was, her only option was to removed her cape and wrap it loosely in its folds. It might stall her defence for a few seconds if she needed to fight, but displaying something like that was an invitation to be mugged.

Tierenan gave her an encouraging pat on the shoulder and vanished into the throng of people. She froze for a second, staring at the door ahead. A merchant's cart carrying large bags of grain rumbled past, and using it as a screen, she took her opportunity. She leapt forwards, ducking and weaving between the traffic. She didn't apologise when people walked into her—she didn't even look at them. She just ran to the mangy tavern and barged through the door. Once inside she took a few deep breaths to calm herself down, then looked uneasily around.

Her dramatic entrance was barely noticed by the tavern's inmates, an even mix of the drunk, the silent and the disorder-ly. There was a group playing cards churlishly in the centre of the room, a large table in the corner housed a rowdy drinking competition, and a number of others sat around the bar, ignoring everything around them in stony silence. Despite their differences they all shared the same unfriendly look about them. She edged towards a table in the corner by the window, brushing past a large, gangly mara at the bar who gave her a scornful glance.

"S-sorry," she stammered, looking to the floor. She turned away; a force grabbed her shoulder and whirled her back round again.

"H'ain't seen you here before," the mara growled, his paws pressing into her. An armour-clad wolf next to him gave her an inquisitive glance from behind his tankard.

"Uh, no. I'm just passing through. I'm sorry, I won't get in your w—"

"You ain't one of the regular girls, are yeh?" he slavered, a wild look burning in his eyes. Faria desperately wanted to him to leave her alone.

"Girls? I'm not—"

The mara leaned closer and took a deep, scouring breath through his nose. "You're *good...*"

A sudden, horrific realisation dawned on her. "Oh, no... No, no, you've got the wrong—please—!"

The mara was just about to grasp her with his other hand when he instead released her with a pained yelp and was hauled backwards: the wolf had dug his claws into the brute's ears and pulled sharply backwards and down. The rodent was now bent over his own back, facing the wolf's severe, disdainful scowl and fierce indigo eyes.

"Paws off, creep," he grunted, throwing him to the floor with a thud. The mara cursed and rocked on the boards, pulling at his torn ears. Suddenly the whole bar's attention was on Faria and the wolf. Rumbles of disdain filtered through the ambient noise, and several bodies began shifting in their seats. The wolf finished the dregs of his drink and gave Faria a blunt look, stepping down from his stool. "Let's go outside."

Unsure, she followed him through the door, not daring for a second to look back at the other occupants of the bar.

Once outside the wolf leaned against the wall. She backed away to the other side of the door.

"Don't worry, I'm not going to ask you for anything. I don't do that, and I know that's not why you're here."

She had been watching him cautiously since they went outside; upon hearing him speak she looked down to the floor, feeling ashamed for creating a scene. She glanced across at him again. His fur was a dull silver, darker on the top of his head and behind his ears. He had a tattoo in the same colour as his eyes, a swirling tribal design on the right side of his face that carried on below his neckline. His armour was charcoal grey and angular in its design. Large shoulder plates poked out from under his tattered jacket, an old grey garment with the sleeves ripped off, reaching down to his ankles. His left arm was armoured only down to his elbow although Faria could plainly see his gauntlets, currently hanging from his belt. His tail wore a thin strip of jointed metal plating, tied with leather strips.

He gave a coarse huff, as if to expel the stress just caused by the fight at the bar.

"That's a bad place for you to be by yourself." He stared onto the street, watching people walk past with mild disinterest, adjusting the strip of black material tied around his head. Bolted onto the cloth was a metal plate, shaped to protect his forehead and temples.

Faria looked away. "I… thought it would be better than being out here." Now she couldn't hide anywhere, and just had to hope that Tierenan would come back quickly so they could move on.

"Dressed like that I'm surprised you even made it this far," he muttered.

Even if he hadn't sounded harsh, she felt irresponsible and naïve all the same. He inspected the battered surface of his high-collared breastplate, covered in dents and scratches. She wrung her hands guiltily.

"I didn't know. Please, I just want some help," she said quietly.

The wolf studied her for a second, then turned back to the street. "I'm not interested. I don't care how you got into your situation, but you're not strong enough to live on the streets like that. You shouldn't be here."

"I know that!" she cried, her voice cracking. "That's… why…"

She clenched her fists as tightly as she could to stop herself from crying. He didn't understand—he didn't even care. Why did she expect that anyone would? She didn't want any of this. It wasn't her fault. Why did things keep going wrong?

The wolf looked a little uneasy at her frail emotional state. Tears were forming in her eyes. She was just about ready to scream and run away when she saw the wolf hand her something. She looked up—it was a bread roll and a lump of chicken, taken from his satchel.

"Ignore what I said," he said, too firmly to be considered kind. "Take this—you look like you've not eaten in days."

She sniffed and wiped her eyes, looking wistfully at the food.

"Take it," he said. "You need it more than I do."

She took it gratefully, and before she knew it she'd stuffed half the bread into her mouth. He chuckled and leant back against the wall. She couldn't eat it fast enough, she'd been so hungry.

"Thank you," she mumbled.

He said nothing, simply watching the streets.

She finished her mouthful, stared at the food in her hands for a moment, and suddenly it all became too much. Tears rolled down her muzzle and onto the dusty wooden porch; exhausted cries trickled from her throat. She forced another clump of bread and chicken into her jaws to stifle her exasperated sobs. The wolf gave her an indifferent glance. She saw, and gave him a defiant glare through her tears, a look that actually seemed to draw a glimmer of surprise from him. She swallowed her food.

"I'll be all right," she croaked. She hated everything at the moment. The Dhrakans, this town, herself for being so pitiful. She wasn't going to stand here and cry through the first proper food she'd eaten in days without having at least some of her dignity left. She was going to become stronger whether she liked it or not. "I just need to get through this."

As the wolf rested himself back against the wall, Tierenan's familiar shape broke through the crowd, with a guard in tow.

Faria watched as the female wolf with elegant auburn and white fur marched up the steps. She wore light archery harness; a metal-plated left arm up to the shoulder and a breastplate of brown leather and white-gold metal. Her scalemail leg armour shimmered in the light. A quiver full of arrows bounced at her hip as she strode. Tierenan sprang to Faria's side. She quickly dried her tears.

"I thought you were waiting inside?" the raccoon asked, doing his best 'mother' impression.

The male wolf scoffed petulantly. "Huh! You two don't know the first thing about this place, do you? Please..." He turned dismissively on his heel and made to go inside, but the female wolf clapped a hand on his shoulder and whirled him back round.

"Kyru! What the hell are you doing? They need our help."

"I'm not doing anything with these," the male wolf grunted. "We don't babysit." He looked to Tierenan. "And what on Eeres is that, anyway? They make armour that goes under your skin now?"

Tierenan was about to explain just exactly what he was and what he could do to people with no manners, when the female wolf stepped in again.

"Kyru!" she scowled, punching his breastplate. "Get your head out of the tankard and behave!" She turned to Tierenan, letting out an exasperated sigh. "This is your friend, I presume?" she asked, gesturing to Faria, who was trying to mentally distance herself from the wolves' argument.

Kyru leant his head against the wall. "She wouldn't have been for much longer."

"She's crying, Kyru!"

"I know that, Aeryn! I just stopped her from becoming some bar-crawler's sick fancy!"

The female raised a hand to halt their disagreement. "Okay... enough. This isn't helping." She turned to Faria, who was wiping her eyes and breathing slowly to try and calm down. Aeryn rested a comforting hand on her shoulder.

"As you heard, my name's Aeryn. Tierenan found me at the marketplace. I gather you need some help?"

Faria nodded. "Yes. Um… is there somewhere we can talk privately? I'm worried about being seen."

Aeryn nodded. "We have a room here—we can go inside."

As they moved to enter, she gave her companion wolf a warning look. "And I'm not leaving you alone to drink ever again, you hear?"

Kyru pushed the inn's door open with great frustration.

From the building opposite, a piercing purple eye narrowed suspiciously, then disappeared behind a curtain.

Chapter Eight

The tavern's accommodation was only slightly more welcoming than the guests. The wood was aged and splintering, but strong. Scars borne on the walls were evidence of repeated brawls along the corridors. Through the ceiling they could hear bangs, crashes and raised voices in one of the upstairs rooms.

"Why would you stay here?" Tierenan whimpered.

"Cheap," Kyru grunted, heading for a room with a sturdy door, still cracked and bowed with age. "There are far worse."

Twisting the key with considerable force to unlock it, the wooden barrier creaked open. The wolf gestured for the others to go on inside while he kept an eye on the corridor. Satisfied that nobody was paying them any untoward interest, he walked inside and swung the battered piece of wood shut behind him.

Two beds and a dusty window were all this room had to offer, aside from a collection of cobwebs around its corners, currently bereft of any local spiders. Tierenan launched himself onto the rightmost bed with great impetus, only to find it had no mattress and that it hurt quite a lot to land on it so hard without cushioning.

Faria sat carefully down on the other, and noticed under Tierenan's bed was a large recurve bow in a specially-made quiver to house it, next to a second quiver full of arrows. At the foot of her bed was a large, double-ended voulge with broad, curved blades and a narrow metal shield about two feet long with bladed edges, the same colour as Kyru's armour. Next to that was an incredibly sharp curved sword with a knuckle guard. An uneasy feeling rose in her stomach; the thought of more violence wasn't an easy one to come round to, and these two obviously meant business. But even so, she could not be protected properly if she wasn't prepared to defend herself as well. That is, if they even decided to help her. Everything held so much risk now, it was almost impossible for her to know what the safest decision was.

"So, how can we help you?" Aeryn asked politely, looking to the two young strays. Tierenan had managed to steal a bowl of nuts from a table as they passed the bar, and was munching them contentedly. Kyru passed Aeryn a disdainful look.

"Isn't that a little presumptuous?" he asked.

Aeryn glared reproachfully back. "Shush. Tierenan," she said, indicating the raccoon, who was looking at Kyru's sword with great interest, "was asking around for a bodyguard. I offered to help but said he wouldn't be able to tell me anything until we got back to the tavern."

"Fine," Kyru grunted. "So whose job is this? His or hers?"

"It's mine," Faria said firmly, noticing that the male wolf's gaze had fallen to her staff. "I need protecting until I get to

Skyria." She stuffed the last bit of chicken he'd given her into her mouth, anticipating another question.

Kyru looked dubious. "Skyria's right across the other side of Eeres. Have you got that kind of money?"

Aeryn banged a fist into his chest plate to silence him. He folded his arms in a sulk. Faria got the impression his temper was going to be hard to denature, although he was asking a fair question. Aeryn looked at her to continue as the fox drummed her fingers nervously on the staff's shaft.

"Money doesn't matter," Faria said, as confidently as she could manage. "It's more important that I find my father. But I... *we* need help getting there."

Aeryn crouched next to her, inspecting the brilliant blue coat and the symbol of the fox's city emblazoned on her sleeve. "This is a Xayall imperial emblem... Shouldn't you be in quarantine?"

"The quarantine's a lie," she growled. She dug her claws into her palms and took a deep breath to continue. She could feel her words being dismissed before she'd even spoken. "The Dhrakans... took over Xayall. They lay siege to it three nights ago and they're using the quarantine lies to cover up their invasion. They're looking for me."

"Why you?" Kyru asked. "Who are you?"

Faria fell silent. They wouldn't trust her if she wasn't honest, but she would essentially condemn herself if they believed the rumours instead. And if they did believe her, revealing her identity would be just as much of a risk if they decided it would be more profitable to hand her over to the Dhrakans anyway. She looked at them apprehensively, twisting her hands around the staff. Aeryn's golden eyes were alight with gentle sincerity. Behind her, Kyru stood with disinterest, still doubtful at her story.

Eventually, she spoke.

"I'm Faria Phiraco, the daughter of the Emperor of Xayall."

Aeryn stood up in alarm. Kyru strode forwards menacingly.

"You know the story, right? The disease in Xayall—"

"It's a lie!" she shouted, silencing Kyru, rising to her feet. Her hands were shaking. "The Dhrakans invaded Xayall looking for me and my father and they decimated it! I managed to escape, but... I need to find him." Her voice started cracking again. "He left for Skyria. I need to find my father!"

Aeryn was shocked. For a few moments she stared at the young fox in awe. Eventually, she shook her mind free. "Why would Dhraka invade Xayall?" she asked quietly. "That's a declaration of war!"

"They're looking for Nazreal," Faria replied, sinking back onto the bed. "And they're looking for *me* because they think *I* know something about it. They've been chasing me since I left the city."

Kyru flicked his claws. He stood oppressively before her, calm and discerning. "There's no proof in that. Nazreal's a myth. There are scores of Dhrakans around enacting quarantine. What's to make us believe you *aren't* their fugitive? We have to be sure we're not getting on the wrong side here."

Tierenan leapt up to shout something rude at the wolf, spilling most of the bowl's remaining contents on the floor; Faria gestured quickly for him to stop. Pulling the staff in front of her, she raked one end along the aged floor. A gentle blue light illuminated the room as the decrepit wooden planks, their fibres formerly gnarled and broken, creaked and twisted until the whole surface of the floor had almost completely reformed.

She looked to the wolves, both of them struck silent in awe. "My father and I are resonators, and the Dhrakans want him, or me, or both of us. I know that's not much proof for you, but it's all I can give you. Please…"

Aeryn could barely believe her eyes. "I'd heard stories, but that is incredible…"

There was a tense silence. In the building across the street, a shadow stood by the window. Just as Faria caught sight of it, it vanished.

"Wouldn't the Senate know about this if it was a lie?" Kyru said sullenly.

Aeryn shook her head, her gaze fixed on Faria's staff. "Not if the Dhrakans were quick enough to send out the quarantine orders. They'd easily be able to stop any information being sent between cities. And with a fake fugitive warrant out… they've pretty much got free rein to hunt as they please."

There was a quiet pause as the two wolves silently considered the situation. Tierenan gazed at them optimistically, clutching the bowl tightly in hope. Faria awaited their judgement, staring at the rippling blue of her staff.

"You against the entire Dhrakan army?" Kyru said, chuckling at the scale of her situation. "That's a hell of an achievement."

Faria looked at him pleadingly. "Please! I can't do this by myself. Tierenan is all I have…"

Aeryn was still reeling from the gravity of the situation. Xayall invaded, the continent in near-lockdown, and they were currently sheltering the fugitive heir to the Imperial throne… She ran her hand over her ears in disbelief. Xayall was undeserving of such a brutal attack.

"I have heard of Nazreal," she said quietly. "But I don't understand why it's so important to the Dhrakans."

Faria's head lowered. "I don't know. It was… As a city it's supposed to have been the pinnacle of the world, however many years ago it existed. Then, it disappeared. A few days ago the Dhrakans told the Senate they'd found something from there, a relic. Everyone wants to know what happened to Nazreal and the lost technology, but Father would never tell me anything about it. He just said… it shouldn't have existed…" she drifted off, feeling herself begin to sink into her emotions again. There was another silence. Tierenan put the bowl and what remained of the nuts on the floor, feeling a little sick.

Kyru chewed one of his claws idly. "Aeryn, it's a big risk, but you've still got military friends in Andarn, haven't you? Could they raise the alarm?" he suggested. "Then we can palm off these two to the army and have it on their hands."

Angry cries in the street caught the group's attention for a second; the large wolf went to the window to investigate.

Aeryn looked a little uneasy at the mention of Andarn. She didn't say anything for a few seconds. "Well… yes… I suppose so," she sighed eventually, looking uncomfortable. A second later though, the shadow of uncertainty disappeared and she turned to Faria with a kind, confident look. "Well, Your Imperial Highness, if we can get you two at least as far as Andarn, I might be lucky enough to get you a military escort to Skyria, and find out if someone can notify the Senate. It's not a promise, but I'll do what I can, and if nothing else we'll make sure you get there safely."

A wide, beaming grin spread across Faria's face. "Yes! Thank you so much! But, um… you don't need to call me Your Imperial Highness. 'Faria' is fine with me."

Aeryn smiled, grabbing her bow and quiver from under her bed. She swept her short sword belt around her waist and fastened it. "Great."

Kyru was still looking out of the window, watching the street intently, while snapping his baldric tight around his armour. "I'm still not convinced, but if you are the Emperor's daughter we'll know where to bring our bill."

He had strapped the shield to his left arm and slung his holstered polearm onto his back, along with a large sack with his and Aeryn's travelling equipment in. Suddenly, watching the trail of movement in the town, his claws flicked in tense realisation. "We have to go. Now!" he barked.

Faria sprang to the window. "Why? What is it?"

A large number of Dhrakan troops were pushing their way down the streets a few buildings away from the tavern, whilst the local militia and opportunist vigilantes tried desperately to force them back, crying out in protest at the storming of the town. The Dhrakan wall responded by punching the resistance to the ground; within seconds a massive brawl had opened up, with people racing from every alley to plunge into the action.

Kyru ripped the door open. "Come on. There's a back entrance."

Tierenan flexed his claws and zipped into the corridor, Aeryn behind him. Faria went to follow and in a quick glance behind her at the figure in the window opposite, she saw two familiar purple eyes leering back at her.

"Faria!" Kyru bellowed. She immediately followed after them.

With Aeryn in the lead, they ran along the tavern's upper floor and turned right to face a locked door. Aeryn tore the sword from her belt and slammed the pommel against the wizened lock. The rusty metal split; another sharp hit knocked it to the floor. The door slammed open, and in seconds they hurtled down the flight of stairs that hugged the back of the building, leading to a back street. Aeryn, Tierenan and Faria made it down and across the alleyway, but just as Kyru reached the bottom of the stairs a muscular Dhrakan shoulder-barged him to the ground. With lightning reflexes Aeryn drew her bow, loosing an arrow into the creature's flank. Leaping up, Kyru slammed the knuckle guard of his sword into its chin, shutting its reptilian tongue between its jaws and cracking its front teeth. It collapsed backwards with a howling roar. The wolf rejoined the others and they sprinted on.

They emerged in the raging streets, with most of Midia's local militia struggling vainly against the invading Dhrakans in all directions, now approaching from the other city gates. The four pushed through the main street into a side alley, narrowly avoiding the weapons and projectiles being aimed at both sides in the fray. As they passed a low fence, a familiar harsh voice piercing the furore made Faria's blood run cold.

"Ignore the townsfolk! Kill them all if you have to, but secure the fox!"

Aeryn heard the cry as well and dropped back to protect the fox, pushing Tierenan ahead. She readied her bow and loosed an arrow, impaling a pursuing Dhrakan in the neck. She turned back to see another leaping from the roof above. The dragon crashed onto the stones before her, his swords readied for a strike. He lunged forwards. Aeryn flinched; the next thing she heard was a dull thud and the sickening sound of blood splattering on the ground. Kyru removed his shield's spikes from the lizard's temple as the creature slumped to the floor.

Tierenan was guarding Faria ahead at a narrow cross-roads, his claws poised to strike. He watched Kyru and Aeryn fend off the approaching dragons from a few metres away, smiling proudly. "I knew it would be worth it!" he beamed.

"There they are!" came a roar from another street. A group of Dhrakans surged towards them at the end of the road to their left. Faria was about to raise her staff to dispatch them when Tierenan swung his arms forward and let loose, his metal fists hurtling through the air. They smashed into the leading reptile, cannoning him back into the rest of his party. Aeryn and Kyru returned and they carried on, running towards the wall at the north-west of the city. Behind them Vionaika was in close pursuit, loading bolts into a magazine on her crossbow.

They reached the wall and immediately began looking for an escape. The gate had been bricked over, the walkway around the top weak and crumbling, and the ladders broken.

"Great! Keep looking?" Kyru growled, glancing over his shoulder. The dragons were approaching fast.

Faria resisted Aeryn trying to pull her away. "No, I can get us through. I hope."

The she-wolf twisted Faria away as a bolt whizzed past the fox's ear and struck the stone. Faria glanced round fearfully to meet the fierce eyes of Vionaika. She turned back to the wall and thrust her staff against it. The stones rippled erratically, wavering with her own fear.

"Just do it! Hurry up!" Kyru barked.

Aeryn drew her bow and shot at the hyena; her arrow lodged itself in the exit hole of the magazine, preventing it from reloading. Vionaika let out a roar of fury and charged ahead, ready to bludgeon the wolf with her disabled weapon. Kyru launched ahead of Aeryn, swinging his sword into the bow's injured stock. The crossbow cracked and split; for a second the hyena was left staring in shock at Kyru through the rain of splinters. With a hefty punch in the stomach he sent her reeling back to her rampaging subordinates. They pushed past their fallen leader, spitting and hissing. Aeryn withdrew, quickly drawing her sword. Kyru raised his blade to meet the approaching reptiles.

"Aeryn, Kyru!"

Faria's call split through the tumult. She'd created an archway in the wall and was beckoning them through while Tierenan grimaced madly for their safety. They sprinted away, the dragons swiping at their backs. Aeryn dived through, closely followed by Kyru. As soon as the wolves rolled free Faria cast her staff into the ground, desperate to stop the dragons. The crystals surged. A wild shockwave rumbled under the archway, sharp pillars of stone burst out of the street towards the dragons like rocky lances. Some managed to leap free, others were pierced at the legs. Vionaika just managed to jump clear, landing on a nearby window ledge. She spat ferociously as Faria sealed the hole.

"Get up!" she yelled at the nearest Dhrakan. "Get out of the city and pursue them, now!"

The dragon righted himself. "Kill the others?"

"No! We may have use for them." She looked back to where the archway had been, and gently touched her stomach where Kyru had punched her. He was strong, and familiar....

"You have gained some interesting friends, Phiraco. Such a pity you are leading them to so cruel a fate."

Chapter Nine

Two long evenings later the four of them had reached the mountainous forest southwest of Kyrryk, the sovereign that shared its borders with Andarn. The terrain was uneven and difficult, layered in cold, hard stones and threatening slopes. Kyru and Aeryn were keeping a steady drudge, already used to the grinding pace of travelling between cities, but Faria would sometimes struggle to keep to their sides with her constant and ever-increasing fatigue. She had to rein in her frequent urges to collapse or give in to the enormous strain on her emotions. She valued the wolves for sticking by her out of trust, and she didn't want to make them think less of her by showing weakness. It was for her they were putting their lives at risk. The young fox was grateful to have any friendly company at all at the moment.

They had stopped at a small settlement in the trees the previous day, and had bartered just barely enough supplies to see them to Andarn. It had been expensive, and Kyru made no small mention of this to Faria at the time. She had fallen into silence for a long time afterwards, fuming, blaming herself for allowing this to happen. She should have been more persuasive to her father to stay. She should have saved Bayer. She should have known something, anything, about Nazreal. Her father's knowledge was completely beyond her reach, and for the first time a sinister cloud began to darken her limited information of his past. She refused to doubt him, however. Scenarios played over in her head for all the things she should have done that would have saved the city and left her father safe. It did little good now, though, and was certainly no comfort when sliding over the uneven slate rocks.

Her major consolations at the moment were Aeryn and Tierenan; Aeryn had already warned Kyru severely about his behaviour towards the young Empress-to-be, and Tierenan simply made things bearable with inane chatter and jokes. But in a way Faria felt she deserved the wolf's criticism; after all, she had failed her sovereign and knew nothing of what was being demanded of her by the Dhraka or her father, and she knew the immense faith in her they were showing even with no proof of her identity, or of any reward at the end of all this except by her own word.

She glanced wistfully at the scenery; the climate here was colder, and the land seamed together with mountains. Tall, thin trees with threadbare trunks and finger-like leaves loomed high in the canopy high above, barely concealing the sweeping rocky peaks in the distance. In her dejection and tiredness she felt they were the teeth of a massive dragon's jaws that would soon be clamping down to trap them all in its gargantuan mouth.

Tierenan, however, was enjoying the surroundings greatly, clambering up and jumping between trees singing how much it reminded him of home, but still attesting most keenly that Skyria was better despite having fewer mountains.

"Why did you leave if you like it so much?" Kyru grumbled, leading.

"It wasn't my choice!" Tierenan counter-grumbled from a high branch. "Some scientists took me here to show off my arms."

The wolf suddenly remembered the raccoon's mechanical limbs, and glanced up to him curiously. "Hmm… quite an asset you've got there."

Aeryn was keeping close to Faria, her bow in her left hand. She looked to the vixen, studying the various rips, burns and muddy stains on her imperial robes. The young heiress looked tired and wan, her wonderful blue eyes heavy with the burdening troubles flooding her world.

"Such a shame…" she said idly. Faria's ears pricked up.

"Sorry?"

"Pardon me, Faria. I was just thinking. I always knew the Dhrakans were aggressive, but I never believed they'd engage in such a war. Xayall holds such a high reputation. It's not hard to see why, looking at yourself."

Faria blushed, although her embarrassment was met by concern for her own lacking knowledge of politics, especially for being the Emperor's daughter. Aside from her recent personal experiences she didn't know how well-deserved Dhraka's reputation was. She brushed aside Aeryn's compliment and tried to hide her own ignorance. "The dragons weren't always like this, apparently. My father says he remembers when it used to be a fairly peaceful nation. I don't know what happened."

"I've always known them to be pushy and squabbling," the wolf said softly, casting a vigilant eye over the trees further away. "At least they were when I was in the military." She regarded the fox's clothes sadly—she could tell under the grime and tears that they had been beautifully made. "I hope you can get your coat patched up somewhere."

Faria looked at herself and frowned, disheartened at how damaged her robes had become. "I hope so too."

The sky was darkening. Behind the mountains the sun was setting steadily, casting the clouds in a deep orange light. A faint yellow hue was still visible in the sky above the piercing summits, and above them the light of the stars slowly began to push through the empyrean.

Kyru stopped. Tierenan, swinging closely behind him, hadn't noticed and vaulted straight into his back with a crash of metal on armour. Kyru stumbled forwards a few feet; the raccoon's rear end collided with the hard, stony ground. He let out a pained yelp and rubbed his lower back. The wolf whirled round, arming himself with a vicious expression that could reduce any child to tears.

"They didn't teach you how to *use* those arms, then?" he growled. "All that technology wasted on a tree-climbing pubescent with the acrobatic skills of a rock!"

"Hey, that's not fair—I hurt my bum!" Tierenan protested.

"Good! Now since you're so blindingly adept at forest life, go pick up some wood. You're at least capable enough of finding twigs in a forest, right?"

Tierenan stood up and marched away, muttering to himself in a sulk. When he was a good distance away, he turned back with a wide smile.

"Wouldn't have hit you if you weren't so bloody fat!" he yelled, before scurrying away. Kyru shook his head, rolling his eyes.

An immense shadow waited silently amongst the mountains in the Dhraka lands, in a hidden valley shrouded by ashen clouds and forbidding jagged peaks. A pit of unbelievable size had been dug into the rock, almost carving the former mountain in two. Within the hollowed shell stood a massive metal sentinel, a dark pyramid, guarding the even more powerful secret that lay at its heart.

Deep within the black edifice, a large chamber cast in a low red light droned with the noise of machinery-clad walls, the humidity stifling as pipes hissed with steam. Chains rattled in the darkness as engineers, scientists, and doctors were all marshalled to their positions around a rocky object about twelve feet high, almost invisible in the darkness. An old, black-scaled dragon with white spines shakily held his palm against the rock and muttered under his breath, as if having a conversation with his shadow. He stopped suddenly and looked to the entrance of the room, through which came a familiar, threatening presence.

"Lord Crawn," he said graciously, bowing his crooked neck. "I am glad you are safely returned."

Crawn ignored his greeting. "Have you made any progress?"

The old dragon turned to the stone and muttered to himself again, then smiled. "She was just about to ask you the same thing, My Lord."

Fulkore rumbled disapprovingly, flexing his shoulders in irritation. "We haven't found either of them yet. The daughter fled during the siege and *he* left before that. We have sent out our best tracking teams to find him." He paused awkwardly. "Unfortunately we have lost control of the prototype that engaged in the invasion."

The ancient black lizard's legs were twitching with age and dread as he whispered into himself. Two powerful entities were held in this room, and being a relay between the two filled him with a fear unlike any he had previously known.

"You... are as useless as your father," he croaked.

Fulkore surged forwards and grabbed him by the throat, ripping him from his feet. "Impudent piece of gristle!"

The old dragon fought to retain his grip on the stone behind him, trembling in fright. "I-it is not me, My Lord! I am just channelling her messages!"

Numerous slaves working around the stone quietly turned away, unwilling to watch another scene of torturous violence. Reluctantly, Fulkore put the old dragon back on the metal grated floor and stepped away. "How long will this take? So far her information has proven little more than superficial. It won't be long before we face the brunt of the other sovereigns for our trespasses. Andarn is a powerful enemy to make so soon."

The old dragon composed himself and mumbled under his breath again, this time speaking more towards the stone. His claws rattled against it with the quaking of his hand. "She says… that it will not be long. She can feel her strength returning. You must be patient, and trust in her information. In the meantime… keep pursuing them. Our spies are on their way."

Fulkore turned away. This was getting them nowhere. He would have to deploy more troops to scour every inch of the continent.

As he went to leave, he heard the old dragon call after him.

"My Lord, she says you would do well to listen. Her plan is already in progress. But you must carry it out as she commands."

The Dhrakan ruler slowly turned around, disgusted at the idea of being commanded like a mere pawn. Nonetheless, he was interested in anything that might yield better results than his already considerable force.

"And, she says," the black reptile continued, "most importantly, that you must not underestimate either of them. They are more powerful than you realise."

A small fire flickered in the darkness, the trees around it dancing faintly in its orange, shimmering light. Around it sat the four on their way to Andarn, talking quietly. They had come across a young wild boar in the half-light and with everyone's combined efforts had managed to catch it just before it reached its den.

"Isn't the fire a little obvious?" Tierenan whistled, poking a stick into its heart.

"We're close enough to Andarn that Dhraka will be more cautious about patrols. We should be safe," Aeryn replied, picking some meat fibres from her teeth.

Kyru nodded in agreement, devouring a shank. "Besides," he mumbled through chewing, "one of us will always be on guard."

Faria looked at her three protectors and felt comforted for the first time since the siege. It was still far from safe, but she was confident in their protection. She smiled tiredly at Aeryn.

"Thank you for this," the fox said, glowing with appreciation. "I can't tell you how much it means to me."

"You're welcome. I'm glad we could help."

"You can buy the drinks when we get to Andarn," Kyru grunted.

Aeryn threw a stick at him. "Considering how rude you were when we first met them you'll be lucky to get anything at all, you pirate."

Kyru threw the stick back at her. "You're just as bad when you drink, you alcoholic! I bet Alaris would have some stories about you in the guard." He was just about to take another bite when a stick hit his wrist—he looked round to see Tierenan looking at him expectantly.

"I like this game!" the raccoon chirruped.

Faria watched the fire as the three others intermittently talked and argued jovially. It was odd, somehow... even despite the pressing shadow of the Dhrakan siege around her, she felt like she belonged, in a small way. She continued thinking for a while, until an errant stick landed in her lap. Startled, she looked up.

"Your turn, Faria," Aeryn said. "Say something."

She fumbled with words for a second, caught off-guard. "So, um… where are you two from?" she spluttered eventually. Kyru looked to Aeryn to explain first, although she looked a little reproachful.

"I'm from Andarn, actually. I used to be part of the standing army there."

Tierenan's face lit up. "Really?! How cool!"

She smiled awkwardly. "Well, for a time… My parents still live there."

"So how come you left the army?" Tierenan asked, drumming his fingers on the log he was perched upon. "Wasn't it exciting enough?"

Kyru let out a derisive chuckle; Aeryn shot him a warning look. "No, it's not that. I was going to be promoted to Captain of Archers, but… it didn't come through. I left about a year ago."

"To put it politely," Kyru said derisively.

"Enough, Kyru."

He shrugged off Aeryn's cautioning look and poked the boar's remains for scraps.

"And you, Kyru?" Faria asked tentatively. "Are you from Andarn as well?"

"Ha! No, not from that cesspit. I'm from a wolf clan in the west mountains of Ohé, near Goraya. I came over here to work as a mercenary—"

"Bandit, you mean," Aeryn quipped, looking mischievous.

He shrugged. "If you like. It makes no difference to some people. Ohé is mostly desert, so there's more opportunity here. I figured I should go where the money is."

A short while later, they stopped talking and quenched the fire. Aeryn and Kyru fashioned the two canvas sheets they'd bartered into bivouac shelters; one for her and Faria, the other for him and Tierenan. The wolves agreed that they would take turns on sentry, and although Tierenan begged to be given a turn, Kyru refused, much to the raccoon's chagrin.

Several hours passed. The forest remained quiet, save for the gentle sweeping of the winds through the canopy and the howls and clicks of nearby creatures.

Faria lay awake, clutching her staff. She was grateful for the chance to rest but in the pit of her stomach the urgency to keep moving crept through her. Could the four of them really outrun the Dhrakan forces? How long would Xayall hold out, and would there be anything left upon her return?

She rolled onto her side to face Aeryn sleeping beside her. It was a tight enough space for one adult, let alone two fully clothed (and armoured) lodgers. Suddenly feeling very self-conscious about the noise she was making, she rolled onto her other side and brushed her nose against the canvas. The fabric smelt musty and unwashed; the earth underneath her dipped and rose in the wrong places for any position to be comfortable. She could hear Tierenan's quiet sleep-breaths a few feet away in the other shelter. Envious, she rolled onto her back again and considered using her staff to make a bed out of soil and tree roots. Ultimately she decided it would be too much effort, and she didn't want to disturb Aeryn.

Armoured footsteps outside her tent raised her alarm. The staff poised, she tentatively looked out of the opening by her head and saw the savage blade of Kyru's voulge resting on the ground. She calmed herself down and watched him tower over her.

"You should be sleeping," he said quietly.

She pulled herself out of the tent slightly. "Sorry. I can't relax," she whispered.

"The floor's no imperial bed, but it's comfortable enough," he replied with a wry smile. "Once you're used to the idea of lying on dirt, that is. Doubt you've slept on the floor much in the palaces."

Faria smiled nervously back, but felt a little bruised at his comment. She got the impression he still held doubts about her story, which was grudgingly sensible of him. "How is it out there?"

Kyru looked over his shoulder. "It's quiet, but you can never really know. You just have to be ready." He rested his voulge against the shelter and picked up a large stick from the ground. Gingerly, he knelt down and poked it into Aeryn's half of the tent, prodding the wolf in the back of the neck. She shook her head and grunted, half-asleep.

Kyru had a playful grin on his face. "She's fun to wake up. She hates mornings." He poked the stick in a bit further and rapped it sharply on her shoulder armour. "Aeryn, you sleepy creature! It's your turn on sentry. Get up."

She turned a lazy head round to him, angrily tore his stick away and snapped it in half, muttering something incomprehensible but discernibly rude.

"Good girl," Kyru sighed, moving towards his tent. "See you later."

Aeryn yawned and stretched, her eyes half-open. Faria watched in amusement as she sloped drunkenly out of the tent, such a dramatic contrast to her usual well-presented demeanour. She looked back at the empty space left in the shelter, then outside at Aeryn, who was now shaking her head and arms to wake up. Quietly, Faria crawled out too.

The wolf didn't notice her until she began stretching, arching her back with a tired groan, catching sight of the fox in her periphery. She jumped slightly, almost reaching for her blade.

"Faria? Shouldn't you be... asleep?" her speech was punctuated with an attempt to stifle a yawn.

The vixen shrugged. "It's, um... still not what I'm used to. I'd feel happier out here talking to someone, to be honest."

Aeryn nodded. "I see. Well, you might as well help me with sentry duty. A bit of drill training for you, perhaps."

They sat, and stood, and patrolled for about half an hour, with Aeryn occasionally making Faria salute and report in. The vixen felt better for pacing around. If nothing else she could walk off some of her anxieties. She sat on a log by the long-extinguished fire, and a short while later Aeryn sat by her, resting her bow across her lap.

"Where did you get that staff?" she asked, running a finger down its intricate golden spirals.

Faria flinched slightly. "My father made it. It was—I mean is—his."

"And you wouldn't be able to use your powers without it?"

Faria couldn't help the apprehension creeping into her smile at discussing her powers so openly. She felt a little like some sort of witch. "No. Well, it's the crystals I need. In the staff they're shaped like this to amplify my resonance and make it easier to handle. Raw crystals are harder to control."

Aeryn nodded, realising that this was an incredibly technical matter that would need a lot of time to properly explain. "Do you know anyone else who can do it?"

"My father…" She regarded the wolf for a moment, assessing her reaction. Aeryn simply waited for her to continue, and with relief Faria leant back slightly, looking to the dark canopy. It was surreal, but comforting in a way, to be talking with her even for meeting so soon. "…and my mother, although she died years ago. There are other types of crystal too, but I can't use them very well. They're not as pure as the blue ones."

"Ah, I see."

Faria looked to Kyru's tent, from which she could now hear two sets of sleepy breathing. She looked around awkwardly for a moment, trying to think of the best way to phrase a question that was brewing in her mind.

"So, are you and Kyru…?" She paused, hoping that Aeryn could fill in the rest herself. It wasn't uncommon for mercenaries to marry whilst on a tour.

Not that it was easy to tell in the dark, but the wolf looked a little flustered. "Oh… no. No. We just travel together. We met in Andarn when I left the army."

Faria nodded, feeling awkward. "I'm sorry. I didn't mean to pry."

Aeryn shook her head. "It's sensible to ask. You're trusting our lives to us, so it's in your interests to know who we are. We know far more about you at this point. I want you to feel safe, Faria."

The young fox smiled. "Even so, I can still be polite."

Taking her sword and running a finger along its edge, Aeryn gave a slight laugh. "You've seen us around the fire, Faria—we're hardly polite. Princess of Xayall or no, you're entitled to be yourself. Didn't you have friends or advisers you'd chat to in the palace?"

Faria fell quiet for a while as the question floated around her mind. All she'd really had were her father, Bayer and Kier. Other servants talked to her when it was their duty to do so, so everything remained rather stilted, and hardly personal. She'd been all but sworn to secrecy over her resonance, and hadn't even been jointly tutored with other children until she was nine or ten. By that time, making friends was difficult—everyone knew her position, but not *her*. Some had been pleasant enough, but many were immature, spoilt by their aristocratic families. She hadn't liked them, and they didn't think much of her quiet reserve.

"Oh, some," she said vaguely, hoping to avoid explaining further. "But actually..." She played with her hands as she worked up the courage to voice her thoughts. "This is the closest I've been to people in a long time, and it's been... nice."

"Aside from the threat of war and grisly death behind you," Aeryn retorted dryly. Faria felt a little deflated.

"Well, yes. But I do mean that. You and Tierenan have been so kind to me. And Kyru, too, even though I don't think he likes me much."

The wolf rested back on the log, looking to the sky, the trees' shadows casting deep chasms in the sky above. "Don't let him fool you. He's harmless enough, as long as you prove you're worth the time."

Faria wasn't so sure, but their meeting hadn't exactly been in the best of circumstances. "Do you enjoy travelling with him?"

"Well, you've seen him in a bad mood, and even outside that he can be insensitive, and brooding, and rude, but... he's strong all the same, and kinder than you might think. There's a lot to him that he doesn't let out." She let out a deep, wistful sigh. "I think he's bored of running around with me though."

"Oh. I see."

An awkward silence descended upon the two. As they sat in the quiet darkness, Faria's thoughts turned to her father and his illness. If he'd managed to avoid the Dhrakans, then he should be at least halfway to Skyria by now. She desperately hoped he was alright. He hadn't been well enough to make overseas journeys for as long as she could remember. Her heart sank when she thought about her city and the state it would be in upon their return, and the lives of all those who were still trapped there.

Before she knew it though, she had fallen asleep. Aeryn sat by her until the sky began to lighten with the emerging sun, whereby she roused the others from their slumber. They buried the remains of the fire and the food scraps under soil, stone and leaves, and in the pre-dawn light continued towards Andarn.

Chapter Ten

Andarn was the biggest city on the Cadon continent, and home to the largest and busiest port. The very centre of the city, around the castle where the king lived, held the grand estates of rich, noble families, most of whom had influence in the government and control of trading circles. Larger estates owned the extensive farmlands surrounding the city, where heaving stacks of crops awaited their harvest. Other merchants owned shipwright businesses as well, to further increase their political and financial clout.

While the city was run by the rich, it was fed and powered by the workers. The number of visitors it received meant virtually all those who lived within the city walls worked within them as well, running shops, taverns, market stalls, entertainment venues: anything a city as large as Andarn could possibly have to offer. Countless traders came from other sovereigns to sell on the streets. The more money they paid for a stand, the better the street they could sell on, and the higher their status rose.

Andarn also had the largest standing army in the known world, working tirelessly to police their city, the sovereign's expansive lands, and to protect Sinédrion alongside the soldiers of Tremaine, its sister state to the north. If the order was given by the Senate, these armies were sent into sovereigns in times of civil war to act as mediators in an effort to quell the violence and encourage diplomatic relations. This was not often welcomed by either side of the war, and had in the past led to three-way struggles for control in an already damaged country.

Kyrryk, a small state sharing borders with Andarn, was in constant competition with its bigger neighbour over a fertile land formerly shared between them. As Andarn grew, immigrants took up the land in order to trade in the city, stealing resources from the already impoverished Kyrryk.

When a civil dispute erupted in the smaller city state some years ago, Andarn was sent to police it on the orders of the Senate, further feeding the small nation's hatred for the encroaching giant. As a result Kyrryk was engaged in a constant subversive war against Andarn, often releasing its criminals into the city's streets on large market days and festivals to create havoc, and trying to take over outlying farmlands and factories by force, bribery or intimidation.

With these problems brewing in the background, other elements were working against the city's position—crime and corruption were rife, as was immigration, fuelled by the promise of leading a successful life within its walls. There was a large shanty town some way out of the city where exploitation was commonplace, with many working indecent hours for virtually no pay, or else forced to beg or steal. Murder was a high risk in Andarn; it was ill-advised to walk the streets alone after dark.

Despite its faults, Andarn remained a vital part of life on Eeres, its influence on people's lives stretching almost as far as the Senate's. Some speculated that it went even further, given that the Senate had little control overseas while Andarn's reputation as a gold mine was well-known throughout the world.

The sharp, clear sky poured its bright sunlight over the sovereign. A strong breeze chased shimmering ripples through the farmlands' crops, the blue sea in the distance pulsing with its serene waves. It seemed almost idyllic, untainted by the looming unrest rolling steadily towards it.

On the brow of a hill that overlooked the sweeping coastal landscape in which the huge city found its home, Faria closed her eyes and took in a deep breath of the fresh, cool air. She could see it up ahead, her respite.

Her ragged, once pristine Imperial robes were grimy and torn, a shadow of their former elegance. Her gloves and jacket had suffered the most punishment from catching on trees, and the dragons' blades. She herself was covered in dirt from the uncomfortable nights of sleeping on the rough forest floors and brushing past the scratch of trees. Her fur was matted, she was decorated with bruises and scrapes, and her hands were constantly shaking from the skirmishes with the pursuing dragons. Thankfully the lizards had shrunk away since they passed into Andarn's borders, perhaps nervous of the larger military presence that could turn their way if they were discovered.

She looked to the others. Aeryn and Kyru were close behind, looking as comfortable in their tarnished state as they did when their armour was clean. Behind them, Tierenan was running from one side of the dirt path to another, making faces at the cows.

"Are you all right, Faria?" Aeryn asked.

The fox replied with a gentle smile. "Yes. I'm glad we're almost there."

Tierenan jumped onto a fence and leaned over, inhaling deeply. He rose back up again, a satisfied smile on his face. "These grasses smell fantastic!" he beamed, looking up just in time to see Kyru casually nudge him over the fence. He landed ungracefully on his head, his extended claws still gripping the wood on which he formerly sat.

"What was that for?" the raccoon spluttered, face squashed against his chest.

Kyru flexed his claw nonchalantly. "Payback for crashing into me. You were too good an opportunity to miss," he said, not able to conceal a satisfied smile at the raccoon's expense. "Thought you'd hear me coming with ears like that. Besides, you're drawing attention to yourself." The wolf continued to smirk as he watched Tierenan scrabble around and stand up, glowering indignantly. The young creature cast an accusing finger at him.

"You, sir, will be arrested!" he bellowed, waggling a vicious claw his way. "I'll report you for trespassing!"

"*Me* for trespassing?" Kyru jeered. "*I'm* not in someone else's field."

"*You* trespassed *me* over the fence!" the raccoon protested, taking a flying leap over to tackle Kyru to the floor. The wolf moved deftly aside and Tierenan skidded across the ground, planting his face in the wooden barrier opposite. While Faria watched the two squabble with mild bemusement, Aeryn's patience was wearing thin.

"When you've finished bickering, *children*, we have a person to deliver."

Faria looked around at the hills and fields, and at the city in the distance. A huge number of ships sat in port while more white sails shone in the sea beyond. "I don't think we need to worry too much," she said calmly. "It seems all right here."

Aeryn clicked her tongue apprehensively. "I wouldn't get complacent yet. Once we're inside the city it may be a different story; even if there aren't any armies, there may be spies. We don't even know if Andarn will be able to help."

At that second, Tierenan bounded over next to Faria and took her hand, smiling gleefully. "Don't worry, Faria! They'll listen to you—you're going to be the Empress of Xayall!"

Kyru clamped his hands around the raccoon's mouth with a fierce look on his face. "You want to shout that any louder, you idiot?"

Tierenan's eyes widened in shock at both Kyru's anger and his own blundering outburst. He pulled the wolf's claws from his face.

"Sorry. I just wanted to be happy for her."

"Then be happy once she's on her way to Skyria," Kyru grunted. "Let's move so we can get rid of you two." He spun on his heel and marched down the hill. Faria took Tierenan's hand gently and smiled at him.

"Thank you," she said softly. It took a moment for the surprise to disappear from his face, but when it did he returned her expression with a wide, glowing grin.

The large, grey walls of Andarn gave off an oppressive sense of grandeur as the four approached it. The huge wooden gates were wide open, and through them the south entrance looked like the mouth of a gigantic creature that had swallowed a city. Down the gatehouse's looming archway they could see the busy layout of the crowded streets, humming with the sounds of carts and thousands of voices. Guards clad in silver and white armour lined the doors, carefully studying everyone who passed by.

Faria suddenly felt incredibly uneasy. She slowed, trying to find a way of obscuring her staff. Kyru, walking ahead, looked behind to see her stalling. He whirled off his long jacket and draped it over her shoulders, making sure that her Xayall emblem couldn't be seen. Even though the old coat had no sleeves and couldn't fasten, it swamped the slight vixen. Holding it shut and clutching the staff to her chest, she gave him an appreciative smile. As they continued past the doors, she couldn't help but notice Aeryn looking put-out by Kyru's offering, and her expression seemed to darken in an unfriendly way as they passed the guards.

Faria couldn't think of anything appropriate to say to dispel the awkward moment, so for a while they continued in silence. Instead she occupied herself in looking at the market stalls they walked by. People were selling grain, nuts, fruits, meat, armour, weapons, paper, feathers, and more than she'd even seen in one street before. She could barely take it all in. Any stallholders devoid of patrons were shouting eagerly for people to come over. Faria found herself looking away quickly from any that caught her eye, ignoring their impelling cries for her to buy something.

A city so huge had a lot of different species to cater for. They turned down a side-street and Faria noticed a bar specifically for bats, with no windows except on the very top storey. Through the glass she could see a table attached to the ceiling with a few cups resting on its 'underside'. Just as they passed, a spindly claw wrapped itself around the mug and lifted it out of sight.

They reached another busy street, this one much wider than the last and lined with tall, grandly-decorated buildings, most of which looked to be inns or guest houses.

The largest and most magnificent belonged to an armourer called Atheus Corraint. Suits of armour in the Andarn colours lined his outside walls, gleaming in the sun. His crest was a massive, illustriously decorated axe crossed with an equally oversized patterned sword, mounted on a shield that was bigger than both. Tierenan began creeping towards it but Kyru pulled him roughly back. Aeryn looked unimpressed.

"It's too expensive for you," she said listlessly. "His workshop makes armour for the Andarn military officers and high gentry. It's all high-detail, custom made stuff. Even I wouldn't be able to afford it."

Kyru shot her a suspicious look. "What do you mean 'even you'?"

She dismissed him with an obstinate flick of her wrist and continued left towards another set of gates, much smaller than the ones at the city's entrance. These were the inner walls that housed the military and government buildings, and the larger estates. Rather than solid wooden gates these were metal railings, black and finished with gold and silver. Behind them was a thick, threatening portcullis, currently open but with its razor-sharp struts poised to plummet shut on any unwanted intruders. A row of sturdy but blank-looking soldiers stood before the grand metal barriers.

"Damn, wrong gate…" Aeryn cursed under her breath. They didn't have time to look for another.

"I'll handle this," she said in a low voice, her hackles creeping up. Obediently they waited back, while she marched purposefully up to the mongoose sergeant, bristling with authority.

"I'm here to see Captain Alaris," she barked. She was slightly taller than the officer, which was fortunate for her intimidation act.

He flinched slightly, taken aback. "The Captain's in the barracks. But you can't go in unsupervised. I'll need to send for someone to guide you."

Aeryn folded her arms, unimpressed. "What, these soldiers are just for display, are they?"

There was a ripple of quiet, amused mumblings behind the Sergeant. He gave a look askance at his soldiers, trying not to look too ruffled.

"No, of course not. Any of my men would make a fine guard for you."

She gave them a cursory glance. "Really? They look more like doorstops at the moment."

The mongoose gave an impatient sigh. "They have their moments. You have a letter stating your business with the Captain?"

Aeryn gave him a hard stare. "This isn't a scheduled meeting. I have an open contract of business with him regarding the borders of Pthiris."

He looked dubious. "So what is your business? If you haven't got the contract I'll need someone to verify—"

"Verify?!" Aeryn roared, quite unexpectedly. Her three companions all jumped, and the soldiers looked startled. "One of our dignitaries has been grievously assaulted while heading into your sovereign through a road that was devoid of your military presence!" she yelled, casting an arm at the nervous Faria, suddenly the assaulted dignitary. "This will not stand! It's only good fortune that they left her with her life that we're here right now, do you understand?"

"Er, well, apologies, ma'am, but it's only protocol to ask—"

"*Protocol?!*" She was getting into her stride now. She continued a tirade of fictional reasons why they should enter the gates as soon as possible. Some of the guards began shuffling away from the entrance in preparation, and to be out of Aeryn's firing line.

Kyru quietly cleared his throat and fixed his attention away from Aeryn, sharing an empathic sense of awkwardness with the guards. Neither he nor Faria could ascertain whether this was an act or if she was genuinely frustrated about something and was using the Sergeant as a convenient punching bag.

"She's not someone you want to be on the bad side of," he said surreptitiously. In a flash of hesitancy, Faria wondered whether it may have had a little to do with Kyru giving her his coat, but gave herself the benefit of the doubt that it was to secure quick entry to the barracks with minimal scrutiny. It was certainly clear that Aeryn was familiar with holding authority here, and knew how to work the soldiers to her advantage.

The gates had already been opened now, and the wolf was still flying a torrent of castigations at the mongoose while he backed away apologetically.

"Our resources have been stretched thin by operations in the Southwest," he grovelled, sweating profusely, gesturing to two guards to escort them.

She straightened, flexing her shoulders in the same threatening way she'd seen Kyru do. It seemed to work. "Well, I'm glad we've found our excuses now."

She turned to the others and flicked her head towards the centre of Andarn. They didn't hesitate, jumping to her side in seconds for fear of being caught in the same cascade of abuse the officer had faced.

Once they were safely away from the gates and on a silent march through the inner part of the city, Tierenan shot her a quick, respectful salute. She gave a short, rather distracted smile and shook her shoulders to rid herself of the tension she'd built up, then turned her attention back ahead.

The buildings deeper within Andarn held an image of a stronger cultural heritage than the constantly-developing main streets. The houses, although aged, were well-maintained and much bigger, interspersed with gardens. There was little mess around, and the drone of the streets behind them was almost completely muted.

Up ahead they could see Andarn's impressive castle, its own walls tall and dispassionately bleak. Next to that was the barracks, a large domed building with a statue of a classical lynx figure standing atop it, brandishing a sword to the sky.

The soldiers escorting them dared not do or say anything that could have incited any comments from Aeryn as they approached the barracks' main stairway. The guards flanking the entrance's massive steps fixed their gaze somewhere over the city, proud and unmoving, a powerful image with their huge spears and forbidding shields.

Faria was in awe at the size of everything. Giving a quick glance over her shoulder she saw a low stone arena inside which a pike drill was being performed with at least two hundred soldiers. She could hear low murmuring voices within the building and the sharp rings of sword clashes echoing through the corridors. They stepped inside.

The flagstones were worn with the marching of soldiers and recruits up and down them. It was a cold building with a rigid, austere atmosphere. As they walked past solid iron doors up a large set of spiralling stairs, Faria could sense an ancient feeling of pride in the ascetic practises performed within the barracks' grounds.

They were led along an upstairs corridor with wooden flooring and antique suits of armour lined up along the walls. Old, faded paintings hugged the walls, depicting tales of heroic battles lost to legend years ago. So great was the presence of military strength along every inch of the building that Faria felt too insignificant to have set foot in it.

Tierenan was just about to touch one of the suits of armour when Aeryn batted his claw away. He gave a disappointed pout, looking eagerly at the intricately-decorated gauntlets. A few seconds later they stopped at a large wooden door with iron latticework across it. One of the guards twisted the handle and ushered them inside.

"I'll get the Captain," he muttered, pulling the door shut behind him.

The centrepiece of the room was a large ebony table surrounded by seats. Around the old grey walls were bookcases lined with scrolls, maps and extensive journals of Andarn's military history. As soon as Tierenan saw the table he made a move to sit on it; Aeryn caught him in mid-air and plonked him down on a chair, giving him a stern look.

"Paws off," she grunted.

"It's only a table," he moaned.

"A little over-protective of this place, aren't we?" Kyru whistled, examining a map of an island he didn't recognise. "I thought you hated it."

Aeryn bristled and shot him a stinging glare. "I don't hate it. We're guests, and we should be careful."

"They should worry," Kyru scoffed. "You could unseat their whole upper hierarchy. How the hell they can even look at you after—"

"That's enough, Kyru!" she bellowed, just as the door slipped open. They all turned to look at once. Large, sharp claws latched onto the edge of the wood, followed shortly after by a strong arm covered in tan scales. A long, grey head poked around the door and studied them with acute eyes. He was a muscular pangolin—an anteater covered in bony scales with a long, sweeping tail—wearing a polished white and silver suit of armour on his chest and legs. On his back was a cloak of sorts, made of strips of metal draped from his shoulders to the base of his tail. Despite his impressive stance, Faria didn't feel threatened by him. In his face was a look of kindness that years of military discipline only helped to strengthen.

As soon as the door clicked shut he looked to Aeryn.

"It's good to see you again, Aeryn," he said, brimming with restrained happiness. "I would appreciate it if you didn't intimidate the patrols so much. You should notify me before getting here. I'll have a hard time bartering you out of prison if someone recognised you."

She sighed impatiently. "Sorry, Alaris. We were in a hurry."

Alaris scratched his chin. "So I guessed. I'm sorry my company wasn't at the usual gate—we've had some interesting developments recently." He tapped his claws idly on the table, looking at her expectantly. "So, what can I do for you?"

Aeryn found herself clutching the rim of her breastplate; Faria could see she was anxious. "It's not for me, Alaris. I'm here for her." She pointed to the vixen, who instinctively stood up and bowed her head to the pangolin.

"I see," Alaris bowed his head in return, turning to address the young fox. "I'm Captain Alaris Hiryu. It's a pleasure to meet you. What is it you need of me?"

Faria reticently pulled Kyru's coat from her and dropped it onto the table. "My name is Faria Phiraco, daughter of Aidan, the Emperor of Xayall. I need safe passage and protection on my way to Skyria, so that I can find my father."

Very quickly Alaris' kind demeanour changed to a calculated, more serious manner. There was a tense pause while he studied the young fox. "I see. May I ask why you need protection?"

Faria watched him nervously. "I'm being pursued by the Dhraka. They attacked Xayall."

"And why has His Imperial Majesty left for Skyria?"

She rubbed her knuckles, trying to grind away her anxiety. "He wouldn't tell me exactly. To meet someone about an artefact."

"How long ago did you leave the sovereign?"

"Eight days."

"And where is your Imperial escort?"

"Aeryn, Kyru and Tierenan are my escort. The Xayall soldiers are trapped in the city—I escaped by myself. I had to…"

Alaris closed his eyes to focus his thoughts, rubbing his forehead. He let out a deep, stern sigh. "If you would sit down," he said. They duly did. The sense of apprehension that had been creeping over Faria since the conversation began deepened as Alaris scratched his muzzle, visibly plagued by uneasy thoughts. He studied her carefully for a moment.

"I have to be blunt. We received word that a disease had been maliciously spread in Xayall," he began, clicking his claws together, "and that the perpetrator had fled, posing as the young Princess. Xayall has since completely sealed its borders until the imposter is found, captured and brought back to the border patrols for questioning." He gave Faria a grave look. "A search of Cadon is about to be underway by order of the Senate, and a number of Andarn's troops are being drafted in to help. To be admitting your identity to me is incredibly dangerous."

Faria was gripping the table anxiously. "Please, it's not true! I'm in danger."

Tierenan sprang to his feet. "It's lies! Faria isn't an imposter!"

"I'm not saying that she is," Alaris said firmly. "But you need to understand the situation. It's an audacious claim to make even in normal circumstances, and, as you say, it's obvious you've been under heavy pursuit already. My first impression, like that of any other soldier that sees you, is that you perfectly fit the dispatch and you are trying to find a place to hide.

My orders are, if I am to find the alleged pretender, to deliver her to the Dhrakans guarding Xayall. Given your claim, I should be bashing down my Commander's door right now with you in chains."

His expression softened at Faria's pleading gaze. "But I know there's more to hear. I would be grateful, now that I've scared you witless, if you could tell me your story."

Tierenan calmed down and Kyru pulled him back into his seat, not taking his eyes from the Andarn Captain.

"There have been a lot of rumours flying around about Xayall that don't make sense," he continued, calmly addressing Faria, who was trying to hide her nerves. He gave a slight smile. "And after all, it would be somewhat suicidal for a fugitive to run into the heart of the biggest military in the world without reason, wouldn't it? Aeryn's judgement is rarely wrong. You're lucky to have her beside you."

Faria definitely agreed, and she relaxed a bit, but still pulled uneasily at the cuffs of her gloves.

"Start from the beginning," he said. "You have come from Xayall?"

She nodded. "Dhraka has laid siege to the city, looking for my father. They—I managed to escape and met up with these three, and we came here... hoping to..." She trailed off, feeling defeated already. It seemed almost pointless to explain herself with such strength of proof against her. She shook her head, clearing away her hindering self-doubt.

"The Dhraka sealed off the city to prevent anyone from getting away," she continued, willing herself forward. "When I arrived at Midia they had started spreading rumours that the city had been quarantined due to disease, and gave out a reward for my capture." She glanced at her staff leaning on the table next to her. "I've been chased since I left Xayall."

"What do they want from you?"

Faria sighed fretfully. "They want to know about Nazreal. They've found an artefact from it, and..."

"And?"

She shook her head. "I don't know what they want specifically, or what they found, but they think I know something that will help them. My father's involved too, but he's on his way to Skyria. He was really worried after the Senate meeting that they might get aggressive. They were desperate for secrets. But he wasn't in the siege, he left before."

"Is he safe?"

"I don't know. That's why I need to find him."

There was a moment of silence while Alaris thought all this through. After a tense minute he took a deep breath and straightened himself in his chair. "Well, there's no doubt you're in a lot of trouble. But whatever Dhraka's reasoning… I still can't verify that you're the real Princess of Xayall," he said slowly.

"Empress-to-be," Tierenan mumbled.

Faria tensed, feeling a pit of dread open in her stomach. She could demonstrate her resonance again, but revealing her secret to the largest army in Cadon could be an altogether greater risk in itself.

"I'm sorry I can't be of more help," he continued. "Although… the Dhrakans have been acting suspiciously of late. At the very least they aren't adhering to quarantine regulations set out by the Senate, and it doesn't make sense that Xayall would choose them to act as their guardians. Our outposts have reported a lot of activity from them too. They've conducted illegal raids within our territory and Tremaine, allegedly caused by 'false leads.'"

He sighed and relaxed in his seat for a few seconds, as if he had been waiting to impart that information for some while. Rapping the table with his knuckles, he stood up and walked to Faria's side. "All right, I'm not going to arrest you. It's a risk that could cost me my rank, but I don't believe our orders have been given with honourable intentions."

At this, a great weight appeared to lift from the young vixen. She rose in her seat, clasping her hands tightly.

"Thank you, Alaris."

"And if what you tell me is true," he continued, "then I'd only be passing you over to the Dhrakans for ulterior motives." He gave her a kind, understanding look. "I don't want to be responsible for making such a mistake. You're very fortunate that there are few people who would recognise Her Imperial Highness by sight," he continued.

"So, you'll help us?" Tierenan chirped, close to jumping up and down in his seat.

"No, he can't," Aeryn said quietly. There was a brief silence.

Kyru glared procaciously at Alaris. "Why not?"

The pangolin cleared his throat. "Aeryn's right. I can't issue any soldiers to protect you because it would still conflict with the Senate's dispatch. If Dhraka found out you were inside the barracks, and not under arrest, it could start a severe diplomatic situation. It is not in anyone's interest to start a dispute. And while *I* believe you, my superiors would be less inclined without proof. You aren't escorted by Imperial guards, your clothes are wrecked, and you've been led here by two fugitives wanted by the Andarn military. At best you would be detained here indefinitely until your father, or Xayall's Council, could be contacted through official channels. In any case, most of our forces are engaged elsewhere, and we can't afford to lose any on a trip to Skyria."

"But…" Faria began shakily, sensing her plans for a safe voyage collapsing around her. The 'two fugitives' statements completely washed over her, but Aeryn and Kyru tensed at its mention.

Alaris caught Aeryn looking at him pleadingly, and from the looks on their faces he guessed Kyru and Tierenan were both trying to think of effective threats to use against him. He chewed his cheek, looking guilty.

"I want to help, but the best I can do is hide you until we find a ship bound for Skyria. I'll have my soldiers enquire at the dock for you this afternoon. But…"

They looked at him expectantly; he wore an apologetic face.

"The only place I know that won't question your reappearance into the city is your estate, Aeryn. Are you happy with that?"

Aeryn looked up at the ceiling in exasperation. "I knew you were going to say that…"

Kyru raised an eyebrow. "*Estate*, Aeryn?"

Chapter Eleven

laris wasted no time arranging a carriage for them. Within an hour they were ready to leave, with Faria suitably cloaked again under Kyru's jacket. The pangolin led them furtively through the corridors to attract as little attention as possible. The dispatch from 'the Senate' was already in the senior officers' grasp, and the troops were soon to be briefed. Finally emerging outside at the rear of the barracks, a plain wooden carriage waited patiently on the street for them. They boarded quickly.

Alaris smiled wryly as he shut the carriage's door. "You know, Aeryn, the next time you see me I may have been demoted."

"Don't be stupid," she replied. "You'll get a commendation from Faria. We'll make you a General."

He grimaced. "No thanks. Too much responsibility for me at the moment. Now go, before you get found out."

Faria leant out of the window, wearing an appreciative smile. "Thank you, Alaris. I can't tell you how grateful I am."

He smiled in reply. "Don't worry about it. Just stay safe, all right?" He gestured to the driver and the vehicle ground into action. He and Aeryn shared a last casual wave before she sat heavily back inside, a sharp, tense sigh escaping her.

Faria listened idly to the sound of the Theriasaurs' feet on the paved streets and the low rumble of the carriage's wheels. She was still shocked that Dhraka's false claims had reached the Senate. Still, it would matter little once they were off Cadon.

Aeryn tapped her foot distractedly whilst staring out at the buildings that passed.

"Um… you don't mind us using your house, do you?" Faria asked quietly.

Aeryn didn't turn away from the window. "It's actually my parents' house. But no, it's fine. I'm glad we've found somewhere safe for tonight," she sighed. With a smile constructed to quell Faria's misgivings, she turned to her. "I think my mother will like you, Faria. She might be able to repair your clothes a bit."

Tierenan gave an impressed whistle. "Wow, what does she do?"

"She's a dressmaker and tailor. She makes a lot of the outfits and robes for Andarn's Representatives."

Faria's eyes widened. "I've seen some of those—they're incredible! She must be amazing."

Aeryn smiled wearily. "Yes, she's very good." She glanced at Kyru, and with his dismissive countenance focused deliberately at the window she looked quietly to the floor, feeling embarrassed.

"Your parents must be rich, too!" Tierenan cooed. "Some of the Representatives pay thousands for their clothes."

Kyru cracked his right shoulder loudly, sending a rattle through his armour. There was a brief, awkward silence.

"Yes… they are," Aeryn said quietly. "My father makes and imports fine materials which then get used in the dresses. They… work well together…"

"*So do you and Kyru,*" Faria thought. Her mind flicked back to what Alaris had said back in the barracks. "What did Alaris mean by 'fugitives'?" she asked quietly.

Neither Aeryn nor Kyru answered. Tierenan gave Faria a suspicious glance. She acknowledged him with a thoughtful frown and leant back in the seat, watching the ceiling rock gently with the movement of the carriage. The remainder of the journey hung in a heavy silence.

After making a sharp turn the carriage passed through a large stone archway, on the other side of which was a long, neat garden with trees lining the road. Aeryn stiffened upon seeing where they were, becoming more tense the further down the path they travelled. Eventually they slowed and turned. Outside stood a palatial mansion, immense in size, presence and dignity. Even Kyru was shocked, although this only worked to amplify his impassive silence.

They'd not been stopped even a second when the building's thick door swept open, unleashing a deputation of valets to assist them and take their belongings inside (not that there was much to take). Aeryn stepped down from the coach first, giving a nervous laugh when one of the staff honoured her with a distinguished bow. Tierenan jumped out and craned his neck back to see the pediment three storeys up, adorned with ornate classical sculptures.

The valets directed them under the large portico and into a grand carpeted foyer bordered by marble tables and huge vases; in the centre stood a gigantic stone staircase that looked like it took up half the building just by itself.

"Are they here?" a sharp, strong female voice with a clipped accent called to them from the doorway to their right. Aeryn spun round to see her mother striding towards them in a magnificently embroidered dress in deep reds covered with golden embellishments, a long train sweeping along behind her.

"Aeryn, dear!" she chirped, throwing her arms wide as she approached. Somewhat sheepishly Aeryn met her with a timid embrace. She was quite a lot taller than her mother; she had to stoop in order to hug her properly. Her mother's large feather and jewel-adorned headdress tickled her nose and threatened to make her sneeze.

"It's been such a long time. You know you can come by home any time you want to, dearest," the older wolf continued, glowing with reserved joy at her daughter's return. "Perhaps with a little more than a few minutes' notice, mind. The rooms are being prepared in quite a panic at the moment."

Aeryn seemed to relax slightly. "Thank you, Mother. I have some guests; I hope they'll be welcome."

"Of course!" she beamed. "Are these they?" She looked eagerly to Faria, Kyru and Tierenan. Aeryn beckoned them forwards. None of them were entirely sure how they should react in a situation such as this; save for Faria, who was practiced enough for dignitaries and Council members, but none who had ever been so friendly. Tierenan's excitement was bubbling away just under the surface as his focus darted from one shiny ornament to the next. Faria could tell he wanted to zoom around the house and inspect everything.

"Mother, this is Lady Faria, from Xayall." Aeryn presented the fox to her mother as politely as she could, suddenly unsure of whether even mentioning Faria's name would be enough to land her parents in trouble. "Faria, this is my mother, Lady Lleyandi."

Faria performed a gracious curtsey, as did Aeryn's mother. "Thank you for your hospitality," the vixen said, feeling very conscious about the state of her clothes in front of Lady Lleyandi's near-regal finery.

"You are most welcome. I must say, you are incredibly pretty."

Faria blushed. "I have to apologise, I'm not… particularly clean. And my robes are rather, um… they've been through a lot recently. I'm sorry."

The Lady leant forwards and inspected Faria's redingote, running her fingers over some of the stains and rips it had collected over the last few days. She stepped back, casting her eyes up and down the bedraggled vixen with a judicious look. After a second, she clapped her hands and smiled.

"I think we shall be able to sort this out, my dear. It is an incredibly well-constructed suit; I would love to get myself into something like that. I shall call for the valets once you have been shown your room and I'll have that from you to mend. We have any number of spare dresses for you to wear in the mean time."

Faria let out a beaming smile. "Really? Thank you!" She bowed her head appreciatively, and then wondered whether it was appropriate etiquette of her position to be doing so. But having been brought up to be modest, it felt a relief to be unknown and bow to others instead of being revered all the time.

Tierenan bounded up next and took an enormous bow, grinning from ear to ear. Lady Lleyandi offered him a new set of clothes upon seeing the state of his shirt, but he politely declined.

"My mother gave these to me; I want to return home with them." He kept looking around at all the finery adorning the room, and tried to discreetly look round Aeryn's mother to catch sight of the decorated corridor she'd walked from. He gave Aeryn a pleading look.

Amused, she signalled to one of the squirrel valets. "This young gentleman would like a tour, if you would."

The raccoon danced around the bemused servant, immediately bombarding him with questions about every ornament and unusually-shaped piece of furniture they walked past.

Lady Lleyandi looked to Kyru expectantly. He stepped forwards and gave a curt bow.

"My name is Kyru Siencyn. It's an honour to meet you."

Lady Lleyandi nodded in reply. "Most kind, and yourself too." Immediately she turned back to Aeryn, leaving Kyru to straighten slowly, looking irked at his apparent rebuff. Faria allowed herself a small grin at his expense; he spotted her over his shoulder and she looked away, pretending to admire the carpet.

"How long are you with us for?" the aristocratic she-wolf asked her daughter, waving for another valet to attend to them.

Aeryn scratched the back of her head apologetically. "I'm not sure. We won't be any longer than two or three days, I should think. We may even have to leave tomorrow morning. It's up to Faria," she explained, giving the vixen a quick glance, "as we're here for her."

Her mother looked a little surprised but retained her formality. "Oh, I see."

"How... much did Alaris tell you about our stay, Mother?" she asked quietly.

Lady Lleyandi opened a small purse and retrieved the folded message from it. "Little, other than to expect your imminent arrival. Why do you ask?"

"There's something I really need to explain to you..." She took her mother by the arm and began walking into a side corridor, leaving Faria and Kyru standing with another squirrel valet. The servant said nothing, waiting patiently for them to issue a command. Kyru thought he looked effeminate, and was just about to make a derogatory comment to vent some of his frustrations when Faria stepped in.

"Excuse me?" She addressed the squirrel more softly than she needed to out of fear of offending him, despite knowing it was his job to minister to her. "Could you show us to our rooms, please?"

No sooner had she finished her sentence than the squirrel had replied with a courteous "Yes, ma'am," and gestured them towards the stairs.

Faria marvelled at the architecture as they passed the balustrades, shining in their marble brilliance. Xayall's buildings had presence, but much less of the extravagance seen in Andarn.

"Isn't this amazing?" she said to the ceiling. Kyru gave a non-committal grunt.

Faria watched him as they were led into an upstairs corridor. He was very tense; he glared spitefully at everything around them as if it was somehow offensive.

"Is... everything alright?"

His irritation was evident by the brusque flicking of his tail. "What do you mean?"

She shied away slightly, warned by the terseness in his voice. "I mean, you've hardly said anything since the barracks, and..."

"Should I be happy to be here?" he growled, resting his left hand on the hilt of his sword, tapping his claws rapidly against it. "We're still in danger, and losing time."

"I mean... you didn't know about Aeryn's family, did you?"

Kyru's pace slowed, face shadowed by frustration. "No. She didn't tell me she had all this. I thought she was just an officer."

Faria looked distantly into the staff's crystal, prismatic in the light from the windows. "Why are you two fugitives?"

Kyru looked aside. He ground his teeth for a few seconds, as if chewing the memory into an acceptable form. "She was due to become a Captain of Archers, a respectable position with a lot of responsibility. But before her promotion she uncovered a conspiracy amongst the higher-ranking officers at the time. They were fuelling another sovereign's civil war with weapons and secrets to influence battles that would increase Andarn's power, and for their own share in the victory."

Faria listened intently, silently.

"She was caught by the conspirators, imprisoned, and blamed for the plots herself. I was imprisoned at the same time for raiding a supply cart. Together we escaped. Although the conspiracy was brought into the open after she left, the roots were deep enough that many of the lower representatives would have been incriminated as well. Leaving the blame with Aeryn was 'safer' than conducting a full investigation to turf out the real criminals, to cover the military's hide in front of the Senate." He gave Faria a glare. "What's one officer in a country full of soldiers? This is the filth of corrupt politics, the greed of those untouched by war but who control it all the same. She would have been given a show trial and a superficial, un-enforced sentence. To prevent her from talking she was offered a place back in Andarn's army. Pathetic consolation," he snorted. "She refused, and kept her fugitive status. We're both wanted, but she far more than I."

Faria didn't know what to say. The idea of such vicious corruption was disgusting, and frightening to think it was so close to the core of the largest sovereign on Cadon. "That's… horrible…"

"But what I don't understand is," he said, struggling to force out the words through his reluctance to speak them, "if she had all this, a family to provide for her, money and influence enough to buy her freedom or pay for a defence, then why the hell did she come with me?" He looked at the window, shining brilliantly in the sunlight. "I haven't given her anything."

Tierenan smashed the tension to pieces as he came whizzing round the corner with an exhausted valet in tow. "Faria, Kyru, this place is fantastic! I'm going to have a bath!" he squawked, completely enthralled. He pirouetted around the fox, then leapt into one of the bedrooms, giggling happily to himself.

For a moment the two stood in silence. Faria looked at her jacket sleeves and pulled at them idly. "I should get these to Lady Lleyandi," she said quietly. As she moved to the door to her bedroom, she turned back to the wolf. "You should ask Aeryn," she said softly, "because I'm sure she wants you to."

She shut the door, leaving Kyru alone by the window. Behind him, just out of sight around the corner, Aeryn held her arms in silence, leaning against the wall.

Chapter Twelve

Dinner was a tense affair. Aeryn had quietly told her mother about Faria's situation, as well as the finer details of her own extended absence. Aeryn's father was none the wiser, and just assumed that his daughter had returned home with some interesting guests. Master Lleyandi couldn't be trusted to keep a secret, as he was rather excitable, so he'd been told that Faria was an aristocrat's daughter 'going through some difficulties', and the others were escorting her.

To make things more difficult, Aeryn's father kept making offhand comments to his daughter about how much they missed her and that she should visit more often, and how he was always on the look-out for prospective husbands for her (Kyru had almost choked on his food at that point). Especially, as he so bluntly put it, considering his 'enormous success' in pairing off her older sister to a wealthy trader in Tremaine. He also offered to take them all on a high-profile guided tour of the city the next morning, which sent alarm bells ringing in everyone's heads. Faria politely declined, saying that they wanted to travel swiftly, and Lady Lleyandi reminded him that he had an important meeting in the morning anyway.

Faria had been given a wonderfully regal dress in green and gold whilst her clothes were being mended. When she was first helped into it by a maid, she was too afraid to move in case she damaged it, and was eating whilst ungracefully leant over her food to avoid spilling anything on its luxurious fabric.

Kyru said virtually nothing for the entire evening. Neither he nor Aeryn looked at each other much, save for a few times when they happened to accidentally glance each other's way at the same time, then stared awkwardly into their food for the next few minutes. Tierenan spent most of the dinner being confused by their cover story, often re-iterating it deliberately and loudly to Faria so he could commit it to memory without any mistakes. He also didn't understand Aeryn and Kyru's lack of interaction, but was excited nonetheless by the prospect of staying in such an expensive building with such lavish attention being paid to him. Just before coming down to the dining hall he'd taken Faria aside, looking astonished.

"They called me 'Sir'!" he'd gasped, then floated down the hallway on a new-found sense of grandeur.

As she surreptitiously rolled back her lace cuffs to take another piece of meat, Faria looked between the two wolves accompanying her and tried to think of ways to get them talking. But since Aeryn was determined to say nothing that would lead her into awkward discussions and Kyru seemed equally determined to say nothing at all, the conversation was stilted at best, so Faria thought it wise to wait until they were travelling again. She knew they wouldn't accompany her to

Skyria, but she wanted to try and help them as much as she could before they parted.

After eating, Kyru and Aeryn went straight to their respective rooms, still not talking to one another. Meanwhile Aeryn's parents talked downstairs with Tierenan and Faria for an hour or so about the Lleyandi family history. It made Faria realise that she knew very little about her own heritage, especially on Father's side. He never talked about it, and since her mother had died when she was three there wasn't anyone else she felt she could ask.

It served as a nice enough distraction for her, but all too soon she began thinking about Dhraka again, that hyena hybrid, the staff, her father, and how they all pieced together. She desperately hoped she would find him quickly.

Once the evening grew dark and her hosts had retired, she made her way to her bedroom and stepped inside, admiring the colours on the walls that appeared even richer in the torches' light. It took her a good ten minutes to fight her way out of the dress, but she triumphed eventually and sank into her vastly comfortable bed. Before she realised it, she had fallen asleep.

The candles in the hallway were extinguished by the valets shortly afterwards, leaving only a tiny light fluttering at the end of each corridor.

Kyru lay in his darkened room with his hands behind his head, tapping his foot on the bed in frustration. He wanted to see Aeryn, but stubbornness was keeping him in place. She was probably asleep anyway. Slowly, he let himself succumb to the silence that swelled the entire house, and closed his eyes.

Snap.

Somebody sprung their hand from the door latch, letting the door drift ajar. Startled, awakened by the sharp sound, Kyru leapt to the threshold to see a figure running down the corridor. In his alarmed state he grabbed his sword from the chair and burst into the hallway, following the shadow. As he moved further and his mind drew back to rationality, he started questioning his common sense: why would an intruder be inside the house? Was it just someone mistaking his room for theirs? Nobody could have broken in… could they?

He quickened his pace. An uneasy feeling crept up his back. The night's darkness still hung oppressively in the windows, and the rest of the house was eerily silent. Keeping his sword in front, he followed the shadow upstairs, and up again to the passageway leading to the roof. A cold wind blew down the narrow staircase. The door was open, swinging gently against the interior wall. Deep grey-blue clouds coursed overhead, and with a sense of foreboding that made the hairs from his neck to his tail stand on end, he crept up.

It took him a second to see the figure standing to the right on the roof, her long nightgown blowing in the wind. She was staring vacantly into the distance, overlooking the centre of the city.

"Aeryn?"

She didn't acknowledge him, standing frozen, catatonic, her gaze fixed on the far horizon.

He took a step forwards. A movement from behind stopped him in his tracks. Kyru whirled round, leading with his sword to take a vicious swipe at the empty air.

"Who's there?" he growled.

"We've met before, albeit fleetingly," a sardonic voice sneered from the darkness. The hyena emerged slowly, letting the shadows fall from her body as she stepped towards the wolf, her crossbow pointing directly between his eyes. "Although our histories have crossed paths generations before we even existed."

"What the hell are you doing here?" he gnarled, digging his claws into the sword's hilt. His tail stiffened; his entire body pulsed with aggression.

"There's no need to be like that." She licked her lips, oozing with derision. "I simply have a request of you." She fixed her eyes on his in an intense glare. "I think you'll like it."

"You have three seconds to disappear or I'll tear out your throat." he barked. "Go and rot!"

She turned to Aeryn and shrugged. "Your choice," she purred rancorously.

A flash of purple, the same lustre as the light from Faria's staff, erupted from a crystal sewn into the ribbon around her forehead. Her eyes gleamed with the same violet hue. Kyru ran to Aeryn's side as she began lumbering towards the edge of the building, still in a trance.

"Aeryn, stop!" he yelled.

She remained unhearing, stepping ever closer to the parapet and the fatal drop over its edge. He wrestled her arm to turn her round but she was unchangeable, like a walking statue.

"What have you done to her?" he roared, rounding on Vionaika with his blade aimed at her neck. She stepped back and pointed the crossbow at him again. The loaded bolt glinted the same purple as her eyes.

"If you want her to live, listen. You haven't got long before she finds her death."

Kyru lowered his sword and glanced to Aeryn, now only a few steps' distance away from the raised stone wall. "If anything happens to her, I'll decorate the city with your entrails," he seethed.

"Kill me and she dies too. Her course is unstoppable unless by my command. I'd think before being so rash," she said, enjoying the growing anger that darkened his face with each passing second. "I want you to join me. You have what I need."

Kyru almost exploded. "Join you?! My honour's worth more than any offer you can make, you twisted harridan! I'm not betraying Aeryn or Faria to your toothless dragons."

"This has nothing to do with those incompetent Dhrakan swine!" she scoffed. "This is for myself." She gave a sharp click with her claws and Aeryn stopped, inches away from the edge. "The only reason I'm working with those impotent dragons is for my own end. They sought me, and with the power I can gain from their discovery I could have an entire sovereign for myself. But as well as that..." she stepped forwards and stroked a claw down her own arm. "...you may have noticed that I'm not of a particular pedigree."

His fur crawled at her proximity. He balefully regarded her scaled hands and lynx ears, alien to the rest of her body. "What are you?" he asked, reviled.

She gave him a piercing look. "There was a creature that, millennia ago, killed over two-thousand people in one night: the Daemon Stalker. Do you know of it?"

Kyru scowled derisively.

Her eyes gleamed with victory. "I, Vionaika, am his descendant! He knew of his impending death, and so passed his abilities through the generations." She flexed her claws, admiring their sharp, ebony talons. "The species didn't matter. Only the strongest creature was selected in order to create the ultimate, perfect body for the new child."

She pointed to the crystal on her forehead. "This is where my power comes from; I'm a resonator."

Kyru leant forwards, teeth bared. "What the hell do you need me for if you've got this great legacy behind you?"

A flare of discomposure flittered across her eyes. "With each generation, the mixing of impure genes with his lessens the power we inherit. Mine are not even a fraction of his. The 'control' exerted by his genetic code also diminishes. I am the first female descendant..." She paused, sidling closer. "...and I need a strong creature to continue my ancestor's legacy. When you struck me in Midia, I felt a connection to you, something in my genetic memory. There is more to your strength than can be seen."

She stared at him hungrily, waiting for a response. She didn't even see his fist flying through the air before it crunched into her jaw and sent her reeling across the roof.

"Disgusting freak," he spat, rounding on her with his blade by his side. "I'll tear you in half for that."

She held her muzzle, her hand quaking slightly as she felt for a broken tooth. Blood dripped from her maw; with rasping breath and eyes filled with savage fire she glared at him.

"Damn you!" she hissed. The crystal on her head shimmered. Aeryn took a massive stride, reaching the parapet at once. Kyru flung his sword away and broke into a run. Vionaika stood up, raising the crossbow at his back.

Aeryn swayed dangerously on the stone ledge. Kyru raced towards her, drawing within reach just as she took one final step and plummeted downwards. Just barely he snatched hold of her wrist, throwing himself against the parapet. He gripped her tightly, desperately. Her unconscious body was a dead weight in his grasp, threatening to pull both of them down to the cold stone below. He grabbed hold of her with his other hand and pulled her up, leaning against the building for support.

Click.

A chill of fear ran down his spine.

A bolt of purple flashed through the air and plunged into his back. He lurched forwards, his eyes wide with terror as Aeryn began to slip from his hands against the pain of the crystal shard drilling into his right flank. With an agonising roar he hauled her back onto the roof, pain slicing through his abdomen like knives drawn across his body. He collapsed against the wall, holding her in his lap. His breath ripping out of him, he gave Vionaika a defiant smile.

"You won't... kill me so easily."

Although visibly disgusted by his resistance, her expression quickly changed to one of sly satisfaction. "It was never my intent to *kill* you," she gloated, backing away into the darkness. "I have merely planted the seed of your fate."

Kyru reached around to the wound in his back. As he clutched the bolt in his claws it shifted; the wood snapped off and the crystal head drilled further into his body. He twisted violently and coughed, a mist of blood spraying from his mouth. He grimaced in pain, clenching his fists, imagining that the hyena's neck was between them.

She had vanished, but her grim, caustic voice echoed through the chill air. "You will not escape. You will find me or you will die, and all your efforts will have been for nothing…"

Kyru leant his head against the wall and cursed himself, cradling the still-unconscious Aeryn against his body.

The dark sky began to brighten. Through the window of Aeryn's bedroom Kyru could hear birds whistling in the trees. He stood over her silently, wondering what he should do. Now Vionaika's control had drifted from her she was sleeping peacefully. As she lay on the bed, breathing gently, he could see the marks of injuries on her arms gleaned from her battles, and the rain of scars on her lower legs that she always kept hidden. He was glad she hadn't awoken as he carried her back down from the roof. It saved him an awkward explanation. But there was so much more to say…

He turned to leave. He took two steps, then a weary voice called to him from the bed.

"Kyru?" she said softly, a little groggy. "Is that you?"

He half-turned to her. His grave expression softened when he saw her. "Yeah… Sorry for disturbing you. I thought I heard a noise."

She sat up and looked around, searching for a possible source. "No, it's just me."

She smiled, and for a second Kyru almost let himself tell her what had happened, that despite the burning pain in his side, and the heavy feeling of inevitability pressing down on him he still wanted to continue with her for as long as he was able.

"Good," he said, almost inaudibly. He moved to the door.

She hugged the duvet around her. "You know…" she started quietly. His hand rested on the handle. He stopped and looked over his shoulder.

"You know… you could stay… if you wanted to," she continued, speaking more to the duvet than to him.

He paused for a second.

"Thank you, Aeryn," he whispered.

Then he left, quietly closing the door behind him.

Chapter Thirteen

Faria awoke to her curtains being drawn open by Lady Lleyandi. Resting herself against the headboard, she sat up and stretched away the tensions of the previous evening. The morning sunlight beamed through the windows, its golden shafts warming the surfaces it touched.

"Good morning, my dear," Lady Lleyandi said kindly, standing by the side of the bed. "Did you sleep well?"

Faria nodded, rubbing her eyes. "Yes, thank you. The beds are really comfortable."

"I'm glad," she replied, running her thumb over a letter she held gently in her hand. "This has been delivered for you."

Tierenan poked his head round the door, having been awake for a while already. He'd managed to hunt down some silver polish and had been busy buffing various bits of his metal plating. He walked in and launched himself onto the bed, narrowly missing Faria's feet. "Is it from Alaris?" he asked, admiring the reflections in his claw.

Lady Lleyandi handed the letter to Faria, who opened it ravenously. "Yes," she said, reading it. "He's managed to find us a ship to Skyria… it's leaving this afternoon. He's warned its captain but we have to make the final arrangements ourselves. It's not a fast ship, but it's the only one in dock."

Tierenan clapped his hands together. "Fantastic! And since it's leaving this afternoon we can have breakfast *and* lunch!" He zipped through the door and made a beeline for the kitchen to get his order in.

Lady Lleyandi smiled. "He does have a wonderful energy, doesn't he?"

Faria placed the letter on her bedside table. "Yes," she said quietly, thinking back to the forest a few days ago. "There's a lot going on in that mind."

A noise at the door alerted Lady Lleyandi. Giving a precise, commanding click of her fingers, a mannequin was wheeled in, wearing Faria's imperial robes. Where before they were almost unrecognisable in their tattered state, they had now been washed, dried, pressed and many of the injuries it had sustained were completely invisible, sewn up to a fine, meticulous degree. Faria's jaw dropped.

"It's not perfect, but it's the best I could do given the time," Lady Lleyandi sighed, examining a scorch still marking one of the cuffs. "I'm afraid they were only very quick repairs, and some of the lining became stitched to the outer layers. Completely removing the burn marks would have meant taking the whole thing apart and placing in a new piece of material, and I didn't have enough in this colour…"

Faria was astonished. "No, no, I couldn't have asked for more! How did you manage to get it finished so quickly?"

Lady Lleyandi fussed over the garment as she spoke, flicking little bits of loose thread from it and stroking over slightly roughed material. "Rips and tears are easy to fix as long as they're clean cuts. It went in to wash as soon as you arrived, then was dry by the time the girls and I set to work on it before dinner. The finishing touches were done this morning while I waited for Aeryn's father to get out of bed."

"Thank you!" Faria gushed, running over to inspect it. "This is incredible!"

Lady Lleyandi nodded appreciatively. "Well, I shall leave you to get dressed. I need to wake up my daughter, which is always a trial." She moved to the door and turned. Faria looked up expectantly as the lady gave her a slightly sad smile. "It has been nice having you all stay, even if only for an evening. I'm glad to know Aeryn's being taken care of."

Faria looked embarrassed. "It's more the other way around, really. I wouldn't have made it this far without her. But I promise that once this is all sorted out, I'll come and visit and bring Aeryn with me."

Lady Lleyandi nodded. "It will be a privilege, Faria."

Before they left, Lady Lleyandi made sure they were well stocked with food, just in case things on the ship 'became difficult'. She even offered to have one of her friends take them over on his own galleon, but Faria declined. She didn't want to get them into any further trouble. Lady Lleyandi did manage to press a black and gold cloak upon her, however. Faria didn't have the courage to tell her that it would probably make her more obvious to people they were trying to hide from; she could get hot enough as it was with the shoulder cape already on her jacket. It was incredibly comfortable though, and gave her another layer of protection.

Aeryn gave her mother a heartfelt goodbye. Lady Lleyandi replied with a light scolding that regardless of the conditions she leaves under, she would always be welcome at home. Tierenan gave the Lady another great bow as he was about to step into the carriage taking them to the dock, thanking her most grandly for the bath.

With no more time to spend on parting, the footman flicked his whip and the Theriasaurs drew the vehicle away. There was a brief moment of sadness experienced by all as they passed the gates, but Faria felt safe knowing that she was finally, undoubtedly on her way to Skyria. She allowed herself a small sigh of relief as she looked out of the window, imagining the reunion with her father and succumbing to the infectious feeling that everything was going to be okay.

Aeryn and Kyru were still keeping their own counsel, for reasons Faria couldn't quite discern. She was just about to break the stony silence when Tierenan all but leapt out of the window with an excited yell.

"Ships!"

A thick forest of masts and sailcloth became visible through the gaps in the buildings. Coloured flags fluttered in the ocean breeze and distant figures could be seen scaling the rigging. Sounds of the shipyard drifted in over the noise of the carriage's travel: shouts, creaks, sails rippling in the wind, the rattle of winches and the rumbling of barrels and heavy crates being packed onto cargo ships.

The carriage pulled to a stop on the main quay and they quickly dismounted, wary of the blur of traffic bustling around them. Dinosaur creatures from Ohé, bigger than Theriasaurs, were lugging carts full of carved stone towards a carrack while a team of muscular sailors hauled at pulley systems to swing more cargo into the ship's hold. Faria had never seen so many sea and marine otters gather in one place, apparently the crewmen of choice. She caught sight of a large, lumbering polar bear marching away further up the quay to a large silver-painted ship. Even carriages moved out of its way, the creature was so imposing.

The four had been dropped behind the cargo ships, looking distinctly out of place. They were too clean, and visibly unfamiliar with the docks. Faria felt each curious look drill into her, once again stirring her uneasiness. She unrolled the parchment Alaris had sent and looked for details of the ship they had been told about.

"It's called 'Marinche', and it should be further down the quay near the Eastern defence turret," she read, pulling the cloak further over her shoulders in an effort to conceal as much of herself as possible. Tucking the letter away, she began looking at the sterns of the ships and their decorative nameplates. Above them she could see various crewmembers looking down on her with puzzled expressions.

"Sailors can be pretty superstitious," Aeryn whispered. "Foxes are rare in port. Some might not give you a second look, but others could really be suspicious of you. We need to be careful."

"Especially as we've no guarantee of safe passage," Kyru muttered, his hand resting on the hilt of his sword with tense guardedness.

Faria said nothing, refusing to deny her chances. She had her chance here to set things right, to find her father and notify Skyria. This was her focus, her drive, and nothing would stand in her way now. She could cast her doubts into the ocean as they left.

They continued walking down the crowded quay, dodging large wooden beams being taken to ships in need of repair, as well as a trail of ornate carvings for a larger, more expensive ship further back. Tierenan inspected a barrel full of fish, sniffing it curiously. Even though lunch hadn't long entered his stomach, he was getting hungry again; thoughts of a leafy salad garnished with fish and seeds began running through his mind. As he looked up he saw a flash of green between the masts—another one of those long-tailed birds he'd seen in the forest. He smiled and ran to catch up with the others.

The ships became smaller the further up the quay they travelled. Faria could see some tiny yachts in the distance and hoped Alaris hadn't made the assumption they were going to sail there by themselves.

"Look, here it is!" Tierenan chirped, immensely proud of his observational skills despite only spotting it himself by chance.

The Marinche was a moderately-sized carrack with simple, unassuming decoration and a figurehead of a maiden lemur holding a globe underneath the foremast. The nameplate was virtually unreadable.

A wooden ramp led from the stone wharf onto the port side of the ship's deck. At the base of it stood a surly ringtail lemur, his arms folded and a peevish look stuck to his face. He watched them approach all the way along the wharf, eyeing them up individually and as a group. Evidently he didn't trust them and moved to meet them before they were even past the sterncastle.

"What do you want?" he grunted.

Aeryn was just about to explain the situation when Faria spoke up in her place: "We're here to meet the Captain of the Marinche," she said boldly, sparking a faint glimmer of surprise from the ringtail. "I believe one of the Andarn guards spoke to him last night."

Far behind them, leant against the high wall that separated the quay from the rest of the city, was a tall, bulky figure shrouded in a cloak. As soon as Faria had entered its view, it had watched her intently, the invisible gaze hidden in the hood's dark shadow.

The ringtail paused for a moment, flicking his nails irately. "Don't remember that. What's your business with the Captain?"

Faria felt the hackles rising up on the back of her neck. She wasn't in a mood to be denied. Her father, everything, depended on this. "My business is with the Captain, and we must speak with him now. We haven't got time to waste." She wasn't used to raising her voice. It was hard to stop it from wavering as she was rarely so forceful, especially to people's faces, and never in confrontation.

He leant back and looked up to the deck. "We're due to leave soon. He'll be busy making final arrangements—"

She took on a darker tone, giving him a fierce look that even Tierenan felt a little unnerved by. "I understand that you are busy," she gnarled, burning with ire. "But please, let us up on deck."

There was another pause while the ringtail considered his options, then grudgingly he stepped aside and gestured up the ramp with his arm. As Faria stepped onto the wood, he suddenly whirled round.

"Wait!"

She looked at him impatiently.

"No weapons. We need to be safe."

Kyru gripped his sword tightly, irritated by the thought of leaving his armaments in foreign hands. Faria almost lost her composure when she realised she would have to hand over her staff. She gave a quick look to Aeryn, who was already laying her bow on the floor next to the ringtail.

"This isn't a weapon." Faria quickly flicked the staff into his vision. "I need to take it with me," she said, a tremor in her voice belying her attempts to stay firm.

The lemur sniffed. "Looks dangerous enough to me. You won't get on board if I don't trust you. Times are rough. We can't risk anything."

Faria straightened and slowly brought the staff from her cloak, handing it to the ringtail with incredible reluctance. Kyru was more explicit in his annoyance, all but throwing his sword, shield and voulge on the floor in a protracted display of dissatisfaction. Tierenan had already walked halfway up the board and was watching them from above, idly flicking his tail.

As soon as Faria's staff entered the light the hooded figure shifted urgently. It stood to its full height and began pacing towards the boat.

"You had better look after these," Faria hissed. The ringtail shrugged.

"They don't look worth selling," he said with a provoking snort, folding his arms once more. Faria took a deep, focusing breath and stepped onto the boarding ramp. It wouldn't be long before they fixed their travel arrangements, and then the weapons would be brought up for her. She would need to be careful, though. She'd told enough people her real identity, and although Skyria was a friendly country she didn't imagine the sailors would be nearly as kind as Aeryn and Kyru. She gave the wolves a quick glance as she stepped onto the deck. She didn't want to lose them now.

The deck of the Marinche was neat and clean, but looked like it had just undergone some fairly hefty repair work. A couple of otters were putting the last of the waterproofing on the wood while others were sweeping the steps to the forecastle. Three crewmembers were playing cards by the wheel and two more, a puffin and a water rat, were studying a map. It was surprisingly quiet; Faria had expected to see more people.

One of the otters glanced up at them. "Captain!" he bellowed, instantly returning to his work.

The door at the stern end of the ship opened swiftly and the captain, a mature, heavily-weathered beaver, strode out. He was slightly taller than Faria, dressed in clothes that, although old now, were once incredibly rich in colour and fashion. His old, battered tail was pinned underneath itself in a loop, a fashion that had gone out of favour years ago. His narrow-brimmed cavalier hat with drooping feathers had seen better days. He scratched his head and looked at them expectantly.

"Yes?" he asked, rather impatient.

"My name is Faria; I believe one of the guards spoke to you last night about—"

"Yes, yes, they did," he interrupted, waving a dismissive claw. "I'm not taking four of you."

Faria glanced quickly round at Aeryn and Kyru to see if they reacted. "No, that's fine. It's just two of us."

"Which two?" the beaver asked, an irritable edge in his voice and a suspicious glare directed towards the two wolves.

"Myself and this one," Faria said, almost politely, as she tugged Tierenan's arm. The raccoon was too busy giving the captain dirty looks to notice.

The coarse beaver looked around. The crew were watching the conversation furtively from their positions. "We're very particular about any 'guests' we have. What's your business in Skyria?"

Faria stood tall, almost drawing even to him in height. "I can't tell you. We just need a guarantee that we'll get there safely." Her voice was firm and decisive. She didn't care for the captain and wasn't going to stand for any dissuasive stalling. "We can keep to ourselves, and I'll see that you're compensated."

The captain said nothing for a few seconds while he drummed his claws on his belt in deliberately slow consideration.

"We have full capacity already. I'll not overload the ship, and we'll have to reduce our rations. We don't cater much for your types," he said eventually, evidently unimpressed by the proposition thrust upon him by Alaris, and hence doing his best to be as uncooperative as possible.

Faria had found a new champion of her infuriation. If the lemur was irritating, the captain gave the word a completely different level of meaning. She almost told him to stuff himself and his precious ship if it meant that much to him, but she managed to calm herself just enough to speak civilly. Aeryn watched her closely as she stood her ground; not an easy task for someone naturally shy and polite.

"I understand it's an inconvenience, but this is more important than you know," she urged pointedly.

On the wharf, the hooded figure had reached the lemur by the ramp. The unsuspecting primate had been too preoccupied to notice the swift, silent hood stalking towards him until it was no more than five feet away. The second he opened his mouth to shout, the cloak whirled in front of him and a golden-scaled fist flew out from under it, striking his face and effortlessly knocking him unconscious. Watching him for a second to make sure he was down, the hooded figure knelt on the stone and inspected the pile of weapons on the floor. It stroked a thoughtful claw down Faria's crystal stave.

Faria was on the brink of commanding Kyru to do something vicious to the captain, who was still playing through his thoughts with painful interminability. Judging by the look on Kyru's face, he wouldn't have needed much prompting. She imagined the old beaver was making them squirm out of enjoyment, hoping that his perceived reluctance would squeeze extra money out of them, or that they would just tire and leave him in peace.

"How much have you got to take on board?" he said laboriously, with a loud sigh.

"Just us, and my belongings on the wharf," she explained, trying to growl as little as possible. Behind her she could hear Kyru flicking his claws and muttering impatiently under his breath.

"Right…" The captain sniffed long and hard, then whistled the air out through his teeth. He spoke with grinding petulance. "I'm not happy about this. We *might* be able to make room for you both *somewhere*. But, uh… you'll need to fit in with the crew. I don't like running a ship with 'distractions'."

This was the first time Faria had been aware of her social standing. If he had any clue who she actually was, she'd make sure he knew how far below he stood. She had never been particularly worried about hierarchy, but she wished she had the power to exert hers right this moment against this irritating, petty creature. Unfortunately, he was her only hope at the moment. Tierenan would be sure to back her up if things became bad on board ship, but even so, the prospect of having to fend virtually for herself again was a daunting one. She knew she would have to accept responsibility for her life sooner or later, as opposed to relying on the constant comfort of an imperial palace or selfless bodyguards.

For now they'd found a ship, and that was enough.

"Good. That's fine," she snapped, relieved to finally reach any kind of agreement. "I'll get my staff and then we'll talk about payment." She had been thinking about her father's stave for the entire conversation, worried if the ringtail was really going to protect it or sell it for booze. She turned to the ramp. Aeryn and Kyru parted quickly for her to stride between them, and suddenly she was faced with the dark hulk of the figure in the hooded cloak.

In a muscular, scaled hand was her staff. She couldn't see the creature's face, but she could feel it staring straight through her. It loomed closer and spoke in a deep, halting voice.

"Where did you get this staff?"

Chapter Fourteen

A tense silence struck the ship. Everyone watched in shock as the hooded bulk closed in on Faria. It was over seven feet tall from head to toe, with a huge humped back that rose even higher.

"Where did you get this staff?" it repeated, more urgently.

Aeryn, Kyru and Tierenan stood behind her.

"What do you want with it?" she asked, staring back into the darkness of its hood, trying to ascertain what it was. The captain and the crew said nothing, watching cautiously so no harm befell the Marinche.

"Where did you get this?" it roared. Faria could feel the force of its voice pushing her backwards.

"It's my father's!" she shouted in reply, not taking her eyes from the shadows hiding his face. "He gave it to me!"

The hood withdrew slightly. She could see the hump rise and fall as it breathed. The scales on its hand and forearm were unusual; golden, with the slightest sheen of silver. The cowl dragged along the ground, completely concealing the creature, despite its immense stature. It looked to Faria's

171

companions, then to the captain of the ship, and then back to her. Rising up, it cast the staff onto the deck in front of her feet and addressed her in a low, intense growl.

"If you board this ship, you will die."

Faria's eyes widened. "What?"

"This ship cannot protect you from Dhraka. As soon as you leave port, this ship will be destroyed."

"Is that a threat or a promise?" Kyru snarled.

The creature was unimpressed. "Neither. A warning."

It was the captain's turn to step in. He strode forwards, for the first time showing some degree of conviction. "What have you done to my ship?" he demanded, shaking his claw. The crew stood to attention as if to rally around him, but still kept their distance.

"I have done nothing to your ship," the interloper explained, his voice imposing even when quiet. "But if you take these passengers aboard, you will be attacked, your ship destroyed, and your bodies left to decay in the sea while the world crumbles around you."

The captain turned incredibly pale. His crew stood dumbfounded as he shrank back, removing his hat to get some air to his head.

The hood turned to Faria. "There is nothing here that will help you."

She picked up the staff and held it to her, now more curious than frightened by the figure before them.

He continued: "Your father put that staff in your care for a reason. You would do wisely not to leave it so readily, or all his work would be undone."

"I didn't…" she began to protest, then realised that he was right—she shouldn't let it go so carelessly. A sense of irresponsibility washed over her. This was all she had of her father at the moment.

Something clicked. She stared at the face inside the hood with fierce intensity. "Wait, what do you know about my father?"

Tierenan crept past the huge cloaked creature to collect the other weapons, anxious they may get forgotten. Behind him, the hooded figure looked out to the horizon, scanning the distance. Faria looked too but saw nothing.

"It is unsafe to talk here," the hood said quietly.

Faria looked to the captain of the ship, who was still a little shaken and now flanked by two taller crewmen. He gave her a wary look.

"We need to set sail for Skyria," she said absently, to nobody in particular. The captain would never accept them now. The hooded warning still rang in her ears.

"I have a ship waiting by the dock," the voice said. "And I can take all four of you, if you so wish."

Aeryn and Kyru gave quick glances between one another as Tierenan pushed past the cloak and handed them their weapons. Faria couldn't help but look optimistic at the unsuspecting invitation for them to follow, and as soon as Aeryn saw her gazing at them both with such hopeful eyes, the decision was made.

"Yes, we'll come too," she said firmly. Kyru looked a little relieved, but still viewed the thing in the cloak with suspicious disregard.

"Faria, I wouldn't be so quick," he warned. "You don't know who he is."

She accepted his concern with frustrated reluctance, as her own questions were beginning to form as well. After all, she hadn't any idea how much he knew of her father, or the Dhrakan siege. She tightened her grip around the staff, reminding herself that every mistake she made could potentially be her, and her father's, undoing.

"Kyru's right," she said, her tail flicking the air apprehensively. "How do we know you're not working for the Dhraka?"

The hooded figure gave a quiet laugh. "I am glad you have at least that much foresight not to trust me straight away." He pushed the hood onto his shoulders with his golden-scaled claws and revealed his face. "But I promise you, I will never side with the Dhraka."

A gryphon with lustrous white and gold plumage stood before them, his elegant features glistening in the sun and sea spray. His long-feathered ears, no longer contained by the stifling hood, stood proud like a split crest of goldenrod with flecks of white running through it. His deep red eyes, burning with an intense semblance of power, also contained a flicker of warmth. The hump under his cloak was his concealed wings.

Everyone gasped; two of the crew ran inside the forecastle at the revelation of such a beast. Faria felt herself blushing at his majestic appearance. Tierenan's jaw had dropped almost to the point of dislocation.

"A gryphon!" he squealed.

Kyru gave up trying to be unimpressed, shaking his head in disbelief. Aeryn joined Faria in blushing.

The gryphon didn't flinch at their reactions; instead he knelt in front of the young fox and took her hand. "My name is Osiris Tallon. I am a friend of your father's, and have been since before you were born. He told me that you might be in need of transport. I apologise for my sternness, but I had to be sure of your conviction."

Faria didn't know where to look. "Oh, I see…"

Kyru folded his arms impatiently, doing a bad job of hiding his jealousy. "I still don't see why we should trust him so soon."

Aeryn gave him an incredulous look. "He's risked his identity to convince us! How many other gryphons do *you* know?" she hissed, prompting a dismissive grunt from Kyru.

Osiris gave Faria an urgent look. "There is only so much I can tell you here," he said, standing up again. "I am also wanted by the dragons, albeit for slightly different reasons." He turned and gestured to the ramp, opening his offer of safe travel to them. "We don't have much time. If you'll follow?"

Faria hesitated briefly as she watched Tierenan bound after Osiris, the doubtful Kyru failing to restrain him in time. The wolf gave her an urgent look, as she was again thrust into a situation she would ultimately have to take responsibility for.

Even though her father's friend was forceful in his introduction, she trusted him. If he already knew Dhraka and how to avoid their soldiers, he could see her to Skyria more safely than any other guide could manage.

"We're going," she said decisively. "This ship would be no good to us."

Kyru felt a flash of pain in his right flank; he was quick to hide it. Unseen by the others he wiped a dribble of blood from his jaw. He wouldn't have a chance of removing the crystal alone. Quietly, he followed Faria.

Osiris looked out to sea. He spotted something again; Faria could see his wings bristle threateningly under the cloak. With a fierce glare he turned to face the others.

"We're out of time! Hurry!"

He broke into a run. Faria and the others followed at pace, bewildered by the sudden urgency. They pushed as fast as they could through the crowded quay. Osiris kept glancing out to sea past every ship, still watching something on the horizon that the others couldn't see. Ahead of them was a set of old stone steps that spiralled up the cliff face at the far eastern end of the dock, leading to the higher regions where the watchtower stood amidst the cannons protecting the city. They hit the steps running, climbing its weathered rise with unfocused emergency.

As they ran, Faria felt Kyru draw close behind her.

"Faria, I need to ask you something," he said quietly. She could barely hear him over the sound of their running.

"Yes?" she replied, more loudly than she'd intended, her breath forced out by the sprint.

Osiris skidded to a halt at a wide, flat part of the stairway. They all stopped behind him.

"It can wait," the wolf muttered.

Below them was the open sea; above them, the lighthouse. Osiris looked around quickly to check for witnesses, then stuck his hand into an ivy-veiled hole in the cliff-face. With a great heave he wrested a stone lever from the wall; in response, a section of wall in front of them jerked out about an inch, revealing carved handholds along its edge. Osiris rolled the slab across, uncovering an incredibly steep staircase leading into the inky darkness under the cliffs.

"Where are we going?" Faria asked nervously.

Osiris scanned the open waters. "There are twelve Dhrakan galleons approaching. If we don't get to my ship quickly we're going to be trapped and decimated." He gave her a piercing look. "Or would you rather stay?"

Everyone turned to the sea. Sure enough, just visible on the horizon, twelve dark, distant shapes could be seen drifting towards them. Faria grimaced fearfully, but without any delay she set down the stairs, the others following. Osiris went down last, pulling the stone firmly back in place behind him, camouflaging it against the cliff.

As soon as it boomed shut the stairway was cast into complete darkness. Faria slowly felt her way down with her free hand against the wall. The rough, uneven stone grazed her hands. She could hear Tierenan's metal claws scraping along just behind her. The darkness below felt almost infinite. Desperate not to trip and disappear forever into its pitch-black well, she sent a gentle pulse through her staff and a soft light illuminated the steep, cragged passage.

After a quick, careful descent they emerged into a huge cave bathed in the shimmering reflections of sunlight beaming through the rocky entrance. In the centre of the hidden bay sat a bulky, odd-looking ship with a patchwork hull, pieced together with different sized planks and dodgy-looking fixtures. The lanterns on the ship cast shadows over the old splintering beams, bits of it lazily patched up with pieces of driftwood. The lower half of the ship was almost completely hidden by barnacles.

"*That's* your ship?" Kyru spluttered. "We won't need to be attacked—that lump of rubbish will destroy itself!"

Osiris gave him a fierce glare. "Do not insult my ship!" he snapped. "You know nothing about her. The Coriolis has never been sunk in over two and a half thousand years of service!"

"'Never' only happens once," Kyru quipped back, prompting a string of unintelligible curses from the gryphon.

"You get on everyone's good side, don't you?" Tierenan quipped to the wolf, prompting a snort from Aeryn. Kyru fumed quietly, making a threatening gesture.

Faria studied the ship carefully as they walked along a rocky outcrop to reach the boarding ladder. She had never seen a galleon designed in such an odd way before. It was longer and wider than any she had known. Considering its length it seemed wrong for it to only have two masts—the main mast in the centre and a bizarre, three-pronged mizzen-mast, angled forwards at about seventy degrees. The sterncastle was inordinately tall, at least three storeys high. The masts were metal, glinting in the water's reflections, as was the bowsprit. On closer inspection it looked like the ship was only wearing a coat of wood, hiding something else underneath it. The gun ports, although open, didn't appear to house any guns.

"Two and a half thousand years old..." she said thoughtfully.

Already on the deck, Osiris nodded proudly. "She's not failed me yet."

"So, are you as old as the ship?" Kyru quipped.

The gryphon shot him a glare. "No. Older."

Faria's ears pricked at his gruff admission, and questions about Nazreal began snowballing in her mind as she climbed aboard, followed by the sceptical wolves.

The wood on the main deck was much different to that on the hull. It was clean, neat, and wore a strong finish that showed dedicated care and maintenance.

While Osiris disappeared into the forecastle to rouse his crew, Faria felt a strange sense of familiarity with the ship. It wasn't a comfortable feeling. It stirred something inside her, a feeling of restlessness and tension, the same that she felt whenever Nazreal's name was mentioned.

Osiris emerged again, followed by some of his crew, ready to set sail. While they quickly busied themselves and various noises emanated from below deck, Faria approached the gryphon, who swung his cloak from his body to reveal his glorious crimson, gold-edged armour and the massive golden wings that had been long cramped by the cloak's heavy fabric. She was taken aback for a second, but her conscience pressed her further.

"Osiris… if this ship is two and a half thousand years old… does that mean… do you know about Nazreal?"

He glanced at her, then continued with his work, marching towards the sterncastle. "We don't have time for that."

"When *will* there be time?" she called after him. He stopped, and the crew fell silent. She kept staring at him. Through her tiredness, her exasperating pain, her eyes burned with a fierce determination.

Although Osiris wasn't facing her, he could feel her gaze.

"Osiris, please… Do you think I can stand this danger without even knowing why I'm being hunted? You were around when the city existed, weren't you? You must have known it!"

Osiris ignored her again, but was still unable to continue inside the ship.

"Your friend, my father, is in danger," she growled, "I'm being chased around the world by dragons and there's something deeply sinister about it. I'm not stupid. Why do they want me, or my father? What is so important about a city that doesn't even exist any more?"

Osiris turned to her. She still stood tall, despite the weight of the emotions pounding on her back.

"Aidan… really hasn't told you anything, has he?" he said quietly.

Faria shook her head.

He looked to the ceiling of the cave, watching the rippling reflections play across the crags. "Nazreal was a scientific city created for the study of the crystals like those in your staff. Once their potential had been discovered and properly harnessed, new technologies were being developed every day. The city expanded rapidly. Crystals were found that could manipulate almost anything. Metal, wood, soil, even flesh. Diseases and old injuries were being healed as if they had never happened. Nazreal became the most powerful entity on Eeres, and, inevitably, power sows the seeds of conflict."

Faria looked saddened. "Do you mean there was a war? Surely with all those advances the world would only have stood to gain, though? Who'd let such a place be turned to greed?"

Osiris' expression hardened. "You're naïve to think nobody would want that power for themselves. It was still just one city in an unfair world. Fear and despair ruled people's minds even with the promise of a better future. People were paranoid. Nazreal was the only place on Eeres that had control of the crystals. If your country, your family, was dying, you would do anything to save it, wouldn't you?"

Everyone listened intently. Faria gripped her staff tightly. She knew the crystals were powerful, but it had never occurred to her that they could have been used so extensively. She had never seen or heard of any larger than the ones in her staff, nor in such huge amounts that a whole city could be dedicated to their use.

"What... what happened?" she asked quietly.

Osiris said nothing, turning away.

"How was it destroyed, Osiris?" she said again, louder, more forcefully.

"I can't tell you that," he replied, equally as forceful. "That is not my duty. When you see your father again, you can ask him."

She froze. "Wait... Father... how much does he know about Nazreal?"

"More than I will tell you," he said curtly. "I was meant to meet him in Skyria, but he sent his bodyguard to me with a letter, telling me to wait here while Kier brought you safely to Andarn. Aidan wanted you protected if things became dangerous. I'd barely had a chance to prepare when I heard news of the attack, and your escape. Searching for you would have been pointless, so I had to hope you would arrive here.

Aidan would never have forgiven me if I left to meet him without guaranteeing your safety first."

Faria couldn't quite believe what she'd heard. "So... did he know Xayall was going to be attacked?"

"Not for certain. We thought they would give us more time, though. I couldn't believe it could happen so quickly. It means they've found something significant, and very dangerous. It was as well Aidan left when he did. With luck we'll arrive together at Skyria." He turned to her and looked gravely at the staff, as if harbouring some kind of resentment towards it. "He also told me he'd be leaving the staff in your care... because he couldn't wield it any more."

"What?!" She ran to Osiris and gripped his hand, a new panic surging through her at the thought of her father's deteriorating health. "He can't use it any more? What do you mean? Osiris, is he all right?"

Osiris laid a claw on her shoulder, forceful but calming. "Don't worry. Your father is the strongest person I've ever known. You'll see him again, I guarantee it."

She calmed down a little, remembering her position. This was all being done for her. She couldn't afford to fall apart. She'd always known that he was ill, but with the Dhrakan threat casting a greater and greater shadow over her, her father's vision of strength was one of the few things she had left to hold onto, a lifeline out of the darkness.

"Once we're in Skyria we'll discuss how to destroy this artefact and end the war," the gryphon continued, flicking his thin, scarf-like crimson cloak to rest between his wings. "There is only so much we can do against Dhraka alone. We, and Aidan, will have time to rest when we arrive. The Skyrians are well-known for their healing skills."

Tierenan nodded eagerly, regarding his arms with thoughtful pride.

Faria wrung her hands. "So, what happens once a plan's decided?"

Osiris gave her a firm stare. "Whatever the outcome, you will be kept safely in Skyria until Xayall is free and the Dhrakans have been suppressed." He looked out at the cave's entrance. "We're losing time. All hands, prepare to set sail!"

He turned to the sterncastle once more and pulled open the door. As he stepped inside, a quiet voice from behind stopped him in his tracks.

"No."

He looked over his shoulder. Faria was standing opposite him, her fists clenched. "No," she repeated, louder.

"No what?" he grunted, determined that the conversation had already finished.

She shot him a defiant stare; suddenly he saw in her the same strength of mind that coursed through her father.

"I won't sit by and let everyone else fight a war for me," she growled. "I know I'm not very strong yet, but…" Visions flashed through her mind of Bayer's injuries, Xayall being ravaged, the intensely serious look on her father's face when he left, the riots in Midia, the approaching galleons. "This is only going to get worse. They're after me, and I will not risk anyone else's lives for my sake." She looked intensely, directly at Osiris, and announced her feelings with loud determination: "Xayall is my home, a place where I will be Empress… and I *will* protect it!"

Her cry echoed through the cave.

Osiris smiled. "You really are your father's daughter," he chuckled. "All hands!" he bellowed. The crew, previously distracted by Faria's outburst, hurried about their duties.

Whilst the cave was filled with the sounds of ship preparation, Faria was still standing quietly where she'd addressed Osiris. She was started out of her trance by Tierenan touching her arm, checking if she was all right. She flashed him a tired smile. He reciprocated with a grin.

"You told him."

They swayed slightly as the ship drifted into motion, creaking and groaning. The wooden hull trembled uneasily as it manoeuvred through the tight cave entrance; the ship itself pitched erratically through the rocks flanking the entrance. Sunlight burst onto the deck, and in front of them lay the open sea…

Kyru, standing at the bow, was the first to see the danger.

The twelve steely-grey Dhrakan galleons were within shooting distance, blockading Andarn's sprawling bay in a fan formation, the rams on the end of the bowsprits held like fists clenched towards the quay. The roars of the dragon cannoneers shook the timbers of the old Coriolis as the ship crawled into the light.

On his throne atop the sterncastle of the largest galleon, Fulkore Crawn let out a terrifying, victorious howl.

Chapter Fifteen

"**O**PEN FIRE!"

The Dhrakan ships began their sideways turn, cannons loaded, gunners salivating. Lit torches hovered over the fuses with quivering flames, hungry to launch their devastation onto the staunch relic sailing towards them.

On the Coriolis, Osiris yelled orders while the crew disappeared below decks to brace for battle.

"Strafe the city!" he bellowed. "That's our runaway!"

Faria, Tierenan, Kyru and Aeryn, unable to help, dodged the rushing crewmembers as best they could. An iguana and a sailfin lizard deftly scaled the sterncastle to attend to the three-pronged mast on top.

A thunderous boom signalled the first barrage. Clouds of smoke erupted from the nearest galleon and a storm of cannonballs hurtled towards them. Most fell short; three passed overhead, but four impacted on the side of the hull, crashing into the old wood. The ship shook with the ferocity of the blows. Kyru grabbed the railing to steady himself.

"Where the hell are the cannons on this ship?" he hissed, trying to see if the gun ports were yet showing any signs of artillery.

"We can't fight unarmed against twelve galleons," Aeryn said, her bow ready just in case they drew close enough for her to shoot.

The second ship opened fire as the Coriolis came within range. Columns of water burst from the sea just below the ship where the iron spheres barely missed punching more holes in their target.

Osiris wrenched open the sterncastle door and glared furiously at the Dhrakan flagship. He could make out Fulkore standing at the bowsprit, the dragon's malevolence like a fire, instilling bloodlust in the fleet's soldiers. The gryphon punched a clenched claw into his open palm and growled.

"Crawn!" They should have left earlier. "Faria!" he shouted.

The vixen turned to him immediately. "W-what?"

"Come with me," he barked, whirling back round to the sterncastle. He glared at the others. "The rest of you get below decks, now!"

They didn't argue. Faria followed close behind Osiris, glancing fearfully over at the ships that were beginning to circle into the Coriolis' path. A constant ripple of cannon shots rumbled from the attacking galleons, sending more of the deadly missiles flying overhead. Two ploughed into the forecastle and another whistled by the mizzen-mast, almost blasting the iguana into the sea.

Osiris slammed the door behind them. Immediately she saw that the Coriolis' interior didn't match the crumbling outer hull. The floor was strong wood like the deck outside, but the walls were a light blue-grey metal, clean and strong, adorned with gold, silver and white mouldings, panels and architraves. Carved into the metalwork was a complex, entwining web of straight lines and geometric shapes. Small lights on the upper part of the walls glowed appreciatively upon her entrance.

Another impact shuddered through the ship.

"Come on!" Osiris snapped, climbing the stairs to her right.

Outside, on the Dhrakan flagship, Fulkore's eyes burned with ferocious excitement as he watched the old ship turn away to avoid the demolishing power of his cannons.

"Keep up the bombardment," he growled to his second-in-command. "Once it's crippled, we'll board it and take the Phiraco child. The rest will be killed."

His subordinate nodded obligingly and signalled the order to the rest of the fleet.

Fulkore turned his attention back to his prey, watching each cannonball, his malicious grin widening with every crushing blow, his mind too clouded by savagery to recognise the ship's distinctive shape.

Osiris and Faria climbed to the bridge at the top of the sterncastle. Jala, the otter quartermaster, greeted them with a quick salute. The room was large, with windows stretching across all four walls. At the front of the room stood a sprawling control panel, covered in levers, dials and switches like a garden of machinery. Mounted on a plinth in the centre was the ship's wheel, a curved W-shaped structure with thick, gold handles. On the wall behind them was a hollow the same size and shape as Faria's staff. Osiris looked at her sternly.

"You need to activate this or we'll be sunk," he told her. She looked to the gryphon for a cue; he pointed impatiently at the hollow. "Your staff! Quickly!"

Another cannonball struck the ship, this time on the sterncastle just in front of the window. She could see more shots hurtling across the deck. She moved the staff into position and, taking a deep breath, pushed it into the slot.

Nothing happened.

"Osiris, what do I do?"

"It's a machine!" he yelled as another cannonball glanced off the sterncastle wall below the window. "Give it some electricity! Come on, Faria!"

Hurriedly, her fingers shaking in the rush of the fight, she focused her mind and shot a burst of electricity down the staff. For a brief instant, she felt the intricate inner workings of the Coriolis. It was incredible. Blue and white streams of energy darted along the control panel. With a whirr, the staff was ejected from the metal gap and the hollow receded, leaving a solid metal plate behind.

Deep mechanical growls sent shudders along the ship; noises of movement shuddered all around them. The splitting of the old wood below snapped the air. Breaking into a triumphant smile, Osiris grabbed a metal funnel next to the wheel and bellowed down it:

"Secure the cargo and ammunition! All available crew to the gun deck and man the starboard cannons. Brace yourselves—we're about to take off!"

"Take off?" Faria yelped.

The Dhrakan cannon fire slowed gradually as they began to notice the strange noise. Fulkore tilted his head and watched the oversized piece of driftwood with a growing sense of apprehension. His sardonic smirk changed to a cold grimace.

The carrack's wooden hull exploded away section by section, casting the ship's aged shell into the waves. The roaring intensified. Loose planks twisted away and the cannonballs that had punched into the hull dropped into the water as the galleon cast off its rudimentary camouflage. With a final eruption of wood and splinters, the Coriolis' true form burst through, a glistening metal vessel of silver and gold, all but untouched by the Dhrakan missiles. All too late the image of the ship burned into Fulkore's vision, a memory reawakened.

"NO! Tallon!"

He leapt at his signal officer, tearing him by the throat and wrenching him forth. "Take that ship down!" he screamed. "Destroy it! Why the hell have you stopped firing?"

The last of the driftwood now floating in its wake, the Coriolis sped through the blue-hued smoke towards the gap between the Andarn cliffs and the furthest Dhrakan warship. Osiris wrested down a large lever on his right. The wheel clicked free and lifted towards him, angling back slightly.

"My ship!" he beamed. "I knew I'd fly you again, you beautiful girl!" He turned to Faria with a gleaming, free look in his eyes. She was clutching the rail by the window, stunned.

"Don't be afraid; you haven't seen anything yet!" he laughed.

Two bright white triangular sails unfurled astride the sterncastle from the three-pronged mast at the top. A third zipped down a line at the centre and shook taught. Five sets of narrow rectangular sails on metal frames folded out from the main mast and swivelled into place, creating horizontal aerofoils over the centre of the ship.

Under the hull four large turbine engines shuddered into life. A thousand years of dust shook free from its temporary resting place and disappeared under the waves. The large ship accelerated at brutal speed through the water as the twelve galleons resumed their frantic barrage.

Eighteen gun ports slid open on the Coriolis' gun deck, each with a gleaming barrel behind it. A single broadside volley from the golden ship thundered into the two galleons they were passing, snapping the keel of one and punching three fatal gashes in the hull of the other. Near the bow, a swivelling gun with a split, spiralled barrel, a thin spike at its centre, whirred into action. A fizzling white ball of electricity sparked up at its centre, grew in size and then streaked off towards the ships like a bullet of white fire. It tore through the sails and mast of one of the ships, setting it alight and sending the Dhrakans aboard into a panic.

Large triangular wings pivoted out of the sides of the ship just underneath the main deck, beginning just behind the prow and finishing in front of the sails by the sterncastle. The Coriolis rose out of the water, a few last cannon shots bouncing vainly off its hull and into the sea. As it climbed higher, two thin rudders hinged from the keel and four stabilising fins folded from the hull between the engines. A few seconds later, the ship began a steep ascent and was out of range, rapidly soaring into the sky.

Fulkore exploded into a blind fury, slashing at flags, punching through the deck and letting out a horrific cry of utter damnation for his escaped prey.

"That contemptuous bird is still alive!" he bellowed, quaking with rage, his breath rippling with the heat of his anger. Perhaps worse than his failure were the words from the black rock echoing in his mind: "*...you must not underestimate either of them. They are more powerful than you know.*"

He pulled his fist from the ring of splinters he'd created in the deck and growled. His second-in-command approached him distantly, wary of his lord's current mental state.

"Sir, your orders?"

Andarn soldiers were ascending the towers to the city defences.

Fulkore cracked his neck. It didn't matter. His final tool that would bring him to glory and destroy the family that had plagued him for generations was already prepared. He scorned himself for not releasing it sooner.

"Have all ships return to Dhraka," he hissed. "We're boarding the Gargantua."

His second-in-command grinned hungrily. "Yes, sir."

Osiris and Faria watched the sky open up before them as they passed over Andarn's cliffs. He let out a gleeful sigh as the ship shook itself steady, blasting away the years of inactivity. Once they reached a steady level, Osiris checked the altimeter mounted on the centre of the wheel.

"Great, we've reached our perfect altitude. We're on course for Skyria."

She nodded silently, still gripped with shock at the sight of the land far below them. The ship was flying. Osiris smiled and gave another command through the funnel:

"Jala, you're at the helm. Somebody show our guests up to the bridge."

A river of pipes and cables lined the dank corridors leading to the black stone's central chamber, where the rock was slowly and meticulously being chipped away by enslaved scientists and physicians.

The black-scaled dragon muttered infrequently into the stone, narrating the scene around him into the pitch-dark surface. A wiry dragon entered the room and cleared his throat expectantly. The black dragon didn't move.

"Yes?" he whispered.

"He has been retrieved," the young soldier reported. "And the Gargantua has been ordered to mobilize."

The black dragon nodded and spoke quietly to the stone again.

"She is pleased," he said. "She looks forward to repaying him in blood for his sins."

Suddenly, one of the scientists on top of the rock broke into a fissure. A hideous low moan crept through the room, its deathly sound infecting every inch, every surface in the stifling darkness. The black-scaled dragon reeled back from the stone in horror, clasping his claws around his head.

"She... she is coming free," he croaked.

It lay before them, trapped in the ore. The part of it they could see pulsated gently, driven by a heartbeat lying deep within its body.

Within seconds a group of dragons moved from the shadows, pulling a large wagon laden with arcane machinery and metal even blacker than the darkness surrounding the stone.

They took one of the large machines and placed it in front of the rock. It was covered in scratches and dents, as if it had been ripped away from something or someone with considerable force. The pipes dragged into the room were connected to it, and tentatively a quaking researcher rotated a few large, ancient dials and pulled down a lever on its side. The device activated, whirring, shuddering, and sparking erratically. Many around it stepped back in fear, only to find themselves blocked by armed guards who pushed them back to their enforced duty.

Small hoses, drawn from the machine, were hauled up to the top levels of the stone and sprayed a small amount of a crystalline blue liquid into the pit. The throbbing object convulsed upon touching it. The rock around it hissed and began to dissolve; the metal and other small bits of machinery were passed up to the top of the rock and work began feverishly to transplant the being inside to its protective armour, piece by piece, too fragile to free in one movement.

The moan grew louder, spreading its macabre echo through the metal corridors, past the thick, black steel walls and out across the mountain range. From the mountain's shadow, a black pyramid, hidden in its coat of stone, began to crawl forth.

Osiris was giving Faria, Tierenan, Aeryn and Kyru a guided tour of the Coriolis, brimming with pride at the mention of every unusual structure or device, and taking great pains to explain everything he could about the ship's construction. It had been commissioned and designed by him. He hadn't wanted just any ship, and this was as close as you could get to perfection, or so he said.

"I can't believe it's made out of metal," Aeryn said, in awe. The panelling was smooth to the touch and well-polished, belying its age. When Faria ran her fingers along it she could feel the same mixtures of metals as in her staff, light but incredibly strong. She wondered if the hull had been damaged at all by the Dhrakan cannonballs.

Kyru was nonplussed. "I can't believe we're *flying*. How the hell does this boat stay up?"

"This *ship*," Osiris snapped, "stays up through the combined effort of its engines, its sails and its aerofoils. It's made of light, strong metals forged by a very difficult and complex process that doesn't exist any more." He cast Faria a furtive glance. "To my knowledge."

"So, what happens if a cannonball makes a hole in it?" Tierenan asked, peering at his reflection in one of the golden panels.

The gryphon gave a derisive scowl. "They haven't, so far. It's the ship's interior I'm more worried about damaging."

"The interior?" Faria chimed, eager to keep the conversation flowing in case he mentioned anything more about Nazreal. "You mean the mechanisms and electronics?"

Osiris nodded, regarding her interest with dubiety. She looked ready to launch into another Nazreal question. "Yes. I don't know anyone who could repair it if anything went wrong internally." He whirled round, flicking his wings. Kyru gave a dismissive click of his tongue, convinced that the only reason the inside of the ship was metal was to satisfy the gryphon's vanity. His armour was spotless, and it was obvious he drilled his crew very hard on cleaning every inch of the ship's casing and fixtures. For a ship that had been at sea for over a millennium, it was inordinately polished.

They were currently walking along the berth deck where the crew slept. At its centre was a long table with fixed stools along its edges, looking like it could comfortably fit sixty people around it. The deck would have looked almost homely, if it weren't for the racks of artillery shells lining the walls. Huge corrugated metal rods over twenty feet long lay secured on the floor, forbidding in their appearance even though Faria couldn't discern their purpose. She meant to ask, but before she had the chance other areas of the ship distracted her and she forgot about them in place of new exhibitions.

Since it was built for Osiris, the Coriolis had decks tall enough for him to stand without stooping. As such, it only had two gun decks, a berth deck and a hold, as well as a number of smaller decks in the sterncastle below the bridge, one of which housed his cabin. Most of the engine mechanisms were at the rear of the ship, under the sterncastle.

They were on their way up back up to the gun deck and their cabins in the wardroom when the door to the surgeon's cabin slid open. From inside came a well-preened but wholly unassuming peregrine falcon with bold, dark eyes masked only slightly by a pair of magnification glasses resting on his beak. He pushed them up onto his forehead with his wing, the flights on which had been trimmed back. A wooden device covered in different-sized articulated hooks was attached to his wrist to form a functional, if basic, hand. He wore a simple leather waistcoat, and green and black leather trousers with feathered strips of leather running down the seams. A silver pendant depicting an egg with six wings hung around his neck.

He regarded them with some interest, taking particular note of Tierenan's robotic parts, then looked to Osiris.

"Vann is doing fine. He only suffered mild cuts from the splintering wood, and some bruises from falling off the mast. I've told him to rest but otherwise we're not suffering anywhere else," the falcon said calmly.

Osiris smiled. "This is Maaka, the Coriolis' surgeon, and my friend." He stepped aside to reveal the four completely to the falcon. "This is Aeryn, Kyru, Tierenan and Faria. They're coming with us to Skyria."

Maaka gave a polite bow of his head. "It's a pleasure to meet you. I trust you're all well?"

Kyru looked surreptitiously to Aeryn and was just about to say something when Tierenan bounded forwards.

"I have a headache," he announced, pointing to the side of his head not cased in metal. Just below his fur was a raised lump, the skin underneath red and inflamed. "It's kind of a sharp pain. I've had it since Faria hit me."

Faria looked shocked, remembering the jolt of electricity she thrust into his head when he attacked her outside Xayall. "Really? Did I do that?"

He smiled, a little embarrassed. "Yeah, you did. But I didn't want to say anything because I knew you'd worry." True enough, she already looked distressed and twiddled her staff restlessly. "I did kinda deserve it anyway," he smirked, idly scratching his metal upper-arm. "So I don't blame you."

Kyru folded his arms once again, shooting the raccoon a disparaging glance. "Yeah, I wouldn't blame you either."

As Maaka led Tierenan into his cabin, the raccoon looked over his shoulder at Kyru. "Maaka, you don't happen to know any procedures that turn ugly miseries into nice people, do you?"

He shut the door before Kyru could reach him; the wolf felt another wave of pain fire up his back and the taste of blood rise in his mouth.

"You better be wearing a bandage when you come out, Tierenan—it'll save you the trouble of finding one when I'm finished with you!" he yelled through the door. Aeryn pulled him away, sighing.

Faria looked around to see Osiris already disappearing up the stairs to the next deck. When she climbed them he was standing expectantly in the corridor, surrounded by a series of wooden doors.

"This is the wardroom," he said bluntly, losing a little of the warmth with which he'd introduced Maaka. Kyru and Aeryn appeared at the step hatch and looked inside the rooms whilst Faria gazed out of the window on the sterncastle door. Ahead she could see the deck cast out before her and the gleaming prow of the ship cutting through the wind. It almost appeared motionless; were it not for the clouds passing swiftly overhead and the breeze rippling the sails, she would have thought they were completely still.

"You can step out if you like," a deep, soft voice said behind her. She turned, startled, to see Osiris. "It'll be breezy though, so be careful."

She stepped back for him to open the door. The large, golden latch clicked loudly as it shifted into position. The door punched open and a fierce wind burst into the wardroom. She managed to push her way through the pressing air current and onto the quarterdeck, shadowed by the bulky gryphon who pulled the door shut with a sturdy thud.

Once out of the doorway, the wind didn't seem as strong. She could counter it if she wanted to with her staff, but the fresh air in her fur was creating a new vigour within her. She walked to the port side and peered over the edge. Hundreds of feet below lay the open sea, the waves shimmering in the sun as if the whole surface was the scales of one gigantic fish.

"It's not as bad as I thought it would be," she said, trying to make out shadows in the water below. "The sea looks so beautiful from up here. I thought it'd be scarier, too." She let out an excited laugh as they overtook a group of gulls flying underneath them.

Osiris leant on the rail. His feathers fluttered calmly in the air's breath as he stared out over the sea, a wistful look in his eyes.

"I haven't flown in years," he sighed.

Faria looked at the clouds beyond. "I've never flown at all…"

Her staff felt icy cold in the breeze. She tightened her grip on the weapon as questions about her father's past and Nazreal burrowed their way into her mind.

Before she could ask anything, he spoke. "I apologise for shouting at you when activating the bridge, Faria. If we'd waited any longer, they would have trapped us. You won't need to do it again. The ship isn't powered by resonance—it has fuel cells—but the device locking the flight mechanism was. Aidan helped me disguise and seal the Coriolis using his powers. If anyone else had taken the ship, they wouldn't have been able to activate it. Only you or he could bridge the connection."

"Oh, I see…" she said quietly. The crystals glinted gently in the light.

"How…" she began. Osiris raised an eyebrow and gave her a quizzical regard. She cast her gaze to the distant line of the horizon, the empty feeling of the future's uncertainty rising in her stomach once again. "How long have you known my father?"

"I first met him when he was about your age," he said quietly, not looking at her.

She could tell this conversation would be hard work. She would only be able to push him so far before he decided it wasn't his 'duty' to tell her any more. "So… what did he do before he came to Xayall?"

Osiris shifted uncomfortably; he cast her a suspicious glance for a second, then turned back to the rolling horizon of the clouds. "He worked in city design, an architect. It was his work that made most of Xayall what it is today. He designed the Tor. And…"

She stepped closer, looking urgently for him to continue. He scratched his ear impatiently.

"He was an incredibly powerful resonator. He could carve entire buildings out of a pile of stone and metal in minutes. He could direct waterways, forge cliff faces... and as a responsible person he was invaluable to the world with and without his resonance."

She held the staff in front of her. The crystal glinted sharply in the sun as if in confirmation of Osiris' testimony.

"But he's not that powerful any more," she whispered, thinking back to her training where he'd only ever been able to demonstrate a small conversion of the staff's energy before becoming ill each time. She pulled her cloak tightly around her.

Osiris nodded. There was a loaded silence for a few seconds. He leant further onto the rails and gave a hefty sigh. "There was a time... he went missing. I searched for him for an age. Eventually he was found wandering the deserts east of Xayall. The carriage that found him was holding your mother, who was then the Empress of the city." He gave a weary smile. "That was the first time they met. He was almost dead when they picked him up. The sickness he had then has pervaded his body ever since."

Faria wrung her hands, looking agitated. "But did they find out what his illness was, or where he got it from? Is there something we can do for it?"

Osiris sighed, his claw unconsciously tightening around the hilt of his rapier. "I... don't know. All we can do is find him and bring him home safely when this is over."

She nodded, still looking sadly at her staff. "Osiris… why do the Dhrakans want—"

The sterncastle door burst open and a loud cry broke over the deck. Tierenan was sprinting across the threshold, his face covered in blood.

Chapter Sixteen

Faria and Osiris reeled back as Tierenan lolloped towards them, crimson dripping from his muzzle. Osiris was about to draw his sword when Faria ran to meet the bloodied raccoon.

He was smiling.

As she approached he skidded to a halt and held out his right hand triumphantly. Cradled in the metallic palm of his claw was a tiny, blackened square block with tiny wires and clips protruding from it. He grinned widely.

"That was in my head!" he sang, watching her pick it up and lay it in her hand, inspecting it closely. It twitched in the wind.

Her ears flattened. "I haven't broken you, have I?" she said anxiously.

He laughed. "It's not a part of me I miss. I feel fine." To demonstrate he began flexing his metal muscles with incredible melodrama, making the loudest masculine grunts he could muster, contorting his face in a series of increasingly bizarre portraits of fake strain. It was a bizarre sight. She could see some of the crew watching, bemused, from the windows. Despite feeling incredibly embarrassed, she couldn't suppress her laughing.

"Stitches make me strong!" he boomed, trying to sound deep and authoritative.

Osiris looked less optimistic. A cold severity sharpened his eyes as they lay fixed on the small burnt-out microchip. "Tierenan," he called. Instantly the raccoon composed himself and stepped forwards.

"Where did this come from?" the gryphon asked, his voice sombre and low.

Tierenan shook his head. "I don't know. My head and arms were metal already, from Skyria. But I didn't have that, and my limbs didn't extend before. They've done some funny things to the rest of me as well."

Osiris remained immovably stern. "Who is 'they'? The Dhrakans?"

The raccoon suddenly became very nervous, the usual cheeriness draining from his body in a few short moments. He pulled anxiously at his claws and shuffled on his feet. "I... don't remember. But they told me I was going to be presented to the Senate. They said it would be a surprise and not to tell my parents. There were loads of us on the boat. When we arrived, I was bundled into a carriage with no windows. They wouldn't tell me anything. I don't..."

"Do you know where they took you?" he pressed, his severe look affecting even Faria. "Tierenan, this thing that was inside you, do you know what it is? Who put it in?"

Tierenan shook his head, his voice so quiet it was almost a whisper. "It... I'm sorry, I don't know... The place I was taken was dark, and the rocks were sort of… like rust. Then they took off my arms, and… and then did something to my head. It…" He paused for a long time, swallowing the flashes of memory that sank into his mind, staring distantly at the deck. "It hurt. That's all I know until seeing Faria walk away in the forest."

He fell silent, looking away from them both, holding his arm as if he were nursing a bruise. Faria rested a hand on his shoulder. The metal was achingly cold. She wondered how much he felt it, whether it hurt when the plating was scorched or frozen, or if he noticed when something wasn't working properly. He barely acknowledged her, instead looking out to the surrounding sky. He was still saddened, but a faint glow of hope rose in his face and his expression softened.

"But I'm coming home now, so it's okay," he said quietly. "I hope… you can still trust me."

On the prow of the ship, he caught sight of a flash of green glinting on the rail. The shimmering bird with the long tail fluttered its wings and disappeared into the sun moments later.

Osiris looked round to follow Tierenan's gaze but, seeing nothing, turned back and sighed, troubled thoughts coursing through his mind.

"I wouldn't worry about it now. Like you said, you're on your way home. I think it's best we get you there as quickly as possible," the gryphon said, his voice still laced with gravity. Tierenan nodded quietly and turned to go back to the sterncastle. Osiris watched him for a moment until seeing Faria's hands, clasped in concern. He sighed, a pang of guilt tugging him away from his stern judgement.

"Wait, Tierenan."

The raccoon eyed him a little frightfully as he approached.

"You're not going anywhere without being cleaned first. I won't have you dripping blood all over my ship. If you get cleaned up properly, I'll show you the swords in my armoury. I designed them myself."

Tierenan's mood snapped so quickly back into place, Faria was sure she actually *heard* it. He rushed ahead, opening the door for the captain and leaping through after him.

The young fox held the black square delicately in her hand and closed her fingers carefully over it. She wanted to thank Maaka on Tierenan's behalf; no doubt the raccoon had escaped in a fit of excitement before he was even finished. Pushing open the sterncastle door, she made her way down to the gun deck.

The deck was quiet save for the drone of the engines and the humming of the wind, although she could hear the lively conversation of the crew sitting amongst the cannons. They seemed a pleasant group, far more so than the Marinche's crew.

She raised her hand to knock on Maaka's door just as the sailors behind her burst into raucous fits of laughter, scaring her near out of her skin. She didn't look round to see if anyone noticed though, instead hiding her flustered blushing in front of Maaka's surgery.

The sliding door stood already ajar. She carefully pressed herself against the frame and peered through the gap to see if the falcon was inside.

He was, but someone else was with him too. She withdrew for a second, then realised who she saw and looked back again. The large silver wolf, hunched over a gurney, muttered something inaudible. In his back was a deep open wound, not bleeding but instead glowing with a faint purple hue not unlike that of Vionaika's eyes. She let out a gasp in shock; immediately Kyru whirled around and caught sight of her. His fierce, alarmed glare stunned her completely. She shrank back behind the door, trying to make herself as small as possible. Her heart was beating in her throat. What was that gash?

Approaching footsteps within the room froze her with trepidation. He'd looked furious. She turned round just as the door opened.

"I'm sorry Kyru, I didn't mean to—"

Maaka tilted his head curiously. She stopped, looking even more ashamed of herself.

"It's alright," the falcon said calmly. "He says you can come in."

She nodded, looking behind her as she entered, hoping that the crew weren't looking her way.

Maaka's surgery was filled with all sorts of complicated medical equipment, some of which she had seen before and others that were completely alien. Scissors, tweezers, forceps, needles and any number of scalpel blades had been attached to metal sleeves that strapped on to Maaka's beak. Some had the capacity to open and close as they needed, operated by his mouth. Arranged in trays on the side were different attachments for the braces on his wrist—blunt hooks, sharp hooks, blades, retractors, callipers; countless other tools glinted in the light of the room, awaiting their turn on the operating table. Larger bits of strange mechanical equipment stood around the walls of the surgery, which itself was spacious enough to have two people being operated on at one time. On mesh-guarded shelves surrounding the walls were dozens of medical encyclopaedias and books on different species' anatomy, along with a few half-unrolled diagrams of skeletal structure and medicine charts. It was bewildering.

Kyru said nothing as she approached, but tapped his claws impatiently on the gurney, his tail flicking brusquely from side to side. She shuffled apologetically forwards, watching the wound throb angrily. It looked agonising.

"Kyru... what happened?"

"I was attacked when we stayed in Andarn," he grunted over his shoulder. "By that hyena thing."

She leaned in for a closer inspection. Maaka flinched slightly at the thought of her getting too close. He withheld stopping her when he saw the crystals in the staff.

"It's reasonably deep, but not irremovable.," the falcon spoke, serious insofar as it was his job to be concerned. "Your organs appear safe from it, but it's sitting close enough to them to be a potential risk. My chief concern is that it's growing veins which are spreading out from the wound. I've never seen it before."

Faria ran her hand over the arm of her glove, turning the possibilities over in her mind. "It's definitely a resonating crystal... I'm not sure what the purple ones do, but I think they're poisonous at the very least. My father said they can be used as a form of control or body enhancement, but I don't know how."

Kyru snorted in frustration. "So, can you remove it?"

Faria shook her head sadly. "No, not these ones. I've never used them before. I could end up hurting you further. I'm sorry."

"I don't care about the pain," he growled. "If it can be taken out, I'll endure it."

She looked aside. "That's not what I meant. It... could kill you."

There was a brief, tense silence.

"So it's death or... what?"

Maaka started placing his tools in small basins to be washed. "It seems like it's the epicentre of the spasms, and I can only guess that it's causing other symptoms as well, either by its chemical compound or, if what Miss Faria says is correct, part of the control exerted by it. I could extract it if you wish, but I couldn't guarantee any adverse reaction. It would be a long operation, would take time to recover from. Whoever put it there would be your best chance at removing it."

The wolf scratched his neck. "Yeah, like that's going to happen." He pulled his shirt back on and jumped to the floor, striding towards the exit. He caught sight of Faria's anguished look and stopped at the door frame.

"Don't worry about me, Faria. You've got bigger things to be concerned about," he said boldly, although she knew he was only saying it to calm her.

"But..." he continued, resting a hand on the door, "...don't tell Aeryn. Please."

She nodded.

The next day, late morning, Osiris was pacing up and down the ship, intense vexation on his face.

"I've sailed this ocean a hundred times! Why the hell can't I find out where we are?" he roared, storming backwards and forwards between the hold and the bridge, followed by a trail of crew members holding pieces of equipment used for monitoring and calibrating the ship's various systems.

Faria and Tierenan had been on the bridge when Osiris had found out they were lost. Both had been shocked to silence at the gryphon's furious tirade and hadn't moved from their places since, despite him not having said a word directly to them. Jala had been reprimanded for not paying attention during his shift at the wheel. His protests to the contrary went unheard as Osiris had, to all intents and purposes, found his scapegoat. Faria was worried the otter was going to be hurled off the ship at one point. After Osiris had gone down to the hold to check the navigation systems, however, he decided that it was an internal problem after all (not that Jala received an apology) and had been working to find the source, and their bearings.

Tierenan peered out of the window behind him. On the port side of the ship he could see a coastline, and he quietly raised his hand.

"Mr Osiris, sir?" he said patiently, while the ruffled gryphon stared intently at the compass. "There's land over there."

Immediately he took the ship's wheel and barked into the communications funnel. "We're landing! Crew to your positions!"

The crew rushed around in a blind hurry trying to prepare the Coriolis. The ship descended beneath the low, grey clouds and made a rushed touchdown in the water; the steering fins only just folded away in time before the ship punched the sea's calm surface. From the crashing noises in the decks below it sounded as if not everything had been strapped down.

A mist hung in the shore's air, shrouding the distance in a grey haze. Old stone buildings were just visible on the hills above the coastline, ghostly in the air.

They sailed slowly along the shallows while Osiris tried to ascertain their position and everyone else watched in silence. After a few minutes of consulting the map, he threw it to the floor in frustration and leant on the window, rapping his claws on the frame.

"We're in Kinuna."

Faria looked briefly to Tierenan, who shrugged. "So... where is—"

"Nowhere near," he scowled. "We'll find the dock and set the navigation systems right again. We've lost a lot of time."

He took the wheel, smouldering to himself about what could have gone wrong. The others slunk out of the bridge and onto the deck.

It didn't take them long to reach the port. Kinuna was a relatively small island between the continents Cadon and Ohé, whilst Skyria lay an equal distance away to the northeast. It held a strong culture and generated a lot of income as a waypoint between the continents. Isolating itself from the rest of world politics acted in its favour, as it became a port for free exchange of ideas and trade, and a popular haven to escape to.

The dock was almost the size of Andarn's, but wasn't nearly as grand. The wharfs were much narrower, wooden, and the buildings were lower and simpler in construction. It didn't need anything more dramatic; Kinuna's residents never felt they had an image to uphold. From all over Eeres, different styles of carrack, caravel and sloop stood on display as if in some nautical display piece. The crew of the Coriolis gathered on the deck to admire the ships they passed, pointing out ones of particular merit or unusual design.

The Coriolis manoeuvred gingerly into dock and was quickly anchored. Although knowing they were off course, the crew were excited by the opportunity to visit the market.

Osiris cracked his shoulders disdainfully at the hushed discussions about leaving the ship. They had no choice but to stay until the systems had been corrected, but he had no intention of this being a leisure stop. Time was crucial.

He nominated several of the crew to remain behind to keep sentry on deck and set the others free to explore, albeit briefly. Aeryn and Kyru left with them for the market in the town centre.

Faria watched them leave, compelled to follow but knowing better to stay. She didn't enjoy the idea of being lost in a crowd again. As she turned back to the sterncastle she bumped into Osiris.

"Faria, I need you, if you wouldn't mind," he said, his normally pristine feathers ruffled with frustration. "I'm not sure how adept your abilities are, but you may be able to help me all the same."

She smiled and nodded, glad to be of use.

As they descended, unbeknownst to Osiris, Tierenan was already on the main deck and buzzing over the thought of exploring Kinuna. He guessed the strict gryphon wouldn't want him off the Coriolis unsupervised, but the increasing temptation was making him lean over the railing in anticipation. As he gazed out over the dock, a flash of emerald green on an awning caught his eye. That bird again...

He checked around him furtively and, with a sly grin, jumped onto the wharf and vanished into the streets.

Kyru had found a clothiers' shop. His sleeveless jacket was almost a net for all its holes. After visiting the Lleyandi estate, he wanted to improve his image for Aeryn. He didn't know exactly *how*, but it was worth a try.

He was surrounded by evening coats and loungewear, feeling very out of place. Nothing looked practical. He needed more of a tough military surcoat, and for that to fit properly he should have been wearing all of his armour. As it was, he only had his leg harness on. It was the most he could tolerate, as his injury was too painful for him to wear more.

He turned to leave, just as a mannequin standing in the back corner of the shop piqued his attention. It was wearing a long, grey, patterned jacket with a high collar and a thick leather band around the waist. Perfect, were it not for the lace-trimmed cuffs lurking on the end of the sleeves. It was a thick, strong material with silk embroidery of sharp, leafy swirls not unlike his tattoos. He stood back for a second and admired it, scratching his muzzle thoughtfully.

"Can I help you?" came a voice. A prim black and white ruffed lemur with a tight white shirt and tawny waistcoat stepped to him, holding himself in a stiff, refined position that didn't look natural or comfortable. Kyru pointed at the jacket.

"Tell me about this," he asked, trying not to drop any hints about buying it. He didn't like dealing with shopkeepers. He was never sure he could trust them, and he disliked their intrusive persuasion to buy something.

The lemur cleared his throat. "This was commissioned by a general who was due to retire to Pthiris. I took his measurements when he was here from Ohé two years ago, but since he hasn't come back to take it and left no address, I've put it up for sale."

Kyru nodded. "I see. Can I try it?"

The lemur nodded. "Of course, sir. He was larger than yourself, though. If it isn't a suitable fit I can measure you up for another."

Kyru scrunched his nose. "I'm not coming back through. 'Big' is fine." He pulled it on over his shirt, ignoring the doubtful look the primate gave him. He shuffled around a bit, pulled it closed across his chest and looked himself over. It would probably fit over his armour, given some persuasion. The sleeves would have to go, though.

"How much without the sleeves?"

The lemur looked blank. "They aren't removable, sir."

Kyru whirled the jacket off and placed it back on the mannequin. "I'm sure they are," he replied curtly, grasping the shoulder seam between his claws and giving it a strong, sudden wrench. The lemur raised his hands in horror as the stitching split open and, seconds later, the wolf held in his hand a former sleeve, frilly cuff drooping sadly at one end.

"What are you *doing*?" he shrieked.

"Seeing if I could take them off," he said, matter-of-factly. "Now, how much for the coat without the sleeves?"

"That is out of the question!" the shopkeeper spluttered, moving to cradle the damaged garment in his hands.

"Why?" Kyru said huffily. "Shows your stitching isn't up to much. And now you have a damaged jacket that you'll have to spend hours repairing. Or I can take it and you can keep the material for the sleeves, saving us both time and money."

The lemur's jaw opened and closed in astonished shock; the words he needed to express his disbelief had not yet been invented.

Kyru nonchalantly flicked some dirt from underneath his claws. "I think it's a bargain."

Kinuna's market wasn't nearly as vast as Andarn's sprawling array of stallholders, but the things on sale here were far more interesting. Tierenan had gawked at a set of swords from Ohé, and his eyes sparkled upon seeing a rack of pistols as fine as he had ever come across (not that he had seen many). Needless to say, he wasn't allowed anywhere near them, and the shopkeeper shooed him away.

He stroked his hand along a length of luxurious cloth but stopped halfway, remembering that he couldn't feel with his hands any more. He had an awareness of touch and the strength with which he did so, but all sensations were the same now. Disappointed but for a moment, he gently took hold of the material and stroked it against his muzzle. It was incredibly soft and light. He smiled at the stallholder, a fat, jolly tiger, and skittered away.

He slowed his pace as he walked up one of the wider streets, ignorant to the looks people were giving him over his mechanical parts. He was far more interested in the market. If he'd had money, he would have bought something for Faria…

Something fluttered past his right ear, swooping in front of him into an alleyway: the bird again! He ran after it and spun around the corner, skidding past a well-dressed couple coming in the other direction.

Barrels lined the alley. He couldn't see the bird any more, but flicked each barrel as he went past to try and rouse it. Glancing around where the alley intersected another, a glint of green shimmered in the passageway to his right. He chased it, almost slipping in a puddle at the junction. His claw latched onto the corner and he pulled himself back upright, eager to catch up.

The path widened into a small, derelict courtyard holding old forgotten crates, decaying straw scattered over the slimy stone. In one corner was a drain, clogged with sludge.

The bird circled over his head, then perched on a figure almost hidden amongst the shadows. Whoever it was sat slouched against the damp wall, wrapped in a dirty blanket riddled with holes. The bird chirruped. He stepped carefully closer, trying to see the figure more closely, when suddenly it moved, turning a head to him with tired, weak eyes.

She, a wiry young ferret, seemed barely to acknowledge him. It felt as if she was staring straight through him. Looking into her eyes, an overwhelming sense of sadness washed over him. Loneliness, weariness, desperation; her fatigue sunk into his heart. And more than that, there was something chillingly familiar about her. He opened and closed his claws as if trying to grasp something to say out of the air.

"Hi…" he whispered.

She lowered her head. He swallowed and looked around awkwardly, surrounded by her poor, desolate environment. The words he wanted to form were lost inside him, trapped by an overwhelming weight in his chest. His cold, empty claws ached for something to offer her, but had nothing to give. The thought of grabbing some food from the market flitted across his mind but he dismissed it quickly, as it would only bring her more trouble.

"My name's Tierenan," he said quietly, managing a smile. "Your bird found me and brought me here."

She said nothing, but the bird flapped its wings proudly.

He waited silently for a response. The sounds of the market echoed distantly along the walls.

"I know who you are. You're one like me," she murmured. "I remember you."

Chapter Seventeen

In the Coriolis' hold, Osiris had pulled out a panel and was busy reconnecting wires and plugs within a big piece of machinery. The power had been shut off for him to work safely, so he was surrounded by a precarious array of lanterns, casting him and the hold in a gentle orange glow.

On the right-hand wall of the hull was a dent caused by a cannonball. The metal was still strong—Osiris admitted he couldn't beat it out himself. Faria studied it for a time, trying to feel the composition of the metals with her fingers.

"I can try, but it may take me a while. I've practiced on common metals, but... since it's almost the same alloy as my staff I've always learnt to ignore it."

"I see," Osiris said quietly, focusing on a clip he'd pulled from the box. "Aidan hasn't taught you to harness that part of resonance, then?"

She looked puzzled, distracted from being about to push the dent back into place. "You mean the metals?"

"No. The resonance itself."

She paused for a second. "That... doesn't work, does it?" She held the staff against the wall and with a low hum of energy the cannonball wound disappeared. "I mean, you can resonate *with* things, but it's just empty power if you don't apply it."

She traced a hand along the hold to find more impact dents while Osiris fumbled with some dials.

"Hmm." He stood up and looked into the darkness in front of him. "That's exactly the point, but the power's far from empty. The alloys in this ship were formed using the resonance energy rather than *a* resonance in particular," he said, somewhat gruffly. "Traditional alloy techniques took far longer and would never yield anything perfect. Resonance, as I understood it, could take only the qualities you wanted to create something new. Resonating with those types of metals separately in the same place just mixes them all together in a heavy mess. What the free energy did was meld them all together into something new, which could then be shaped under a resonator's control as he or she saw fit."

She pushed another dent into the wall, although a slight ripple was left in the surface. She felt the metal again and tried to smooth it over. "Oh... I didn't realise."

He laughed. "That's probably not a bad thing—I'm sure Aidan was wise not to frighten you with it. But you weren't the only one who didn't understand them. Wars were fought over the crystals before anyone knew how to use them, even before Nazreal. The world was uneasy, which was why I sought to distance myself from it by building my own ship."

"How did my father come to learn about all this? There's barely any knowledge of Nazreal's techniques in the world now." She paused and looked to where Osiris was working. "Did you show him?"

Osiris gave a quiet, indignant huff. "Aidan knew enough about the crystals not to need my help. The techniques have always been part of the world; it's just a case of knowing where to look. Xayall and Skyria have been lucky to find most of the artefacts so far, and he was the one that brought them all together, as much as he could."

Faria looked thoughtfully to the ceiling. "I see. Then what else has been found from Nazreal?"

Osiris sighed; she couldn't tell if he was irritated with her questions or just lamenting over the panel. "Mostly metalwork in some form or another; some small bits of machinery, holdings for crystals. A few medicines and cultivation techniques have been passed down, mainly in Skyria. The Coriolis is probably, hopefully, the largest existing single piece from that time."

Faria's ears pricked up. "You mean there were other ships?"

"Not like this one," he muttered.

She nodded thoughtfully, daydreaming about the magical ships that could once have roamed the seas and skies of Nazreal. Osiris stuck his head back into the panel he'd been working on and started twisting a large dial with strange symbols into various different positions, comparing the readings on a compass attached to his belt.

There were so many things Faria knew little about, most of which she'd discovered in the last few days: the tragedies and conflicts in Nazreal's history, and the overwhelming responsibilities of the tasks ahead. Just touching the Coriolis' hull she could feel the memories of age burned into its fabric. It was the same haunting sensation she got holding her father's staff.

"It's a shame that so much was lost. Do you think we can ever get it back?"

"The less people know, the better," he grunted. "Resonance was too powerful for our world."

"But think of the good it could do!" she sang, her voice echoing into the hold. "I've had resonance my whole life, but I always felt so aimless with it, so isolated. And there must be more. So many people could survive, and sovereigns grow. If it was controlled, I'm sure it could be used responsibly."

The gryphon gave a gruff snort into the panel. "I've heard that before. Nazreal was built virtually on those beliefs... and as a lie to cover ulterior motives. Don't fool yourself with hope—nothing has changed. People are dying of the same diseases, and the same wars appear over and over again."

She watched him continue working in the half-dark, his movements becoming sharper and harder the deeper the conversation went. She looked at her staff sadly.

"For every new discovery, every good intention, there'll be a way of corrupting it for selfish ends," he muttered. "Just like Tierenan."

She shot him a concerned look. "What do you mean?"

He wrenched something violently in the panel, throwing an echoing boom around the dim hold as he hit the frame with his fist. "Tierenan's arms and the metal plates attached to his body are similar to Nazreal's technology." His tone darkened. "That chip you knocked from his head regulates electronic impulses, changing their form to affect a command in a circuit, or a body. Where one gives him control of his arms as any normal creature, another can gain control over *him*. Even though you broke it, he may still be influenced by it in some way. We don't even know why the Dhrakans wanted him."

In the candles' nervous light, Faria stared silently into the darkness.

Tierenan stared blankly at the ferret, mind racing.

"I'm… like you?"

She stood up and let the blanket slip from around her neck. Underneath the dirty rag, Tierenan saw the unmistakeable shine of metal plating running up her neck and along her shoulder, into which a perch exactly suited to the bird had been carved. It ruffled its wings and Tierenan saw that it too was metal, with small glass eyes and twinkling green paint.

"You escaped as well?" he asked, hope building. "How did you make it here? Did you need help getting home? I can… help…"

He trailed off as she looked to the bird, saying nothing, retaining her solemn, soulless gaze. She ran a finger down its back and it fluttered appreciatively.

"Do you remember your mission?" she asked quietly.

He froze, hot apprehension crawling up his back. Deep memories echoed through his mind. "No," he said, firm but anxious. "I'm free of that now."

For a brief second she looked envious, a wistful shadow crossing her face. "I see…" She studied the bird, now flitting from finger to finger. "You don't remember me, do you?"

Tierenan stared, desperately trying to spark recognition from the face before him. He'd lost most of the memories of his capture by the Dhrakans, for better or worse, including those of the others still being held captive there. He shook his head sadly.

She stood still, a silent acceptance of his guilt. The bird tilted its head contemplatively. The two remained standing for a while, she staring into the middle distance, impassively silent; he pulling awkwardly at his claws and casting her cautious glances. The colour of her fur was barely visible underneath the dirt coating her face. She was a mixture of browns and whites, incredibly pretty, but very thin.

She held her hand to him, and the bird hopped onto her open palm. "This is Tikku. I've been told to give him to you," she said forlornly.

He looked up quizzically. "Why? What's happening?"

She gave a faint smile. "Don't worry, this won't change anything. It's best that you don't remember. I wouldn't want to."

"Wait, what do you mean? What happened?" he pleaded. For a brief instant her name flitted across his mind. He couldn't steal it into his consciousness, but something welled up in his memory, layered under his waking thoughts.

"Tierenan…" She looked straight into his eyes with a piercing loneliness. "I won't see you again. They've not finished with you yet. I'm glad… that you found freedom, at least for a while. I will dream of mine, after your wishes."

"No, stop! Please, tell me your—"

The bird took flight and flew across his vision. Instants later she had vanished and he was alone, Tikku circling around him, twittering gently. Tierenan held out a finger and the bird rested on it with a gentle flap of his wings. Overhead the skies were beginning to clear.

He looked to the bird and smiled as it bristled its wings, tiny whirring sounds humming from its body.

With the Coriolis repaired, the crew had returned to the ship and were making speedy preparations to continue to Skyria.

Aeryn stepped onto the deck and looked about, holding a dagger she'd bought at the market. Its sharp, awl-like blade flicked the light from its edge as it turned, with a second, shorter blade jutting at an angle from its base, and a fang-like spike twisted onto the pommel. It looked vicious—she was sure Kyru would approve. As luck would have it he stepped up the boarding ramp that very moment, and let out a betraying sigh of exhaustion when he reached the railing. Seeing Aeryn, he quickly tried to ground himself, but it was too late for her not to notice his haggard appearance.

"Are you all right?" she asked, moving towards him. He held out a hand to stop her coming too close. She looked a little put-out. "What, get lost in a bar?"

He gave a tired laugh. "Yeah, right. I'm fine. I just… ran to get here," he said between breaths. He leant against the railings and unfurled the jacket he'd bought, now minus both sleeves. "What do you think?" he asked, watching eagerly for her reaction. "I got a discount for damage."

She approved it with a nod as visions of him wearing it flashed across her mind. "It'll suit you well," she mused, unable to hide a sly smile. She then revealed her dagger and presented it to him. "What about this?"

He threw the coat onto his shoulder and took the weapon in his hand, lightly bouncing it on his fingers to feel its weight. With the point, he drew a slow arc in the air in front of him, then turned it backwards in his hand and did the same again. He ran a finger along the blade's edge and the grip, admiring the pommel spike.

"It's got a good balance," he said, handing it back, unable to take his eyes from her smile. "A little brutal for you, isn't it?"

She flicked her tail. "I can be just as brutal as you if I want," she replied coyly. He laughed.

"I'm sure you can."

He moved to put his jacket in his cabin, and to lie down. The crystal throbbed in his back with heightening intensity. He would collapse if he didn't rest. But a hand tugged at his sleeve, halting his advance. On turning, he was surprised to see Aeryn shyly let go, turning the blade over in her hands.

"Actually, I'd like to learn how to use a dagger properly. If you could… help."

He sighed quietly, the pain in his back no match for his affections to her.

"Sure."

Osiris strode onto the deck, looking around impatiently. "Is everyone accounted for?" he bellowed. Jala moved to his side with a list of crew members firmly in his grasp.

"Almost, sir. We're just waiting for Tierenan."

The gryphon ruffled his feathers irritably. "I knew he'd wander off, bloody striped liability. Somebody go and—"

At that second a familiar skittish figure bounded up the boarding ramp and skidded to a halt at Osiris' feet, puffing with exhaustion. Tierenan gave the gryphon a nervous, apologetic smile. Osiris sighed irascibly.

"We almost went without you," he grunted.

The raccoon scratched the back of his head, looking sheepish. "Sorry, Osiris. I got lost in the marketplace."

The gryphon eyed him suspiciously for a moment, noticing something stuffed into his pocket. He considered interrogating him about it until Faria appeared, greeting the young creature happily. His misgivings hid themselves for the moment. Perhaps he was just too paranoid for his own good.

"Fine," he boomed, marching up the deck. "Prepare to make sail!"

Kyru stopped him midway. "Did you find out what was wrong with the ship?" he asked.

"The instruments were misaligned," Osiris muttered. He took a few steps to the sterncastle then turned back, looking to Tierenan. "Somehow."

Overhearing, the smile faded from Faria's face. She couldn't think on the cause for long, for as the ship drifted gently away from the dock, she felt a secretive tug on her arm. Tierenan cast a searching look across the deck to make sure they weren't being watched, then carefully pulled Tikku from his pocket and displayed him to Faria, cupping the green bird gently in his hands.

"Wow, it's beautiful!" she gasped, watching the light play on his iridescent feathers. Kyru heard her exclamation and looked over; Tierenan saw him and stuck his tongue out derisively. The wolf snorted and shook his head.

"Where did you find him?" Faria asked quietly.

Tikku looked up at his new master and gave a brief chirp. Tierenan tensed slightly. "He was in a street by the marketplace. Cool, isn't he?"

She nodded. The bird turned to her next, giving her careful scrutiny. She smiled. In reply, he beat his wings and gave a cocky swing of his head.

A swell caught the boat. Excited, she turned to the Coriolis' heading and felt her heart lifting again. They were heading to Skyria, finally. The anticipation of seeing her father again felt enough to fuel their vessel by itself.

Faria closed her eyes. "Finally. We'll be there soon, I promise."

Chapter Eighteen

The waters of Skyria were almost still in the early evening light. The sky above them was deep blue as the setting sun rested in a golden haze, running a line of vermillion across the borders of the horizon.

Osiris had ordered against flying to save their diminishing fuel supplies for later, and though they had been lucky enough to encounter a strong headwind it had still been three days' hard sailing. Faria repeatedly pressed him about the delay, insistent on travelling faster. Eventually she'd relented, and spent most of the journey on deck watching the horizon.

Tierenan sat with her, pointing out particularly interesting clouds and waves. She was too busy scanning the distance to respond much to his impassioned chatter, not that he minded. He played with Tikku in his hands, watching him hop from one claw to the next, and then fly onto his metal ear. Occasionally the bird would circle around the ship and disappear over the sea, to return an hour or two later.

Meanwhile, at the centre of the deck, Kyru was training Aeryn in the use of daggers. She listened attentively, watching his movements carefully and copying them as precisely as she could.

He had a sword in his right hand and a dagger borrowed from one of the crew in his left. "I wouldn't use them the other way if you can help it. Shields oppose your right hand, and you'll barely scratch them with that. Block with your sword until you find an opening. Trying to attack with a dagger alone is an easy way to get an injury."

She looked a little put out. She knew how weapons worked—she had been through Andarn's military school. It was just that nobody taught them the specifics of dagger fighting.

"But what if I need a dagger in this hand?"

He looked blank. "What do you mean?"

"I *mean*," she stressed, "what if this was all I had? Are there any sure-fire techniques?"

He shrugged. "It's just a small sword. Your best advantage is once you're past your enemy's blade. If that was all you had, your best bet is to reverse it, defend with the blade down your forearm and go for a lock or disarm." He paused for a moment, fixing his gaze on the dagger. "Once you're inside, strike anywhere vulnerable. The neck's the quickest kill."

She nodded, turning the weapon over in her hand. This hadn't been the bonding experience she'd hoped for. She glanced his way a few times in the awkward silence, trying to catch his eye. Kyru moved in a slow, deliberate kata, plotting out moves in his mind.

As she watched the billowing sails glow in the sinking sun, she heard him sheathe his sword. He turned and paced towards the edge of the deck. She followed, a little shyly.

"You don't need me to tell you where to attack someone," he said. "Most of it's instinct, and you're good enough not to need my help." He paused as he reached the railings, looking restless. "I mean, you're…"

She stood next to him, trying to hide her nervous anticipation. "Mmm?"

"…you're the best archer I've known."

"Oh…" She closed her eyes and smiled, letting a small laugh escape. "Thank you."

A wave of pain shot up his back. He tensed, trying to suppress the blood welling in his throat. A second later it faded, but small aftershocks pulsed through his body. He felt a hand touch his shoulder in concern; he looked back to Aeryn and smiled. Relieved, she smiled in return. They watched each other for a few seconds, until Kyru's smile faded and he looked away, fear of what the damage could cost him becoming more painful than the crystal's effects themselves. Aeryn moved next to him and looked down to watch the water break and froth under the Coriolis' bow.

"Where do you want to go, Aeryn?"

She gave him a nervous glance. "What do you mean?"

He looked out over the sea. "Now you don't have a military career, where can you go? Is there somewhere you want to be?"

She played a claw idly over the railing, thoughtfully. "My father always wanted me to start my own branch of the business. He said I could choose any of the factories he owned. I always hated that, because I wasn't making anything for myself, just riding on his name. I wanted to be a soldier and joined the army to protest, in a way, so my rank would be a badge of *my* abilities. I could show him and anyone else who asked what I could do of my own merit. Besides, I hated administration, and I'm useless at crafts. Now…" She looked across the deck to Faria, staff in hand, and Tierenan next to her. "…I'm not sure. It's funny what life can throw at you. I suppose I'll be happy wherever I find myself needed most."

She looked back to him. He had a strange, almost regretful smile.

"I see… That's good."

He turned away, about to leave.

"And you?" she called softly. He stopped, not looking around to her. Instead he let his gaze be caught by the clouds floating above them. He dug his claws into his palm.

"I didn't come over to Cadon just for money, you know that. I was looking for… something else."

She gripped her dagger tightly. "And… did you find it?"

"Yeah…" He looked down. "Yeah, I think I did. To be honest, Aeryn…" he started, quietly.

He paused. Tierenan was standing ahead of him, grinning madly.

"What?" the male wolf asked, cantankerously.

Tierenan kept grinning.

"*What?*" Kyru gnarled, even more irascible.

"I have a new nickname for you," he jibed. "Paintyface McGrowl, grumpiest wolf on the sea!"

A maddened expression spread across the wolf's face. "Oh, really?" He marched towards the raccoon who, sensing hostility, sprinted off in the direction of the sterncastle. Kyru broke into a run, ranting after him: "Paintyface, is it? You're Dead McDrowned when I catch you, you walking broiler plate!"

Aeryn rested her head on her hand, leaning on the railings, and gave a deep sigh.

"Idiot…"

Suddenly, an excited cry rang across the deck. Something had appeared in the distance, and Faria saw it.

"It's there!" she yelled. Skyria was finally within reach.

Perched gently on the bowsprit, Tikku gave a bright chirrup and took flight, disappearing behind the ship. Faria didn't notice. She sprinted down the deck to tell Osiris.

The bridge door flew open and she burst inside, alight with excitement. "Have you seen it?"

Osiris wasn't as reciprocating in her enthusiasm. "Yes, I have."

She moved to the front-facing window of the bridge, pressing her hands against the glass.

"Do you think he's been waiting for long?"

"I couldn't tell you," he said quietly.

She stared intently at the distant shape, and the interminably slow rate at which it crept into view.

"I hope he's all right."

Osiris didn't reply.

The island of Skyria was the capital of its archipelago sovereign. Each island was connected by massive bridges spanning the ocean gaps between them. Surrounding the city stood a large defensive wall, attached to which was built a huge stone dock to the north. The sovereign was a symbol the world over for its most prominent and awe-inspiring presence: the enormous trees growing in its land, hundreds of feet tall and as wide as a galleon's length. The largest of them, making up the huge governmental and spiritual centre of the island city, reached higher than Xayall's Tor.

It was nearing twilight when the Coriolis drifted up to the waters a few hundred meters from Skyria's south-western sea defences. The sails folded in and the ship swayed to a halt on the ocean's calm surface. Faria could barely contain her excitement, pacing backwards and forwards across the prow of the ship and looking anxiously to the bridge where Osiris was briefing Jala about something she hadn't been allowed to hear. After minutes that seemed to her like hours, he strode onto the deck.

"Why aren't we docking?" she asked, trying to be calm through her impatience.

He gave her a dismissive look. "Jala will handle it. We've lost enough time. Now, are you ready?" He turned around and knelt down, showing her his back for her to climb onto.

She wrapped her arms around his thick, feathery neck and held on as firmly as she could manage. He shunted his armour further up his body, moving it and her into a more secure position. With a great movement, he spread his wings and broke into a run, each swoop of his magnificent gold and white pinions creating a massive gust of wind. Even though it was a terrifying experience, the rising excitement forbade Faria to close her eyes. In seconds, they were airborne.

"Osiris!" she yelled, holding on to him and her staff with all her might, her breath rushed out of her by their height and speed. "This is incredible!"

"I know," he said, beaming. "Why do you think I was born a gryphon?"

Suddenly, he lurched to one side. Attached to his leg was a metal claw, with Tierenan reeling himself along it, looking both determined and guilty at the same time.

"Sorry Osiris!" he called. "I can't swim."

Faria could feel the gryphon's indignation ripple through his body. She gave the raccoon a quick glance; he was looking straight ahead, at the home rapidly coming to meet him.

They swept over the waves and rose up, soaring to the height of the wall and ascending past its crenellations, giving Faria a glorious view of the land below. The upper levels of the city were connected by horizontally-growing trees into which stone walkways were embedded, transplanted onto the trunks of the central giants. Intricate stairways, paths, ladders and lift systems wound up the outside of the trees, while far below at ground level stone-built buildings nestled between their massive roots. It looked so serene in the twilight, protected by the shield of leaves above. Before she could lose herself in the wonder of its construction, Osiris swooped down.

An assembly waited upon the walls, attending their arrival. The entire Skyrian Council stood before them, trailed by torch-bearing guards and countless scholars, all eager to catch a glimpse of the young Princess and her guardian. Slipping from Osiris' back to stand before them, she froze when she saw the size of her audience. A mature red panda, the High

Councillor of Skyria, stood forwards and bowed his head in respect.

"It is an honour to meet you at last, Your Imperial Highness," he said in his quiet, proud voice. She bowed nervously in return, conscious of the silent, awed crowd ahead.

"I'm, er... it's a privilege to be welcomed here. I'm glad your sovereign is safe," she said in reply, wracking her brains to think of the things foreign dignitaries tend to say. The panda smiled and stood up, regarding her kindly.

"You are most gracious, Your Imperial Highness."

She clasped her hands anxiously around her staff and looked to the trees beyond. Just as she was about to ask where her father was staying, Osiris strode forwards.

"Irien, I apologise for my impatience, but we have pressing matters to discuss."

Irien nodded. "Yes, I understand. We have a lot to tell you."

As he spoke, Tierenan, having been hiding behind Osiris for a suitable time to make his dramatic re-appearance, whirled into view with a great flourish.

"I'm home!" he cried, opening his arms.

Astonished cries rippled through the Skyrians. The gryphon gave him a murderous glare for interrupting, his ire for the moment trapped within his clenched fists in front of the Skyrian dignitaries. Two voices, a male and a female, pierced the crowd above all others, and a pair of raccoons desperately pushed themselves forward.

"Tierenan! Tierenan!"

Faria stood back as they raced up the steps, leaping forward to their son. Before Tierenan could even outstretch his claws they had swept him tightly into their arms, all falling to their knees in an overwhelming, passionate embrace. His mother was crying, holding him protectively against her. His claws shook with the emotion pouring through him. There was so much he wanted to say. He wanted to tell them about the adventures that he'd had, the friends he'd made, but all that came out were stuttering cries, muffled by his family's embrace.

Irien shook his head in disbelief. "Osiris, did you know our young raccoon was captured?"

Osiris ran his claw over his ears, trying to hide his frustration. "No. Faria found him."

The male raccoon knelt before Faria, gleaming with joy. "My name is Taban, and my wife is Zia," he said, brimming with emotion. "Your Imperial Highness, thank you, thank you for bringing back our son." He was so emphatic in his gratitude that she felt incredibly flustered, especially as Tierenan had more found her than the other way round.

"He's been a great companion," she said as Tierenan emerged from behind his mother, maintaining his gleeful smile even when his eyes glistened with tears. "I wouldn't have made it here without him."

The young raccoon nodded excitedly, pulling gently at his mother's arm. "But Mum, Faria's amazing! She saved me from the Dhrakans, and…" he trailed off in a babble of excitement, giving wild gestures to important parts of his story.

"So he was captured, then?" Osiris muttered.

Taban nodded. "Some months ago a group of scholars formed a conspiracy to give our knowledge to the Dhrakans, in exchange for a share in the artefact's discovery and any spoils that came from it. So they took Tierenan, among others."

"That's right!" Tierenan said, accusing the absent conspirators. "They said I was going to be shown off to the Senate as an example of our advances in medicine! They... made us leave so quickly. I didn't want to go without saying goodbye, but they said you already knew... it was a secret, and you were leaving just behind us..." He hugged his mother tightly, apologetically. "I'm sorry..."

"By the time we'd found out what had happened, they'd left Skyria," Irien said darkly, "and our ships couldn't pursue them into Dhrakan territory. Tierenan wasn't the only one we lost."

Taban looked back to Tierenan. "I had almost lost hope of seeing him again."

Faria was herself close to tears at Tierenan's reunion. She longed for that same experience with her father, somewhere on this island. He must be resting deeper inside. She moved to Irien, eager to be taken to him.

"Why did they take Tierenan?" Osiris asked, his single aim to retrieve the information he needed.

"For the artefact." Irien glowered at its recollection. "They needed to understand the workings of mechanical limbs. One of the scholars reappeared ten days ago on one of our smaller islands, half-dead. He explained what they had found."

Osiris' eyes widened. For the first time, Faria saw a shadow of fear in his gaze. "What do you mean, limbs? What have they found, Irien?"

"It's not just 'what', Osiris. It's 'who'."

A deathly silence fell over the conversation. Osiris' mind raced. His hands pulsed with apprehension. What escaped him was barely a whisper:

"Raikali…"

Faria looked between the two, scared cold by the harrowing, drained look on the gryphon's face. Irien stirred.

"And I'm afraid that isn't all," he said quietly. "They have also resurrected the Gargantua."

Osiris shot a vicious glare at Skyria's High Councillor. "What do you mean *resurrected*? That thing didn't escape Nazreal's devastation! It was destroyed, Irien! Everything was!" he roared, closing on the red panda. Irien held up a hand to stop his advance.

"Osiris, calm down! This is what we have been told. It changes nothing of the disastrous truth. Both Raikali and the Gargantua still exist and are in the Dhrakans' hands."

The congregation fell into a deathly silence. Osiris was rigid with rage, his eyes deep and vengeful.

"I had expected perhaps a weapon, or a power source. But Raikali… Aidan, you…"

He whirled round and stormed to the wall, throwing wide his wings.

"Osiris, wait!" Faria shouted after him. "Why don't we talk to my father first? We might be able to work out a plan!"

Irien came forward to her. "Your Highness, the Emperor isn't—"

"Enough!" Osiris bellowed.

Faria looked to the gryphon, afraid of his overflowing anger but spurred by a greater fear for her father. "Osiris, where is he?"

He didn't reply.

"Osiris!" she shouted to his back. "Tell me! Where is my father?"

"Your father…" He paused, trying to quell the bile in his throat. "…is not here."

Faria fell silent. She looked down at her staff, which was pulsing in rhythm with her ever-growing anxiety. "Then where *is* he?" she growled.

Osiris kept looking out to sea, at the Coriolis that was now silhouetted against the deep red sky. "I don't know."

She charged forward, grabbing his arm and pulling him round to face her. "That's a lie!"

"*It is not!*" he boomed, shaking her from him. "Aidan was supposed to come here so that we could destroy the artefact together. Had I known what it was… I should never have let him travel alone."

She swallowed hard. Her blood ran cold. "So… he's…"

"I don't know where he is. At best he is lost somewhere, at worst he is already being held by Crawn."

Tiny swirls of wind began sweeping around Faria's feet, her resonance mounting with her rising emotions. "Then we have to rescue him!" she cried. "He-he could be alone, or they could be torturing him! Please, Osiris!"

He rounded on her. "*We* are not doing anything, Faria!" he barked. "*You* are to remain here in Skyria like he asked!"

Her hands were shaking. "You lied to me."

"I did not," he said firmly, resentfully. "He asked me to take you to Skyria and I said that we *might* meet him here. I made no promise to you about what was to happen. That was *your* assumption. I was acting on his request."

"But you *knew*!" she roared, staring fiercely.

"I knew no more than you did!" he replied, equally as loud. "Do you think for a second I wanted him to be left so vulnerable?"

"Then why did you risk it?"

"I thought we had more time! Time to infiltrate Dhraka, time to find their artefact and destroy it before they would launch a strike!"

There was a tense pause. The ferocity in his eyes subsided slightly, and his voice sank sadly. "He wanted you to be protected. When I heard about Xayall, even though I knew he was their target, I could do nothing until I found you, or even knew who you were. That's why I was so suspicious when I saw you at the dock."

She shrank down slightly, feeling the tears well up in her eyes. She forced them back. "But... why didn't you tell me?"

"Because I hoped that he would be here too. And if he had, then none of it would have mattered."

She looked at him. For all his fierceness and the hard, almost impenetrable sternness he plated himself with, she realised that he was as concerned for her father's safety as she was. The staff's crystal coursed with gentle light.

"I want to save my father."

He knew it was useless to argue. He sighed deeply, his defences melted. "You're much like Aidan, you know. I couldn't win against him, either."

She turned to Tierenan, who smiled. As her fond feelings toward the raccoon's companionship welled in her mind, she wrung her hands to courage up a worthy goodbye.

Before she could speak, a deep, low rumble shook the air. The wind swirled with the smell of fire. In the sea beyond, the water trembled as a huge shadow emerged, rising, surging upwards towards the surface. As the waves bulged and split, the metal demon broke through the ocean.

The pyramid's mechanical roar shook the trees as it burst from the water, steam hissing from the massive vents running up its sides, its pitch-dark shadow eclipsing the golden Coriolis.

Faria stumbled back, eyes wide with terror. Orisis' blood ran cold as ice.

"The Gargantua…"

Chapter Nineteen

The Gargantua loomed over the ship as a colossal deathly horror, rumbling, clanking and hissing in rhythms that sounded like an enormous living creature. The group on the shore watched, horrified as the dwarfed carrack lowered its sails and began a desperate bid for freedom.

"No… no…" Osiris' voice was a ghost, his eyes glazed as he stood, catatonic. Faria clasped her hand to her mouth to prevent herself from screaming. Tierenan clung fearfully to his mother.

The Coriolis had only turned a short distance before a huge doorway slid open at the Gargantua's base like a huge insect's carapace. Large crescent-shaped structures slid out through the pyramid's gaping maw and lowered into the water, sliding round and underneath the helpless ship to trap it. Metal rods spiralled into place from the gigantic shackles, locking against the Coriolis' hull. Slowly, the structures began to retract and Osiris' gleaming ship was pulled into the midnight darkness of the Gargantua's interior, at least twice as high as the golden vessel itself. The doors rumbled shut, closing with a thunderous boom that punched across the waves and into the hearts of all who were watching.

Its dark purpose complete, the Dhrakan's hellish ship turned slowly away, retreating across the waters.

"Osiris…" Faria croaked, fearing she would collapse at any moment. "Osiris… we have to do something."

The gryphon watched the ship complete its turn, still frozen to the spot. It felt as if he'd been ripped from his body. He could do nothing but watch as the horrific, un-slain Gargantua swallowed everything he held from his previous life on Eeres.

"Osiris!" Faria cried. "Please!"

Her desperate voice shattered his trance. He shook his head clear and looked to her urgently. "Come with me. We have to board it before it has a chance to descend."

She nodded, and without a second thought, leapt onto his back again. Next to them, Tierenan broke free from his mother's grasp and took hold of Osiris's waist. Zia took his arm pleadingly.

"Tierenan, please wait!"

He shook his head. "I have to go. I need to help them."

Taban rested a hand on Zia's shoulder, which Tierenan then covered with his own metallic claw.

"I'll come back, I promise!"

Osiris readied himself, and, as Tierenan gave one last loving glance to his parents, the gryphon took to the air. Taban and Zia held each other tightly as they watched their son disappear after the dark megalith. Irien bowed his head, hoping against hope that they would survive. If they didn't, Eeres was destined for a terrible fate.

The Gargantua was already some distance away. The engines were deafening; as it moved it left devastating, powerful waves in its wake. It choked the air with columns of acrid steam that smelt of burning metals; the caustic stench seared Faria's nostrils. Breaking through the noxious cloud, the trio landed near the top of the pyramid. Faria struggled to maintain her balance against the Gargantua's forward motion, grabbing hold of a metal plate and flattening herself against the side. Osiris scanned around for signs of sentries—nothing.

"Damn them for pursuing us!" he shouted over the rumble of the engines and the whistle of the wind. "We have to find a way inside!"

"I can create a door," Faria yelled, still holding herself down. "But you'll need to keep me steady."

Osiris grasped her shoulders and leant into her while she plunged the staff into the black metal. The panel was thick and strong, difficult for her to resonate with completely, but she managed to mould an opening. With one last look for guards, Osiris guided Faria inside and then leapt down himself, followed quickly by Tierenan.

As soon as she hit the deck, Faria took cover between two large metal struts next to the breach. Once Tierenan was inside, she turned to seal the hole, her ardent focus overruling the pain in her arms. As the wall twisted back into place, the noise of the wind disappeared and the external rumblings of the Gargantua became a softer but ever-present groaning, shuddering from every surface of the vast ship.

Osiris looked around and drew his rapier. "Hardly changed at all," he growled.

Faria gripped her staff tightly, feeling her fur stand on end. The deep light cast distorted, eerie shadows on the walls. "Osiris, what is this thing?"

"A fortress built before the fall of Nazreal. It was conceived as a mobile city capable of protecting any sovereign on Eeres, but the Dhrakans took the design and turned it into a siege engine with enough artillery to level a mountain," he hissed venomously. He turned and fixed Faria with a deadly stare. "Faria, you understand that this place is filled to the brim with Dhrakan soldiers."

She nodded, anxious.

"There is something else in here, a creature more evil and more deadly than anything that ever walked on Eeres. If she sees you, Raikali will kill you. She will kill your father and everyone around you if you give her even the tiniest opportunity."

She nodded, still in a daze of fear. Spurned, Osiris grabbed her shoulder. "Focus, Faria! You have more power than you allow yourself! You must not let her gain control of you. We have to escape this place together, and you are the strongest weapon we have, but you must trust in yourself and focus your resonance! If you doubt yourself even slightly, we will all be lost. Do you understand?"

She took a deep breath. All of them, had risked all they had to protect her, to bring her here. She would not fail them. "Yes, I understand."

"Good. Let's move." He stood tall and moved forwards, led by the point of his sword into the darkness. Faria and Tierenan stuck close behind him.

He stopped at a corner, flattening himself against the wall to peer round carefully and check for guards. The Gargantua had enough potential to house, equip and sustain up to three thousand troops for a month, not including its ordnance supplies. He did not want to risk being found if it was fully garrisoned.

The way was clear. He swung across the gap between the intersecting hallways and beckoned for the others. They followed, both giving cautious glances along the corridors around them. The three continued onwards, turning down strangely empty passageways. The floor was a metal mesh; underneath it ran bundles of pipes and cables, buzzing and hissing discontentedly. Malevolent iron doors flanked the corridor at regular intervals. Overhead were gently roaring ventilation shafts, billowing stale air into their faces. They were lucky not to have seen any Dhrakans yet, although the numbers swarming the Coriolis below must have been colossal, Faria thought.

"Do you think the others will be all right?" she whispered as they drew to another junction.

"I hope so. The Dhrakans will be angry to find you're not on board, though. What worries me is they knew exactly where the ship was. Skyria was lucky to escape being decimated."

Something moved in the steam ahead.

A shadow appeared, darkening, forming shape as its owner lumbered near. Osiris threw his arm back to halt Faria and

Tierenan, but it was too late. The dragon burst through the veil of steam, drawing his sword.

"Intruders!" he shrieked, swinging his blade towards the gryphon.

At lightning speed Osiris thrust out his arm and lunged, sending his rapier through the lizard's head with devastating accuracy. The Dhrakan gurgled and slumped to the floor with a boom that shook down the metal corridor. Seconds later they heard echoing yells and the pounding of footsteps coming their way. Osiris looked urgently to Faria.

"Get away!" he bellowed. "Find the crew and free them! I'll make my way to the engine room to stop this infernal machine."

Tierenan nodded and ran past Faria, trying to pull her into the corridor to the side. She stopped, watching Osiris.

"Faria, come on!" he hissed.

"Stay safe, Osiris!" she called, disappearing with Tierenan into the steam.

The gryphon bristled with determination as Dhrakans appeared all around him.

"I've waited a long time for this…"

The harsh metal walls were rough with dirt and corrosion, lit in a dirty green. The sound of the Dhrakans sealing the cell doors still echoed around the dank brig. The cages' ceilings were low, almost too low to stand in properly. The floor was a sharp, uneven mesh, and the only furniture was a broken, twisted bench. Directly below them lay the machinery that propelled the Gargantua; a cacophony of rumbles, clanks and whirring shook their entire level. Water dripped from the ceiling; the whole room smelt of oil and fumes. There was another stench embedded in the walls and bars of the cell, a gut-turning echo of blood and flesh.

Aeryn sat silently against the wall, the only occupant of her caged room. In the cell to her right was Kyru. Fears for him flooded her mind. He'd been hit during the ship's capture; blood cascaded from his mouth, and as the only female on the ship she'd been isolated from him and the crew when thrown into the cells.

There had been no point resisting. Before the ship was even inside they'd been swarmed upon and forced into surrender with ruthless efficiency. The few who tried to resist paid for it. Maaka was attending to the serious injuries as best he could without any of his tools.

Hulking Dhrakans stood at either end of the corridor, heavy shields and short spears firmly in their grasp, quivering hungrily when the promise of inflicting pain chanced across them. On their patrolling marches before the cells they sneered in reviled contempt for the prisoners, and struck the bars with their shields.

She could hear hushed voices from the next cell and strained to listen, unable to make out the words over the machinery below. Resting on her knees, she leant back against the wall.

Behind the dividing wall, Kyru was on all fours, shaking uncontrollably. His knees weak, he rocked as he tried to resist the convulsions that threatened to tear his stomach apart. Sweat stung his eyes. His ears burned. His skin was rippling alternately hot and cold and it took all his strength just to stay up. Maaka was knelt next to him with a grave expression.

"There's nothing I can do for you here, Kyru. I honestly don't know how long—"

"That's fine," he whispered, spitting thick blood onto the floor. "I… had a feeling it would turn out this way."

Suddenly he lurched upwards with a huge seizure; a gargling yell of pain sent another wave of blood spattering through the mesh and onto the pipes below. Aeryn closed her eyes fearfully, clawing a hand against the wall in a vain effort to try and be closer to him. Kyru threw his fist on the floor and cursed himself. If this was the price he had to pay for saving Aeryn, then it was worth it. He only wished that they could now have been somewhere else, if these were due to be his last hours.

"Perhaps… I should have told her," he rasped.

In the ventilation grate above the brig's heavy door, beady glass eyes watched silently. An instant later, they disappeared, fluttering into the darkness with a beating of small, metal wings.

Faria and Tierenan pounded along the Gargantua's corridors, diving away from approaching shadows and hurling themselves between vertical pipes to hide. Where possible Faria created swirls of steam to mask their flight, and so far they had remained unseen. The Dhrakans were rapidly on the move, however, and every corner presented itself with a fresh threat of another bladed gaze.

They came to a narrower passage with a pipe-filled alcove; here they pulled in and rested, their breathing heavy but silenced. Faria leant her head against the wall.

"This place is monstrous…" she whispered.

Tierenan peered around the corner behind him. "It's huge. I don't think we're anywhere near the others yet." Just through the steam at the other end of the passageway he could see a much larger, highly-lit room, in which he caught sight of a familiar metal mast. He pulled Faria closer and pointed ahead.

"Look, it's the Coriolis!"

Cautiously, they sidled out of the alcove and crept to the threshold, keeping tight against the wall. The mesh walkway in front of them circled the second floor of the massive chamber. Down below they could see Osiris' golden ship, pinned by the Gargantua's brutal vice. Dhrakan guards marched brutishly up and down its length, occasionally running their blades along the deck or the metal rails. There were at least fifty guards in the docking bay on the various levels, all vigilant against any intruder's breach.

Faria felt her heart skip. "We'll never get past without a fight—they're everywhere!"

Tierenan clicked his claws on his palm nervously. "*We* wouldn't, but *I* might," he said, tracing a path down to the ship with his eyes. He looked at the walkway below them; it looked like he would be able to fit underneath it.

"What do you mean?" she asked, apprehensively.

He pushed her back into the alcove. "You hide here, okay? I'll get down to the ship and see if the crew are still aboard. I won't try anything violent by myself, I promise."

"I don't want to hide!" she hissed. "I can't just be passed around like I'm made of glass when I can fight as capably as anyone else!"

Tierenan looked at the docking bay again. "Faria, it's not about fighting right now. Even all of us together couldn't take on all the Dhraka in here. Finding the crew is the most important thing, so we can free them and get everyone out safely." He took her shoulders. "And like Osiris said—we lose everything if we lose you."

Faria was speechless. She looked at him for a few seconds, then gripped her staff with renewed determination. "All right," she said firmly. "But hurry, and come back as soon as you've found out what's down there. I'll keep myself as well as I can."

Tierenan nodded affirmatively. With her help, he prised open the mesh flooring and dropped onto the pipes below. There was just enough space for him to crawl along on his stomach. The pipes were scalding hot against his fur and loose segments rattled when he moved over them. He could see the corridor below him through tiny gaps in the plating. A Dhrakan walked past slowly, lifting its nose curiously as if catching a strange scent. Quietly, the raccoon pulled himself along to where the pipes met the docking bay and turned right, squashing himself behind the metal tube. He flattened his tail, anxious that it didn't give him away.

As Faria watched him disappear, she prayed that he wouldn't get caught. She took a deep breath, preparing herself for what fight could come to either of them if they were found. Her staff ready to strike, she backed into the alcove.

Inside the docking bay, Tierenan froze again to let a Dhrakan soldier pass overhead, then continued his journey in synchrony with the dragon's oppressive footsteps. He couldn't risk looking over the pipe to check for guards, but he could hear their muttered conversations about the state of the Dhrakan lands. He continued until he reached a pipe that descended behind the walkway below and straight to the floor of the bay, where large supply crates had been hurriedly loaded and left in a disorderly manner across the hold. Tierenan paused for a second, plotting his route carefully. As soon as the path was clear, he skittered down the pipe and slid directly behind a large metal box. He glanced out quickly, then skipped to the next container, watching all around him. The dragons above hadn't noticed his climb, and the boxes were welcome cover for the moment. The Coriolis was now above him. He crawled underneath the machinery that held the ship in place, and to his fortune discovered a torn drainage port in the base of the crescent vice. He leapt in, almost hitting his head on the keel.

He paused for a moment to examine the shafts that pressed into the hull like massive blunt drills. His blood rose as he heard the golden vessel creak with the pressure of the bolts holding it up. Gathering himself, he clambered over the beams to a gun port and squeezed inside moments before a Dhrakan glanced down at the ship. Seeing nothing, the guard continued on his patrol.

The Coriolis' interior was mostly untouched, and distressingly empty of crew. A few artillery shells rocked gently on the gun deck's floor and a cannon had been displaced by part of a clamp, but there were few signs of struggle.

Voices murmured below him. He laid himself flat on the stairs, looking secretively through the gaps. Two dragons were lounging on the berth deck, ripping open food supplies and throwing around the crew's possessions. Tierenan was tempted to evict them from the ship in anger, but remembering Faria, thought better. The crew weren't on board anyway. He had just pushed himself up and was heading for the gun ports when an idea struck him. He bounded towards Osiris' cabin.

The captain's quarters were full of lavish materials and strange golden artefacts. A large painting of a landscape littered with cliff-faces and flocks of different avian races hung across one wall, reminiscent of treasures lost through the centuries. Tierenan had seen it briefly when Osiris had presented his array of swords, which was just what the racoon was on his way to collect. They'd have a better chance of escaping if they were armed.

He crept up to the highly-decorated sword cabinet and pulled it open. Seven gleaming swords hung before him, each with an intricate trigger mechanism to affect some hidden ability or other. He grabbed the biggest of the rapiers and swung the baldric over his shoulder. As he reached for another, a voice from outside the door froze him in his tracks. He darted behind it just as it swung open and the two dragons strode in, grimacing in disgust.

"This is rubbish," one spat, his revolted gaze falling on Osiris' nest-like bed near the window.

The other was equally as unimpressed. "It'll be worth something to those bastards in Pthiris. We can squeeze decent money out of them."

Tierenan crept round the door and sprinted to the gun deck, the quick clicking of his claws on the boards just enough for the dragons to notice. He heard them start into action behind him and leapt through the gun port, dropping to the basin of the clamps with an echoing thud. As the reverberating sound faded to silence around the hangar, the heavy footsteps of the soldiers drew closer...

The last Dhrakan fell at Osiris' feet, a deep slit cast in his throat. He had stopped counting the soldiers that attacked, focusing his thousands of years of sword skill into giving them quick, efficient deaths. He panted heavily, wiping the sweat from his feathered brow. One had managed to strike his wing. It dripped with blood, staining his plumage. He looked around and, hearing a slew of soldiers approaching in the distance, vanished in the steam.

Faria waited silently in the alcove. The hot, stuffy air next to the pipes was uncomfortable to stand in, and deadened her senses. Her eyes were unfocused and the constant rattling of the metal was masking the other noises she was trying to listen for. She kept moving from one side of the alcove to the other to adjust herself, always watching for a sign of Tierenan. She dared not move to find him.

Bang.

A noise from the docking bay shot fear through her body. Had they found him? She moved out to see, but as she did a

Dhrakan ran past, colliding with her and stumbling to the ground. She landed hard on the metal opposite him but stood up straight away, panic fuelling her desperate movements. Before the dragon righted himself, she stuck him with the electrified tip of her staff and bolted into the dark passageways. She cursed him for his blind discovery, and desperately hoped Tierenan would escape and find her.

As she careened down the halls, glimpses of movement flickered in the corridors to the side of her. She had to hide, or else fight everything that pursued and waited for her.

A piercing yellow eye glinted in the shadows far behind her. With huge wings barely clearing the walls, the menacing giant began his pursuit.

Kyru opened his eyes. Someone had leant him against the wall. He wasn't even aware of passing out, or how long he'd been sat there. He wearily looked around.

Nothing had changed. The guards still stood at the ends of the brig, making clear their jailers' pride by flicking the javelins menacingly in their claws.

He rested his head against the wall, looking along it. He knew that Aeryn was behind him, somewhere in the adjacent cell. For the forbidding metal barrier between them, she might as well have been on the other side of the ship. He crawled to the bars.

"Aeryn?"

There was no answer. He sat back against the wall and sighed, his eyes drifting closed.

"Kyru?"

He shuffled against the bars, startled. Suddenly he'd lost the words to speak to her. He sat silently for a few moments, unsure if the cold feeling in his legs was the crystal or anxiety at hearing her voice.

"I'm... sorry."

She pushed herself against the wall of her cell, trying to get as close to him as possible. The guards were watching, their intrusive leers diminishing what little privacy they had.

"What do you mean? This isn't your fault, Kyru."

"That's not... what I meant," he murmured. He leant his head against the wall and looked up to the corroded ceiling, letting out a deep, sad sigh. "When we were in Andarn, that hyena attacked me during the night. She shot me with a crystal... It's poisoning me."

Aeryn's hand slid to her neck in shock. "So... can you remove it?"

He paused. The crystal twisted within him as if to prove how deep it lay. "No."

She turned and rested her back against the wall, her eyes deep with a sad, vague look resting somewhere between despair and hope. "Why didn't you tell me?"

He didn't know. Of all the things he'd wanted to say to her, this and one other were the ones that evaded him most when he felt them strongest. He was silent for a few moments. All he could think of was her. If he'd left her to be killed on the roof he would have died anyway.

"I thought I could free myself from it. I wanted... to tell you, but if I was going to die then..." he paused to quell the lump in his throat, "...then I wanted to be with you, happy." He smiled tearfully as he leant his head back, thinking of her.

"You are my something greater, and the greatest thing about me." He gave a quiet laugh. "I'm a pain in the neck, right?"

She was crying. She hoped he couldn't hear. Through the bars she slipped her hand, reaching for him. He did the same and they took hold of each other. In the dark, festering cells, the warmth of their hands soothed their pains, even though the wrenching thought of him being taken away brought a new burning sadness. She looked at the ceiling, staring defiantly through her tears.

"I'll save you. I promise."

Faria stopped running, wheeling into a room to hide. She knew stopping was dangerous, but running blind with Dhrakans patrolling the corridors was an even surer way to get captured.

A forest of pipes lay before her, stretching into the darkness. Each of them had a pressure indicator on it, and along one wall was a huge deck covered in an array of taps, levers and switches. Some were broken; others spat flecks of hot water. Occasionally one of the pipes would release a burst of steam into the room, then drift into silence as the pressure fell.

The door swung open. Before she could finish her turn to see, a vice-like grip clamped around her throat and lifted her to the ceiling. She flailed her staff to strike, but it was torn from her grasp and thrown to the floor.

Fulkore grinned madly.

"Found you, Arc'hantael!"

Chapter Twenty

Fist clenched around her throat, Fulkore slammed Faria against the wall, the metal at her back buckling under his strength. She struggled for breath, digging vainly at his claws. The dragon's scales were like glass blades, raking her hands as she pulled at them. He growled victoriously.

"It was a wise choice to run, but no prey ever evades me for long."

She hauled herself up on his claw, gasping for breath. "I… I'm not Arc'hantael. My name is Faria Phira—"

"SILENCE!" he roared, breath steaming with anger. "How dare you shake off your vile history with such casual lies?" Pressing her further into the wall, he cast a vicious glare at her staff. "That weapon belongs to your father. You are accountable for his sins as much as he is; your ignorance is inexcusable! You will pay in blood for the attempted destruction of the Dhrakan Empire!"

"I don't know what you're talking about!" she cried.

Fulkore's face twisted to a reviled grimace. "Sickening that you do not even comprehend the legacy of suffering your father handed you," he snarled. "When he constructed that baneful city we were granted a share in its government, an inalienable right which he then denied us. This war is the fate he chose for this world."

"You're wrong," she hissed. "My father never wanted a war over Xayall!"

"Disgraceful spawn! This has nothing to do with your pathetic Xayall!" he roared, his glistening teeth inches from her face, pulled up into a ferocious sneer. "If your father did not want a war he should have killed himself back in Nazreal when he murdered my people!"

"Nazreal? That's impossible! My father wasn't—"

He threw her to the ground with brutal force. She rolled and crashed into a pipe, landing the hard, hot metal in the small of her back.

"Just like your treacherous father," he spat, striding towards her. She tried to reach for her staff but, paralysed by the blow, she couldn't move before Fulkore clamped her neck in his claws and ripped her from the floor. "Your lies are the same. For every second you live, Arc'hantael, you darken the memories of the millions of proud Dhrakans executed in your name. The ones destroyed in the earthquakes were lucky compared to those of us banished underground by the radiation for thousands of years. I shall enjoy feeding you both to Raikali."

She stared back at him defiantly, thrashing in his claws. "Both? What have you done with my father?" she growled with all the breath she could manage.

His face broke into a twisted, maleficent, sickening smile. "He is here, on the Gargantua." Her eyes widened in shock.

He drew her in closer, his grin cracking with greater sadistic satisfaction. "But I cannot guarantee how much of him will be left!"

"No!" she screamed, punching desperately, hammering into the rocky scales of his wrist. He smirked at her powerlessness and turned to grab the staff.

It had gone.

As he swept round to find it, a loud click broke through the steam; a steely shape spun through the air, clouting the vicious lizard in the jaw. Another flew past his face and latched onto the hand clamped around Faria. The claws clenched shut with a crunch, blood spread from the gouges. Fulkore's arm sprang back in painful recoil and he released the vixen. As she dropped to the floor Tierenan sprinted round and threw the staff into her arms, pulling her away. Fulkore lunged for them, fists pounding into the empty space inches behind them. His tail whipped over their heads, slicing the control deck. They hurtled towards the door. Fulkore reeled for a pursuit but stopped as another figure stood before him, rapiers flashing in the steam. The dragon rose to his full height, his eyes burning with a hatred deeper and more frightening than Faria had ever seen. Osiris raised his swords.

"Faria, find Aidan and bring him to the Coriolis," he said, his cold gaze unmoving from Fulkore's grim visage.

"All right. Be careful!" she called back, disappearing into the corridor, Tierenan at her side. Osiris allowed himself a wry smile.

Fulkore's long tongue danced over his razor teeth. "You should have died a long time ago, accursed bird."

"I will not die before you, Crawn. If you were already dead, I would only be disappointed it wasn't me that killed you," Osiris growled.

"Two rapiers?" the dragon sneered. "I'm insulted. Have you really become that desperate?"

"Not desperate," the gryphon seethed, his blood boiling. The abhorrence he felt for the dragon filled every fibre of his existence. "All the blades in the world would never be enough."

They leapt at each other. Fulkore tore at the air with his claws, slashing wildly. Osiris dodged past them and thrust his swords at Fulkore's chest. The Dhrakan's hardened breastplate withstood the heavy blows; he brought his open claw into the side of Osiris' neck, slamming him away. Osiris rolled free, followed by a kick from Fulkore. He blocked it with his arm and swung his free blade to the dragon's back. The dragon whirled around to catch the sword in his palm. Before he could strike again Osiris lunged forwards, led by his sword. The point glanced off Fulkore's breastplate, and with the gryphon now directly in his path the dragon opened his jaws and struck forwards, sinking his knifelike teeth into Osiris' left wing. In a flash Osiris retaliated, plunging his sword into the dragon's flank. Fulkore let out a fierce howl. Released, the agile gryphon dived aside as Fulkore spun again to face him.

Blood oozed from their wounds. Fulkore flexed his claws, balling them into mace-like fists.

"Your skull will shatter in my grasp," he hissed. Steam billowed from his nostrils.

Osiris flexed his wings. "Not before your heart is pierced by my blade!"

Faria struck her staff against the grated flooring. A ripple of metal cannoned towards the Dhrakan standing before them; the rolling sheet flew open like a net and snapped tight around him in a barbed snare. He shrieked and fell to the floor. As they passed, Tierenan landed a swift blow on his head, rendering him unconscious. They carried on ahead.

"*He's here,*" she thought. "*Father's here, and I can save him.*" Around every corner she could feel herself closing in on him. So much was she concentrating on it that she didn't hear Tierenan call her. It was only when he grabbed her shoulder and hauled her back that she saw what he was directing her to.

Dripping through the pipes above them was a sticky, blue-green substance with a slight luminance. She ran her fingers over the small pool on the floor and it buzzed at her touch—immediately she knew it was imbued with crystal.

Carefully, she touched the staff to the leak's source and closed her eyes. She could feel its path through the ducts, following it back up through the ship. Along, up, weaving and sucking through small, tight pipes, then—

Her eyes opened suddenly. She almost fell over and Tierenan ran to stabilise her.

"What happened?" he asked urgently.

She shook her head, the crystal's turbulent map still pulsing in her mind. "I... I'm not sure. I think I've found my father."

The guards in the brig stood restlessly at their duty. Far above them they could hear distant yells and the rushed pounding of troops. The Coriolis' crewmates looked to each other suspiciously.

"Do you think something's happened?" Jala whispered furtively, trying not to attract the guards' attention.

Maaka shrugged. "Unlikely. They're probably preparing to dive back underwater."

The otter watched the guards for a moment. They were exchanging apprehensive glances and looking up to the ceiling, as if studying the movements of the noise. "I don't know much about Dhrakans, but they don't look happy. Maybe Osiris has taken a Skyrian ship in pursuit."

Maaka plucked a broken feather from his wing with his beak. "He does like to make an impression. With their distraction, we should put ourselves to good use and break free the Coriolis. I've had all I can take of this place."

Still leaning against the wall to Aeryn's cell, Kyru watched and listened, his mind in a stupor. He wasn't sure if he was awake or just watching a vivid dream. Either way if they tried to escape, he'd be a burden. Dead weight. He couldn't even see properly. The slightest turn of his head sent the world into a blur, taking a second or so to come back into focus. His hearing faded in and out and he barely had the energy to move his hands.

Aeryn had retreated into her cell a while ago. He could hear vague movements, investigative taps and bangs, but couldn't place them.

Ever since they'd been flung in here, she'd been searching for a weak point in the cell, but could find no cracks, not even the slightest loose bolt to prise free. She sat on the metal bench, tapping her feet agitatedly, scouring every surface for even the tiniest chance at freedom. A sigh escaped her as she slumped against the wall, exhausted but desperate for an opening.

A bang snapped the air above her as something punched through the ventilation duct. A second later a flash of green swooped down and landed on her hands.

Tikku. In his mouth was a key. Aeryn's jaw dropped.

"Where did you come from?" she whispered. Tikku hopped to the wall and quickly scratched a single word into the metal plating with his beak:

'Feith'.

He hopped round and flapped his wings, then disappeared back into the vent.

Aeryn didn't stop to consider the message. She scrambled to the edge of the cell and beckoned the others forth with a piercing hiss.

"I've got a key!"

Maaka pushed through to the wall next to her. "How on Eeres did you get that?"

"Tikku brought it to me through the grate above my cell. I need you to back me up while I try it." She glanced hurriedly over to the jailors. One of them caught sight of her and let out a cry, striding forwards with a vicious snarl on his face.

"Quick!" she rasped. "Distract him!"

Jala, who had been just behind Maaka, grabbed the falcon and hurled him backwards with a rolling kick. Taken by surprise, Maaka's reaction needed no drama, as he shouted and landed amongst the other crewmates, fluttering angrily.

The two began a shouting match, while the others joined in with equal volume. The guard stopped by them, for a moment forgetting Aeryn.

She leapt to the door and jabbed the key into the lock. With a desperate twist she opened the cell; instantly the dragon saw and thrust his spear, a violent jab through the bars. She grabbed the gate and threw it against the polearm's shaft, snapping the wood and sending the point spinning into her cell. Diving back in, she picked it up and launched herself through the door, tearing at the guard's eye. The other Dhrakans were already on their way. As the first dragon fell, Aeryn threw his keys to Jala, who set about unlocking the other cell door.

Another guard lunged towards the wolf. She dodged his spear, drawing her makeshift knife up and into her attacker's forearm. The dragon howled in pain and tried to batter her with his shield, flailing madly. It missed Aeryn by an inch. She swung the cell door open into the passage and twisted behind it to avoid the rain of blades thrust towards her.

Moments later the rest of the crew broke free and swarmed the remaining dragons, beating them unconscious and stealing their weapons. More would arrive any second, their battle too loud to go unheard. She moved into the crew's cell and took hold of Kyru, supporting him with her left arm. He felt his body tear apart with every movement but willed himself up, determined not to impede her.

"We need more weapons," Aeryn said firmly, as the crew armed themselves with the shields of the fallen dragons.

"There'll be plenty coming at us," Kyru said, his voice a harsh whisper. "They won't let—"

The crystal in his back was raging. He arched forwards, a storm of pain wrapping around his abdomen. Blood oozed from his jaw. He gripped Aeryn's hand tightly. If he could not follow her, he would not let her be lost with him.

Following the memory of the path instilled in her by the crystal liquid, Faria and Tierenan moved quickly. There was activity everywhere. The Dhrakans were on alert. The sound of claws clicking on mesh and the sinister rattle of armour echoed menacingly through the metal halls.

They came to a walkway in an immense circular room: the power station of the Gargantua. Stifling heat pulsed in the heavy air. A tall, domed structure loomed before them, almost disappearing in the swirling dark vapour above. Down below was a sprawling mass of machinery, deafening with the thunderous rolls of its gears and the hissing of steam. Underneath, and feeding the dome, was an enormous reactor, the primary source of the Gargantua's monstrous energy. Most of the Dhrakans in the massive chamber were attending to the core and the four secondary generators around it, but soldiers stood everywhere.

Hewn into the forbidding dome ahead was a thick doorway flanked by four guards. Within it lay the end of the crystal's path. Faria quickly pulled Tierenan behind a large pipe before they were noticed.

"We need to get inside," she whispered, gritting her teeth until they almost ached.

They studied the walls of the huge domed pillar. It looked to have been built out of welded bricks of metal, too strong to try and breach. High in the metal of the dome she saw a billowing ventilation grate, big enough for the both of them to climb into.

Now for a distraction.

She peered out from behind the pipe to study the rest of the reactor room. Near the next entrance along was a large expanse of the room's outer wall, free from pipes.

Willing the energy through her aching, bleeding hands, she pressed her staff into the wall's plating behind them. A nest of ripples travelled along the metal surface to the large open area, blossoming with an orange glow, turning quickly into a pulsing, molten bubble. At the same time a second ripple shot into the dome's wall and formed a stepladder from the walkway to the grate.

Below, the Dhrakans had noticed the bulb of burning metal and started a panicked rally to cease operations. As the bubble reached a critical size, Faria gave it one last burst of heat and pressure. With a colossal boom it exploded, showering the room with flecks of red hot steel, rupturing pipes and the gears laid underneath and spewing hot liquid onto the lower level. Emergency bells rang through the chamber; the engines slowed to minimum output. The Dhrakans by the chamber door leapt up and sprinted to the erupting fissure.

Safe with the sentries distracted, Faria and Tierenan bolted to the door and flew up the stepladder to the ventilation grate. As he ripped off the metal grill, a horrible feeling took hold of Faria's body; a chilling, terrifying emptiness. She clambered into the vent and slid forwards. In front of them was another grate. They pressed their faces against its slats.

The room was barely lit, the moving shapes inside like shadows against shadows. The blue, luminescent crystal shimmered at the centre of the room, dripping over a tall, sinister figure and into the floor. It was here Faria saw the origin of the terror that sparked in her earlier. It was akin to a black hole standing before her, engulfing, consuming the essence of the crystals. She was unable to make out its shape completely. Jagged and strong, with a head almost shark-like in its menace. When the dim lights, disrupted by her explosion, flickered back on she saw it: a black suit of arcane armour, with each section smooth and sharp as if it were a blade that could cut the very air around it. Beneath its black surface it held a bloody, crimson hue, caused by the crystal serum merging with the hideous, soul-emptying energy contained within. It was female, and held the enhanced muscle structure of a cat. When it turned its head, Faria could see the grim recreation of a fierce lioness's head. Her breath caught in her throat upon seeing its dark red eyes, infinitely deep pools that pierced with threats of intense suffering.

The others in the room appeared disquieted by the noise outside the chamber. The scientists by the creature's lower left leg, still encased in the rock, hurried back to their job attaching segments of tube and wire to the armour already in place. A dark, corroded skeleton and rotting flesh, the core of the reconstructed being, was just visible underneath their encasement.

Faria was rigid with silent fear. Before the figure, once standing but now crumpled to his knees, was another presence, his hands chained to tall posts either side of him, head hung low, eyes shut in a trance of pain, unmoving. His robes were torn and marred with blood. A web of scars both ancient and new covered his body. Faria had to strangle her own cry upon seeing him.

A deep, chilling voice hit the room.

"Your friends are not amusing, Aidan."

She recognised it instantly: the voice, the dark shape in her dream. Raikali…

"I can understand their wish to escape death," she said, seething with derision. "After all, many tried to escape Nazreal before it disappeared. Even me. But while I was lucky enough to find a protective shell, millions of others were sent screaming to their graves, by you."

Aidan said nothing, remaining unmoved, hanging from the posts.

"There is a way to atone, Aidan," she continued, breathing vengeance. "Tell me where Nazreal is."

His eyes remained closed. He didn't respond. Suddenly, Raikali threw her fist forward.

"You wouldn't have been stupid enough to destroy it!" she roared, her voice quaking the metal. "Where is the city? What have you done with Nazreal?"

Faria watched desperately as her father slowly, through his excruciating pain, raised his head to stare into the lioness' soulless eyes with proud defiance.

"You lost your right to Nazreal, Raikali. I will never give it to you."

She smiled rancorously, a twisted expression made more sinister by the metal constricting her face. "You have little choice, Arc'hantael. I have defied your piteous judgement thus far. It will be found. The only choice you have is whether you die after I find it, or before."

"Then it doesn't matter if I tell you. If I remain silent at least there's a chance you'll be stopped before you reach it."

She clenched her fist. "Nothing will stop me! I will not rest until I return the world to its rightful place and reset the destruction you have caused."

"The world you are pursuing would have destroyed itself. You shouldn't pretend to be so self-righteous. All you want is a world to control, to dominate and constrict to your own twisted will. Eeres has healed. It no longer needs Nazreal."

"How dare you!" she screamed. "Eeres has no choice! My power will grant the safety it longed for. How often do you see the signs repeating themselves every day, Arc'hantael? The wars, the conflict, the despair that confronts so many in this crippled existence. It is inevitable." She pointed an accusing claw at him, eyes shimmering with hate. "You yourself are guilty of the greatest act of vivicide in history! Were all those lives worth your cowardice to accept our birthright to evolution and technology?"

"I never intended to kill them!" he shouted back. "I wanted to destroy Nazreal and Nazreal alone! It should never have existed! The world should have grown by itself, without the meddling of the crystals."

"So you would condemn us to live in the dirt? Thrashing vainly in the darkness for the best place to die?" Raikali's voice lowered, growing even darker and more poisonous.

Aidan leant back, casting his head to the pitch-dark ceiling above. "The world is stronger than you think. We survived before Nazreal and we have survived since."

Raikali let out a hideous laugh. "Then you are guilty of the two worst crimes known to Eeres: both the construction and destruction of that wretched city!"

"I have always thought that," he retorted, bitterly. "Nazreal was created by a need for peace and a genuine quest for knowledge. But the potential for powers and technologies presented to us was too much for most to understand. Greed, ignorance, hate; all corrupted it. It had to be taken away."

"A charlatan's logic. If greed is so intrinsic to nature then you have no hope of changing it. All you have done is delay the inescapable. But under my supervision the world would be controlled, allowed to develop at a pace that keeps it safe from such irrational desires. Everyone deserves their world to be a utopia."

"Utopia?" Aidan spat. "Controlled? Is this how you fooled the Dhrakans again? You aren't even attempting to hide your manipulation of a machine world that you can repress and advance at your own will. That version of Eeres would only fester under your feet. The greed that destroyed the world millennia ago is only present in you, Raikali. Nothing will change as long as demons like you exist to drive the world to ruin, with your name screamed from the rooftops."

She was overcome by revulsion, glaring murderously at him as he spoke. "Foul hypocrite!" she shrieked. "Guards, take him! Hoist him up!"

Two Dhrakans advanced on Aidan and took hold of his arms, pulling him to his feet. Faria's heart beat painfully in her throat. Her staff began glowing wildly, emitting a high ring. Aidan kept his defiant stare drilled into Raikali.

"You have already ruined the world in the name of your justice," the lioness spat. She raised her arm, pointing her claws directly at his chest. "I shall enjoy watching the life ripped from your body, like you ripped the flesh from mine."

At that second the grate burst from the wall, transforming into a volley of needles that shrieked through the air, raining on the dragons' arms with a thousand tiny stakes. Aidan dropped to the floor. Tierenan and Faria leapt from the grate, facing the dark menace and her coiled, reptilian guards. Raikali cast them a terrifying, abhorrent look.

"The staff! Arc'hantael's daughter!" she bellowed.

Faria raised her father's weapon.

Chapter Twenty-One

Blood flashed across the walls, streaming from the Dhrakan body that crashed to the ground. The crew of the Coriolis stormed through the grim passageways, cutting their jailers with vicious strikes, the trail of bodies in their wake growing larger by the minute, and the furious roars of the pursuing soldiers resounding ever nearer. They had lost several to the brutal chase already.

The ship's maze of corridors led them to more conflict at every turn. The Dhrakans were rampant—even their own shields weren't enough to hold them back. They pounded again and again on the stolen metal barriers, hacking, slashing, tearing them to pieces with their blades. The crew were defending on all sides. Aeryn's strikes were limited to her one free arm; on the other was Kyru, who could do nothing except push himself along with her. His body was growing heavier; more and more he had to rely on her to carry him, and he could feel her slipping away from the rest of the crew.

"Aeryn, leave me."

"Never."

She slashed a dragon across the face as it leapt at them from a side passageway. It slumped against the wall. Ahead of them a blockade of shield and spear-bearing Dhrakans marched into place with the vicious rattling of metal on metal. Past the lizards' glowering eyes, they could see the dock that held the Coriolis and their one remaining chance at freedom.

She glanced at her recently slain Dhrakan. A bandolier of grenades hung from his shoulder, a lit piece of match smouldering behind the strap. In a flash she ripped the belt of explosives free. Resting Kyru in a side corridor, she plunged the burning match against the grenades' fuses.

"Everyone, take cover!"

The crew split into the side passages, hugging the wall. She hurled the smouldering bandolier at the Dhrakan shield wall, whose operators were so solidly in place that they didn't have time to move. The grenades exploded in a thunderous volley above their heads. Aeryn felt the shockwave punch down the corridor next to her, slamming the walls and forcing the breath from her chest, the explosion's deafening sound swamping the rest of the battle. Moments later came the smell of charred metal and thick, sharp smoke.

The way was clear. They wasted no time recovering from the devastating blast, and sprinted, shields first, into the docking bay. Aeryn grabbed Kyru around his chest and hefted him into the corridor.

"Come on, we're nearly there," she said, her determination to save him as sharp as the blade she still grasped.

"You… you have to leave me!" he croaked.

"I told you, I won't," she growled back. The burnt metal floor, buckled by the grenade, hissed and sparked with the destroyed pipes beneath.

He tensed. His breathing slowed suddenly, becoming heavy and harsh. "You won't… have a choice," he rasped.

"What does that mean?"

They broke into the docking bay. Fights were crashing all round them. Some of the crew were halfway to the ship. She looked around hurriedly, trying to plan the safest route to the Coriolis. A figure appeared beside them. Whirling her sword to it, Aeryn caught sight of Vionaika's mad grin.

"It means that the prize is mine!" she cackled. Aeryn went to lunge with her sword but Kyru lurched away, coughing and retching wildly. Instantly, Aeryn stopped her attack and turned to help. In a second, he spun round and landed a hefty kick that sent her reeling against the wall. Kyru drew himself tall, arms shaking, a mad, unfocused gleam in his eyes. Blood dripped from his muzzle.

"Kyru?" she called.

He didn't respond. Not a flicker of emotion touched his face. He clenched his fists and strode clumsily towards her as Vionaika let out a triumphant laugh.

The pipe ruptured as Osiris shoulder-barged Fulkore through it, spraying them both with scalding steam. They skidded along the floor, ripping at each other's throats with their claws. Fulkore tore a fistful of feathers from Osiris' back; the gryphon pounded his fists on the lizard's face, trying to smash the fire-hardened scales. The two creatures traded millennia of burning rage in their crushing blows. Their roars and growls reverberated around the room, each impact of their fists and rip of teeth could be felt in the pipes.

At last, Osiris broke free and turned back for the swords he'd thrown clear when the fight came too close. Fulkore followed, the taste of both Osiris' and his own blood fuelling his insatiable thirst for violence.

Osiris grabbed one of the blades and immediately spun back around. His other was some distance away. Fulkore continued his charge, claws ready to plunge into the gryphon's head. With little time Osiris dived away to his second weapon. Fulkore thundered past him and slid along the floor, unable to stop himself. As he turned Osiris lunged, impaling the dragon's left hand on a pipe. Deftly, he flicked the point of his other sword to press underneath Fulkore's throat. The dragon gave him a mad stare.

"You could never hope to kill me, Tallon."

"I never needed hope, Crawn. I *knew* I would slay you." He flicked a trigger on the hilt of the rapier at Fulkore's throat; the end of the pommel twisted out. Just as he released his left hand to grab the switch, the dragon's warped, cruel expression stopped him.

"This isn't the first time you've let yourself succumb to revenge, Tallon," he growled, a dark, sinister grin creeping across his face. "I remember the last time so well. Perhaps Arc'hantael will be more forgiving for your failure than your betrothed was!"

Osiris' eyes widened with rage.

In that brief second Fulkore's neck arched back, the back of his throat rippling with yellow light. Osiris noticed just in time, withdrawing his sword from Fulkore's claw as the acidic yellow flame streaked past, searing his arm. Regaining his focus to rescue Aidan and Faria, he sprinted away as Fulkore howled triumphantly into the darkness beyond.

Faria stood boldly before Raikali.

"Let my father go." she growled.

Raikali let out a derisive laugh. "This is payment for sins past; there is no escaping my judgement. He deserves more pain than I can ever bring him. At the very least I shall kill him, and then you." She glowered blackly at the vixen. "A troublesome legacy I was not expecting."

Faria bolstered her staff, grabbing it with both hands. Energy rippled through the crystals. "I will be more than troublesome if you touch my father again," she hissed.

Raikali's face twisted into a grimace of rage. "Kill her! Take the staff!" she yelled.

"Faria, be careful!" Aidan cried. The Dhrakans around the edge of the room leapt forwards. Faria wrenched her gaze from the monstrous Raikali and spun her staff around, thrusting it into the floor. Pillars of metal burst up in front of the advancing dragons, trapping them in a thick steel cage. Tierenan threw his fists into the stomach of one coming from the right, while Faria ran forwards and cast her staff into the breastplate of another, fusing it into one solid piece of metal and locking him in place like a living statue.

Raikali's crystal-flooded veins began to glow. The pipes in her back throbbed violently as Faria fought her way to her father. She aimed her claws in an arch in front of her and, the serum spitting and bubbling beneath her, they extended at bullet speed, slicing into the floor by Faria. They missed her legs and head, just barely. She slipped past the quaking blades as they withdrew for another attack.

Tierenan aimed an opportunistic punch at Raikali to stall her claws. She grabbed his fist with lightning reactions, the strength in her palms enough to crush the steel in his in a second.

"Defective worm," she hissed.

Tierenan gave a defiant smile.

Faria barrelled to her father. Her mind raced; she was shaking with fear. She had to protect him. She had to protect Tierenan, and the staff, the Coriolis, Aeryn, Kyru, Osiris—she couldn't lose them now. She fumbled at the chain, trying to sever it with the staff's glowing blade.

Tierenan could feel Raikali's strength pressing against his arms, threatening to dislocate his shoulders. He ripped his fists free and ran to Faria. The cyborg lioness raised her talons again. Aidan saw her.

"Quickly, Faria, my left arm. Free it!"

The serum spit and burst.

Faria swung the staff down. It bounced off the chain, the sharpened blade dulled by her overpowering rush of fright. She struck it again. This time it split through, scattering the chain fragments over the floor.

"I'll tear you to pieces!" Raikali shrieked.

Her claws tore the air, shrieking towards them, aimed straight for Faria's eyes. Aidan ripped the staff from Faria's grasp and held it aloft, his palm against the crystal. Centimetres away the blades froze dead in the air, trapped within a blue-green shield blossoming in front of her. Energy spewed from the staff into the barrier, both it and Raikali's claws quivering with its unstable energy. The lioness drew them back and tried to punch them in again, shrieking in rage. Aidan's glowing eyes bore her a ruthless glare.

"You will not touch her!"

"Curse you, Arc'hantael!"

Faria watched, awestruck, as her father's shield resisted the blows again, and a fourth time. But the barrier was shrinking—he was weakening.

"Faria..." he grunted, his arm twisting and quaking, unable to withstand the enormous amount of energy needed to save them. She grabbed hold of the staff and emulated his energy, boosting its path through the crystal. Instantly the shield strengthened and spread. Through it she glared at Raikali, who withdrew her claws, her grimace distorted with hatred.

Aidan let go, too hurt to continue. The shield disappeared but Faria's own rage cascaded into the staff the longer she stared into the metal visage ahead. Around them formed a chaotic pulsing orb of blue-green electricity, pounding the air with its convulsions. Raikali readied her claws again, Aidan now the target of her wrath.

Faria saw.

"Don't you DARE!"

Resonance energy erupted from the tip in a blinding explosion. Waves of blue lightning pierced the Dhrakans standing nearby, fusing them to their armour and the floor. Raikali's armour protected her from the resonance's fusion but the force still slammed her back, nearly ripping her foot from its root in the stone base. She let out a hideous cry of pain.

"Faria, stop!" Aidan shouted.

She looked to him desperately, unable to prevent the already swirling points of light from gathering into another destructive sphere. He took her hand and prised it from the staff. Streaks of energy flicked from her hand as the orb sputtered and evaporated. Her whole body stung with the energy's toll. With a last burst of his own strength, Aidan sliced through the chain binding his right arm and dropped to his knees, exhausted.

Tierenan grabbed them both and pulled them towards the door, barely giving Faria enough time to take the staff. Shakily, she placed the weapon's tip at the centre of the huge metal arch and cast a burst of energy at it. With a colossal boom the doors crashed out, ripped from their hinges, thrown into the chamber below. Their way clear, Faria and Tierenan ran down the walkway, carrying Aidan between them.

Raikali, reeling from the pain of her near-dismembered foot, sent a vain claw slicing after them. It couldn't reach.

Her deadly stare burned through the darkness. They would not survive.

Kyru slashed at Aeryn with his claws; teeth bared, a constant low growl rumbling in his throat. His swings were wild and clumsy. She kept dodging away, having already cast aside her sword to avoid wounding him in retaliation.

His last swing, a backhand punch, landed her against a stack of crates that rocked as she thumped into them. Her head was swimming. Why was he attacking? Did he even recognise her? He drew back for a flailing punch at her face. She pulled herself away and ducked behind another crate as his fist splintered the wood.

Watching him at the other side of the platform was Vionaika. Seeing a chance, Aeryn leapt from cover and tore forwards. Before Vionaika knew it, Aeryn was upon her and a deep scratch was laid in her face. The hyena threw the wolf's arms away and bayed viciously, flying at her in a volley of scratches, punches and kicks. Aeryn blocked and lashed back with equal fury. Kyru stood some distance away, poised but not moving to one or the other. The barren, vicious look hung on his face.

Aeryn launched for the hyena's ear, trying to rip it off. Vionaika blocked and jumped back. "I should have killed you in Andarn!" she spat.

"Killed me? I'd have eviscerated you if I'd seen you near Kyru!" Aeryn flared back.

Vionaika laughed torturously. "Ha! He didn't even tell you that *you* were the bait I used to trap him! How unfortunate," she glowered, her eyes lighting up with sadistic glee. "He saved you from death on your pretentious mansion's roof, a situation I put you in while you slept, helpless. You were pathetic, so easy to trap. What threat are you to me?"

Aeryn's vengeful snarl only made the hyena more triumphant; every inch of her grin made Aeryn bristle with rage.

"I'll murder you!" the wolf roared. She grabbed Vionaika's arm and clamped her jaws around her wrist, her sharp teeth aching to taste vengeance. Vionaika screamed, pounding on Aeryn's head to force her release.

"Bitch, let me go!"

Aeryn closed her eyes, her teeth deep in the flesh of the hyena's arm. She swiped at Vionaika's throat and pulled with her muzzle, trying to tear her arm off. Vionaika kept clubbing her knuckles against Aeryn's head, splitting the skin. Blood poured down Aeryn's face. As Vionaika lunged for the wolf's eyes, something grabbed her free arm. She looked around. Kyru stood beside her, her arm trapped in his grasp. As Aeryn released her jaws, he rocked back and threw his other fist into Vionaika's chest, impacting her with a thunderous crack. The hyena fell to the floor. Stunned and injured, Aeryn stumbled too, falling against the nearby crate. She lifted herself up and gave one last, swift kick to Vionaika's stomach before turning to Kyru. Taking hold of each other, they made flight for the ship.

The *Coriolis'* crew had freed the guns. They loosed the cannons into the walls of the docking bay, plunging the dragons into chaos as they tried to attack and evade at the same time. The barrels of the ball lightning generators whirred and spat with electricity, frying Dhrakans in mid-air and scorching holes in the Gargantua's hull.

Bursting onto the walkway above and behind the ship came Osiris, seeing the entire battle at once. On his left were the docking bay controls. He sprinted forth, batting away two Dhrakans who tried to dive-bomb him. The guard protecting the controls took an opportunistic swing at Osiris, who punched him aside and threw him over the edge.

Osiris studied the levers quickly. With a hefty swing he pulled back the largest of them and the gargantuan doors opposite groaned and swung open, revealing the night air ahead of them. He ripped another two levers down and the two crescent clamps holding the ship thundered into action, slowly relinquishing the dauntless Coriolis.

At that moment, a thin Dhrakan leapt at him over the railing. Osiris dodged the flailing swords and head-butted the unprepared lizard, who staggered back against the wall. Pushing his full weight against the sprung levers, Osiris tore them from their fittings to prevent their escape being reversed, then leapt along the walkway.

His eyes were fixed on the ship's deck as he ran. He couldn't see Faria or Aidan anywhere. If they weren't below decks, then—

An explosion shook the gantry. Ahead of him came Tierenan, Aidan and Faria bursting from their makeshift doorway, a slew of Dhrakans snapping at their tails. He chased after them.

Below them the ship was still loosing its cannons, now lifting in an unstoppable arc towards the sea.

Aeryn saw the Coriolis begin its ascent. There was only one platform she and Kyru could reach in time if they hoped to board it and escape: the furthest. She bolstered him against her body and strengthened her stride. She kept her eyes on the ship constantly, pulling herself towards it, Kyru tightly held against her. He clutched her shoulder.

On the walkway opposite Faria's pursuit, a block of archers took position along the railing and loaded their bows, taking aim at her group and Osiris. The arrows shrieked through the air, piercing the grate floor. Impaled pipes bled with steam; arrowheads sparked and mashed against the thick metal walls. Tierenan knocked one aside with his claw; behind him Faria created a current of air to deflect them into the Dhrakan pursuers. Osiris was having the most trouble avoiding them, his injured wings unable to constrict any further. He pushed through the dragons, using the creatures as shields.

"Aidan! Faria!" he called, wrenching the last Dhrakan's neck aside to reach the trio. Supporting her father, Faria turned, and at that instant a dragon landed between them with a lit grenade in his hand. Tierenan skidded to a halt and whirled back round as the lizard cast the bomb at their feet.

"Look out!"

The explosion engulfed the walkway. Shards of metal rained from the blast, smoke flooded the area. The archers kept their sights trained on the cloud, watching for survivors.

As the smoke cleared, the walkway had been ripped in two. Pipes underneath spewed water and steam; several cables lay dangling underneath. On one side of the rift were Aidan and Osiris; Faria and Tierenan on the other. Faria had summoned a shield just in time and Aidan had barely managed to do the same, although both were still thrown back a considerable way. Osiris had caught the older fox, taking the brunt of the impact to save him.

Faria's head throbbed. She couldn't hear anything. Opposite the gap she could see Osiris pulling her father up. The gryphon pointed wildly at the Coriolis and yelled something she couldn't hear.

"I'll fly him to the ship! Tierenan, take Faria!"

Holding Aidan firmly in his claws, he leapt onto the rail and spread his wings, diving into the fierce hail of arrows and swooping onto the Coriolis' deck.

An arrow whipped past Faria's face. Something pulled her from behind—Tierenan wrapped his claw around her and they both climbed over the railing. With the mizzen-mast now directly ahead of him, Tierenan aimed at one of the prongs and fired his free claw at it, latching onto the yard. He leapt down, a storm of arrows hitting the floor in their wake.

The two of them swung down at break-neck speed. The raccoon retracted his claw to stop them hurtling straight over the deck, but once they were safely over the Coriolis he fired his other fist, grabbing the main mast to slow their flight. Osiris caught Faria before she hit the deck, pulling her straight towards the sterncastle. Through the chaos below, she saw two figures moving along the walkways next to them. She grabbed the rail in horror.

"Aeryn! Kyru!" she cried.

Aeryn heard her. They were at the base of the gangway now with time to spare, but Kyru was stumbling with every step. His head hung low and he was barely breathing.

"Come on, Kyru!" she shouted, hauling him up another step. He flinched. With his free arm, he grabbed onto the metal fence and began pushing up with all the strength he could manage. The Coriolis drifted past at an unforgiving pace. Some of the crew appeared, reaching out their arms to bring them in. Kyru could hear Aeryn next to him and the concerned cries quaking above; the rest was a blur of painful noise. He forced his eyes fully open and looked up. They were close. They could make it yet. He pushed through the hollow deadening in his legs, focusing all his energy on every step they took.

Suddenly, a wave of pain more intense than anything he'd felt before shot through his back. For a second he blacked out, his left leg was paralysed; his breath was forced from his body. His throat seized up and his arms burned like fire. But all he could think of was Aeryn. She had to live. He let out a terrifying, strangled scream.

"Kyru!" she cried. "We're almost there! Come on, please!"

They were three steps away from the Coriolis with the sterncastle approaching fast. As soon as that passed, they were lost. He looked to Aeryn desperately as they climbed one more step, and she reached out for Osiris' hand. Arrows struck the deck around them; another pierced the gryphon's cloak. Soldiers sprinted rapidly up the gantry behind them.

Kyru took a massive breath and closed his eyes. With a sharp movement he pulled himself from Aeryn, knocking her forwards at the same time. Before she could move, with the final reserves of strength fading from his body, he grabbed her. His arms quaking, feeling that they would snap at any second, he thrust her into Osiris' grasp.

"I'm sorry, Aeryn!"

For a moment that seemed an eternity, the two wolves watched each other across the railing. A second later they were apart, and he was out of reach.

She wrestled against Osiris' vice-like grip. "Let me go!" she screamed. "Kyru!"

Faria raised her hands to her muzzle in horror while Tierenan raced up the sterncastle steps and leant over the barrier, holding out his arm for Kyru to grab. Arrows thundered into the deck around him, but just before he could fire his claw the Coriolis lurched forwards and broke through the Gargantua's doors, landing in the sea.

Kyru watched the ship disappear into the darkness, ignoring the soldiers fast approaching him. She was safe. That was all that mattered.

A huge wave of relief flowed over him, washing away his strength. He collapsed to the floor. The soldiers before him stopped when they saw him fall.

Aeryn screamed into the darkness at the Gargantua from the golden ship's deck. With the sounds of battle now behind them, her painful cries were more piercing than any of the explosions.

"Kyru! I'll find you! Don't you dare die!"

Osiris placed a claw on her shoulder. Instantly she launched into him, punching his chest plate. Tears streamed from her eyes.

"How dare you leave him? How dare you? You should have grabbed him, he should be here!" She fell to her knees, pulling at his armour. Her whole body shook with her cries.

On the Gargantua, the soldiers parted for a shape to move through them, approaching the wolf. Kyru's eyes were almost closed, the darkness swirling about his body. He could just about see the figures surrounding him. As the shape emerged, he fell icily cold. A dark feeling opened deeply in his stomach. The freezing black swamped his senses completely, leaving him paralyzed, lost within his body.

"I told you what your choices were," a voice told him in the darkness, sickening, oozing with derision. "I knew you wouldn't disappoint me…"

Faria went to her father on the Coriolis' deck. He was staring out to sea, while behind them Tierenan did his best to comfort the grieving Aeryn.

"I'm… really glad you're safe, Father," she said quietly.

Aidan turned to her and smiled. His left arm was bleeding. She could see something blue and gold sticking out of the flesh of his forearm—his pendant, hidden inside him when he was first captured. Just as she went to examine it his eyes closed and he fell backwards, landing unconscious on the deck.

"Father!"

Chapter Twenty-Two

The shadowy grey skies over Xayall were a bleak reflection of the hearts of its people. The city had been abandoned by the occupying Dhraka when it became clear the fight lay elsewhere, and although it was free again it was left desperately crippled.

The Coriolis had landed in the river a short way north; quickly afterwards a carriage was hailed from the city to rush the deathly weakened Emperor of Xayall back home and into the physicians' emergency care.

Aidan had been rushed to his bedroom and was quarantined for the first few hours so he could be attended to. Faria had been beside herself, with even Osiris unable to calm her. Tierenan and Aeryn sat outside with her but the atmosphere was grim, nobody able to breathe the slightest comfort. Tierenan paced nervously between Aeryn, Faria and Osiris, searching for any hint that he could ease their sadness. Tikku sat silently on his shoulder.

Inside Aidan's bedroom the surgeons had examined him closely, tended his wounds, wrapped him in warming bandages, administered potions and pored over manuals, although no solution could be found to stabilise his rapidly failing condition. Eventually Maaka emerged, dishevelled and sombre. Faria and Osiris rose at once, both looking to him with clinging urgency. Faria wrung her hands.

"Is… he all right?" she asked weakly.

Maaka looked away. "I've been talking with the Xayall physicians. He's been ill for a very long time. Longer than anyone could have anticipated." As he continued, Faria's hands shook more and more, she fought back the explosion of cries building in her chest. "As such… with the exertion placed on his body, he's got very little strength left. His body is… failing."

"Failing…" Osiris said quietly. It was an alien word for such a person.

Faria drifted to the door and rested her hand on it, feeling for her father's presence. The wood was cold and unwelcoming, but she could still sense him inside, faintly.

"Can… can I go in?" she asked, her voice a whisper. Maaka nodded.

The door opened silently at her touch. She knew her father's room well. But where his warmth radiated from it in days past, everything now felt grey and unfamiliar, like a house stripped of all its furniture. Its smooth marble floor reflected the dull clouds shrouding the sky. The green drapes were blowing slowly, ghost-like in the wind. It terrified her. Her father's canopy bed, surrounded by the hushed Xayall physicians, was lit in a soft orange by the sparse, flickering torches on the walls.

The doctors moved away as they saw her approach, bowing respectfully. The chilling silence gripped at her as she walked. It took forever to reach him.

She stopped. This couldn't be real. Someone had made a mistake. Her father couldn't die. Not yet…

She felt a hand on her shoulder. Osiris said nothing, still looking to Aidan, shrouded by the rippling curtains. The gryphon's gaze was distant, the usual sternness washed from him. She stepped forwards again, now coming to the bed.

As soon as Aidan saw her he smiled tiredly, his eyes glistening. His breathing was shallow. The wound on his arm, inflicted by himself to hide his pendant, was bandaged but still bled softly. His whole body rocked with his breaths, as if each took all his remaining strength to force through. The colour in his eyes had faded further, almost a pale green now. But they were still *his* eyes, and they still brimmed with love at the sight of his daughter.

"Faria," he whispered, reaching out to her. She took his hand and held it tightly. "I'm sorry. I think… I've worried you a bit."

She trembled in reply, trying to withhold her tears. "Heh, yes… but you're here now. It's okay."

Osiris avoided his gaze. Aidan gave him a look askance.

"You're looking ruffled, Osiris. Get into trouble?"

The gryphon laughed, still looking to the balcony. "Idiot. Like you're one to talk."

Aidan smiled, looking at the canopy above him. "I guess you're right."

There was a pause, and Faria stood up. For a second she left her father's side and ran to the corridor, beckoning to the others. They walked in quietly and Faria took them to his bedside.

"Father, these are my friends. They protected me while I was looking for you. This is Tierenan,"

The raccoon smiled and politely waved.

"And Aeryn,"

Aeryn bowed respectfully. "It's an honour to meet you, Your Imperial Majesty."

The fox gave an appreciative nod to them both. "Thank you for protecting Faria. She means the world to me."

"She's incredibly strong," Aeryn said proudly. She was still fighting back her own pain of losing Kyru, but for Faria, she kept herself calm. Faria needed her strength.

"Takes after you, Aidan," Osiris murmured.

"Damn. I know I'm in trouble if you're complimenting me, Osiris," Aidan replied, taking hold of the pendant around his neck. It was gold, a ring with wing-like carvings on its upper quarters. In the centre was an eight-pointed star, and mounted onto the ring's lower edge was a crystal prism. He was silent for a few seconds, staring ahead, lost in a memory. A second later he let go of the pendant and looked up at the ceiling.

"I'm sorry for getting you involved in this, Faria."

She hesitated. It wasn't the fact that she was involved. It was that it had happened in the first place, and that wasn't his fault. "No, it's all right," she said quietly. She looked at the floor, deep in thought.

"You would have died if she wasn't," Osiris grunted, a hint of irritation in his voice.

Aidan sighed. "I should have died a long time ago…"

Faria turned sharply, a shocked and forbidding glare in her eye. He squeezed her hand. "Sorry, I didn't mean... This is difficult for me."

"This isn't exactly easy for us either, Aidan," the gryphon muttered, folding his arms.

The questions that had been clawing at Faria's mind were working into her throat. She didn't know if she should ask him. She wanted him to be stronger. One thought kept burning into her consciousness, and every time it did she wanted to shake it away and be rid of it: the dreadful fear that rose in her chest, the creeping knowledge that she would soon, very soon, lose him. Unknowingly, she gripped his hand tighter. He gently stroked her arm.

"Faria, are you all right?" he asked softly. One of the physicians took a chair and placed it behind her. She sat down, turning the vortex of words over in her head, swallowing her tearing emotions as much as she could.

"Father, in the Gargantua... they called us 'Arc'hantael'. What does that mean?"

Aidan shivered slightly. The hairs on his neck bristled. "That... is our heritage," he said solemnly. "My real name is Aidan Arc'hantael. Phiraco was your mother's name. I took it on to try and hide us." He let out a small, sarcastic chuckle. "Didn't really work, did it?"

She thought for a few moments. "But why is that important? Your name... they already knew you as Arc'hantael? Was that when you were researching Nazreal?"

Aidan sighed. "No, it runs far deeper than that. The last time I was called Arc'hantael was before Nazreal was destroyed."

She shook her head. "But that was—"

"Two thousand, five hundred and three years ago," Aidan said grimly.

A crushing, deafening silence hit the room.

She stood up, dropping his hand. She felt sick. "They said you built the city…"

"Yes. They were right. And I destroyed it too," he growled through his teeth, the ancient, bitter anger rising in his throat. "Along with the hopes, dreams and lives of millions of people on Eeres."

Everything she had heard about Nazreal suddenly flooded her mind. The ascension, the destruction, the cataclysm, the technology, the search, the stories; the key to everything was her father. The burning words of Fulkore and Raikali seared her mind. Millions died. An entire civilisation virtually wiped out.

She looked at him. Suddenly now, where she had seen such strength in his eyes, all she could see was his aching sadness, the burden of the responsibility he'd been carrying for so many years. She sat down slowly and took his hand again. He held hers appreciatively.

"What happened?" she eventually asked. He looked pained in response, she was unsure if it was because of his physical state or the resurgence of his memories.

"In Nazreal's time, Cadon and Ohé were one continent. It was struggling to come to come to terms with peace. Seven main sovereigns, and thousands of tribes and cities. Food was difficult to cultivate. All sovereigns had agreed to outlaw eating of other sentient species, but tensions rose high all the same. Fierce battles raged over fertile lands. In the end they were taken by those with the greatest armies. Above all this, two sovereigns were working together to find long-lasting solutions for peace; Skyria and Mahrae.

"Mahrae was the smallest of the nations, held together by a strong community and an affinity for knowledge. It never held interest in war. Most of its leaders were scholars and scientists. It was in Mahrae that the crystals were first discovered, where a large amount of the debris from the moon fell.

"Once they were looked at more closely, the people of Mahrae found that the children born in areas with a high proportion of crystal shared a connection with it and could change the crystals' shape. Resonance." He gave a distant smile. "My parents were young resonators. Over the years crystal was discovered in more locations around the lands, and more abilities were being found to go with them. Their potential was seen immediately, so the old sovereigns raced to establish diplomacy before war broke out."

His face fell to a darkening expression. "Inevitably it did. It was only after an army's complete massacre by vigilante resonators that it was decided a new, independent city would be built to study the crystals, shared by all sovereigns."

"Nazreal," Faria whispered.

"We shouldn't have been so optimistic. By this time I was an architect and builder. I constructed buildings for those who'd been misplaced by wars, caused ironically enough by what gave me my gift. The houses I built weren't always accepted."

"You weren't short of other offers, though," Osiris said pointedly.

"No," he replied. "But I didn't want to make weapons. So when I was approached to design and build Nazreal, I welcomed the opportunity. And, as…" he paused to let out a dismissive puff of air. "…allegedly one of the 'greatest' resonators around at the time, representative of Mahrae and ally of the gryphons, I was put on Nazreal's council to control its development. Osiris was on the council as well," (a remark at which Osiris looked a little awkward) "as were Raikali and Sarr Crawn, Fulkore's father. Raikali was the first Queen of Gauros, her sovereign of lions. She saw Nazreal as the foundation of a great new world, and relished the importance she was given. Crawn was the Dhrakan Emperor at the time, by brutal coincidence."

Osiris rolled his shoulders in irritation at Crawn's mention. He gave Faria a warning glare. "That whole race is bad blood."

She shuddered, still feeling Fulkore's vice-like claws around her neck.

Aidan appeared to fall faint for a moment; he grabbed his pendant tightly and closed his eyes, the crystal flickering faintly. His hand became deathly cold. Faria gripped it tightly, trying to pull him back to her. She couldn't lose him now. After a few seconds it warmed again, and the crystal fell dormant.

His eyes opened, only half-way this time.

Tierenan rubbed his forearm idly, a nervous reaction. "So… what happened to Nazreal?" he asked tentatively. Aidan rested himself into his pillow. His body was becoming stiff and heavy.

"It was fine, for a while. It started off quite small, but as more resonators gave themselves to its cause it grew, slowly. Eventually those from other sovereigns forgot about their previous nations and focused on Nazreal as if it was the only place in the world. I constructed new buildings, expanded the city walls, and made research tools and equipment."

He gestured to his staff, leant against the wall by the bed. "That was originally intended as a universal energy transform- er, capable of changing any form of energy into any other. Since discovering electricity, something was needed that could store it, change its output to something more useful and back again if reserves fell short. It was the first in a line of devel- opments that lead to Nazreal's destruction." He stopped for a moment to regain some energy. His voice quietened, slowly becoming thicker and heavier.

"Raikali was a resonator as well, just like us. She wasn't as skilled as I was, but she harboured an aggressive drive to see progress. I was content to develop my skills and carry out the menial tasks while she saw to the city's organisation. She arranged the Dhrakan garrison to protect the city. There was no question we would be kept safe if another sovereign tried to attack. But unfortunately, it wasn't outside that was the problem…"

"So she betrayed you?" Faria asked nervously.

"Not as such," Aidan replied, his breaths more laboured now. He was shivering. "She… there was an experiment she was overseeing, a secret, that went wrong and affected her resonance abilities. It warped her mind. She began seeking more control over Nazreal's assets and made a pact with Sarr that their two nations would eventually take over Nazreal and turn it into a joint empire. The Dhrakans themselves had kept back a few of the better scientists and, from my work, developed nuclear fusion reactors, putting them to work in their new war machines."

"You mean the Gargantua?"

"And others. As part of the pact, Raikali had been given a reactor and placed it under Nazreal's central tower. She altered the building's structure, turning it into a gigantic cannon capable of firing a resonance energy beam at anything on the planet. At the same time, tensions mounted between the gryphons and Dhraka—"

"You don't need to tell them that much, Aidan," Osiris bristled defensively. Aidan gave an understanding nod.

"The Dhrakans were stripped of their share of Nazreal. They were allowed no part in it and were banished from the city. Not that it mattered. They had already begun an insurrection and were bringing the Gargantua's sister ship Leviathan to besiege Nazreal. I found Raikali's fusion device by chance, while she was murdering the council. Once I had discovered what it was, I asked Osiris to take as many as he could out of the city in the Coriolis while I worked on disarming the tower."

A coughing fit struck Aidan. The doctors moved closer; he halted them with a staying hand. "Don't…" he wheezed. They stood quietly back. Faria held his hand to her muzzle, pale with worry.

He continued, his words coming quicker as his strength faded. "I had to rid the world of Nazreal in any way I could. I fought Raikali outside the tower as the Dhrakans broke in. I couldn't stop her, but we both entered the chamber containing the fusion device. She activated it, my disarming incomplete, the tower no longer a cannon but a cataclysmic, unfocused resonance bomb. She fled, but I stayed to stop it. Its unbalanced energy could have destroyed the planet, blown it apart. I tried to contain the energy surge as best as I could, but... In the end I channelled the energy through my staff, and myself, to try and move Nazreal to the moon, out of reach of everyone, and save Eeres."

The faces in the room were frozen with shock, save Osiris, who seemed to be reliving the horrific memories as painfully as Aidan was.

"I failed..." he whispered. "The resulting energies split the continent in two and thrust the two halves across the planet from each other, while Nazreal ripped across the planet's surface. Most of the world was killed by the earthquakes and tsunamis. It was complete devastation. Not many survived outside the Coriolis."

He turned to his daughter, a desperate look of urgency shadowing his face. "There's something I haven't taught you about resonance, Faria. What you felt in Raikali's chamber was the crystals' own energy. It's incredibly dangerous. It can burn through or fuse anything, everything together." He looked pointedly at Tierenan's arms. "Even metal to flesh. Once the energy within them gets to certain levels it starts taking more from its surroundings at a devastating rate. It grows, consuming more and powering itself until it burns out, by which time it can vaporise half the planet. I only just managed to stop it."

Faria felt like a ghost as his story came to its conclusion. He had endured all this for so long... "How did you survive?" she breathed.

He let out a slight laugh. "I'm not sure. I think the resonance protected me, almost, kept me frozen. I was alive but in a trance, drifting through the rock that encased Nazreal until eventually, I broke through and the energy dissipated, leaving me in the desert."

The faintest of smiles reached his lips. "I thought I had destroyed the world. If your mother hadn't been riding through and seen me, I would have died not knowing any better. Kaya was a descendent of the survivors taken from Nazreal, a resonator too. I told her everything. I showed her what was left of the city, and we made a decision to protect it. We created a seal over its resting place that can only be opened with that staff, and every so often we would return to study small artefacts and place them in false ruins to help the world in its struggles."

"Then Raikali? How did she survive?" Osiris asked gravely.

"As she fled she reached the Leviathan and absorbed the entire pyramid to create a shell for herself—the black rock. But her resonance was distorted, so as a cost of protecting her, it burned away her body. Had the Dhrakans never discovered her she would have been nothing but dust in a few years."

Faria was shaking with anxiety. "But, you're all right, aren't you? Your resonance is pure, so your body won't be eaten away, right?"

Aidan turned to her, tears of apology welling in his eyes. "Faria… I'm sorry… I just don't have the strength anymore."

She leapt onto the bed and threw her arms around him. "I… I'm sorry, father. I wasn't fast enough to save you. I just… isn't… isn't there something we can do? Stay just a little longer. Don't die. Please?"

Aidan couldn't move. The tears rolled down his face as Faria sobbed into his chest. Tierenan clasped his hands over his muzzle to stop himself from crying too. Aeryn turned away.

"Faria… I need you to be strong for me. You have to protect Nazreal. *You're* the person who can stop the world from falling into destruction again."

She shook her head. "Not without you," she cried. "I can't do it without you!"

Osiris pulled Faria back from Aidan as he struggled to speak. She kept hold of his hand, crying uncontrollably.

"Faria, listen to me. Nazreal is in the wasteland to the east, deep inside the huge mesa behind the mountains. It's still there; you can't let Raikali get inside!"

Faria nodded, shaking with grief.

Aidan's breath rattled weakly from his chest. He struggled at the pendant around his neck, pulling it shakily from him.

"Faria, take this… your mother made it for me. It's kept me alive." He looked at her again, still able to summon strength from his love for her even as he was dying. Another wave of tears streamed from his eyes. "I love you so much. You gave me my life again. Of all the things I've had in this world, you are the most precious to me."

Faria pulled herself from Osiris and embraced her father one final time. "I love you too, always."

"I'm… sorry that I couldn't… do more for you…"

She pulled away, staring into his eyes, their colour now faded even further. "I don't want you to worry about me,

Father. I'll miss you… more than the world, I'll miss you. But I'll try, Father. I promise I'll try." She buried her head in his chest again.

Aidan gently laid back, his eyes falling closed.

"Thank you… Faria…"

Faria felt his stillness. She froze for a second, then pulled herself up to look at the old fox. He looked so peaceful now. The tiredness that ravaged his body for so long seemed to have lifted from him. He looked young, almost happy.

She cradled her head in her hands, unable to hold back her tears any longer, while Tikku spread his wings and disappeared into the cold, open sky.

Chapter Twenty-Three

Xayall lay in uneasy, dark silence. In the mausoleum, a short but grand tower near the Tor, quiet preparations were underway for the Emperor's funeral. There weren't enough hands to plan a proper service amongst the repairs needed for the city, and time was not on their side. The Gargantua had been seen covering land a day ago, rendezvousing with reinforcements. It would not be long before Dhraka returned, teeth bared and cannons blazing. Even without the deadly machine, in its current state Xayall could be taken in hours. The troops depleted, the walls smashed; it was a grim picture. Some six hundred troops were still able to defend the city, but the Dhrakan rearmament meant it would never be enough.

Aeryn had thrown herself into blockading the gates and wall breaches. The soldiers were arming themselves, forming ranks in anticipation of the onslaught. She helped as best she could, finding ways to distract from thoughts of Kyru. She kept telling herself he wasn't dead, that she would save him. But every so often she would stop and look up at the dim fires illuminating the Tor's windows, wondering after the bereft young vixen she'd escorted here, and the even further-reaching loneliness she must be facing.

Faria was too heartbroken for sleep. Instead, she drifted emptily through the tower. Nothing belonged to her; not the Tor, not even her hands or her eyes. Everything she saw seemed like images played to her with no real substance, as if it was happening to someone else. It was a listless, aching catatonia. She couldn't tell if she was awake or dreaming. For her, the night was endless.

She hadn't been able to find Bayer, which had pushed her despair further still. Nobody could tell her where he went during the battle. Nor had anyone heard from Kier. While she was just able to keep herself from fearing the worst, not knowing was perhaps even more horrible.

Tierenan had been following Faria at some distance, making sure she was safe. He felt in some small way responsible for her grief by being so optimistic early in the journey. But then, hope wasn't a bad thing to hold onto, even at the most desperate of times. He had tried approaching her with words of comfort but lost them whenever he drew near, her penetrating sadness so deep he feared anything he said would simply disappear, and she would withdraw even further.

In the early morning darkness, the torches in the corridors burning faintly to their wooden stock, he finally approached the young vixen. She was leant against an open window's stone pillar, feeling the cold wind ripple through her fur. She didn't react upon his approach, saying nothing, staring distantly at the night.

He pulled at his claws awkwardly. "F… Faria, I'm…"

"I'm sorry I took you away from Skyria," she said sombrely, now looking halfway between the window and him, fixed on neither. Her eyes were tainted with a deep, cold loneliness.

He pulled his fist to his chest, as if trying to mould his feelings into something tangible. "No, *you* shouldn't be sorry," he cried. "I was just..." He fell into silence, looking about awkwardly.

"You don't have anything to be sorry for," she whispered. She looked back out to the window. "I wouldn't have seen him at all if it weren't for your help. I'm... really grateful." She clutched her father's pendant tightly at her chest. "Once this is over... I'll take you back to Skyria, I promise."

He felt so incredibly small stood next to her. He bit one of his claws to suppress his welling emotions. Desperately, he wanted to tell her that everything would be all right...but he knew it wasn't true. He'd never known such sadness as this before, that complete loss of hope.

Slowly, he turned to leave. A gentle, almost faint hand on his shoulder stopped him. Faria wiped away her tears and swallowed her cracking voice.

"Tierenan, could you stay with me? I mean, if you don't mind..."

A wave of relief showered him. Although trapped underneath the exhausting burden of loneliness and the legacy of Nazreal, he could see Faria, herself, still struggling through. She was immeasurably strong. He gave her a proud smile and leant on the window next to her, looking over the torches lighting the city streets and at the shining silver moon above them, casting soft white beams through the passing clouds.

"The moon looks fantastic tonight," he said quietly.

She nodded. "Yes…" She paused, stroking her pendant thoughtfully. "You know… the crystals in my Father's staff came from there."

He gave her an incredulous look. "You went all the way up there? How did you do *that*?"

She let out a quiet laugh. "Heh, no, we didn't go up. They came down. They all did…"

The sun rose behind the overcast skies; the ashen clouds were a grim promise of the day to come. Not long after light, the sentries on the north gate blasted their trumpets, the sound echoing desolately through the landscape's trembling silence.

An army was approaching.

A Xayall sentry, a bearcat, sprinted to Faria and knelt before her. "Your Imperial Highness, we have a large convoy approaching the city."

She gave him a suspicious regard. "Not the Dhrakans?"

He shook his head.

"Open the gates," she commanded.

The guards took their positions throughout the city. Faria, Osiris, Aeryn and Tierenan stood at the base of the steps in front of the Tor with two rows of Imperial guards stationed in formation on either side of them.

The huge wooden barriers drifted open with a low rumble, and the approaching force ahead of them drilled into motion as a spearhead aimed at the city's heart.

A huge train of soldiers in gleaming white and silver armour marched staunchly through, their rumbling footsteps resounding powerfully throughout the crippled city: the Andarn army. Among them were carried great stacks of wooden stakes for mounting barricades, and long, Theriasaur-drawn carriages for transporting the wounded.

The four of them stood, amazed at the approaching procession. At its head was Alaris, and proudly flanking him were Kier and a stiffly-walking Bayer, still suffering from his injuries. As soon as she saw them Faria wanted to rush up and embrace them, but reluctantly held herself to the ground. She was now head of state; she had to retain dignity in front of the Andarn soldiers.

"There are two whole battalions there…" Aeryn said quietly.

Osiris smiled. "Aidan was always good at pulling favours, too."

The Andarn army reached the gates of the plaza and, with Alaris' raised arm, came to a thunderous halt. He, Kier and Bayer marched forward.

The pangolin, dressed now in his full suit of armour including a sleek, articulated helmet and specially-made gauntlets, bowed respectfully in front of Faria, lowering himself to one knee. Kier and Bayer did the same.

"Your Imperial Highness, I have been asked to bring relief and protection to your city," Alaris said in a formal yet kind address. "I trust it will be accepted."

She let out a calming breath. "Yes, Captain Alaris. Xayall thanks you for your assistance."

Alaris stood up and smiled. "Then we shall get to work. I'm glad to see you made it safely home."

His words, although purely well-meant, stirred in her emotions she had worked hard to repress. "I, er... we encountered some difficulties. The... the Emperor..." She took in a deep breath and clenched her fists, looking anywhere for something to focus her attention on. She couldn't look at her family's bodyguards, without whom she wouldn't even be there to address them. She felt she'd disappointed them. Eventually, she looked down to her empty hands. "The Emperor is dead. His interment is today," she said, her voice barely a whisper.

Kier and Bayer both stood up, shock flooding their bodies like icy water. Kier remained silent, looking at the ground by Faria's feet. Bayer stared blankly ahead, eyes wide with painful realisation.

"I'm... glad we've not missed it," he said quietly. He looked to Faria, saddened but holding his warrior's pride. "His Imperial Majesty was always an inspiration. It has been an honour serving him. I hope to continue my service protecting you, if you so wish."

Faria nodded, keeping her jaws tightly shut to stop a cry bursting from her throat. After a deep sigh, she calmed herself. "Thank you, Bayer. I'm so glad you managed to escape."

Bayer gave a slight smile. "Thanks in no small part to yourself, Your Highness—your storm of splinters and dust clogged the crossbow's gears. After that, it was my best fortune that Kier broke through the siege. He took me to Andarn, where I was able to rest."

Kier bowed his head humbly, although started when Alaris gave him a pat on the shoulder and shoved him forwards. "It was his efforts that exposed the Dhrakan's counterfeit dispatch, raised the alarm and brought our army to you."

Faria stepped towards Kier and took his hand. He blushed, taken aback.

"Thank you for protecting us, Kier. I'll forever be in your debt for rescuing Bayer, and for serving Xayall, me, and my Father so well." She smiled gratefully, although her eyes still flowed with wistful sadness. "He'd... he'd be so thankful to you, I know it."

Kier nodded respectfully. "Thank you, Your Highness. My duty to you and your family is my greatest honour."

Alaris gave a smart salute and bowed his head in reverence to Faria. "We'll leave you to your preparations, Your Imperial Highness. I'll have my soldiers attend the ceremony."

"Thank you, Alaris," she said quietly.

Only a few short hours later, Faria was standing on the path to the mausoleum in a long black gown, Osiris by her side. Behind her was the large silver casket that carried her father, laid on a beautiful funeral bier. The metal coffin was adorned with golden wings and leafy borders, a large fox head symbol on its lid. She hadn't looked at the casket for long; the knowledge that her father was sealed within it terrified her. On either side of her stood the troops from Xayall and Andarn, each respectfully silent, and behind the coffin were Kier, Bayer and the members of Xayall's governing council,

Aidan having no family other than Faria. She realised, painfully, that she was all that remained.

The clouds continued to roll impassively overhead. A voice called softly from behind her, belonging to the High Councillor conducting the service.

"Your Imperial Highness, we haven't much time. Shall we begin?"

She looked to Osiris. The gryphon's steely gaze was fixed on the building ahead. Slowly, she took a step, and the parade behind followed at her steady pace. She barely noticed the soldiers saluting their weapons on either side of her. Each step closer to the mausoleum filled her with increasing trepidation that this wasn't right, that they'd made a mistake. He should be here. He shouldn't have to be buried.

She caught sight of Tierenan and Aeryn in the row at the front when they reached the courtyard before the mausoleum. Tierenan was crying; he confessed that he'd never been to a funeral before. The tears clung to his metal claws as he brushed them away, cursing at himself for getting so emotional. Faria was grateful to him for being able to express what ceremony was currently forbidding her.

Aeryn laid a reassuring hand on his shoulder. "Don't be ashamed, Tierenan. Funerals aren't for the dead, they're for those left behind."

He nodded tearfully, unable to tell her he was crying for Faria anyway.

As Faria ascended the steps and reached the door of the Mausoleum, she, Osiris, Kier and Bayer flanked the threshold as the pallbearers slid the casket from the bier and marched up to the chamber. Once inside, they manoeuvred the coffin into position over a stone sarcophagus, carved with beautiful designs of animal deities and the Xayall emblem at its centre, with Aidan's name at its heart.

Seeing his life, his body, turned into just a name on a stone carving made her want to crumple at the injustice. She wanted to rip the coffin apart and shout her father's body into life again, telling him how much she loved him, how much she still needed him. But with the rumbling seal of the sarcophagus' stone lid, so went the sealing of her final hope. The pallbearers left silently, and behind her the High Councillor began reading a speech. She knelt in front of the stone tomb. On either side of her, in further chambers, were other members of the Imperial family. Aidan had been buried next to Kaya, her mother. It was a comfort to Faria in some small way, knowing how much he must have missed her.

She felt Osiris kneel next to her. His head was bowed, his eyes closed. She wondered if he too was holding his emotions in check, or whether years of life had hardened him against such losses. They both said nothing for a time, while behind them the High Councillor's speech continued, echoing in the courtyard.

"Faria... I'm sorry I couldn't tell you about your father, and Nazreal..." the gryphon said solemnly.

"It's all right," she breathed. "It must have been hard to carry that secret with you... for you both."

He looked at the sarcophagus, watching it as if the images engraved on it were moving in their tableau. "I didn't want you to think less of Aidan. He wasn't a murderer."

She wrung her hands. "I know..."

His head bowed again. He sighed mutely.

"Osiris… I don't know what I should do," she said quietly, looking to the floor.

He opened his eyes. "What do you want to do?"

She almost thought he had been expecting her question. She wrung her hands, clenching them into a ball in front of her. What she wanted and what she knew she had to do were two independent concepts, not pulling against each other but not mixing. The gap left by her father's death pressed a permanent coldness to her body. She thought about the fight her father had put up against Raikali, even when he was so close to death.

The lioness' grim visage appeared in her mind. *She* was responsible for it all, not her father, who had only wanted to help the world and all who lived in it. She looked at the sarcophagus in front of her, the stone carvings echoing faintly of his memory. He would have liked it.

"I want…"

Outside, Alaris turned to his soldiers and raised his arm.

"Andarn, a salute for the Emperor of Xayall!"

In response, the troops of Andarn raised their spears high and let out a great, roaring cheer, once, twice, three times. Faria felt the strength in their voices, a strength she feared she would never hold herself.

"I want to stop Raikali. I want to keep her from Nazreal. I want…" she looked to the ceiling of the Mausoleum, on which were paintings of Eeres and depictions of the starry heavens above them. "…to protect the world."

Osiris nodded, then turned to her and bowed his head. "Then that is your answer," he said kindly. "Aidan… was the closest friend I had." His usually piercing eyes were misty with sadness. "I met him when he was young, and even though we shared relatively little time together I have always carried my friendship with him as my greatest possession. I believe in his spirit, which I have already seen in you." He looked to her. "Faria, I swear to protect you and fight for your world as long as I live. You are the future of Eeres."

She looked out to the courtyard. The service had finished, and in the doorway stood Aeryn, Tierenan, Kier and Bayer. They all looked to her.

"Thank you, Osiris," she said tearfully. "Kier," she moved to the fox; he jumped at her address.

"Yes, Faria?" he said, a little flustered, forgetting to call her by her title and looking panicked at having done so.

"I want you and Bayer to take the civilians out of the city. I don't want them caught in the battle."

He responded after a pause, "Yes, Your Highness." She could tell that he almost refused. "But will you have enough soldiers? You'll need all the fighters you can spare, and you'll be at most risk above all others. I'll gladly fight with them to protect you."

She shook her head, slowly learning the authority of her position, fuelled by Osiris' pledge. "Even a victory won't mean anything if Xayall doesn't survive. The buildings can be rebuilt, but its citizens can't. Please, Kier, Bayer."

Bayer hung his head. He knew his injuries were holding him back. He wanted desperately to stay but, if he admitted it, it would only result in his further injury, and loss of the lives he wanted to protect. He stood as tall as he could to address her.

"We shall guard them with our lives, Your Imperial Highness."

They turned and descended the steps. She looked to Aeryn and Tierenan, a little awkwardly. She didn't want to see them hurt, but knew they wouldn't be bound by Imperial duty to carry out her order.

"You can go too, if you want," she said, not looking as if she wanted them to leave at all. "I can have someone take you back to Andarn—"

"I'm staying," Tierenan whistled, smiling once again. "I've helped you this far; it wouldn't be fair if I didn't stay to the end."

Aeryn nodded. "I'll stay too." She stepped forwards and knelt in front of the young fox. "Thank you for choosing us as your guards, Faria. I can think of no-one more deserving to rule, nor one more honourable to serve. And I mean that as a soldier," she smiled as she took Faria's hand, "and a friend."

Ignoring ceremony, Faria hugged Aeryn. Eager not to be left out, Tierenan jumped in too, causing the three of them to sway violently and almost topple down the stairs. They broke apart, still standing close to each other.

"I know Kyru would say the same if he were here," Aeryn said.

"Bet he wouldn't join in the group hug, though," Tierenan muttered, giving Faria a nudge with his elbow. She allowed herself a smile as she looked to the wolf.

"We'll find him, I know we will."

A clattering of armour rang in the tomb. Sprinting up the steps in anxious haste came a coati scout.

"Your Imperial Highness, the Gargantua is approaching the city!"

Chapter Twenty-Four

A deafening rumble pounded the air, a relentless thunder that rolled ever closer as the black shape charged towards the city. The Gargantua's huge caterpillar tracks crushed trees to splinters. Pillars of black smoke spewed from its walls, choking the sky. The mechanical pyramid's snaking trail of destruction through the forest left nothing but dust and shattered ground in its wake. Ahead lay Xayall, visible above the canopy, a contemptuous symbol for the Dhraka to aim for. The fires inside the machine burnt furiously for its annihilation. With deadly precision, four massive cannons spiralled from the upper portion of the black pyramid and locked into place, the city sighted along its rifled barrels.

The soldiers on Xayall's walls watched the hulking machine's approach. Weapons firmly in their grasp, they prepared to repel the dragons that would fly against them. Aeryn was on a rooftop by the walls, leading a section of archers. In front of them was a staunch row of wooden shields they could shelter behind, currently holding thousands of arrows to be loosed into the fray.

She tightened her grip on her bow, her mind still racing with thoughts of Kyru. They had to beat the Dhrakans if she had any hope of finding him again. For them to retreat would mean to lose him forever. She would face the onslaught and dive into the Gargantua herself if it meant she could rescue him.

A thunderous explosion sounded in the distance. The soldiers tensed in alarm.

Flashes of black shot across the sky; a rain of cannonballs stormed through the air and slammed into the city, punching holes in buildings, fracturing stone. The archers leapt behind the shields, two of which shattered in the projectiles' impact, showering those behind with piercing shards of wood. Several soldiers were blasted from the walls, their armour no match for the missiles' solid iron blow. The remaining troops looked to each other nervously; their ranks began drifting into disarray.

Alaris, holding firm on the north-west wall, gave a sharp command.

"Open order until the ship nears the walls! Stand ready!" he bellowed.

Aeryn turned to her block of archers and raised her bow. "Archers, ready! Take aim at the boarding platforms!"

The black machine roared as it drew closer, like a demon raging to its prey. Xayall braced itself. The cannons fired again, their iron hail once more pounding into the city's defences. The battle had begun.

The maps twitched nervously in the breeze in the Tor's grim war room. Faria had been taken downstairs to be placed in her armour; she was due to return soon. Tierenan had stayed behind to guard the room, being left alone. He ran his hand along the table's smooth surface, pouring over the hastily-scribbled diagrams strewn across the oaken platform.

A high whistle alerted him. Tikku swooped in through the balcony and circled his head before landing on the table, hopping between the papers, inspecting them curiously.

"I wondered where you were. It's about to get danger-ous," he said quietly, gently scooping the bird into his hands. "You should fly somewhere safe."

The bird let out a panicked chirrup and pushed against his claws with its wings. A flicker of electricity sparked from it. Tierenan yelped and released his grip; the bird swept round him in an arc and landed back on the table, scanning the documents more quickly. Tierenan went for it again; it leapt over his hand and dove towards his face, claws reaching for his eye.

"What are you doing?" he cried, swatting it with a heavy backhand. The bird hit the table with a thud, scrambled around and righted itself. It froze for a few seconds—he leapt on it and held it tightly. The lenses in its eyes flickered, tiny whirs and clicks streamed from its head. Then, in a garbled, tinny voice, it whispered:

"*Kill me.*"

Tierenan froze. "What?"

"*Last chance to help you. I betrayed once, no time. Had to save you from Gargantua. Followed you since first siege.*"

"You... you were tracking me..."

"*Knew your movements. They know everything. It was you they followed, through me. I'm sorry. Kill me.*"

"They followed me… but I thought Faria broke-"

The bird let out a burst of electricity; Tierenan could see his hands closing tighter and tighter around the bird's tiny body.

"Stop it! Tikku, stop it!"

Faria burst in with four guards, her protectors designated by Osiris. Over her black robes she now wore a metal breastplate, vambraces and shin armour.

"Tierenan, what's wrong?"

"Faria, help, I can't stop! Tikku, he's-"

With a splintering crack, the bird's body split apart, tiny shards of emerald scattering across the floor. The clicks and whirs died, and the bird's eyes stopped moving.

Faria's hand shot to her mouth. "Tierenan, what have you done?"

Tierenan stood, frozen in shock.

"Faria…" the raccoon said weakly.

The booms of the cannons rumbled in the distance. The Gargantua was almost at the walls.

"Faria… I've betrayed you."

The Gargantua's cannons rained their devastating blows into the city. Buildings exploded in clouds of brick, wood and dust. The soldiers were helpless against the machine's impenetrable armour. Its mechanical stench billowed out before it. It rammed forwards, churning the ground, almost by the river's edge.

Alaris raised his huge, double-handed sword.

"Close ranks! Prepare to engage!" he bellowed.

The Gargantua lurched forwards, breaching the river. The defenders took hold of their spears and shields, gritting their teeth, bracing for impact.

The monster touched the hillside under Xayall's walls.

Suddenly, an explosion from underneath the leviathan's tracks scattered searing-hot metal far into the trees; the whole pyramid rocked violently with the force of the blast. The Coriolis, hiding in wait further down the river behind the city, swayed in the water, its bowsprit, now in two rail-connected halves, pushed out to the width of its hull. The split metal pole steamed, glowing bright red. The water around the ship hissed with its radiating heat.

Osiris gave a triumphant cry where he was stood on the bridge and punched the air. The railgun still worked.

The Gargantua's rear engines fumed and growled as it fruitlessly tried to continue its ruinous drive ahead, pushing its shattered, melted front tracks deeper into the river and muddy hillside.

"We've halted their advance!" Osiris yelled into the communication funnel. "Get ready for immediate take-off! Prepare the gun decks!"

The pyramid's huge black doors shuddered and slid open. From its sinister darkness came the ferocious howls of the Dhrakan soldiers standing aboard the hulking crescent platforms. Immediately upon seeing the Xayall and Andarn guard before them, hundreds of winged monsters took to the skies, screeching hungrily.

"Archers, shoot!"

Aeryn's order was followed immediately. A storm of arrows shrieked through the air and pierced the bodies of the Dhrakan vanguard. The archers reloaded quickly, the crossbow snipers at the front picking off the airborne menaces while the longbows kept the infantry under a constant hail of arrows. She loaded her bow with lethal efficiency and loosed an armour-piercing arrow straight into the jaw of a dragon diving for the archery line. It plummeted onto the street below. She drew another arrow from her quiver and shot again, hitting another directly in the heart.

More Dhrakans poured from the vast hold, even more crazed than those in front. The metal boarding platforms rumbled forwards, pushing onto the outer walls of the city and breaking the battlements like they were old chalk. The Dhrakan foot soldiers began their violent assault, swinging their blades wildly at the necks of their enemies.

Alaris' spear block held its points at the invaders; some dragons were pushed to their impalement by the bloodthirsty rage of those behind. The polearms stabbed, thrust and ripped at the ones attacking from the sky. The Andarn pikes were a strong, brave defence that kept their wielders well-protected and their attackers wounded. In a matter of seconds, though, the battlements were close to over-run. Clashing metal and screaming voices saturated the air above the ominous drone of the Gargantua.

"What do you mean?" Faria asked, her tone darkening. The blood rose in her veins as the noises of war crept into her ears, the struggle on the battlements already resounding in the Tor. The soldiers rushed to the balcony, arming themselves.

She kept her stern eyes on Tierenan. He gave her an apologetic look, then fixed a grave stare on Tikku.

"These birds… I remember them," he said solemnly. The tiny green creature twitched in Faria's hands. "The Dhrakans gave them to the captured children."

She watched it, concern creeping up her chest. "Tierenan, what are they?"

"They're machines that can control other machines. Tikku was the one that altered the Coriolis' navigation systems, and more than that…" He tightened his claw. Tierenan looked intently into Faria's eyes. "It's been following me ever since I left Dhraka. They can lift information from our heads. They're spies, Faria!"

For the first time, Faria saw his face darkened by anger, a deep contortion of resentment that frightened her to see him wear. "Even though you destroyed my control chip, he's followed and told them where we were every step of the way. It knows everything about our journey."

Faria stared at the bird. "That means…" she whispered.

He gritted his teeth. "They already know where Nazreal is!" He was shivering. "I'm sorry, Faria… I should have realised," he whispered. He looked down to the destroyed bird. His confidence was shattered. He had wanted nothing but to protect Faria, and for him to be taken advantage of so easily, he felt he too deserved to be lying in pieces on the floor. "I've betrayed you, everyone…" He looked to his claws, covered in tiny flakes of iridescent green metal. "I've been so stupid."

Faria straightened, looking out to the balcony. "No… it's not your fault," she said distantly. "They were coming here whether they had their answers or not. It was only a matter of time. All they need now… is me."

The sounds of battle were so much fiercer than those she still remembered from the first siege. She gripped the staff tightly and it glowed uneasily in her hand. Her father's pendant pulsed urgently on her neck.

The Coriolis burst into the sky behind the city and swept around the Tor in a wide arc, heading to broadside the Gargantua. It sailed opposite the black behemoth and opened fire. Shells ripped through the air, pounding the thick armour of the Dhrakan battleship.

The Andarn defenders tried desperately to stem the flow of dragons, to halt their advance into the city, although occupation was no longer the invaders' ambition. Instead, the brutal and complete massacre of anything that stood against them was their sole purpose. The flying monsters clawed at the Andarn troops' backs and swooped for the archers, their arrow reserves already running critically low. More were being winched to the rooftops by soldiers below, under attack themselves from opportunistic warriors broken free from the main fray. Aeryn impaled one lizard with a swift arrow shot. It lodged in its wing, sending it spiralling into a wall.

The Gargantua's cannons shifted upwards, the golden Coriolis now in their sights. With a terrifying burst they fired, missiles hurtling towards the flying ship. Osiris had seen the huge barrels move and steered the ship away just in time as the shots skimmed under the hull. A single shot from those cannons could critically destabilise the ship and bring it out of the sky. They had no shield to hide behind in the air, nor a surface to break their fall. He brought the ship around for another attack. They would have to circle the Gargantua to avoid its fire. As he watched the city sweep below, six more cannons spiralled from the Gargantua's other sides and faced the Coriolis...

Aeryn watched the ship climb away, glad it had escaped the cannons' wrath so far. Hundreds of dragon archers filed out of large doorways under the machine's massive ordnance platforms. Crossbows already loaded, they took aim at the soldiers below and loosed their bolts with devastating accuracy. Whole lines of defenders fell, allowing the encroaching Dhrakans to push even further. Aeryn raised her bow at them.

"Archers!" she roared, "Take down their crossbowmen! Protect the line!"

The archers responded willingly, loosing their next volley at the railing above. Some Dhrakans fell, but more remained. A few turned their attention now to Aeryn's block, trying to snipe at them behind the pavaises. As the two units exchanged shots and scored equal numbers dead, she saw something amongst the Dhrakan crush on the walls. A flash of grey through the scales and blades. Her heart jumped.

A heavy bolt thundered into the shield by her face. She growled and loosed an arrow into the offending dragon's stomach, then scanned the battle for that same streak of fur. Had he escaped?

Suddenly, a scream from the support group below ripped through her. She darted to the edge to see, drawing her bow, and—

Kyru.

Clad in black Dhrakan armour he sliced through the guards with twin swords, a blur of speed and agility with frightening skill. He pushed through the spearmen with terrifying ease and sprinted up the street towards the Tor. She watched after him, rage churning inside her, not at him but at Vionaika's manipulation against his will and honour. She grabbed the winch rope to leap to the ground when a crossbow bolt ploughed into her right shoulder armour, grazing her arm. She staggered back and tore it free of the metal. On the street, the baneful hyena whirled away with a sardonic grin, following Kyru along the street. Aeryn growled viciously, again taking hold of the rope and descending to the street.

"Take command and keep supplying the archers!" she yelled to the captain as she sprinted after Kyru.

Faria dug her claws into the balcony railing. Even with only four soldiers protecting her she felt she was denying the defenders of valuable troops, and for her to be apart from the fight felt even more a condemnation of their hopes. She could do so much with her resonance. The Coriolis' railgun had thwarted the Gargantua's movement but the Dhrakans were still formidable in their numbers. Tierenan watched beside her. She could tell he felt the same as he tapped his claws agitatedly on the stone, his eyes fixed with grim observance.

Aeryn coursed through the streets, Vionaika and Kyru some way ahead. She could smell the vile hyena under the smoke and steel. The Tor lay ahead, its doors barred firmly shut by huge wooden barricades. She tried to steady her bow to take aim at the hybrid's neck as she ran, but the pounding of her feet on the paved roads jostled her too greatly. She stopped, the hyena in her sights. Opening the bow to full draw, something crashed into her back. Her arrow ricocheted off the ground and broke, spinning into the air. A dragon with huge knuckle-dusters faced her as she leapt back to her feet. She dropped her bow, drawing her sword with vicious rage.

"I don't have time for you!"

The dragon cackled and leapt forwards. She rolled under his outstretched fists and drew her blade across his unprotected abdomen in a deep slash. He screeched and tumbled forwards, clutching his entrails. As he writhed, more Dhrakans flew low overhead. She snatched her bow from the stones and sprinted onwards.

The Tor's guards readied their spears upon seeing Kyru approach. The wolf leapt high into the air, parrying the spear points that marked him, and thrust his swords into the helmets of two of the guards. His two blades swept through the air and slashed the neck of the one next to him while on the other side the guard was met with a brutal kick. The Dhrakans that swooped overhead landed and began assaulting the other soldiers.

Vionaika stopped at the plaza threshold, pulling a large bolt tipped with an oily mass of cloth from a holster on her back and loading it onto the bow. Taking a smouldering match cord from her belt, she lit the wad. The oil burst alight with a roar. A second later she pulled the trigger and the bolt flew at the door, flames rippling from the blazing head. The burning cloth split as it hit the wood; its powdered interior mixed with the blazing oil and a violent white explosion shattered the entrance. With the soldiers occupied she ran inside, closely followed by Kyru. Aeryn arrived to see them enter the breach and dived in after them.

Faria and Tierenan felt the explosion at the base of the tower. Two of the soldiers by the balcony turned and ran into the corridor. The others stood on guard, weapons ready. Her staff pulsed in warning.

Outside, the Coriolis' circling of the Gargantua rendered the ship's valiant defensive efforts useless. The hulking black cannons had the shining galleon constantly on the move. Osiris couldn't find a safe point to let the carrack's guns hit their marks and give cover to the Xayall soldiers. Dhrakans still poured from the pyramid, their numbers dwindling but still clashing forwards with a full army's strength. He looked ahead to the bowsprit, which had folded back into its usual shape.

"Prepare the railgun for a second shot!" he bellowed. "We're going to fire it right at the reactor!"

Jala's concerned voice echoed through the tube. "We're running short on fuel, Osiris. Are you sure we can manage it?"

Osiris pulled the ship violently upwards; a cannonball hurtled between the mast and the sterncastle. "*Manage?*" he hissed. "Do you understand the consequences if we lose? We'll be dead if we don't destroy it!"

"Yes, Osiris, sir."

On the upper gun deck, six of the crew hauled one of the massive metal rods from under the storage rack and held it to the delivery tube under the bowsprit. The bow clanked and whirred, the angular mast at its head tilted down and separated to a space a little wider than one of the ammunition rods. Nestled in its two halves were rows of semi-circular electro-magnets. Buffer rails extended sideways from underneath the bowsprit at each end to cushion the outward force caused by the projectile's release. The crew didn't load it yet; the Coriolis needed to be in position, and the captain would need to give the order.

Osiris cracked his shoulders, gripping the wheel of his beloved ship tightly in his claws. "We can do this…"

Faria peered over the balcony's edge to see the fighting at the base of the Tor. She couldn't see clearly the events, aside from the rushed clamour and frantic movement of fighting. The two soldiers who left hadn't yet returned. The other two stood resolutely by her, Tierenan as well, although he wandered from door to balcony in a tense, nervous patrol.

Suddenly there came armoured footsteps in the corridor. The soldiers readied their weapons. A second later the door burst open and twin blades were upon them, stained with the blood of their companions, hilts held in a death-like grip by the frenzied Kyru. He tore and slashed, their blades barely able to keep up with his.

"Kyru, stop!" Faria yelled. Quickly, she raked the staff's edge on the floor. A fountain of stone moulded from the wall and made to catch him. He was too fast—he ducked underneath and leapt up into a soldier's chest, punching the wind from him and bowling him to the floor. He stood on the breastplate of his disabled foe and turned to the other, slashing wildly. Tierenan shot out his claw to stay the wolf's hand but in a flash something whistled from the door and deflected his aim. Vionaika ripped back the lever on her repeating crossbow and shot another bolt straight for his head. He ducked away and lunged forwards, but she swiped the crossbow's stave into his stomach, sending him staggering back.

A small hatch opened at the top of the Gargantua. A black figure strode through it and observed the battle below. She flexed her claws and leapt into the air, blue-green orbs of crystal forming from her palms.

Faria pointed her staff at Vionaika and charged the energy in its tip. Tiny sparks danced over the crystal's edge, growing rapidly larger. A second later a streak of electricity spat from the staff, straight at the hybrid. It missed its mark, however: the hyena's metal crossbow stave diverted the arc and the lightning cracked into the wall-mounted torch, which exploded in a crash of embers and brick-dust. The hyena shot another bolt at Faria. A tornado-like gust of wind swirled around the fox, flinging the dart against the wall. Vionaika reloaded for another shot when an arrow struck the wood on her crossbow, almost knocking it from her hand. She twisted the arrow out with a grim scowl.

Aeryn, bow loaded, aimed it at the hyena's head. Just as her fingers were slipping from the string Vionaika dived away, leaving Kyru in the wolf's sights. She realised too late, and punched her bow desperately upwards. The bow's lower limb caught the arrow shaft, flicking it clear of her former companion. Kyru saw her; he punched the closest soldier unconscious and began a death run to her, salivating madly. She made a grasp for her sword but he was upon her too quickly. She dropped her bow and grabbed his wrists, his mania-induced strength pinning her against the wall.

"Kyru!" she cried. "Kyru, stop! It's me!"

The purple crystal on Vionaika's forehead glinted with satisfaction, her eyes awake with the thought of spilling

Aeryn's blood. "He won't hear you!" she cackled. "He is mine now, and soon you will be no-one's."

Faria slashed her staff at hyena's legs. Vionaika dodged, and as the staff hit the floor Faria noticed an unfamiliar, ominous whine. To her right she saw a blue-green line creeping around the edge of the room, snaking between the bricks. It spread from behind her in both directions, looping around the room. Vionaika saw too and dived to the floor.

"Get down!" Faria shouted. Tierenan dropped to the stone; she ducked behind a chair. Aeryn swept Kyru's legs out from under him with a powerful kick and they both crashed to the ground.

Instants later, rays of blue light streamed from the lines, slicing through the air and dust like a huge blade. In a shrieking explosion that pushed Faria hard against the floor, the whole section of the Tor that lay above them split and shattered, sending rubble crashing down to the streets below. Splinters of stone, curtain, metal, glass and wood rained on the amputated war room. Faria pulled herself up, shaking from the impact of the rupture. Dust cloaked the area; she could barely see the sky. Through the fog of devastation, a dark shape flew towards them. She felt a deep coldness in her chest.

Raikali flexed her claws again. The blue-green orbs disappeared from her palms and she pushed herself towards the dismembered Tor, her armour's blue-flamed engines roaring at her back.

Tierenan punched his right fist into his open palm, a threatening growl rumbling in his throat. He and Faria glared at Raikali as she swooped to the wall's edge.

"The disgusting Arc'hantael lineage," the black lioness seethed. "Time to destroy the last of it."

Faria flew into a rage. She swung her staff at the macabre Raikali, whose engine bursts lifted her effortlessly free. The more she avoided the attacks, the fiercer Faria became. She launched ice splinters, hurled lightning arcs and cast whirlwinds at her, revenge for her father's death the forefront in her mind. Tierenan's punches and violent grabs at the lion's legs missed every time. Faria could see only the dark shape ahead of her, gloating, just out of reach.

"I won't let you live!" she screamed, melting a collapsed suit of armour into red-hot pellets that she launched at Raikali. "You killed my father! You corrupted Nazreal! You razed Xayall!"

Raikali drew back her claws, ready for a diving strike. Faria's staff quivered as a deeper blue light rippled under the crystal's surface. "I'll tear you from the sky!"

Osiris slammed the control wheel upwards. The ship's bow descended, pointing straight at the heart of the Gargantua.

"Load the railgun!"

The crew below hurled the metal rod into the delivery chute and slammed it shut. The chamber folded into the ceiling and the bowsprit's halves surged with lightning. Ladders of electricity flicked up its length, growing thicker and more powerful. The whining hum of the gun's charge rose above the noise of the engines. For a moment, that was the only sound that filled the gryphon's ears, and then—

At the touch of the trigger the white-hot iron rod burst from the railgun's barrel, followed by the piercing shriek of its launch and the sonic boom of its flight. The bowsprit halves cannoned outwards with the force of the blast, glowing red hot. Twisting in the air as it flew, the rod pierced the Gargantua's armour as if it were paper. It struck the reactor with a glancing blow, destroying two support columns and rupturing one of the secondary reactors on the periphery. The machinery underneath buckled and split apart, the molten wound above triggering fires and explosions in its wake. The reactor blistered with searing hot metal; immediately a dirty grey liquid spewed from a pipe above it, flooding the radioactive heart and stripping it of its power, along with the rest of the fortress. The machinery ground to a halt. One final, mechanical screech marked the Gargantua's ultimate death as the pillars supporting the internal structure buckled, destroyed by the railgun, the floors inside twisting and breaking in a devastating haemorrhage of distorted metal.

The explosion stunned the battlefield. Dhrakans turned to their dying fortress to see their brethren spilling out in fear, wounded and gasping for breath. Seeking their moment, the defending officers signalled the command to push back, and the combined forces of Xayall and Andarn began forcing back the confused and startled Dhrakan attackers. The Coriolis was slowly sinking in the air, the power used to fire the railgun a huge drain from its engines. Osiris kept hammering levers to pump new life into it, but he was unable to slow the ship as it drifted and groaned ever nearer to the city below.

At the Gargantua's pinnacle, he noticed something move. The peak swung open and a small rotor-propelled craft lifted into the sky, heading swiftly for the Tor. To his horror he saw the decapitated tower and bellowed down the communications funnel.

"Get the power back! *Get the power back!*"

Raikali drove her body into Faria in a thundering shoulder barge, sending her sprawling against the wall. She hit her head hard, a painful shock rippling through her body. Her staff spun to the floor. Tierenan leapt for the lioness; she caught his head in her claw, digging the sharp talons into his scalp. Faria tried to move but an instant later she found herself pinned against the brick by Raikali's piercing talons. Vionaika grabbed the staff triumphantly.

"Let her go!" Tierenan yelled, swinging for his captor. Although his attacks struck with futile force, she was not amused.

"Pathetic creature. You betray me with such disgusting ignorance."

He gave her a pained, sardonic glower. "My betrayal's better than yours. You tried to enslave the world."

Her face contorted with anger. "Filth!" she hissed.

Faria pulled frantically at the claws holding her to the wall, trying to free herself. She sliced her palms on their razor edges but remained trapped, condemned to watch the torture in front of her. Blood trickled down Tierenan's head where the claws pressed into his skin.

Raikali stood reviled at his defiance. "I won't even take pleasure in killing you, pitiful disgrace."

"I'd rather die than live in your shadow," he spat. "You tortured all those children. You made me betray Faria! You should be torn to shreds!"

She paused, contemplating his features. "And to think you had such promise."

Tierenan looked quickly to Faria, his eyes wide. "Faria, don't give up! You mustn't let her—"

Raikali's claws extended, punching through his head. Blood spilt onto the floor. Tears of horror fell from Faria's eyes as the lioness' talons retracted, dropping the limp Tierenan to the ground.

"Tierenan!" she screamed. "Tierenan, no!"

The dull throb of rotor blades hit the air. The Gargantua's small scout ship hovered by the Tor's edge. A door kicked open. Fulkore stood menacingly at its threshold.

"Get in," he growled. "The Gargantua's crippled. We have to leave."

Raikali gave a derisive scoff. "Fine." She gestured to Vionaika, who pulled a small cloth from a pouch on her belt. She scooped out a handful of shimmering purple dust from it and threw it viciously at Faria's face. Her limbs seized up. She tried with all her strength to leap down and tear Raikali's throat from her body but her arms and legs remained unmoving. Faria let out a stifled, raging growl, glaring furiously at her captor. Raikali ignored her, grabbed her forcefully and strode to the ship. Behind them, Kyru rose to his feet and followed Vionaika obediently on board. His movement stirred Aeryn. She sat up, the world in a blur, and looked around.

"Faria?" she groaned. She saw the fox being hauled onto the small ship, desperation pouring from her eyes, and stood up just as the door slammed shut.

"No!" She jumped forwards but the ship had already pulled too far away to jump to, and burst away over the trees to the east. She staggered forwards, her eyes shifting to Tierenan's mangled body. He was still breathing, although only just. In the cityscape ahead, the Coriolis struggled towards them. It looked like it would disappear over them, as it was beginning to pick up speed. Quickly, she dived for her bow and drew an arrow onto it, then loosed it towards the bridge.

Osiris saw the arrow sweep past the glass; he turned to see Aeryn standing over Tierenan. The colour fell from his face.

The ship swooped low over the Tor. Maaka and Osiris leapt out, the falcon attending straight to Tierenan's wounds.

"We can still catch them," Aeryn said resolutely to the gryphon, gripping her bow tightly, watching the black machine in the distance.

Osiris watched it too, his steely gaze burning with wrath. "We won't have another chance. If we don't stop them, Raikali will get what she wants."

She looked to Tierenan, brimming with anger-fuelled determination. "I have no intention of returning if we fail," she said quietly.

"That makes two of us."

He took hold of her and leapt skywards, opening his wings and flying onto the Coriolis' deck. Seconds later the ship rumbled away.

Chapter Twenty-Five

The black escape ship shuddered relentlessly over the trees, its heading plain.

Faria looked about anxiously. The ship had high metal sides with tiny, dingy windows and an open roof. The wind roared overhead, its biting cold stinging her ears. Kyru stood by her, an unwavering guard in a most unwelcome sense. His wide, unblinking eyes were glazed and bloodshot. His mouth hung open, breath rasping from his throat. Opposite her stood the despicable Vionaika, the staff a hostage within her grasp.

Tierenan's shattered, bloodied body haunted Faria's vision. She tried to shake it from her sight but his grievous and torturously undeserved fate burned at her heart. Raikali, the tormenting malefactor of these images and those of her father's past was by Fulkore at the controls. Faria's rage was strong enough to make her paralysed hand quiver with the will to strike the foul creature right through the head. She hated her for the scars she'd carved on the lives around her. She hated her for taking away the lives she loved, her father, her world, for decimating the sanctity of the planet.

Raikali's claws clicked impatiently on the thin hull. Fulkore bristled at her presence.

"This had better be right," he growled as they passed over the low, barren mountains that bordered Xayall at crushing speed. His battle armour appeared to make him even larger. A hulking axe with a long, serrated blade sat by his side.

"Arc'hantael would not be so misleading on his deathbed," she sneered. She shot a venomous leer at Faria, who glowered madly back. "Useless as he was."

Faria forced her mouth open an inch. "How dare you!" she hissed.

Raikali whirled round and strode towards her, bladed fingers at the fox's throat.

"How dare *I*?" she hacked. "*I* am going to restore this world to the glory that it was torn from by your miserable father!" She stroked one of the razor edges under Faria's chin. "His death a thousand times over would not be enough to quell the infernal pain he gave me. Even yours will be a mere shadow of satisfaction."

Faria glowered defiantly, straining away from the point cutting into her jaw. "You're nothing but a murderer," she scoffed.

Raikali leaned inwards, her face becoming even more sinister with a dark, quiet anger. "If I was, there would be nobody left alive," she whispered. "You survive for one task more, and the others are spared out of insignificance. It was only because your father foisted the staff on you that we had to pursue you. But since he became so pathetically impotent in his powers, it would always have ended up this way. I would be insulted to share in Arc'hantael's heritage if this was *my* destiny."

Both of Faria's hands were shaking now. Her eyes shone with unimaginable anger; so strong was her fierce glare that even Raikali felt the slightest apprehension toward the young vixen.

"I will stop you, as long as I have breath in my body," Faria gnarled through her clenched teeth.

The lioness turned away dismissively and walked to the front of the ship.

It hadn't even been an hour since they fled the battle, but too soon they broke free of the mountains and reached the open wasteland. Up ahead was the gigantic mesa, drawing near. The shadowy rock, almost a mile high, had never been scaled, and the terrain surrounding it was almost completely impassable, cut off by unusual swirling winds that buffeted the waste's borders and threw the grey dust around in a perpetual sandstorm. Nothing would grow on its sand, and it had long been abandoned to try building around or beyond it. For centuries nobody had questioned its existence as a sinister megalith at the base of Cadon, a silent sentinel over the world, watched nervously from a distance. Now its secret was known. Inside its jagged, sheer-edged shell, lay Nazreal.

The early evening sky was reddening behind the clouds, like a fire in the heavens. As the sun lowered beyond the horizon it cast the world into an ever-darkening, ever-warning shade of crimson. It was as if Eeres itself knew of the impending horrors waiting to rip the world apart once again.

The ship rocked and trembled as the winds ripped against its hull. As the immense rocky plateau smothered their view of anything else, Faria saw it as the approach of an incredible sleeping monster, soon to be awakened from its terrifying stillness.

Fulkore eyed the sands below suspiciously. "These winds aren't natural."

"One of Nazreal's remnant defence mechanisms," Raikali spat. "He wasn't lazy enough to believe the mountain would be left alone without dissuasion." She scanned through the coarse, swirling mists at the cliff face for signs of an entrance. Just visible below their flight line, by a small jut of rock, she saw a large, twisted steel plate embedded in the mesa wall and a narrow stairway leading to it from the desert floor.

"There!" she barked.

The winds still surging about them, the black craft drew dangerously close to the colossal wall of rock and hovered above the outcrop, which was just wide enough to support it. It touched down unsteadily, and the rotors whined to a halt. Raikali leapt out first, flexing her cable muscles as if to draw the ancient atmosphere into her body. Kyru threw Faria out of the hatch, straight into the mechanical lioness's claws. She grabbed the vixen by the scruff of the neck and thrust her at the torn metal plating in the wall. Even though distorted and beaten by years of artificial sandstorms, the ancient symbols and intricate carvings were still visible, albeit faded on its surface.

"This is part of Nazreal," Raikali said, bitterly. "This is the world's true destiny. And you are going to help me restore it."

"I'll never help you," Faria snarled.

Raikali let out a piercing, mocking laugh. "You have no concept of your powerlessness, child."

She strode ahead through a tall, tapering crevice with a footpath levelled at its base, Faria dangling from her claws. Vionaika and Kyru followed. Fulkore turned to the desert, axe slung over his shoulder. Just beyond the storm, he could see a golden shape in the sky, the same one he had seen so many times before. His eyes narrowed. A shiver of anticipation rippled through his body and his teeth glinted in a wicked, vicious grin.

"So, this will be our final reckoning…"

He turned and marched for Raikali.

The Coriolis was losing speed. Osiris fumed at the wheel as the fuel gauge stuttered and shivered its way down to the lowest possible level. An alarm bell rang behind him as the needle sank into the warning area.

"Damn it!"

The mesa was still far off, imposing despite the distance. He punched the throttle lever forwards and the engines roared weakly once more, a last-ditch sprint to catch up with Raikali. Aeryn stood next to him, itching to strike her blade through Vionaika's vile, gloating face. They both stared at the towering mesa with strengthened resolve.

"Faria won't make it easy for them," Aeryn said quietly, holding her sword firmly.

Osiris shook his head. "No. But we have to help her. Even with her abilities she can't hope to overcome so much alone."

A piercing rumble sounded in the depths of the Coriolis. The engines whined and spluttered, their fires exhausted.

Osiris ran to the console and pulled back on the wheel, lifting the ship to a slow, gliding descent to the sands. Unable to carry its desperate cargo any further, the Coriolis crashed into the desert and wedged itself in the dunes, listing woefully. Osiris and Aeryn jumped outside and onto the deck, shielding themselves from the battering sands.

Osiris flexed his wings. "We can still make it."

Aeryn slung her bow and quivers over her shoulder and climbed onto his back. The gryphon turned to his assembling crew.

"Follow us on foot! We'll give them everything we can to protect this world!"

They responded with a unanimous cry of support.

A resolute growl resounding in his throat, Osiris threw wide his wings and leapt skywards, swooping towards the outcrop and the metal that glinted through the storm in the red light of the sky, careful to make allowances in his movements for the buffeting wind.

At the end of the crevice, dug into the mesa's edge, stood two narrow doors about forty feet high. They were a bleak white-blue, but in the light glimmers of crystal could be caught rippling over them. As they approached it seemed to crawl over the doors' surface in waves. Faria couldn't tell if they were metal or stone. Their imposing height and thick construction was a forbidding message to anyone attempting to enter. Raikali handed Faria roughly to Kyru and approached the door, holding out the back of her right hand to stroke the air above the gate's surface. It buzzed with a strong, purposeful static energy. She withdrew upon sensing it.

"I thought so."

"What?" Vionaika asked impetuously. "This door shouldn't be too big for you to destroy."

Raikali glowered at her. "It isn't the door, fool! There's one last deterrent in place. This is where you'll actually come in useful, Vionaika."

The hyena looked sceptical. "What can I do against that?"

Raikali clamped her hand around Faria's arm and twisted her around like a rag doll to face the door. "Control her. Use her powers to open the door. I wouldn't be surprised if Arc'hantael had prepared the entire mesa to collapse if the lock opened incorrectly."

Vionaika looked reluctantly at Faria, then forced the staff into her hand. The hyena removed the crystal ribbon from her head and twisted it roughly around the fox's neck, uncaring of whether it might cut her. The purple gleam in her eyes strengthened as she began taking control of Faria's movements, although the strain of taking over two bodies at once was evident. Kyru began to sway; Faria's forced movements were unbalanced as Vionaika marched her to the door in robotic, mismatched steps. She tried desperately to resist the violent contortions pushing her body forwards against her volition. Her attempts to drop the staff were futile, as her fingers remained firmly curled around its shaft. It pulsed erratically, aware of her struggle but similarly helpless to resist.

The energy swirled around the door, then swept down the walls either side. To Faria, it felt like it stretched over the entire mesa, even laced into the storms surrounding them. At chest-height was an indentation over the crack between the huge gates, exactly the shape of her staff. Tiny pores of crystal lined the concave surfaces of the hollow. Gently but shakily, she pressed the staff into place. A brief glimmer of resonance energy spat from the weapon, but it instantly fell dormant again, Faria still holding it to the door's lock.

"What is it?" Raikali growled impatiently.

Vionaika looked around nervously. "I don't understand the mechanism. It's too complex."

Raikali wrenched the hyena by her shoulder and ripped the ribbon from Faria's neck, then crushed the crystal to dust between her palms. "Useless creature!" she rasped. Then, to the horror of both Faria and Vionaika, a green-blue mist erupted from Raikali's claws and wrapped around the terrified hyena's neck and shoulders. Vionaika croaked and gasped, quaking desperately. A channel of the resonance vapour streamed straight back into Raikali, who whirled round and slammed her crystal-covered palm against the back of Faria's head. Instantly the fox felt herself bracing for a massive explosion of energy. Seconds later, an arresting light bloomed in the stave and a huge web of crystal veins spread from the staff's centre. For a moment the blue streaks lit up the entire doorway. The wind behind them dissipated, dissolving the storms to a deathly stillness. The energy veiling the mesa vanished, and the doors became as lifeless as any normal stone.

Raikali sucked the blue mist back inside her shell, giving Vionaika a disdainful look as she fell to her knees, gasping for breath.

"If you cannot use your powers properly, I will use them for you." She sneered. "It appears you share neither your ancestor's intelligence nor his strength. My efforts to find you have been wasted on a mere shadow of what I expected."

Vionaika, still shaken by Raikali's power, was about to launch into a bitter rebuff, but as she stood up Fulkore appeared behind her.

"The Coriolis has landed in the desert," he grunted. "Tallon will be here soon."

Faria's ears pricked up. Osiris was coming? Her body was still restricted, not only by Vionaika's poison but also by Raikali's invasion of her limbs. She tried to turn but she was met by the lioness, who ripped the staff from her grasp.

"This abomination's destruction is long overdue," she grimaced. With a vicious twist of her claws the staff buckled and split, shattering the crystal veins over the sandy ground. Faria watched in despair as the tiny blue spirals cracked along its length and split at the head, the golden shaft crippled and torn. The light pulsing within it withered and died, and with it, a great deal of Faria's hope. Raikali threw it tempestuously to the sand and, taking Faria by the neck, thrust open the doors.

The column of light split the vast cavern in two. The sprawling cityscape of Nazreal opened up before them, with buildings more beautiful than Faria had ever seen. Even with their crumbling structures and broken walls they still presented themselves with extraordinary nobility. Tall, elegant towers stood silently in the darkness, with long, arching causeways leading from their hearts to connect them to other towers around the city. Everything was of the same white-blue material as the doors outside. Even the smaller buildings were ornate and distinguished, punctuated by remnants of fountains and graceful staircases that led to the higher levels. At the centre of the covered city lay a central tower, almost identical to Xayall's Tor. But for all its archaic splendour, the devastation had rendered it a ghostly echo of its former self. An eeriness hung in the air, along with the penetrating sensation of being watched by a vast, invisible crowd. Every surface was covered in a fine layer of blue crystal residue, with large clumps of solid crystal thrust from the ground and the walls of the buildings. They looked like giant hands trapped under the earth, reaching for an escape.

Huge chasms carved the city into several pieces, connected only by the remnants of stairways and arches. Some of the buildings and the city's outer walls were now grafted to the vertical sides of the mesa, the structure of Nazreal distorted and stretched by Aidan's ancient apocalypse. Faria could feel the memories of those who had walked along its streets in the dust on the ground. Pressure hummed in her ears, like the distant shouts of thousands of people crying for her attention. A crawling cold sensation spiralled up her legs.

Raikali's face broke with a twisted, maleficent grin. "Yes!" she cried triumphantly. "My city! My world!"

Fulkore regarded the environment with disdain as they trudged through the ruined streets, suspiciously eyeing scraps of black armour decaying on the ground. The buildings were desolate, their inhabitants vaporised.

"The city's empty. There's no glory in this dilapidated husk."

Raikali spun round. "Not yet, Crawn," she hissed. "But you remember it, don't you? The technology, the power! Once I reshape the world, you will have all the resources you need to exact your revenge on the ones who destroyed Dhraka, and I will return to my place at the head of a glorious empire. I will make Eeres the worthiest place in the Universe."

Faria looked at her incredulously. The death that hung within the walls, on the ground, shadowing every room; she would unleash it?

"Reshape the world? You can't!" she cried, prompting the lioness's metal claws to tighten around her neck. "The world has grown since Nazreal. It needs to stay as it is! If you try and change it back you'll—"

Raikali roared and threw Faria against the nearest wall, her eyes aflame with rage. "You know nothing of what I will achieve! You haven't known death! You haven't known the torment that has haunted my body for two thousand years! You never knew what the world was capable of, and your father tore this city from its world before it had a chance to ascend! I will change it back to its former glory; morph it into its lost shape! It will grow and shine once again!"

Faria heaved herself to her knees. She raked her claws on the dust-covered stone. "I won't let you. I haven't known your pain, but I know my own, and my father's. He, and I, have faith in this world that it can choose for itself where its future lies. It will grow to its own glory!" She rose to her feet, her hands shaking. "And I will do everything I can to protect it from you!" She rested her hands against the wall behind her, bracing against the brick.

Raikali's anger surged through her metal plating, crawling as if it were her skin. She stiffened, her claws flicking angrily by her side. She took a step forwards.

"RAIKALI!"

A deep, vengeful roar rumbled through the buildings. Osiris and Aeryn thundered up the wide main street, their weapons drawn, the gryphon's cry echoing in the stone above. Raikali looked to Fulkore and Vionaika.

"Kill them!"

They needed no telling. Fulkore's face split with a sadistic grin as he whirled his deadly axe through the air. Vionaika loaded her crossbow, snarling poisonously as she and Kyru sprinted away. Raikali turned back to Faria and lunged forwards, aiming for her neck once more. In a second the wall behind Faria lit up and she phased through it, leaving the lioness clawing at bare stone. She drew back her fist and punched right through, an explosion of blue light cascading from her knuckles, clearing away half the wall in front of her. As the dust settled, Faria had disappeared.

"You cannot run, Arc'hantael! I will shower this city with your entrails!"

Faria sprinted through the streets with the wall's dust still tingling on her fingers. She could feel the city thrum with the pounding of her feet. She had found a magnificent weapon to use against Raikali—Nazreal itself!

Chapter Twenty-Six

The wind whistled in Aeryn's ears as she hared down the deserted street, dodging rubble and contorted pillars of crystal. Sword in her right hand, bow in her left, she would be ready to drop either depending who met her first. Osiris had taken to the air not seconds before to find their targets more quickly. She could hear his powerful wing beats nearby.

Leaping over a fallen column, something huge tore towards her. In a flash she ducked down; a massive axe split the stone above her head. She rolled clear to see Fulkore rip his blade free of the brick, his face twisted in spite. She backed away, readying her sword.

"That won't help you, pest," he boomed. He gripped the axe with both hands and broke into a crashing, ground-shaking run. She barely had time to jump away—his speed was incredible. He rumbled past and swung the axe across her, the air in its razor wake slicing past her tail. She turned again. He spun on his hind claws and drew the blade back, aiming to cleave her in two. As she prepared to jump, a blur of white and gold slammed between them. A crash of metal hit the air.

Osiris stood before her, his two rapiers pushing against the axe's lethal serrations.

"Aeryn, go!" he yelled. "Find Faria!"

In a second she was gone, bounding up the steps ahead. A rabid grin spread across Fulkore's face.

"Want your death to go unwitnessed?" he sneered.

"There are things more important than my death," Osiris spat. "Like yours."

Fulkore gave a cruel laugh. "You will never kill me, Tallon. I will live in your nightmares forever!"

He broke their block and swung back, circling the axe in his right claw and slashing it down towards Osiris' legs. The gryphon leapt up high, twisted in the air and swooped downwards, blades aimed at Fulkore's throat. The dragon swept his axe up just in time, knocking the blades clear of his body. Instantly Osiris flicked round to slam his armoured shoulder into Fulkore's jaw. The dragon reeled back, throwing a crushing fist into the gryphon's backplate. Osiris landed a few metres away, skidding on his feet.

Fulkore wiped the blood from his jaw. "Those foul wings will be paraded above my throne after I rip them from you!"

Osiris drew his rapiers en garde. He had finished with his threats.

This was the end.

A massive, fractured staircase stood before Aeryn as she ran towards it. On either side of it lay gaping chasms, within them a creeping darkness that seemed to spread up their rocky walls. The oppressive silence swathing the city was broken only by her footsteps and clattering armour.

Two figures appeared at the crest of the stairs above, silhouettes against the crystal residue's faint light. Before she could prepare her bow, the taller of the two raced down, swords whistling through the air. She dropped her bow and wrenched her dagger from its scabbard. Kyru's double swords sliced for her; she blocked but only just, the force of his blows jarring her arms. Sparks flicked from the blades.

Above, Vionaika watched. Grinning.

The boom of splintering rock resounded just behind Faria. She could feel the force of the impact juddering through her feet. She darted round corners, skidded along alleyways and leapt over toppled walls, the relentless machine behind her obliterating the structures that stood in her way with burning blue light. As she turned another corner the wall behind her shattered, a shower of debris shooting down the street. Raikali's engines burned with her fury, her fists throwing the walls aside with equal malice.

"Your death shall be my glory!"

Faria stood at a crossroads, desperately trying to find the next way to turn. The whoosh of flame from behind caught her ear; she turned to see Raikali rising from behind the last building, her claws primed and drawn back, ready to strike. She looked right at the fox, crimson eyes blazing.

"There you are!" Raikali screamed.

She cannoned forwards, pulling back her right fist to prepare for a devastating punch. Faria swept her arm across the wall to her left; an arching barrier of crystal formed above her. Raikali's bladed claws smashed through but Faria had already run ahead. Again Raikali leapt up for another attack, but with a thrust of her hands against the walls on either side Faria sent two crystal spears up to meet the lioness, who spun in the air and smashed them to splinters. It wasn't hurting her, but it slowed her enough to give Faria some headway.

The street ahead opened to a large plaza. Suddenly, Faria's shelter had gone. She turned to see Raikali's black shape launching from the streets. Her claws gouged the stone, ripping blue sparks across the ground.

The claws drew back and instantly thrust forward again, aiming to trap the vixen in a cage of blades. Faria rolled backwards, slamming her hands against the floor. The ground split and hinged up either side of her, closed over like a shield. Raikali's claws pierced the stone but penetrated no further. Faria scrambled out and made her escape, sprinting along the torn and cratered plaza. She could hear Raikali cursing, firing up her engines. Half a building remained ahead, with a strong blue hue in its empty windows. If she could just make it...

"Enough, child!" the lioness roared as Faria's desperate approach to the doorway neared its end. She threw back her arms and the claws grew to dagger-size, imbued with the blue glow of the crystal vapour. Faria dived into the ruin just as Raikali cast her metal fists forward and carved the side of the building to pieces. It ruptured and exploded, sending debris in all directions, collapsing the top half of the ruin inside where the lower half formerly stood. She withdrew her claws and watched the demolition subside.

The decimated fragments settled. The cloud of dust was still billowing out, but at its centre was something odd: a glowing, pulsing sphere, increasing in size. Before Raikali could identify it the dust swirled in a powerful vortex and a platform rose out of the rubble. At its pinnacle was Faria.

Her eyes shone with the resonance cascading through her. Bolts of blue lightning streaked from her fingertips, tearing up the ground below. She stood on a pillar of crystal, drawn from the dust around her, rushing to the stem like water drawn into a fountain.

The entire mesa began to quake. A huge, jagged ring of crystal spiralled from the city around them, a circular tidal wave of piercing lances directed straight at Raikali. The lioness' eyes widened in disbelief as Faria let out a defiant yell.

"Die, Raikali!"

She threw her arms forward. The thousands of lances she'd formed all burst forward, shrieking through the air. So many flew at the target at once she couldn't tell if they'd pierced her. They kept flying, each one smashing into the ever-growing sphere of lances in front of her. She watched anxiously, determined to see the orb fall and shatter, to break the demon trapped inside.

A crack appeared in the crystal. Moments later Faria's attack split and dissolved, morphing into a whirling ring of crystal blades that circled the lioness's outstretched arms. Her face threatened death.

Faria balled her sparking fist to strike again but Raikali was quicker: in moments the bladed ring had formed into two conical missiles that careened towards the column. They smashed it, severing Faria's platform from its base. She plummeted to the ground, just brushing the crystal with her hand, forming a platform for her to slide free. As she righted herself to run, six blue spears pierced the air, catching her clothes and pinning her to a broken wall below. As the stone impacted her back she saw Raikali searing towards her. A black claw closed around her neck.

"I am through with your games."

The crystal javelins dissolved into shackles that bound Faria's arms behind her back. They constricted around her metal vambraces; she couldn't touch them. Raikali ripped her viciously from the wall and dragged her along the ground by the back of her neck. Faria wrestled vainly against her grip, but it would not relent.

Ahead lay Nazreal's central tower…

Kyru's frenzied attacks continued in a ceaseless barrage. Aeryn could barely counter as he forced her to retreat back towards the buildings, his blades overpowering her. She defended against him as best she could, but her reluctance to hurt him put her at a serious disadvantage.

She leapt around him as he tried to land a double blow down on her head. For an instant she saw the purple stone throbbing in his back and lunged for it but he was too quick, blocking her blade with his, baring her a vicious snarl. With every move away Vionaika would step closer, as if her tie to the crystals was limited by distance now that her forehead crystal was missing.

Sensing this, Aeryn bolted away from the hyena. Kyru followed at break-neck speed; she spun around and blocked him, then deftly circled behind him to push them both away from Vionaika.

Aeryn began her attack, hacking and slashing desperately at his blades to force them out of his grasp. He retreated, if only slightly, and the further she pushed, the closer she came to landing a hit. The purple hue in his eyes weakened, his moves slowed. She took a heavy swing at his sword to knock it away and tried to tackle him, when the glow suddenly strengthened and an enhanced viciousness speared his actions to a new level; she had to break away and retreat. Turning, she almost met with Vionaika's crossbow swung for her head, inches from her eyes. The bloodlust washed over Kyru; he clashed his swords against each other with vicious rancour.

He burst forward, and Aeryn was forced to block another flurry of sword sweeps as the hyena presided sadistically by, loading her crossbow. Slowing him down would be impossible if she kept so close. She had to separate them, or else impair the hyena.

Vionaika's crossbow was trained straight on Aeryn's chest…

The axe raked the ground under Osiris' legs as he leapt clear of Fulkore's rampant swing. He prepared to make another dive with his rapiers, and in the same movement Fulkore brought the axe up in an arc, sweeping over his head. Osiris dodged in time for it to miss his body, but the spiked blade ripped into his right wing, tearing flesh and feathers from it and sending him into a rough, staggered landing on the ground. His wing shook painfully, the intense pain burnt through his shoulder and back. Fulkore's maddened grin widened even further, his lizard tongue flicking excitedly.

"Grounded at last, Tallon!" he gloated, swinging his axe in triumph.

Osiris took his right sword into a high guard position and pointed his left directly at Fulkore. He tried to ignore the pain. It was swamping his consciousness; every move he made prised the wounds open with stabbing, piercing agony. He had to end this and reach Faria.

The two circled each other. In their brutal, tortuous fight they had travelled to a wide rift in the ground, infinitely deep and infinitely dark, on an unpaved circle of land littered with rubble. The gryphon stroked a claw along the ornate handle of his right-hand sword, the same he had used against Fulkore in the Gargantua. This was his weapon of justice, constructed in millennia of burning hatred.

A yellow heat burned in Fulkore's throat. He opened his mouth and with a sickening roar spewed his acid flame towards Osiris. The gryphon jumped aside, using a nearby wall to springboard himself towards Fulkore. The dragon raised his axe to meet him; the blades clashed together in the blue-hued darkness.

There was a snap of metal and a crunch of armour. Blood dashed the ground.

Nazreal's central tower stood forebodingly in the darkness, a sentinel whose grand heritage had been stained with deathly shadows. It cast fear into Faria's heart. She could hear Raikali's breath rattling heavy in her chest as they approached, the remnants of her body sensing the site of her last struggle in the lost era.

Around the tower lay the scars of a previous battle. Huge, sweeping ripples had been cut through the buildings, as if their stone was water for an instant but solidified immediately afterwards. In the centre of a group of buildings opposite was a huge, sphere-shaped void, with the surrounding brick drawn to its edges like a whirlpool. She could distantly feel her father's energy.

Raikali, her death-grip still at the scruff of Faria's neck held her aloft to face the gigantic megalith. The young fox could see the crystal veins lying dormant in the tower's structure, cast from deep underground to the incredible height above. The wing structures at the top were trapped in their jagged web, the very tips surrounded by circles of crystal rods aimed at the sky. The air lay still and heavy around it. A low, faint mist coated the ground. There was a stifling humidity in the atmosphere, and an electric buzz to the earth. The strength of the resonance was unbelievable. Faria could feel it pressing into her from everywhere, like a heavy shroud draped over her entire body.

At the base of the tower was a deep, misshapen tunnel with small clumps of crystal creeping from its walls. It was steep, and from its twisted shape looked to have been melted into existence rather than carved or built.

"This is the gateway to my ascension," Raikali purred, her voice twisted with a disgusting sense of pride at her own cruel ambition. She looked scornfully at Faria. "And you are its key."

Faria clenched her fists. "I'll never let you succeed!" she spat through her teeth.

Raikali picked her up and cast her inside the tunnel. Faria fell a short way, grinding her face along the rough wall.

"Your defiance is tiresome," the dark voice growled. "It is not a matter of choice. It is inevitability."

Faria hauled herself up and ran at Raikali, aiming for a desperate headbutt that might knock her down. The black lioness merely grabbed her by the neck and threw her down again, slamming her head on the ground. A large cut split open under the vixen's right ear. She cursed herself for her lack of strength, her powerlessness against this demon that had ruined her life. All she'd been able to do was run away and stab at the flames of Raikali's pursuit. The untouchable menace had wrapped itself wholly around her now, and she was left with nothing to resist.

Raikali grasped her neck and continued deeper into the tunnel.

A blue light illuminated the twisted pit. Faria could feel the intensity of the crystals getting stronger and stronger.

The passageway came to an abrupt stop and before her opened up a large, round chamber, its walls completely covered in crystal. A distorted metal pathway, led to the centre, a void where there was space for an object that had since disappeared. More distorted walkways leading elsewhere had been ripped free. The room's shape was like the nuclear heart of the Gargantua. Faria's fear trapped her as effectively as the chains that bound her arms.

"The resonance chamber," Raikali breathed, indulging for a moment in its incredible, oppressive presence.

She strode to the centre, where a bundle of severed cables stuck from the ground. Her body stiffened, and something inside her shoulder made a whirring noise. Her left hand stretched from the forearm and thrust into the nest of wires, which moments later snaked up her distorted limb and plugged into the vertebrae below her thorax. Her eyes flashed victoriously.

"And now, child," she cried, holding Faria aloft by the throat, a maniacal grin splitting her evil face, "My ascension begins!"

Her open mouth began to glow. Faria watched in terror as the blue mist spewed from Raikali's maw. The crystal vapour swept into Faria's body and latched onto it. It felt as if it was pulling her apart, like her body was being torn away from the inside. Faria let out a horrific scream, the overwhelming pain searing along every inch of her. Her shackles dissolved, eaten by the crystal vapour. She grasped madly at Raikali's claw to try and free herself, the burning in her arms making her thrash uncontrollably as tears came unbidden to her eyes.

The mist swept back into Raikali, forming a vampiric loop of resonance theft, draining from Faria and feeding the lioness. The glow under her black armour pulsed with ever-increasing strength, the resonance enhanced by the reactor below. She threw back her head and let out a shrieking, victorious laugh.

"This is it, Arc'hantael!" she screamed. "I will bring Naz-real back to the pinnacle of Eeres' existence, with me as the beating heart of a new world!"

The crystals around them began to shine. A high-pitched, discordant whine filled the air. Faria felt the energy ripped from her body. She tried desperately to resist, willing herself to keep hold of it. But the more resonance that was stripped from her, the weaker she felt herself becoming. At the heart of the earth below she could sense a deep, colossal rumble working its way to the surface.

Aeryn thrust her blade at Kyru. He parried it aside, slashing for her right shoulder. She flicked his blade sideways and spun behind him, a crossbow bolt shooting across her flank as she moved. Vionaika wrenched back the handle to reload and readied another shot. Kyru got there first, though—he lunged at Aeryn, and although she blocked, the force of his attack sent her reeling back to the top of the massive staircase they were fighting above.

Another bolt whizzed through the air, piercing Aeryn's leg. She cried out, barely holding her ground. She knew where her opportunity lay, and she would not waste it. She just needed him to attack once more...

"How is your love now?" Vionaika mocked, throwing her crossbow's aim towards her again with palpable malice. "He won't hear you. As long as I control him he will remember nothing of you except your painful evisceration by his own hand. And with that, I will control him forever!"

A wry smile appeared on Aeryn's face. "You're wrong. As long as Kyru is alive he'll keep fighting your influence. He would never let himself become a pawn for such a grotesque mongrel."

Vionaika roared angrily. "Kill her! Slice her to ribbons!"

Aeryn took in a deep breath and braced herself, holding her sword and dagger in front of her chest. He lunged forwards.

She took both his blades with her armoured left arm, which she wrapped around them both at lightning speed, locking them against her side, elbow and wrist. In that same second, she twisted her whole body round and threw her sword directly at Vionaika. Distracted for a second by the wolf's halting of Kyru, Vionaika didn't see the blade, which hit her leg and cast a deep cut through her shin. She let out a piercing shriek. This was Aeryn's chance.

With Vionaika focusing on her pain, Aeryn saw the purple in Kyru's eyes fade and he stood unmoving before her.

Already facing away from the stairs, she pulled him back with all her strength. She rolled backwards, holding him tightly. The two cascaded down the enormous stairway, their armour crashing, buckling and scraping all the way down. Aeryn's arrows spilt over the steps. Vionaika watched dumbfounded from the top as they skidded to a halt some way from the last step. Covered in bruises and scrapes, her armour in tatters, Aeryn struggled but managed to pull herself up, dagger still miraculously tight in her grasp. Opposite her, Kyru shakily stood, twitching erratically. She reversed her dagger and ran at him. He lumbered forwards, holding only one of his swords. Vionaika could feel her grip on him weakened; she leapt down the steps. Aeryn powered forwards, raising the dagger.

The two collided.

For a moment, neither of them moved. Kyru's sword had sliced into Aeryn's side. Vionaika's eyes lit up with delight.

"Yes! Now finish—"

Suddenly Kyru staggered back, letting out an agonising scream. He writhed around to his back, clawing desperately at his right flank. Clutching her side, Aeryn threw the dagger to the floor. She'd hit her mark. The blade had hit the crystal and broken it in two. Kyru clawed and dug at it like an injured animal, growling torturously.

Vionaika shook with rage.

"Vile bitch! How dare you!" she screamed. She loosed bolt after bolt at Aeryn, who darted from side to side, ascending the steps to reach her bow. She plucked her fallen arrows from the ground as she went.

Kyru ripped the largest hulk of crystal from his body and held it in front of him. The purple hue swirled from his eyes, melting into thick, purple tears.

"Aeryn…"

She scraped her bow from its resting place as a bolt clipped the stone by her foot. Dodging aside, she loaded her bow and drew it, loosing an arrow just past the hyena's shoulder. Vionaika flinched away, her bolts emptied, scrabbling for another magazine as Aeryn prepared her final shot, aiming down the arrow's shaft to straight between Vionaika's eyes. The hyena was too quick, and slammed the magazine into place, shooting one from her hip at Aeryn's shoulder. It glanced off her armour but disrupted her stance. The arrow swung wildly off its nook. Vionaika pulled the reloading mechanism back in place, her aim right at Aeryn's head.

"You failed!" she roared.

From below her came a powerful sweep of movement. Kyru's blade swung straight through Vionaika's arm, sending the crossbow and her severed hand tumbling to the ground. She shrieked in agony; he cast his elbow into her stomach with devastating force. She crumpled to her knees, barely able to breathe. As he stood, she pulled a knife from her belt and drew back, aiming for his open wound. He spun around and locked her wrist, just as Aeryn released her fingers from the bowstring. The arrow streaked through the air and thundered through Vionaika's left eye and into her skull. She shuddered, her dagger clattered to the stone. A grim whisper rasped from her throat as she gave the two wolves a final, gnarled glare and slumped to the ground, dead.

Kyru and Aeryn looked to one another for a second. Shakily, he sheathed his sword. "You found me," he croaked.

She gave a pained smile. "My turn to wake *you* up, Kyru." She tried to take a step towards him but her knees failed; with a cry she collapsed to the stair. He rushed down to her and rolled her into his arms, both sitting, bleeding on the steps.

"I didn't deserve you keeping your promise," he said quietly. "I told you I was a pain in the neck."

She smiled, tears rolling down her face. "You idiot. I love you."

A deep rumble shook the mesa. They looked up, alarmed. "Faria…" he whispered.

Osiris collapsed back against a fallen pillar. His swords had snapped, and his chest had been sliced deeply by Fulkore's axe. The deep chasm lay mere feet away from him.

He watched the hulking reptile stalk towards him, his own injury leaving only his massive right arm to wield his axe; his left had half of one of Osiris's rapiers sticking all the way through it. His own breathing was heavy, tied with spatters of yellow liquid from his craw, his fires spent. He had a deep cut across his abdomen and the shredded membrane of his wings had been torn into by the gryphon's furious claws.

He advanced further, then stopped, resting his axe on the ground, tapping his claws on the handle in cold anticipation.

"Is this it, Osiris? This is how our eternal battle comes to an end?" He let out a snort of a laugh. "Somehow this is not how I imagined."

Osiris would not give him the pleasure of a retort, instead staring at him with a fixed, unquenchable hate. Even seeing the dragon dead before him would not end the pain that had burned within him for so long. He played with the broken rapier blade in his right hand, flicking the hidden trigger.

Fulkore swung the axe over his shoulder and advanced closer, his immense shadow cloaking the injured gryphon.

"Where is your pride, Tallon? No last aria of justice? A most honourable opponent beaten to silence with not even death's last gasp to serve his memory?" He ground his teeth in irritation. "Such a disappointing finish."

He tugged the axe upwards. Osiris saw the dragon's arm muscles tense as the swing pulsed into action. In an instant he lunged from the pillar, wrenching the end of the pommel from his rapier and placing all his force behind the remaining shard of blade. The metal splinter penetrated the armour and pierced the Dhrakan's chest just under his heart. Fulkore's axe dropped from his grasp in mid-flight, spinning into the ground. He staggered back, the blade lodged in his breast, blood seeping from the wound. Osiris's eyes blazed with ignited revenge.

"I hereby rid this world of you," he spat, venom in his voice. Fulkore's shaky claw reached for the hilt to try and remove it from him. Osiris continued, the device in his hand almost crushed by his own anger. "A curse upon my life that I can never lift, I destroy your existence in the same way you obliterated hers."

He held the small switch in his palm.

"Goodbye, Fulkore!"

He smashed it between his hands. A fuse, unseen in the dim light, sparked and whistled within the pommel. Before Fulkore could reach, it burned out, and a white-hot explosion illuminated the area.

The dragon let out a diminishing roar. The force of the explosion threw him back to the chasm's edge. He stumbled and fell; the growl of his death and the ripple of flames disappearing into the dark silence below.

Osiris listened to it fade. A strange stillness overcame him. He reached out for a wall to support him as a wave of pain creased him in two.

Suddenly, the ground shook. He looked about him and saw the central tower begin to glow. Everywhere, bits of the crystal were pulsing with an ever-increasing intensity of light. The blue dust that smothered the floor shook, rising into the air. A horrible realisation of Faria's fate struck him, and he began a frantic journey through the ruins.

The resonance chamber shook with the deafening whine. The crystals' luminance was a blinding white that began to turn the walls red hot with their radiance. Raikali's howling laugh was the only noise to pierce the crushing sound. Faria couldn't even hear herself scream. She could feel the entire planet quaking beneath her, twisting, wrenching, breaking apart. The scream of millions of people all over Eeres shook in its core. She could feel the seas rising and swirling as her stolen power began to take hold of the trapped world. The two continents would soon shift towards each other, crushing lands between them, causing them to break apart and dissolve into the oceans.

Faria couldn't breathe; the pain was like being at the heart of a white-hot fire. Her struggles against Raikali's arm had become little more than twitches, her energy now torn from her and forced into the world below.

"*No…*" she thought, her mind racing through the pain. "*No, I can't let this happen.*"

She wrenched her hands up and grabbed hold of Raikali's arm, pulling with what little reserves of strength she still had buried within her that Raikali couldn't yet reach.

Something burned on her chest. She struggled to pull it free, trapped underneath her breastplate. Her claw caught on a chain. She pulled it, and her father's pendant clinked into her hand. The crystal hummed appreciatively. It was glowing, but in a power isolated from the lioness's circuit of leeching and annihilation. It was *her* energy, alone and untouchable. She grasped it tightly in her hand and focused all her effort into reshaping it. It lengthened, sharpened, narrowed into a sharpened spear in her hand. She threw her arms into the air and held it in both fists. Raikali watched, suddenly very aware of her movements.

"What are you doing?" she roared. Vengefully she increased the flow of blue mist between them, draining Faria's energy faster, more violently. Faria screamed again, arching her back with the pain of the resonance being further torn from her body. She roared at her demonic captor, the crystal blade still firmly in her grasp.

"You should have disappeared with this city, Raikali!" she screamed. "The pain, the hatred you feel, is of your own creation! The world… *will never be yours!*"

She brought her arms crashing down onto Raikali's wrist. The shining blue dagger pierced the armour. Faria suddenly felt the resonance energy rippling through her again. She took hold of it before Raikali could steal it away and willed the crystal into violent, bladed explosions. The crystal serum in

Raikali's arms solidified and burst into thousands of razor-sharp spikes that punched through her armour and shattered her skeleton. Raikali shrieked in agony as her body splintered, the glowering horror in her eyes fixed on Faria's dauntless stare.

Her body destroyed, Raikali fissured and split with a final roar, showering the room with thousands of tiny glass-like shards. Faria fell to the twisted metal floor. As the crystal's radiance faded and the rumbling subsided, the room was cast in a dim blue light. Deep below, the planet calmed to a slumber. Faria felt the ground beneath her cooling, and her ears were soon ringing with the calm silence of the deserted city.

Her breath returned. She felt the air cooling her body with every inhale, although she ached so much that she could barely move. She felt like she'd been burned alive. She gazed into the reflections of the crystals in front of her, shakily holding out an exhausted hand to stroke its smooth surface.

"I did it..." she whispered. Her muzzle wet; a mixture of blood and tears.

She slowly closed her eyes.

A voice called her name. She could hear it but didn't have the strength to respond. She tried to force her eyes open. The voice called again.

Osiris rushed down the tunnel, his voice cracked with worry. He burst into the resonance chamber and saw Faria prone on the ground. His heart sank.

"Faria!" he called again, kneeling down next to her. The gryphon stroked a hand over her cheek. She wearily opened her eyes; he could not have been more relieved. Osiris let out a massive sigh and smiled graciously.

"Are you all right?" he asked.

She shrugged faintly. "I was… going to ask you that."

He looked about. Shreds of Raikali's armour littered the room. The pile of splintered crystal by the cables in the centre lay dormant. Bits of the shards broke off and crumbled like drying sand. The lioness' dark, ominous presence had vanished.

He scooped the vixen up in his arms and held her tightly. "She's gone. You've saved the world, Faria."

She rested her head against him, utterly fatigued. She just wanted to sleep. "There's still so much to do, though…" she said quietly. "Xayall… Nazreal…"

Osiris smiled. "You can worry about that later. We have the luxury of time, now."

As he carried her out of the ruined city they came across Aeryn and Kyru, helping each other towards the city's exit. They rushed to Faria, who cried upon seeing them both again. Together they walked out to the darkening skies and were met by Osiris' crew, who helped shoulder them the rest of the way. Osiris kept hold of Faria, and as she looked out over the wide world spreading out in front of her in the gentle night sky, she fell into a deep, calm sleep.

From the Author

Thank you for buying, and reading through, Legacy. It means a great deal to me, and I sincerely hope you've enjoyed it. Whether it was your kind of novel or not, I'm always appreciative of honest reviews. A writer is little without an audience except to himself, so it's nice to know what's working. Feel free to get in touch.

About the Author

 Hugo lives with his wife Madison in Raleigh, North Carolina. He was due to study Psychology at university before deciding it was too scary and went to Chichester College to study performing arts instead.

He has performed in several professional theatre productions, as well as a few documentaries, and was an extra in *The Young Victoria*.

He constructs his own Steampunk costumes and regularly attends any conventions he can as his original character Phoenix the Blade, who is to feature in his forthcoming Steampunk novel, *Firesong*.

Hugo has always been interested in writing – his older sister used to write and illustrate stories for him when he was very young to keep him amused. He is a big anime and manga fan, with a large collection of DVDs and an even larger collection of soundtracks from anime, films and video games.

Legacy is Hugo's first novel.

COMING SOON

If you enjoyed reading *Legacy*, keep an eye out for Hugo's other forthcoming titles in the Resonance Tetralogy:

Book Two: Fracture

Book Three: Ruin's Dawn

Book Four: Resonance End

...and The Song Chronicle of Thera (a Steampunk series)

Firesong – The Ballad of Phoenix the Blade

Moonsong – Fugitive of the Snow

Therasong – Heart of the World

Lightning Source UK Ltd.
Milton Keynes UK
UKOW04f1831120913

217111UK00001B/6/P